THE CROSSBOW STALKER

A serial killer strikes in the heart of England

TONY BASSETT

Published by The Book Folks

London, 2022

This book is a work of fiction. Names, characters, businesses, organizations, places and events are either the product of the author's imagination or are used fictitiously. Any resemblance to actual persons, living or dead, events or locales is entirely coincidental.

ISBN 978-1-913516-28-4

www.thebookfolks.com

The Crossbow Stalker is the second standalone title in a series of mysteries set in the Midlands. Details of the other books can be found at the back of this one.

Chapter 1

George Roscoe saw the Bowie knife glinting in the sunlight as he stepped off the bus.

He gazed across the car park at a curly-haired man sitting behind the wheel of an ex-US Army Jeep, polishing the blade.

Beside him was a man with a ponytail, laughing and drinking from a can of lager. Both men had jet black hair and olive skin, and were in their late twenties. They could have been brothers, relaxing in the fine April weather.

George needed to walk past them in order to reach the high street. But, as he approached, he realised the two men were focussed on a bearded stranger in a blue shirt and jeans who was strolling towards them.

'Here he comes now,' the first man muttered as his eyes lit up.

The peace of the afternoon was suddenly shattered as the two men screamed insults at their victim. The newcomer tried to run but the pair were too quick as they chased him around the cars.

The ponytailed man, who resembled a burly nightclub doorman, grabbed his shoulder and began punching him.

George was shocked by the men's show of violence. He and two male shoppers tried to wade in and pull them apart. But they were too late to stop the curly-haired knifeman lunging at his victim, yelling, 'That's a warning.'

George, lacking in confidence despite his six feet in height, held back for a moment. But finally, out of concern, he forced himself forward and squared up to the knifeman.

'Leave him alone,' he demanded.

'Don't give me no trouble,' the man retorted, running towards the Jeep. 'I know where you live and I'll come and sort you out.'

By then, a crowd had gathered, and the thugs drove off.

George was worried about the victim on the ground, writhing from a wound to the left arm. 'Are you all right?'

Blood was seeping through his shirt.

'The bastard stabbed me.'

A woman, who ran a cafe on the other side of the car park, pushed her way through the crowd of onlookers.

'Someone call an ambulance. Come on, love. Let's get this wound cleaned up.'

George followed as they weaved their way among the cars. 'What was all that about?' he asked, peering anxiously into the man's face.

'I don't know. I must've done something to upset them,' gasped the victim, who was slim, aged about thirty and with short, brown hair.

Once he was assured the injury looked like a minor slash wound, George tapped him on the back.

'I'm going to see if those men are still around. They shouldn't be allowed to get away with mindless thuggery like that.'

He sprinted down a cobbled alley leading to Queensbridge High Street, where he gazed around in vain for several minutes. Uncertain where the men might be – or even if they were still around – he turned right along a route which would lead him past the only major supermarket and the police station.

He tried to imagine how his father Gavin, a detective chief inspector, would have reacted. At the age of twenty-three, he'd single-handedly tackled an affray in Birmingham before back-up arrived. George would reach that age in two years.

'I should've done more,' he muttered.

Then, as he stepped from the pavement to make way for some passing shoppers, he caught a glimpse of the khaki-coloured Jeep. It was parked on the opposite side of the street, some distance ahead.

No sooner had he seen the rather neglected, mud-splattered vehicle than its engine roared into life. The thug with the ponytail strolled across the street from the supermarket carrying cans of lager and jumped into the passenger seat.

Then the driver performed a U-turn and it drove slowly along the high street towards George with part of its canvas hood fluttering in the breeze.

He drew a quick breath when he saw the driver's face – the man who'd threatened him a few minutes earlier.

George took a photograph on his mobile phone as they roared away, leaving a cloud of dust in their wake. He then made a note of the registration number in his diary.

When George returned to the car park, he found the cafe owner had bandaged the man's upper arm and had sat him down at an outside table.

The middle-aged woman shook her head as she turned to George. 'His name's Oliver,' she said before adding, 'The ambulance will be here in a minute.'

Oliver glanced up. 'I've told you I'm all right.'

The woman tutted. 'We'll see what the paramedics say, shall we? I reckon you'll need stitches.'

George studied the photo on his phone. 'I've just seen them in the high street. Look.'

Oliver peered at the sharp image and shrugged. He was reluctant to speculate on who the men might be. He slurped his tea and kept his head bowed, all the while staring intently at the grey cobbles.

Then he smiled at George. 'Thank you for stepping in.'

George shook his head. 'I didn't do anything, but I think you should tell the police.'

'Do you?'

'Definitely. Those guys don't seem to have any regard for the law. Next time it could be worse. They might kill someone.'

He sat down beside him. 'I'm George, by the way. I can email you the photo, if you want. It might help trace them.'

'Thanks. I'm grateful,' said Oliver with a broad grin. 'Give me your number and I'll call you if I need it.'

After leaving the cafe, George bought some cauliflower and broccoli for his mother from a vegetable stall in the Warwickshire town. Then he walked along the bustling high street, clutching his shopping. He passed all the main shops and some black and white Tudor cottages.

Eventually, he reached the doorway of his mother's seventeenth-century restaurant, the Apollo Tearooms. His sister Melody, in a black and white outfit, could be seen through the window, darting between tables.

Blonde-haired Helen Roscoe emerged from the kitchen, wiping her hands on a teacloth. 'Did you get what I asked for?'

'Yes, Mum,' he said, handing her the two carrier bags. 'I was a bit delayed. A man got stabbed in the car park.'

She looked concerned. 'Is he all right?'

'I think so. A woman bandaged his arm while we waited for the ambulance.'

'Must have been a bit scary for you.'

'Yes. There were two men. I shouted at one of them to leave him alone.'

She frowned. 'George, you've got to be careful. They could've gone for you as well.'

'I don't know. I came away feeling I should have done more.'

She shook her head. 'God, I don't know what this town's coming to.'

As he followed his mother into the kitchen, George recalled the menacing words of the curly-haired man. 'I know where you live.'

He was convinced they'd never met before. They were just empty threats from a man who was clearly no stranger to aggression, he thought.

Chapter 2

Two weeks later, Detective Sergeant Sunita Roy was climbing the stairs to the CID office when she spotted Brett Dawson smiling at her from the landing above.

Dawson had just been promoted to the rank of Detective Constable with Heart of England Police after leaving the uniformed branch. 'I haven't seen you for a long time, Sarge,' he said. 'Where've you been hiding?'

Her long hair swayed as she reached the final step. 'I've been helping Tom Vickers on a drugs case.'

'Sounds interesting.'

'It wasn't. A lot of hanging around for people to show up. Then when they did show up, you sometimes wished they hadn't.'

He laughed. 'I can imagine.'

'Congratulations on your promotion, Brett.'

'Thanks. I'm really pleased.' He began to blush. 'Look, Sarge, I'm not very good at these things. It's just that we've been on a few jobs together and we seem to get along. I was just wondering if we could maybe go for a drink one night?'

The twenty-six-year-old sergeant looked embarrassed. 'You can buy me a drink one evening in the Golden Fleece.'

His confidence began to ebb like sand in an egg timer. 'That's not the same. Half of CID are usually in there. I'd like to go somewhere, you know, somewhere we could have a quiet chat. Maybe a meal.'

Sunita shook her head. She enjoyed his company but found him rather immature. As for his platinum blond hair, earring and acne, the jury were still out. 'Well, that's very kind of you, Brett. I'll have to think about it.'

She took a few steps towards the double doors that led to the CID department. 'I'm busy this week.'

Crestfallen, he called after her, 'Maybe next week? When you're not so busy?' but his pleading went unheard.

Detective Chief Inspector Gavin Roscoe was leaning over a computer screen, briefing one of his team, when his sergeant strolled towards him.

'Just the person I need,' he called out in his slight Birmingham accent.

Sunita was slim with luscious, black, flowing hair and eyes like dark pools. She gave a friendly smile as she approached.

'Yes, sir?' she murmured.

'Just go and sit in my office. I'll be right with you.'

Moments later, he found her staring out of his window, watching the cars outside arriving and departing. He came in and shut the door before settling himself down in his executive chair.

He grinned. 'I'm glad that drugs operation is out of the way. Something's come up. A man has made a report at Queensbridge nick. Seems someone's developed a grudge against him. He's had acid poured over his car and he was stabbed by two men in the town centre earlier this month.'

Sunita frowned. 'No way, sir. Will he be OK?'

'Luckily it was just a small wound to the arm.'

Sunita was intrigued. 'How long's this been going on?'

Roscoe, a stout copper's copper with the ruddy face of a man who enjoys a drink, shrugged. 'I'm not sure. A few weeks, I think.'

Then his desk phone rang. 'Excuse me while I take this call. Yes, Khalid? There's no sign of him at the shop? Go and have some lunch and try again in an hour. And if that fails, try him again an hour after that.'

He put the receiver back on its cradle. 'Where were we? Oh yes, the campaign of harassment. It's been going on for a few weeks. The guy's called Oliver Bufton.'

'Where does he live, sir?'

'He's in Biddington. D'you know it?'

Sunita shook her head. She'd been working in CID for a year and was still familiarising herself with the area.

'It's a hamlet between Queensbridge and Worcester. Go round and have a chat. The stabbing was on 5 April. My son George was a witness.'

'That must have been frightening for him,' she said.

'Yes, it was. Somewhere I've got the picture he took on his phone, of the men's vehicle.'

After searching his drawers, he found a colour printout of the Jeep. 'Here you are. It's a Willys-Overland Army Jeep. You know, from the Second World War. It had false plates.'

Sunita studied the photograph. 'A bit brazen, sir. Gallivanting around in a vehicle like this. They can't have been worried about keeping a low profile.'

'No. One of our team's done a trawl of CCTV cameras in Queensbridge but, unfortunately, there are no clear images of the stabbing.'

'I could call round this evening if you can give me the full address, sir.'

'It's Woodlands Cottage in Rose Lane.'

'Sounds a bit posh, sir.'

The chief inspector, who was beginning to feel every one of his forty-nine years, leaned back in his chair.

'I've been told he's out tonight, but he's got a day off tomorrow and is free at ten in the morning, so can you drop by and see him then?'

* * *

As the chief inspector's navy-blue BMW glided past the scented, green meadows on the outskirts of Queensbridge, a soft rain fell. Storm clouds threatened while he turned into the narrow, tree-lined lane, and reached the driveway of his 1930s detached home, The Willows.

After locking his car in the garage, he noticed the front lawn was beginning to look unkempt. 'Needs a mow,' he muttered as he passed the leaded light windows and unlocked the front door.

Helen emerged smiling from the kitchen. She reached up to kiss him on the cheek. 'Hi, darling. How's your day been?'

'I've known better,' he grumbled while glancing through the open living-room door at their son George, who was watching the television news. He was lying on the brown leather settee, brushing his fair hair out of his eyes.

Her smile faded. 'You know the man George saw getting stabbed near the market? George bumped into him again in town today. He was complaining the police have done nothing.'

'Really?'

Their son turned the sound on the TV down and stood up.

'Dad, Oliver Bufton has only had one phone call from the cops since being attacked.'

As the beep of the microwave drew Helen into the kitchen, Roscoe put his briefcase down and strode over to his son. He took a seat near the open brick fireplace.

'It's only just been reported to CID and one of our team is meant to be seeing him tomorrow. Can you go over what happened again?'

His son described every detail he could remember. Roscoe got up and walked across the red patterned carpet towards the far end of the room. He stared out into the garden.

'You shouldn't have tried to confront them. You might have been stabbed too. You should have just called the police.'

'But you told me that story about the affray in Birmingham.'

'That was a long time ago. There weren't so many knives on the street. And I was in uniform with back-up on the way.'

George shrugged. 'I think those two thugs had possibly been lying in wait for Oliver.'

His father nodded. 'Very likely. They might've been looking to settle a score.'

George leaned forward with a solemn expression. 'It was the shameless way they acted that got to me.'

'That Jeep must have really stood out in Queensbridge.'

'Yes, that's true. It wasn't in mint condition.'

George sat on the settee again. 'Dad, there's something else I wanted to tell you.'

Roscoe turned round to face him. 'OK. I'm listening.'

'Dad, you know I've been wondering about whether to go into farming or the hotel business? For the first time, I'm thinking about the police.'

Roscoe smiled. 'Go on.'

George leaned back. 'What happened with Oliver made me think. Maybe I should try to make a difference.'

His father stepped towards him. 'I'm not sure how your mother would feel – having two members of the family in the force, George. You've had a one-off experience. Give it a while. You might not have the same opinion next week – or next month.'

George shrugged. 'I think I will, Dad. I was shocked when I saw the man with the knife. Oliver was lucky. He could have died. I hope that thug gets caught and taught a lesson.'

Chapter 3

Ricky Stanton clambered into his sports car in Stratford-upon-Avon and set off for his girlfriend's house.

The Londoner was in a celebratory mood. He'd been striving for success since the day he left school. Today, more than twenty years later, he'd been thrilled to learn he'd been named his firm's top-performing salesman.

To mark the occasion, he was planning a romantic trip to Paris with his girlfriend, attractive fashion photographer Angelina Moretto. He hoped she was free that coming weekend. She'd recently cancelled some of their social plans – blaming her busy work schedule.

When he reached her house near Queensbridge railway station in his yellow Lotus Evora, her front garden was a riot of colour. Bold blue irises mingled with mauve hellebores and yellow daffodils. He failed to notice the curtains in the front bedroom upstairs twitching as he parked on the street, which sloped down gradually from the main road at the top.

Brushing against a bright yellow forsythia bush, he approached the front door and rang the bell. The chimes echoed through the house. How did she manage to keep the garden in prime condition when she led such a busy life? he wondered. He'd not yet been entrusted with his own front door key. Perhaps that would come later in their relationship.

Former model Angelina took several minutes to come to the door of the house in Oakdale Road. But eventually, she appeared, casually dressed in a T-shirt and slacks, and invited him in.

Ricky at once sensed her attitude towards him had changed. She normally flung her arms around him with an exuberant Latin-style welcome and kissed him passionately. Not this time. And, as she led him along the corridor to the kitchen at the far end of the house, she merely asked how his day had gone.

When he mentioned his sales triumph, her response was muted. Angelina, who was twelve years younger than him, simply muttered, 'Well done.'

He reached out to touch her hand, but she moved away from him.

'And how's your day been?' he asked.

'So, so,' she replied. 'I should've gone to Birmingham, but the retailer I was due to meet was sick and the meeting had to be called off.'

'That's a shame. Listen, Ange, I thought we could go out for a meal tonight. You know, to celebrate my sales figures.'

She shook her head. 'I'm feeling a bit tired.'

'Ange, is there anything wrong?'

She sat down at the wooden kitchen table. 'Ricky, I'm very sorry. I'm truly happy for you, I really am. It's just that... Oh, I don't know how to say this...'

'What, darling? What is it?'

'Ricky, I think we should have a break for a while.'

'You've found someone else. Is it that swanky guy, who's got dreams of going on the stage?' He recalled catching her once in town, chatting outside a shop with the electrician and part-time actor, Oliver Bufton.

She shook her head and looked blank. 'No.'

He glared at her. 'Why then? What's happened to change things between us?'

Angelina looked down at the red, quarry-tiled floor and, for a moment, said nothing. Her silence filled him with foreboding.

‘I just feel that maybe our relationship’s run its course. I think I need to be on my own. My life’s too hectic to devote time to anyone else right now.’

Ricky put his hands on his hips and scowled.

‘I was going to take you away on a romantic break,’ he shouted. ‘I was on the point of getting the tickets. It was going to be a surprise for you.’

‘Ricky, I’m sorry. Maybe if we could leave things for a few weeks...’ Her voice trailed off.

The furious salesman took a few paces towards the front door before glancing back at her.

‘No, don’t let’s bother,’ he insisted. ‘You’re totally unreliable. I don’t know what I ever saw in you. I deserve someone better.’

He stormed out of the house without looking back, slamming the door behind him and causing the sash windows to rattle.

‘What’s the bloody woman playing at?’ he asked himself. ‘One day she’s all over me. Then the next time I see her, she’s as cold as a Moscow night.’

Seething with resentment, he stood outside on the red-brick pavement for a few minutes, considering what to do. His exit had been rather sudden. Should he go back and try to talk her round?

He marched up to the front door and pressed the bell.

Two minutes later, he heard the sound of feet trudging along the hallway towards him. The door swung open. Angelina stood there with an agitated expression, her hands on her hips.

‘What d’you want?’

‘Look, Ange, let’s talk this over.’

‘I’m sorry, Ricky. I’ve tried to explain I need a break.’

He edged his right foot closer to the doorway. ‘Ange, the last six months have been the best of my whole life. You mean everything to me. Don’t I deserve to be treated better than this?’

‘Ricky, I’m sorry.’

The toe of his shoe was touching the internal doormat. 'Just give me one good reason why you don't want to see me.'

'I just need more time to myself. Our relationship has become a little... suffocating, Ricky. I'm now going inside.'

She attempted to shut the door, but his foot was blocking it.

'Ricky, please take your foot out of the doorway.'

'I will when you give me a proper explanation. Is it Oliver Bufton?'

'Take your foot out of the door or I'm going to get very angry with you.'

She struck the door aggressively against his foot, causing him sharp pain and forcing him to step back. Then it slammed in his face.

He thought of pressing the bell again but was beginning to see she was adamant. Swearing to himself, he walked back to his car and prepared to drive home.

How on earth am I going to live without her? he thought as tears started to well up in his eyes. 'Maybe I'll phone her tomorrow and she'll feel different.'

He started the car. 'If I find out in a few days' time that bloody woman's seeing someone else, there'll be hell to pay.'

* * *

As Ricky Stanton made a three-point turn in his Lotus, he didn't notice the curtains quiver in Angelina's bedroom.

'It's all right – he's gone,' she announced as he sped away up the street.

At these words, a man in nothing more than a pair of black Calvins clambered out of the wardrobe like a character in a comedy film. Both he and Angelina stifled a giggle over the close shave they'd just had.

'I couldn't hear much,' he said. 'But I got the impression he's none too happy.'

'I've finished with him,' Angelina said. 'All he talked about was his bloody cars and his bloody sales targets. Right now. Where were we?'

'Come here, my precious, and I'll remind you.'

Chapter 4

Oliver Bufton's home, an isolated thatched cottage in a narrow country lane, was shrouded in a silvery mist as Sunita Roy's white Peugeot 208 drew to a halt outside. She parked on a paved area to the left of the building behind a red Ford Fiesta, which, she assumed, belonged to Bufton.

She checked her warrant card was in the pocket of her jacket and then stepped out of the car. Out of curiosity, she strolled over to examine the Fiesta. Red paint had been stripped from part of the bonnet, leaving grey patches across the metallic surface. 'That must be the acid damage,' she muttered to herself.

After locking her car, she followed a stone path that led to the oak front door of Woodlands Cottage, admiring some red and yellow roses as she passed.

Sunita rapped on the brass lion's head knocker. It was answered by a man with short, cropped, brown hair in a blue denim jacket and blue jeans.

She smiled at him as she produced her ID.

'Oliver? I'm DS Roy. May I come in?'

'Of course. You're right on time. It's just turned ten.'

'I hear you vaguely know my boss's son, George,' she said, stepping onto the hall carpet. Like the car, it appeared to have been damaged.

Bufton stroked his beard as he edged backwards. 'George?'

'Yes. The guy who took the picture of the Jeep.'

'Oh George. That's your boss's son? Come in, anyway. You're welcome.'

Smiling broadly, he led her into a small living room with green floral-patterned wallpaper which was modestly furnished with a light-brown, three-piece suite, a rectangular table and chairs and an old-fashioned oak sideboard. Rear windows offered views across open fields.

She made herself comfortable on the settee.

'So you've recovered after what happened two weeks ago?'

Bufton nodded. 'Yes. The arm still aches from time to time. I was more shaken up than anything else.'

Sunita took out a small notebook and began writing. 'So these two men have some kind of grievance?'

'They must do.'

She frowned. 'I noticed the damage to your car.'

'Yes. That happened a week before the stabbing. Look, I called the police because I needed some advice. Someone's out to get me.'

She put down her book and clasped her hands while listening intently. 'That's quite a claim.'

'But it's true, and the worst aspect of it is I don't know who and I don't know why. I only dialled 999 after George suggested I should. But I realise the police don't have much in the way of resources and stabbings happen a lot. I'm probably wasting your time.'

Sunita picked up her book again. 'You're not wasting our time, Oliver. Can you first of all tell me a little about yourself?'

Her host sat down in an armchair near the front window. He grinned. 'Well, I'm thirty and I work as an electronics engineer in Hanley Wood. I live here in this rented cottage and both my parents are dead.'

She nodded. 'Have you got any brothers or sisters?'

'I've a brother in Bromsgrove who works at Longbridge and a sister with two children who lives in Stratford.'

‘Are you married or in a relationship with someone?’

‘No, I’m not married, but I recently began a relationship with a woman in Queensbridge and we’ve been seeing a lot of each other.’

She stroked her chin thoughtfully. ‘Tell us about your car.’

Her host glanced through the side window to where his car stood. ‘I was parked on the hard standing here, close to the lane. When I got up in the morning, it was damaged. I never heard a thing. But that’s not all.’

She nodded. ‘I saw your hall carpet was damaged.’

‘Yes, some bastard poured bleach through my letterbox.’

Sunita looked up from her writing. Despite his tale of misfortune, she observed Bufton still managed to smile. Perhaps he was one of those people with a constant smile.

‘Have you any idea at all why anyone would be doing this?’

Bufton shrugged. ‘No idea at all.’

‘How long have you known your young lady?’

Bufton blushed in embarrassment. ‘I’ve known her about two months and I’m absolutely besotted with her.’

‘Could she have anything to do with these events?’

At this suggestion he seemed annoyed.

‘No. Definitely not.’

‘I take it your young lady is unmarried?’

‘Divorced.’

She was becoming impatient. ‘What I’m trying to get at – in a rather clumsy way – is to ask if you’ve possibly put someone’s nose out of joint? A previous boyfriend?’

‘I suppose it’s possible, but it doesn’t seem to be just one person involved in this campaign of harassment. I mean, two men were involved in the attack in Queensbridge. Is there anything you can do to help?’

At first, Sunita was uncharacteristically unsure what to say. Then she managed to collect her thoughts.

'I think you need to discuss this with your young lady to start with,' she said. 'See how she reacts – see if you elicit a clue from her reaction as you describe the events to her. You obviously need to be careful whenever you leave home or arrive home. Look around carefully when you're by the front door and make sure you've got good locks. Are you going away for Easter?'

'No. I'll either be here or at my girlfriend's place in Queensbridge.'

'A good idea is to change your patterns of behaviour. Alter the times you leave home and leave work, and try to put your car away from your normal parking spots. Meanwhile I'll have a word with our colleagues at Queensbridge Police.'

Bufton smiled. 'It would be extremely helpful if a patrol drove round here a few times during the night.'

She nodded. 'Unfortunately, there are cost implications there, but I'll see if something can be arranged.'

She felt intense sympathy for him. He was battling to cope with daily life while under the shadow of fear. And until now the police had given only a lame response.

'I'll do the best I can for you, Oliver,' she said as she rose from the settee.

She was preparing to leave when some framed photographs on the oak sideboard caught her eye. Without a word, she strolled over to look at them. One showed a blonde woman in her twenties in a graduation cap and gown. The other showed the smiling face and shoulders of a dark-haired woman sitting on a beach.

'These your sisters, sir?' she asked.

He hurried across. 'No, no, no. This is my new girlfriend,' he said, picking up the seaside pose. He hurriedly slipped the graduation photo into a drawer. 'I don't know why I kept the other one there. She's just someone I used to know.'

'Anyway, I'd better not keep you, sir.'

Bufton grinned. 'Thank you, Sergeant Roy,' he said. 'I'll follow up what you've said. That all sounds very sensible.'

She took a final gaze round the room. 'Please do, and if you need any more help at any time, please contact us.' She handed him a card. 'This is a direct phone number to our office.'

As she stepped outside, Sunita noticed a strange object on the ground near the doorstep. She knelt down to inspect it.

Bufton stood watching her from the hallway. 'What is it, Sergeant?'

'It's a dead crow.'

Chapter 5

Later that same day, Frank Baker took his rucksack from his hall cupboard and opened the front door of his ground-floor flat. It was shortly after two in the afternoon and he was late for his meeting with his friend Vernon.

He hurried through the middle of the Troutbeck estate, passing the dull, grey, pebble-dashed houses, until he reached the park which lay beside the main Worcester Road. His friend was already waiting for him on a bench inside the park, close to the entrance gates.

Elfin-faced Vernon smiled and shook his head. 'You said you wouldn't be late.'

'Yes, sorry,' said Frank. 'I lost track of time.'

The older man took a bottle of cider from his rucksack, and they began drinking from it in turns.

Frank began to laugh. 'I was lucky. I'm sure the check-out girl knew I'd nicked it, but I was out of the store and away before they came to their senses.'

When they'd finished the bottle and discarded it on the ground, they set off in the direction of Queensbridge town centre. Frank and Vernon had been born and brought up in the town. They knew every highway and byway. They'd also both served short sentences in the same young offenders' institution after committing similar offences – burglary, theft and criminal damage.

After following several back alleys, they reached the large Victorian detached and semi-detached houses close to the station in Oakdale Road.

A house surrounded by high hedges near the top of the road was their first target.

'There's no car in the drive. Probably no one in,' muttered Frank as he tried the doorbell. He had an excuse ready if anyone answered. They were washing cars in the area. He'd got a sponge and a duster in his rucksack if proof were needed. The house stood silent. Nobody came.

He led Vernon round to the back garden before taking a large screwdriver from his bag and sliding it beneath the wooden frame of the heavy sash window. To Frank's relief, the lower sash moved upwards a few centimetres and they realised the window was unlocked. The pair placed an old garden chair close to the window, raised the lower sash and peered inside.

It was a small, neat family kitchen with light-blue cupboards, pine worktops and a small pine table and chairs. They clambered in, crept through the hallway and peered into the front room, which was bright and spacious with ornate furnishings. The house was as quiet as a funeral parlour. They put a bottle of Southern Comfort, a games console and a radio in the rucksack and brazenly walked out through the front door.

Near the garden gate, the pair, both in their early twenties, stopped and crouched down on the grass beneath the high hedges, swigging from their bottle.

'That went OK,' said Frank, and they both burst out laughing. 'Let's try the house two doors down with the red door. It's got a side alley.'

Again, they hoped they'd be able to prise open a rear sash window with their screwdriver, but this time all the wooden-framed windows were firmly locked.

Frank, once dubbed 'West Warwickshire's one-boy crimewave' after being locked up for a spate of break-ins, frowned. 'We don't want to smash the glass. Makes too much noise.'

They were about to leave when he tried the back door handle – in case the householder had had a memory lapse and forgotten to lock it. To their astonishment, it opened.

Vernon laughed as they sneaked inside. 'Some folk are idiots.'

The men realised at once they were in a less elegant and more bohemian home than before. The kitchen was in a poor state of decoration. A long wooden table with eight chairs stood at the centre of the room. A grubby cooker, fridge-freezer and kitchen cabinets stood beneath the two sash windows they had tried to jemmy open.

Frank crept into the drab hallway and began climbing the stairs. He stopped halfway up, pressing a finger to his lips.

'I thought I heard something.' A minute passed. All was silent. 'No, it's OK.'

The front bedroom was plainly furnished with beds, wardrobes and chests of drawers.

Then Frank became excited. 'Look at this, Vern.' He was examining a gold necklace, two gold rings and a gold bracelet which he'd found in a drawer. He slipped them into his rucksack. 'These must be worth a bit.'

The middle room contained nothing of interest, but they were astonished when they entered the back bedroom. Most of the walls were covered from floor to ceiling with photographs of celebrities. Sofia Boutella, Sasha Lane and Rowan Blanchard were seen parading on the catwalk while Beyonce, Lady Gaga, Justin Bieber and Ed Sheeran were pictured at society events.

Then suddenly the stillness of the afternoon was broken by the sound of a car door slamming in the street outside. Frank raced to the front bedroom and peered out as the driver of an ex-US Army Jeep was in the process of parking outside.

'They're back!' Vernon cried.

He opened the rear bedroom window. Luckily, there was a sturdy, black drainpipe close to the window.

'Come on!' he said, raising the lower sash fully and kneeling on the ledge. He grabbed the downpipe firmly with both hands and hauled himself onto it. Then he slithered down the pipe to the ground.

Vernon had never clambered down a drainpipe before but had scaled ropes in school gym classes. He too manoeuvred his way down to the concrete.

They were about to run off when they overheard a conversation between a man and a woman in the kitchen. Step by step, crouching down to keep below the windowsills, they inched their way round the corner of the house in the direction of the front gate.

'You realise I've got a steady boyfriend, don't you?' the woman was saying. 'This is just a special occasion, a one-off.'

'You're such an angel,' the man replied.

'Let's go upstairs,' said the woman. 'I want you in my arms.'

The two men outside chuckled. Cautiously, Frank raised his head to peek into the kitchen. A man with curly black hair in his mid-twenties was standing with his arms round an attractive, dark-haired woman of about thirty.

The olive-skinned man was stripped to the waist and kissing her passionately. Frank was struck by the man's vague resemblance to the footballer Cristiano Ronaldo.

Vernon kept his head down. 'What's happening?'

Frank laughed. 'There's a couple kissing.'

Again he peered over the sill as the couple moved towards the hallway door, undressing each other as they went.

'Bloody hell!' said Frank. 'They're getting their kit off. Looks like Ronaldo scores again.'

'Let me see,' said Vernon, standing bolt upright.

At that moment, the bare-chested man spotted the younger man's face and raced to the kitchen door.

'What's the matter?' the woman cried.

'We've got company!' said the man, racing outside and pursuing the pair out of the garden.

He was puffing and panting as the pursuit continued up the street. 'Come here, you little bastards!'

He chased them until they reached the main road. But Frank and Vernon were too nimble and the breathless man was forced to give up the chase.

'He might be fast on the pitch, but he couldn't catch us to save his life,' Frank joked to himself as they tore along the alleys of Queensbridge.

Chapter 6

A few days later, Sunita Roy was hurrying along the pavement towards police headquarters, her hair and open grey coat billowing behind her in the breeze.

All the while she was unaware she was being watched. Tom Vickers, newly promoted to the rank of Detective Inspector, had just parked his white Audi A3.

Her frenzied figure was running diagonally across the St James Street car park as the slightly overweight detective inspector stepped out of his car.

'You're in a rush this morning, Sunita.'

Startled for a moment, she slowed her pace and laughed. 'Oh it's you, Tom. I wanted to write up a report before the boss shows up.'

Vickers, who was around five feet ten inches tall and with short brown hair, glanced at his watch. It gave the time as five past ten. 'I was going to say. You're not late.'

Vickers locked his vehicle and accompanied her to the entrance steps.

'Haven't you brought your car today?'

'Couldn't get in the car park. Left it down the road.'

He shook his head. 'It's about time the top brass did something about the lack of parking.'

She nodded and smiled. He looked smarter since he'd shaved off his dark, ginger moustache, cut his hair and begun wearing his charcoal-grey suit.

'Look, I'm sorry that drugs operation was such a pain, Sunita. I'd like to buy you a meal some time to make up for it.'

She returned his smile. 'Thanks, Tom. I'd like that.'

'You know you're always welcome to call round at my office for a coffee.'

Half an hour later, when she'd finished writing her report, she received a call on her mobile phone. It was her chief inspector, calling from his car's hands-free phone.

'I'm on my way to Biddington. Someone's been shot. I'm praying it's not our friend Oliver. Can you join me there?'

'I'm on my way, sir.'

* * *

As she began the twenty-five-mile journey to the Worcestershire hamlet, she cast her mind back to the disquieting moment she found the dead bird, and when Bufton had emerged from the cottage to examine the carcass.

'I can't help feeling it's some kind of omen,' he'd remarked.

Sunita had tried to reassure him. 'I believe crows act as messengers between the world of the living and the dead. When they're found lifeless, it stands as a warning. It means there's a change coming.'

But her words failed to placate him. He was convinced the men harassing him had left the dead bird. Now there'd been a shooting. She drove through Queensbridge with a sense of foreboding.

As she reached the village of Norton Prior, she turned right, crossed the bridge over the River Avon and followed the winding country road until she saw the sign for Biddington. After a short distance, she reached a road junction beside a small green.

Her fears for Oliver Bufton's welfare grew as she saw that Rose Lane, to the left, was cordoned off. A young constable was standing by a signpost, directing traffic.

'DS Roy. Can I drive through?'

'Sorry, Sergeant. It's very restricted up there. The lane's very narrow. It's best if you leave your car here.'

After following the constable's suggestion, Sunita set off on foot along the lane, peering across open fields through gaps in the hedges as she walked.

As she passed a bend, Woodlands Cottage came into view. Four police cars and a white van were parked in front. A white tent had been set up round the doorway. Two SOCOs were at work in a field across the lane.

Roscoe emerged from the back of the cottage, clutching a clipboard.

He shook his head. 'Oh, there you are, Sergeant. I expect you've heard what happened.'

'No, sir.'

'Someone's been shot in the heart with a crossbow bolt. I'm afraid it looks like it's our poor old friend Oliver.'

Sunita had suspected Bufton had come to harm, but hearing the manner of his death caused her to draw a sharp intake of breath.

'Oh, how terrible,' she said.

'A delivery driver discovered the body. We'll need to find him.'

Sunita gazed around. The cottage was on the brow of a hill. The lane sloped downwards to the west. Where the ground levelled out a short distance down the hill, she noticed a farm gate on the left-hand side and then a clump of trees.

She turned back to find the chief inspector having a discussion with PC Derek Underhill from Queensbridge police station. He was asking whether the delivery man was still around.

Underhill, an amiable, softly spoken constable in his late twenties, nodded.

'Yes, sir. He's over there.'

He pointed to a sullen-faced man standing by the side of the lane. Roscoe waved to him.

'Two minutes,' he called.

He then led his sergeant over to the tent, where they found Home Office pathologist Dr Silas Reynolds and a young assistant.

'Ah good. You've brought your young sergeant along,' said the doctor, who was dressed in white overalls. Round his waist was a white, waterproof apron and he had white, rubber gloves on. 'We've no idea at the moment who the man is.'

Roscoe clasped the tent flap. 'Sergeant, would you mind taking a look? You've met the man.'

Sunita leaned inside and was shocked to recognise the pale, white face and short, cropped brown hair of Oliver Bufton. He was sprawled across the ground with his right hand on his chest, dressed in a blue denim shirt and blue trousers.

She took a moment to compose herself before emerging into the bright sunshine, shaking her head. She spoke in a whisper.

'Yes, it's him. Oliver Bufton.'

Her mind returned fleetingly to that morning, just a few days earlier, when Bufton had described the hate attacks while doing his best to smile.

Sunita's hands crept to her face. Roscoe, concerned for her, put his arm round her shoulder.

'Are you all right, my dear?' Dr Reynolds asked.

She tried to smile. 'I'll be fine in a minute. It's just a jolt to the system. That's all. When an incident in Rose Lane was first flagged up, we hoped and prayed it wouldn't be him. I was talking to him barely a week ago, giving him advice.'

Roscoe had a solemn expression. 'That's right, Silas.'

'Despite the nature of our work, death can still hit you like a bombshell, Sergeant,' Dr Reynolds said. 'It affects me too – and I spend most of my life peering at bodies.'

The chief inspector cast his eyes to the ground. 'I'm going to be blaming myself over this. We got Queensbridge police to arrange occasional patrols round here. It clearly wasn't enough. We should have done more.'

Reynolds patted him on the back. 'Don't upset yourself, Gavin. So he lived in this cottage?'

'Yes. He was renting it.'

Reynolds shrugged. 'He died fairly quickly. The bolt entered his body at the right atrium and, judging by the angle of trajectory, it would've been fired directly across the lane.'

Sunita frowned. She recalled the unlucky moment she discovered the black crow. She stared at the ground beside the tent, half expecting to see it. But it wasn't there.

The doctor yawned and stretched out his arms. 'There are signs your Mr Bufton tried to remove the projectile from his chest but failed.'

Sunita looked blank. 'Why would someone use a medieval weapon like a crossbow instead of a gun? Aren't they heavy and cumbersome?'

'That's true, my dear, but firearms are difficult to get hold of since tougher licensing came in. No licence or registration is required to own a crossbow, so they're becoming more popular. Tens of thousands of people use them across the country at archery clubs.'

Roscoe frowned. 'How do we know the bolt was fired with a crossbow and not a longbow?'

The doctor stared towards him. 'Crossbow bolts are shorter and heavier.'

'All right. Let's have a look at the bolt,' said Roscoe.

'Well, it's bagged up, but I can retrieve it,' said the doctor. 'We're getting some photographs printed which show the deceased with the shaft embedded in his chest.'

The pathologist stepped inside the cottage and returned with two plastic bags. He held up one of them, which contained the bloodstained bolt.

'This is what killed him,' he said, 'The shaft is fifty centimetres long, crimson and made from carbon.'

Roscoe pulled a face. 'The blades on the bolthead look sharp.'

Reynolds nodded. 'They are. The fletchings – the wings at the back – are crimson, yellow and white.'

Sunita frowned. 'It's frightening to think that someone could dream of using a missile like this to kill another human being.'

'Have we got any idea of the time of death?' asked Roscoe.

'Between 8.00 a.m. and 10.00 a.m.,' the doctor said. 'But there's something else I've got to show you. This white handkerchief was found in the victim's mouth.' The doctor brandished the second bag with a flourish as if he were a magician demonstrating a trick.

'And in the corner of said handkerchief, voila! A large, embroidered letter *C*.'

Roscoe studied the material through the see-through plastic.

'It's quite lavish and hand-stitched in silver thread. I believe they call that a floral script monogram.'

Reynolds grinned. 'Quite the expert, Gavin!'

'No, it's just that I read a book about it once. It's because of the tiny flowers in the design. It looks as if the murderer's name might begin with C… although I'm not sure why he'd want to advertise it.'

Chapter 7

The morose, grey-haired man who discovered the murder victim lying on the ground by the cottage door was impatient to resume his round of deliveries.

'Can we do this another time? I've got a vanload of electrical parts to take over to Stratford.'

Sunita shook her head. 'I'm afraid we can't. This is a murder inquiry, sir.'

The two detectives led him a short distance away from the frenzied activity taking place around the white tent so they could conduct their interview with him.

Walter Newman, who was forty-seven and occasionally shook his head while speaking as though suffering from a nervous twitch, worked for a firm called Pawson and Son in Stratford.

The chief inspector smiled weakly. 'Can you tell us what happened this morning?'

Newman nodded. 'What a terrible sight to find. I was driving up the lane. It's a shortcut I sometimes use. I'd been to Gloucester and was on my way to Queensbridge to make some deliveries. Well, I came up the hill and there's this man lying on his back outside the cottage. I thought he might've had a heart attack or something because he wasn't moving.'

Sunita interrupted. 'What time was this?'

'Just before ten o'clock. I stopped my van and went to have a look – you know, to see if I could help. Oh my God! There was no pulse and there was a crossbow bolt poking from his chest. So there was nothing I could do. D'you know? I'd never seen a dead man before. I was shaking when I got back to my van, I can tell you.'

Sunita nodded. 'So you dialled 999 from your van?'

'Yes.'

Roscoe patted his shoulder. 'You did well. If he'd still been alive when you reached him, I'm sure you'd have done your best to save his life.'

'I definitely would, sir. But, sadly, that wasn't to be.'

'Did you see anyone else around?' asked Sunita. 'Was there any other vehicle around?'

'No. Not that I recall. Only the Fiesta over there,' he said, pointing to Bufton's car at the side of the cottage.

The sergeant took the man's address and phone number and, just before he left, warned him they might need to interview him again at a later stage.

She turned her attention to her boss. 'Are you all right, sir?'

He nodded. 'I'll be fine. This has shaken us both up.'

'Yes, sir. Mr Bufton was a nice, friendly guy. Sir, don't you think we should go into the field opposite and find the spot where the killer was standing when he fired?'

'Yes. We'll do that now.'

They walked down the road to the farm gate and began studying the muddy terrain between the lane and the entrance to the field.

'There are vehicle tracks here – fresh, if I'm not mistaken,' said Sunita.

He nodded. 'Yes. Whoever it was, he almost certainly came in a vehicle and may well have parked it here.'

'We have our scene photographer at the cottage, sir. I'll get him to take some pictures.'

Five minutes later, she found Roscoe had passed through the gate and was exploring the field. She followed his lead, taking care not to step in the mire.

They found two members of the forensic team working beside the hedge that lay directly opposite the cottage door. A small section of thick grass had been cordoned off. A woman was crouching down, taking samples of earth and grass. There was a large gap among the thorns which afforded a direct view of the doorway.

'We've found marks in the mud,' the woman explained as they approached the police ribbon. 'So it looks like the person with the crossbow was waiting around here for the victim.'

Roscoe nodded. 'There's no question this is the spot where the killer fired their weapon. They'd have had an unimpeded view and the angle of trajectory entirely fits.'

Sunita smiled at the woman. 'Any other forensic clues? No signs of the bow being placed on the ground here?'

'No, Sergeant. We've made a thorough search, but nothing,' the woman said.

'Well, the killer must've knelt over the body after firing the bow, because a handkerchief has been placed in his mouth.'

The woman nodded. 'They could easily have passed through the hedge here, stepping over the fence and wire to reach the road. But we've examined the whole area and there's no forensic evidence so far.'

Before the detectives left the scene, they decided to have one last word with Dr Reynolds, who was washing down his plastic trousers with disinfectant beside the dead man's car.

'Silas,' said Roscoe, 'I just wanted to check with you. Was Oliver still alive when the handkerchief was placed in his mouth?'

'Yes, probably, Gavin. But the handkerchief wasn't used to choke the victim, if that's what's in your mind.'

Sunita watched as the chief inspector paced around, staring at the ground and thinking. She'd rarely seen him so agitated.

'So the handkerchief was used as some kind of signature act to celebrate the killing,' he concluded. 'He wanted to leave his personal stamp on the scene, claiming the victim as his.'

Reynolds nodded. 'That's right, Gavin. The same thought had occurred to me.'

Chapter 8

Gavin Roscoe was staring out of his office window at the mothers and children in the recreation ground across the street two days after Oliver Bufton's murder when someone knocked on the door.

Sunita Roy, in a smart grey suit, opened it a fraction. 'Would you like a coffee, sir?'

'Thank you, Sergeant. Make it a strong one.'

A few minutes later, as they both sat sipping hot drinks, she mentioned she'd received a call from DI Vickers.

Roscoe nodded. 'Yes, I've asked him to help us with the Bufton case. What did he say?'

Sunita leaned back in her chair. 'He's making inquiries about the handkerchief and crossbow bolt.'

'Yes, that's right. He's a good operator,' said Roscoe.

'He told me he's also been studying pictures of the tyre marks left by the farmgate. Is your coffee OK?'

'Yes, the coffee's fine, thank you, Sergeant. Do you want to tell me what you've found out?'

'Oh, yes, sir. First thing today I finished listing the contents of Bufton's pockets and rucksack. In the pockets of his jeans he had a comb, a diary, some business cards showing the name Avonshore Electricals and about three pounds in change. In his jacket pocket, he'd got a leather wallet containing a bank card, a twenty-pound note and a picture of a dark-haired woman – possibly his girlfriend. The rucksack contained screwdrivers, a meter, cable and other electrical equipment.'

'Has the team got anywhere with the relatives?'

'I'm not sure, sir. PC Underhill was making inquiries about family addresses. We contacted Bufton's brother in Bromsgrove – he's the guy that ID'd the body. Bufton also has a sister in Stratford and we're making efforts to trace her.'

Roscoe said, 'It sounds like a lot of hard work's been going on. Anything of any help in Bufton's diary?'

'I'm not sure, sir. DI Vickers has been reading it.'

'What about Bufton's car?'

Sunita was expressionless. 'I think Forensics have been examining it. Have the media team been issuing lots of press releases about the murder, sir?'

'Yes. We'll be giving out the victim's name shortly – now that we've informed next of kin and had the body identified. We've had to mention the crossbow bolt in one of the earlier press releases and, of course, the papers have gone crazy about that. But so far we're holding back on the finer points – and we're not revealing details of the handkerchief and vehicle tracks. There's a new trainee who's moved over from uniform. He's liaising with the family, along with Derek Underhill, so we'll know more shortly. Anyway, come and have a look at these.'

The chief inspector picked up an envelope from the table and pulled out ten colour photographs showing a naked couple. The sergeant stood up and leaned over his desk.

'We found these yesterday in one of the drawers in the sideboard at Woodlands Cottage,' he said. 'They're of Bufton and some well-built blonde, both in the altogether.'

Sunita grinned. 'Bufton in the buff, sir.'

Roscoe laughed. 'Yes, you could say that! The point is we need to find out who this fine-looking woman is. In fact, we need to find out a lot more about his life.'

She nodded before returning to her seat. 'Hopefully, the diary will help us.'

'Yes, it may. I've had a quick look. Lots of names, but we can't be sure at the moment how they all fit into his life. The woman in the picture could be Lucinda Thomson from Stratford or Angelina Moretto from Queensbridge. But there are other women's names too. There's a girl with the surname Lewis and the name of a record company next to her.'

Somehow, from the back of her mind, Sunita recalled the words spoken by Bufton at Woodlands Cottage.

'Sir, Bufton seemed infatuated with a woman that he'd just formed a relationship with. Do you remember when I briefed you about my visit there? He said he was "absolutely besotted" with her.'

Roscoe nodded. 'Yes. It's vital we find her. You told me she was in Queensbridge.'

'It could be the Moretto woman, sir. There's an address in the diary in Oakdale Road, Queensbridge. He's written "A" next to it.'

'That must be her.'

Just then his desk phone rang.

'Chief Inspector,' he replied. 'Is that right? What? In the back of the car? Not much else? OK. Thanks for your call.'

He turned to his sergeant. 'That was Alice Ling in Forensics. There was nothing of much interest in the car. But they did find a flyer from Pawson and Son, the electrical suppliers...'

Sunita raised an eyebrow. 'That's the firm Walter Newman works for.'

Roscoe nodded. 'Well, they're a big local firm and perhaps it's no surprise that people have the firm's leaflets in their cars – especially if they're in the same business. It doesn't mean Bufton necessarily knew Newman. Newman certainly didn't mention knowing Bufton when we interviewed him.'

A few moments later, Roscoe's phone rang again. This time Tom Vickers was on the line.

'Sir, I had a quick word with Oliver Bufton's brother, Leonard, after he left the mortuary. He says he knew nothing of Oliver's recent life. He'd not seen him for six months.'

'Family rift?'

'No, I don't think so. They just both led busy lives, like most of us.'

After ending the call, DC Omar Khalid knocked on the door and presented their boss with a slip of paper.

'Here's the address you asked for, sir,' said Khalid as he smiled and left, closing the door behind him.

The chief inspector jumped up from his seat. 'Come on, Sergeant. Do you fancy a trip to Stratford? I've just got an address for the Thomson woman. We could visit her, call in at Shawley Green on the way back to see Walter Newman again and visit the Moretto woman in Queensbridge as the final visit of the day.'

'Good idea, sir.'

Chapter 9

Sunita Roy had only once before visited Stratford-upon-Avon, famous throughout the world as William Shakespeare's birthplace. As a child, she'd travelled with her parents to see Anne Hathaway's Cottage, the five-hundred-year-old childhood home of the Bard's wife.

The town also held fond memories for Roscoe. He'd proposed to Helen, who was three years younger than him, during a candlelit meal at one of the hotels.

But as his BMW brought the pair to the town's outskirts just before midday on the Wednesday morning, their combined spirit of optimism based upon happy memories quickly evaporated.

They discovered Oliver Bufton's former girlfriend, twenty-five-year-old Lucinda Thomson, had moved away, leaving her ground-floor flat in the town's Drayton Avenue to a new owner who had been there for the past year.

However, after knocking at nearly every flat in the block of twelve, they eventually found a woman who recalled that Lucinda's older brother, Robert, lived in nearby Lodge Road and Roscoe decided they should call on him. With the assistance of DI Vickers back in CID, they found an address for the brother's three-bedroom semi-detached house.

Sunita felt thirty-year-old Robert Bray appeared anxious as he took them into his small front room.

'I just saw on the Midlands TV news that Oliver Bufton's been killed. Have you come about that?'

'Yes,' said Roscoe, showing his warrant card. 'We gather your sister knew him.'

Robert nodded. 'Do you want to sit down?'

Roscoe made himself comfortable on a shabby, brown, two-seater settee between the door and the bay window. But Sunita said she'd prefer to remain standing and stepped across to the mantelpiece. She'd noticed a framed photograph of the same chubby blonde woman with a fair complexion who'd appeared without inhibitions in the photographs found in Bufton's sideboard. She made a mental note not to disclose to Bray that they'd seen her in far more revealing poses.

She smiled. 'Your sister's a good-looking girl.'

'Yes, Lucinda was always the prettiest girl among her friends growing up. Shame Bufton was such a bastard.'

'How do you mean?'

'They were together for four years and got engaged. They were talking about marriage and looked at a house together. Then he suddenly got cold feet. She was devastated. He finished with her a year ago and she's never got over it. In the end, Lucinda had a breakdown. She's now gone to live in Spain with our parents. She's never forgotten how much he hurt her.'

Sunita's smile faded. 'We're very sorry to hear about her unhappiness. Could you explain something? How come she's got a different name from yours?'

He folded his arms. 'My sister's surname used to be Bray. She got married when she was quite young to a man named Thomson, which explains her current surname. He was a rat as well and she divorced him.'

Sunita gazed at him. 'How long was she in hospital after her breakdown?'

'Off and on, for about six months.'

Roscoe shrugged. 'So the point is you've got a serious grudge against Mr Bufton?'

'Well, I didn't like the way he treated my sister, but I didn't feel strongly enough to want to kill him – and certainly not with a bloody crossbow. But he fancied himself with the ladies. I shouldn't wonder if there aren't dozens of people with a grievance against him.'

Sunita frowned. She knew grudges could last for years. Maybe a lifetime. She could recall the many fierce arguments she'd had with her parents, who'd once been desperate for her to marry a man from India.

'We all tend to fall out with people from time to time,' she said. 'But, thankfully, the vast majority of us get over our problems and move on.'

Roscoe smiled. 'Well said, Sergeant. Anyway, I don't think we need to take up any more of your time, sir.'

As they walked back to the car, Sunita was quiet.

'You all right, Sergeant?' Roscoe asked. 'You look a million miles away.'

'I'm fine. It's just I think he knows more than he's telling us. I get the feeling he's holding something back.'

'Yes, I thought that as well. He was fairly guarded in what he told us. Anyway, we've got more people to see.'

Their next visit was to the picturesque village of Shawley Green, which lay halfway between Stratford and Queensbridge. Sunita had never been there before and Roscoe had only been there once, which had involved a trip to the village pub, the White Swan, for a darts match.

A short distance from the pub was a large village green surrounded by a cluster of charming black and white cottages – some crowned with thatched roofs.

Walter Newman's two-bedroom, red-brick cottage was in a side road leading from the green. A dog could be heard barking as Sunita strolled up the brick path to the door and rapped loudly on the knocker. Newman opened the door slightly and peered round.

'What d'you want?' he demanded.

'We need to ask you a few more questions,' she explained as the chief inspector joined her at the door.

'You can't come in at the moment,' said Newman. 'In any event, I've told you all I know.'

Sunita was annoyed by his attitude. 'We didn't realise at the time that both you and Oliver Bufton were involved in the electrical business.'

'Yes, but I don't see what that's got to do with anything.'

Roscoe frowned. 'So you knew Oliver Bufton from your work? Why didn't you mention that when we spoke before?'

Newman shook his head. 'No, I didn't really know him.'

'What does that mean?' said the chief inspector. 'You either knew him or you didn't.'

'I knew him by name, but I'd never met him. Put it like that.'

'You deliver electrical parts to all the electrical businesses around the south Midlands but you've never spoken to a man who works for Avonshore, one of the largest companies?'

'I don't know everybody.'

Sunita was close to losing her temper. 'The murdered man had one of your leaflets in his car.'

'He might've had one of our leaflets, but he didn't get it from me. Look, if I'd recognised him, I'd have said so.'

The chief inspector touched his sergeant on the shoulder.

'All right. We'll leave it there for the moment.'

Just then the face of a friendly cocker spaniel appeared round the door.

Newman became even more irritated. 'Sammy! Get back inside.'

Sunita was gazing through the open doorway. 'One more thing, Mr Newman,' she said. 'I see you've got a longbow in your conservatory.'

As the spaniel had edged the door open a little, the sergeant's eyes had peered along the passageway, right to the far end of the house. A brown, hand-made longbow could be seen propped up against a window.

'Yes, I'm a member of the Wackos,' he said.

A puzzled look spread across her face. 'Sorry, what are the Wackos?'

Roscoe smiled. 'Warwick & Queensbridge Company of Archers.'

Newman nodded. 'Been a member for, well... must be ten years now. But never used a crossbow. Never been interested.'

As they returned to Roscoe's car, Sunita was shaking her head.

'I can't quite make him out, sir. He didn't show any surprise when we revealed Bufton worked with electrics.

On top of that, it was he who found the bolt in the dead man's chest, but he never mentioned he was an archer. Might be worth looking into his past.'

Roscoe nodded. 'It was also strange he didn't want us to go in. He could be hiding something.'

'Or he may have simply wanted to stop the dog getting out,' Sunita suggested.

As they got into the car, Sunita realised their last visit of the day – to Miss Moretto's home – would have to be handled delicately.

'Sir, Miss Moretto's likely to be distressed.'

He nodded as he started the engine. 'That's why I'm glad, Sergeant, that you're here. If I was turning up alone, as a hulking great bloke, I might well have the door slammed in my face.'

Chapter 10

It was the second week running that the dark-haired woman had had to make the five-minute walk from her home to the town's police station.

On the first occasion, Miss Moretto had been reporting the theft of her jewellery. Her present mission was just as urgent – what on earth had happened to her boyfriend? He'd failed to make contact with her since he left her home on Sunday night. She was hoping and praying he'd not fallen victim to some terrible accident.

She climbed the stone steps at the front of the red-brick building and approached the reception desk. The burly sergeant invited her to wait in an interview room.

'Someone will come down and attend to you shortly, madam,' he told her.

After she'd spent a few minutes waiting on a chair by the window, PC Derek Underhill emerged in the doorway.

'It's Miss Moretto, isn't it?' he said, entering the room and closing the door behind him firmly.

'That's right. We met the other day. No news about my jewellery?'

'Sorry, no. But the local paper came to see you, didn't they? I hear they're running a report tomorrow.'

Angelina nodded. 'I know. Let's hope that leads somewhere. But I'm not here about that. This time I'm worried about my boyfriend, Oliver Bufton.'

The constable became solemn. He took a deep breath. 'I'm so sorry. I didn't realise he was your boyfriend.'

Her face was blank.

'You know Oliver?'

He frowned. 'You haven't heard, have you?'

'Heard what?'

'I'm awfully sorry, Miss Moretto. I'm afraid you won't be seeing him again.'

'What on earth d'you mean?'

'I'm afraid Oliver Bufton has passed away. It happened on Monday morning.'

'*Dio mio!*' she screamed. '*Era l'amore della mia vita. La mia vita è giunta al termine.*'

PC Underhill had poor knowledge of Italian, but realised she cared deeply for the dead man and was distraught at her loss.

She fell forward onto the small table in front of her with her head in her hands. When seconds later she sat up, her face was red and bathed with tears. '*Olly era il mio amore... mio amore!*' she screamed.

Her cries of woe alerted the desk sergeant and, moments later, two female constables rushed in and tried to placate her. Reverting to English, she cried, 'How can this be possible?'

PC Underhill fetched a box of tissues from the reception desk.

'All I can tell you is we're investigating how he died. Look, I think the best thing is for us to take you home. You only live round the corner, don't you?'

'By the station,' she sobbed.

'We'll take you home and make you a nice cup of tea.'

He whispered to one of the two women. They nodded and assisted Angelina as she left the room and was led out to a police car. Within a short time, she'd been driven home and was being consoled by the two women.

The desk sergeant asked PC Underhill, 'Was her boyfriend the poor man shot with the crossbow?'

'That's right,' the constable said. 'It's been in two of the national newspapers and everyone in Queensbridge is talking about it. She must have a bit of an isolated life. Somehow she missed out on the news.'

'It wasn't our job to inform her. But if she'd been married, we would have sent a welfare officer round.'

'That's right,' said the constable. 'Talking of which, do you know the number for welfare? It looks like she's going to need a bit of help.'

* * *

Shortly before six, Gavin Roscoe and Sunita Roy arrived in Oakdale Road. While he searched for a parking space, the sergeant stood at the gateway of Miss Moretto's house admiring the begonias and fuchsias flourishing in the front garden.

After a few minutes, as the scent of the flowers wafted towards her over the early evening air, a black cat peered cautiously out of the neighbour's gateway. Then he sidled up to her and nuzzled her trouser leg. As Sunita crouched down and stroked the animal's head, the chief inspector arrived at the gate.

'Is she in?'

'I haven't tried the door, sir. I thought it best to wait for you. I've just checked with Underhill. She was informed earlier of Bufton's death and has taken the news rather badly.'

'That's a shame. Makes it harder for us.'

The chief inspector strode up to the red door and rang the doorbell. But it was not Miss Moretto who responded. The door was opened by a middle-aged woman Roscoe recognised immediately, family liaison officer Pam Listers.

He broke into a smile. 'It's a surprise to find you here.'

Her eyes glazed over. 'I didn't think it would be long before you turned up, sir.'

'Do you know my new DS?'

Pam laughed. 'Of course. We met a few months ago. How are you?'

'Fine, thank you, Pam,' Sunita said.

She raised her hand and ushered them back into the front garden. 'I've just given Miss Moretto a sedative and she's gone to bed,' she said in a hushed voice.

Roscoe tutted. 'That's a nuisance. We desperately need to speak to her.'

'Have you been with her long, Pam?' Sunita asked.

'A good few hours.'

'Shall we go inside anyway, sir, and have a chat with Pam?'

Roscoe nodded and the pair followed Pam into the dark, narrow hallway.

She whispered, 'You'd better come through to the kitchen. It's the only room that's just about habitable.'

Pam's open laptop was perched on the far end of the kitchen table.

'Right. Make yourselves at home. How's the family, sir?'

'Much the same. Mel keeps tapping me for money. She wants to go to the fair tomorrow. George is toying with joining the force.'

'George would make a good copper,' Pam said. 'Wish our two lads would settle down.'

Pam, who liaised between detectives and families affected by serious crime, continued, 'You've no idea how upset Miss Moretto was when she discovered the man murdered in Biddington was Mr Bufton. She'd only known him a short time, but she worshipped the ground he walked on.'

Roscoe frowned as he sat at the table. 'Rather a strange combination. I mean, a glamorous fashion photographer and an electrician.'

'Yes, I know. But apparently there was more to him than meets the eye. He had charm, good looks and a very caring nature. He'd been to drama school and had ambitions to become an actor. He was only doing electrical work to pay the bills while he looked for stage work,' Pam said.

Sunita joined Roscoe at the table. 'Did you manage to find out much about Miss Moretto? For instance, details of her private life?'

'Not very much, I'm afraid. She worked for an agency in Birmingham. She had a short-lived marriage to a man named Carlo. That was annulled six years ago. Since then she's had a number of boyfriends.'

Sunita said, 'Wasn't there meant to have been a man with her when she was burgled?'

'I asked about that. She said he was an odd-job man, come to fix the washing machine. He tried to chase the burglars, but they got away.'

Sunita took out a small, black notebook and began writing. 'Why did she come to England in the first place?'

'Her work drew her here. She began by taking photographs for an Italian agency in London and then, three years ago, a job came up in Birmingham,' Pam said.

Sunita nodded. 'Did you ask why anyone would want to kill Oliver?'

Pam took a seat beside the laptop while she considered her answer. 'Not exactly, but I asked her about the men in her life and she was very guarded in what she said.'

Sunita shrugged. 'I suppose she didn't want you forming a bad impression of her.'

'Possibly. She was a little scared of one man, but she wouldn't give me any details. She implied he might be stalking her.'

Roscoe shook his head. 'Bloody nuisance. That knowledge she has could be key to the whole case.'

Sunita wondered whether Miss Moretto had any relatives in England.

'She went upstairs before I could ask her,' said Pam. 'But I've found this.'

She collected a postcard from the kitchen worktop and placed it on the table in front of the two detectives.

Sunita picked it up. 'Someone's had a Roman holiday – the Trevi Fountain, Sistine Chapel and the Colosseum.'

'It's addressed to Miss Moretto. I found it behind the kettle.'

'My Italian isn't very good,' said Roscoe. 'But I'll have a go. It looks like it says, "Dearest Angelina. Having a wonderful time in Roma. Marco's children, Elisabetta and Rosetta, have grown so much. They're now aged five and six. You must come and visit me again when I'm back in Stratford. Love, Cristina".'

Pam grinned. 'Not bad for a man with poor Italian.'

Sunita stood and wandered round the room while the other two were engrossed in conversation. She noticed a piece of white paper had been pinned to a corkboard behind jars containing tea and coffee.

'I think I might've found Cristina's address, sir,' she said. 'There's a note here saying Cristina Lorenzo, Applewick House, Cumbernauld Road, Stratford.'

Roscoe smiled. 'Well spotted, Sergeant. This Cristina is obviously a friend or relative. We must take a note of that. Might be helpful at some stage. Right, folks. I think it's time to go.'

Sunita nodded. 'We'll obviously have to come back when Miss Moretto's in a state to meet people.'

'Yes. I might send you along here sometime tomorrow, Sergeant. I take it you're going soon, are you, Pam?'

'Yes, sir. I thought I'd just tidy up for Miss Moretto and then head home.'

Roscoe got up. 'How's Raymond?'

'Fine, sir. Looking forward to retirement, like me!'

'Don't blame you. How long have you both served?'

She gave a broad grin. 'I've done twenty-nine years and he's done thirty-two.'

'It's time they let you go,' said the chief inspector, rising from his seat. 'You should have time off for good behaviour.'

'I'll miss everybody when we go,' she said.

'We'll miss you too,' said Roscoe.

Chapter 11

The sun was slowly fading from the sky, leaving in its wake a golden haze across the western horizon, as Tom Vickers' car drew up outside the roadside pub.

He smiled at his passenger. 'I hope this is all right, Sunita.'

She smiled back. 'We'll soon see.'

The new landlord of The Wheatsheaf Inn, just outside Redditch, had spent a great deal of money refurbishing the building after it had been neglected by the previous owners. The inspector had chosen to take Sunita there after remembering they provided hearty meals at reasonable prices.

A waitress showed them to a table by the window and brought them menus.

'You've been a bit quiet during the journey,' said Vickers as they sat down opposite each other. 'Is everything all right?'

'I've been thinking about poor old Olly Bufton. It was such a shock to see his dead body. I keep feeling we let him down. It was obvious someone was out to get him.'

Vickers, who was six years older than her, smiled reassuringly. 'You weren't to know how things would pan out. Lots of people get threatened and nothing comes of it.'

'I just wish I could've done something to save him.'

After ordering their meals and a bottle of chardonnay, Sunita adjusted her hair. 'How have you been getting on with the tyre tracks near Woodlands Cottage?'

'We've got one really good impression. It was a seven fifty by sixteen tyre.'

'That means nothing to me.'

He nodded. 'It's a tyre that's mainly used on Land Rovers and some military vehicles. The tread's slightly worn on the inner edge.'

As their waitress poured the wine into two glasses, Sunita asked, 'What does that show – that the vehicle's tracking needed attention?'

'Yes, probably, although there are mechanical problems that can lead to excessive wear in that part of the tyre.'

Sunita nodded and sipped her wine. 'What do you make of the handkerchief with the letter *C*?'

'Well, Dr Reynolds says it's a linen handkerchief – probably from Northern Ireland. Thorough tests have been carried out on it, but nothing of interest was found. Obviously, there was saliva from the dead man's mouth, but there's nothing from tests to link the item with any other person.

'I've been in contact with a number of manufacturers. From the weave structure and the style of the capital letter, it's unlikely we could find precisely where it came from because there's no packaging with it, of course. We could get the plods over there to trawl round the factories, but the chances are they'd only be able to find out the general area where it was made – not the actual mill. There's no laundry mark or any identifying label.'

Sunita smiled. 'So we've hit a bit of a brick wall there?'

'Looks like it, Sunita. As for the crossbow bolt, they come in all colours. Some crossbow users prefer a bright colour like a deep red because they're easier to find in rough terrain. A friend of mine in Wolverhampton reckons the killer could've used a hunting crossbow. They can be used for killing deer. Strictly illegal, of course.'

Sunita watched as he sipped his wine. 'That bowman must've been a crack shot. It requires a bit of skill, if you're hiding behind a hedge, to jump up and fire across five metres straight into a man's heart.'

He put his glass down. 'I agree. I think we might be looking for someone who's been shooting bows since childhood or practised for years.'

As the waitress brought Sunita's grilled salmon and served Vickers his chicken pie, he revealed he'd been asked to visit the archery club on the following Monday.

'It's in a place called Shawley Green in the heart of the countryside,' he said. 'It's the only place for miles around where you can learn to shoot with a crossbow. I'm hoping they're going to give us valuable information.'

Sunita cut into her salmon. 'That's the village the boss and I went to on Wednesday to see Walter Newman.' She ate a mouthful of fish and then said, 'I've been wondering if Bufton's love life was the trigger for his murder.'

'Why do you think that?'

'He'd known Angelina Moretto for two months and told me he was obsessed with her. The harassment only started after he began dating her.'

Vickers frowned. 'So had he replaced another man in her affections? Yes, I can see where you're coming from.'

'Jealousy is a very powerful emotion, Tom. But while that looks like a sensible line of inquiry, the man himself seemed sure that his new relationship was unconnected with all the incidents. A comment from Pam Listers has also stuck in my mind.'

'Is that the family liaison officer?'

She nodded. 'Yes. Miss Moretto told her she was scared of a particular man. It's vital to find out who that was.'

'Haven't you and the boss spoken to this Miss Moretto?'

'No. She's been under sedation. I think I ought to go and see her sometime this weekend. One of the DCs has been round a couple of times, but there's been no reply.'

Vickers finished a mouthful of pie. 'You take your job very seriously, don't you, Sunita?'

She nodded and smiled shyly. 'Yes. I want to make something of my life.'

'You will do,' he assured her. 'You've got all the right qualities to go all the way to the top, if you wanted to. I'm so glad you were able to come out with me this evening.'

She laughed. 'I got tired of saying no.'

'I hope we can do this again.'

'I'd like that.'

Chapter 12

Tom Vickers was pleased to return to work after an exhausting Sunday spent helping a friend decorate his house. He was looking forward to breathing in fresh country air at the archery club.

But his car was even more sluggish than usual as he drove away from his home in Halesowen and approached Shawley Green. It rattled and clattered along the road. He hoped it would continue running for a few more months so that he could save up enough to meet the inevitable repair bill.

After a few minutes, he spotted a sign on the main Stratford road showing that he needed to turn left for Warwick & Queensbridge Company of Archers. He followed the narrow lane through woods until he reached a clearing on the right-hand side and drove into the club car park.

As he emerged from his car clutching a manilla envelope, he noticed the clubhouse was a single-storey building. A sign outside gave directions to the reception desk, changing rooms, armoury, a trophy room, an indoor hall, a members' lounge and a cafe. Floodlights had been installed for evening archery sessions.

The clubhouse overlooked a huge sports field where twenty targets had been set up ninety metres away. Several archers were practising with longbows as he walked towards the main doors.

Vickers smiled at a teenage girl sitting behind the reception desk. 'Is there someone I can speak to?'

'What's it about?'

'I'm from Heart of England CID. I need some information about crossbow shooting.'

'I'll see if Jasmine Turner's available.'

Moments later, a smiling blonde woman in a white, floral-patterned blouse and blue jeans approached and introduced herself.

'Hi. I'm Jasmine, the club secretary,' she said.

'DI Vickers. I just need a few minutes of your time.'

'Shall we go somewhere quieter? Would you like a tea or coffee?'

'Coffee would be good,' he said.

After asking the receptionist to make two coffees, she led Vickers into the lounge with a row of floor-to-ceiling windows and a set of glass doors overlooking the archery field. They sat down in armchairs either side of a small table.

Jasmine flicked her long hair out of her eyes. 'I gather you want to know about crossbows? Is this because of the murder the other day?'

He nodded.

'Well, most of our members shoot with short bows or longbows and many of them frown on the use of crossbows. But we've got a small group of enthusiasts who regularly use a crossbow.'

'Why is there opposition from longbow users?'

Jasmine shrugged. 'All sorts of reasons. One reason, believe it or not, is they were used by the French in the Middle Ages while the English used longbows. You wouldn't think that could be a factor, but it is.'

Vickers grinned. 'They've been in use for thousands of years, haven't they?'

'Yes, not here, of course. The club only started in 1950. They were used in wars in Roman times and these days they're used for hunting in the USA.'

As their coffees arrived, he looked around and realised the club enjoyed vast grounds. He caught a glimpse through the windows of a lake shrouded by reeds, shrubs and trees.

'How many of your members use crossbows?'

'I'll have a look at our records, but I think it's around thirty. Some come regularly – others less so. I'll have to introduce you to Laura Pitchford, Charlene Jones, Lucy McKie or Tom Millwood. They're all regulars here with the crossbow. We've even got a lad on a community scheme, Frank Baker, who's been introduced to the crossbow.'

Vickers raised an eyebrow. 'Wasn't he the one-boy crimewave?'

She laughed. 'That's right.'

He pulled a colour photograph from his envelope. 'Look, I wanted to show you this picture of a particular crossbow bolt we're interested in.'

Jasmine studied it for a few moments. 'It's crimson, isn't it? It looks a bit like the ones our members use.'

His eyes lit up. 'Really? That's interesting.'

'Yes. Some of our members say it's easier to find them in the rough. Actually, we had a break-in a month ago and a batch of our bolts were taken.'

'Did you report this to the police?'

'Yes, your colleagues in Stratford dealt with it. We also had some cigarettes stolen from the cafe. The premises are a bit isolated, as you've no doubt discovered. We've got a security firm making regular patrols, but they aren't here all the time. Someone smashed a window at the back and got in.'

'Do you know if Stratford police had forensic tests done?'

'They sent a forensic woman round. She thought she might've picked up a couple of fingerprints, but we've heard nothing more. Apparently, there are a lot of burglaries going on at the moment and there's only a slim chance of catching them.'

He was excited to hear about the break-in. He wondered if it could be linked to Bufton's murder.

'Do you think this one could be from the batch that was stolen?' he asked.

'There's a good chance. We ordered a large consignment of crimson bolts with red, yellow and white fletchings.'

Jasmine examined the photograph again. 'That murder in Biddington was terrible, wasn't it? Have you got any clues yet about who might be behind it?'

'I can't go into details, I'm afraid, for operational reasons,' the inspector said. 'I'm sure you'll understand. But I need to ask whether you've got any suspicions about any of your archers.'

Jasmine shook her head. 'We collect a lot of information when people become members. It's true we don't check into criminal backgrounds, but we're like a family here. We'd soon get to know if a member had no regard for the law. I can't swear that all our members are angels, but I can't think of anyone who'd use a crossbow to commit murder.'

'Have you banned anyone recently?'

'We had to eject a couple of men in February when they got drunk. They'd arrived a little the worse for wear and, while here, they drank more. They're now banned.'

'Perhaps you can give me their names later,' he said. 'So you think the killer must've been a practised hand?'

'Yes. I tell you what. I think it would help you to speak to one of our crossbow regulars. You wait here. I'll go and see if one of them's around.'

The inspector put his photograph back in the envelope and sipped his coffee. A few minutes later, Jasmine reappeared with a shy woman with long dark hair who was in her late twenties. She was accompanied by a smiling, confident younger woman with short, dark hair and black-framed glasses. The inspector stood up to greet them.

'Hello, I'm Charlene,' said the shy woman, reaching out to shake his hand. 'How are you? All right?'

Jasmine glanced at her proudly. 'Charlene's been winning lots of competitions. And can I also introduce Lucy McKie?'

The inspector smiled and shook their hands.

Jasmine patted the detective on the shoulder. 'Is it OK if I leave them with you? I'm needed at reception.'

As she left, Vickers showed the two archers his photograph and they confirmed it resembled the kind of bolt they used.

'This could be from the batch that was stolen,' said Charlene. 'It's got the same colour fletchings. We've ordered some more, but they're taking ages to come in. They're made in Derbyshire.'

'How long have you been using a crossbow then?' he wondered.

'Only about six months, but I seem to have a natural flair.'

'Could one of you show me how to fire one? I've never seen one in action before. I know my guvnor would want me to examine one and find out how they operate.'

Charlene beamed at him. 'Absolutely. I've just placed my crossbow at reception.'

After collecting the weapon, she returned to the table.

'This is my favourite one. It's a recurve crossbow – a bow which curves forward at the ends. The rules here are the bow must be a recurve, the draw weight has to be under ninety-five pounds and it's got to be cocked by hand.'

The inspector picked it up to gauge its weight. 'It's heavier than I expected.'

Lucy interrupted. 'You can get them fairly cheaply. A reasonable second-hand one would set you back two or three hundred pounds. But mine's a sturdy, well-built one and cost a lot more. Would you like to watch us shoot?'

He nodded and followed them out of the clubhouse.

Charlene took up a position sixteen metres from a standard archery target, cocked her crossbow and loaded a bolt. Then the inspector heard a click and the shaft skimmed through the air before piercing the golden bullseye.

He beamed in surprise. 'Good shot!' he cried before Charlene struck the edge of the bullseye with two further shots.

She smiled. 'This bow isn't too difficult to cock and quite accurate, as you saw.'

Lucy stepped forward. 'Can I borrow yours for a moment, Charlie?'

Charlene nodded and handed the crossbow over. Lucy then struck the bullseye with three shots, improving slightly on her rival's score.

'Just a bit of luck there,' Lucy mumbled.

Charlene frowned and took the device back. 'It's a good all-round crossbow – very practical and very easy to use. You get something like sixty metres per second out of it. It packs a powerful punch and it would be quite capable of killing someone if it got into the wrong hands.'

Chapter 13

'Good morning, darling!' Larry Holland bowled into the room and gazed out of the patio doors towards his lush, green rear lawn. The grey-haired, forty-eight-year-old businessman found his wife sitting at the oval table in the large dining room of their Warwick house, eating grapefruit.

She beamed at him. 'Good morning, dear. It looks like another bright day. Have you got much planned?'

He nodded and then announced in his gravelly voice, 'Yes, I've got a busy morning. I've got to be in the office at ten o'clock and I've got meetings all day. By the way, you haven't forgotten I'm going to be away at the end of this month, have you?'

Virginia – or Ginny, as she preferred to be called – pressed her forehead with her left hand as she paused for a moment to think. 'Is that the Lift and Escalator Exhibition?'

'Yes, I'll be away between 28 May and 3 June.'

'So you'll be away for the bank holiday weekend?'

'Yes, there's a lot of work involved in setting up the stand. I want to be there to supervise and I've also been invited to make a speech. Sorry, dear.'

She picked up a piece of buttered toast. 'Remind me again where it's being held?'

'Aberdeen.'

'Oh, that's right. Aberdeen. I wouldn't have thought there would've been enough people interested in mechanical lifts to make it last a week.'

He ignored that remark. What did she know about lifts?

'Why they've got to hold it in Aberdeen I'll never know – when they've got the wonderful exhibition centre in Birmingham, which is so central for the whole of the UK. I hope you'll be all right while I'm away – not too bored. You tend to get bored easily, don't you, dear?'

Ginny looked surprised that the idea of her becoming bored could have entered her husband's mind.

'Of course not. I've got the residents' association business to see to. I can visit our two nieces and I'll have a chance to spend a bit of time with some of my friends.'

Larry found she had placed some letters beside his placemat. Using a table knife, he slitted the first envelope open. A credit card bill.

'How much? This can't be right!' he exclaimed. 'It's over two thousand pounds!'

Blonde-haired Ginny, who looked relaxed in her white-towelling dressing gown with white faux-fur slippers, gazed at him.

'What's that, Larry?'

'It's your bloody shopping, by the look of it. You've been ordering online again, haven't you? Look at this lot – Andersons, Jersey halter dress and flared trousers; Andersons, two trouser suits and a pussy-bow blouse; Andersons, a lurex top and a loose-wrap dress. You must think money grows on bushes in the garden. Bloody Andersons!'

Ginny was furious that Larry was questioning her fashion spending.

'You want me to look good when I'm with you, don't you? All women need to keep up with the trends. Some of my friends spend far more than me.'

Larry glared. 'Maybe their husbands haven't got a huge mortgage. Look, Ginny, we can't go on like this. You're spending money we need for other things.'

Ginny stood up angrily. 'Who was talking the other day about buying another car? It sometimes seems you only want me around to skivvy for you and keep your home nice while you want all the money spent on yourself. I spend a few hundred pounds on nice new clothes and you resent it. Well, I've had enough.'

She picked up the glass milk jug, which was in the centre of the table. Then she marched across to the end of the table, where her husband of twelve years was sitting in his smart, dark-blue suit.

'Be careful,' he shouted. 'The gardener will be here in a minute.'

Ginny was not worried that their part-time gardener might hear them arguing. Although her husband rose from his chair in an attempt to escape, he was not fast enough.

She succeeded in pouring most of the milk over his head before stomping back to her chair. For a few seconds, the irate husband remained standing by the table, allowing the semi-skimmed milk to cascade from his head and shoulders onto the carpet.

He scowled at her. 'You've really done it now. That was a step too far. I'll have to get showered and changed and will be late for work.'

Then he stormed off upstairs. Ginny, who had started to become used to the rows that had beset her marriage, tried to continue with her breakfast as though nothing dramatic had happened.

She took a sip of tea. She gathered a spoonful of marmalade from the jar and smoothed it across her toast. She took several mouthfuls, but finally gave up. She'd lost her appetite.

Judging by the way their lives had played out before, she knew few words would be spoken between them for the next few days. Then there would be a thaw in the atmosphere and, gradually, their relationship would return to normal.

Until the next time, she thought. But would there be a next time? And for how much longer could she endure this hollow shell of a marriage? She took some of the plates to the kitchen and threw the remains of her toast into the waste bin.

Chapter 14

For several days, Sunita Roy had been trying without success to speak to Oliver Bufton's girlfriend, Miss Moretto. She had called at the house at various times of the day – even at 6 a.m. on one occasion. All her efforts had failed.

As Tuesday, 9 May dawned, she resolved to make one last attempt to take a statement from her.

It was nearly seven in the evening when she arrived in Oakdale Road, looking for a suitable parking space. She eventually found one and walked up the street to the house with the red door.

But although she pressed the doorbell several times and could hear its sound echoing around the house, there was no response. Had she gone to stay with relatives? Had she gone back to Italy?

After so many futile visits, Sunita was now determined to solve the mystery of Miss Moretto's apparent disappearance. Although she was on her own, she decided to explore the garden and rear of the house.

Gingerly, she crept along the side of the building until she came to the back window. She glanced in, but the kitchen appeared unchanged from her visit with the chief inspector the previous week.

She gazed along the fence, where there were overgrown flower borders, unclipped bushes and dense foliage. She also cast an eye over the rear garden with its tall grass surrounded by more neglected flower borders. Nothing there seemed notable, except that there were two ladies' dresses, some underwear and two bras hanging from the washing line.

'Well,' she said to herself. 'Nothing ventured.'

She tried to turn the chrome handle on the back door and was astonished when it opened. Cautiously, she stepped into the kitchen. 'Miss Moretto!' she called – almost expecting the lady of the house to come parading down the corridor towards her, asking what she wanted.

Somehow she doubted that would happen, but she called the householder's name again. Her plaintive call remained unanswered.

Sunita opened the door to the hallway and walked to the foot of the stairs. It had not yet reached dusk, but she turned on the hall light to give herself greater vision. She turned another switch for the landing light.

Then, with trepidation, she mounted the stairs and gradually reached the top. Her best guess was that the homeowner was in the back bedroom – her photographic studio – working on a project. But she was not there.

Then she tried the middle bedroom and the front bedroom. She was not there either. Sunita, becoming concerned at what she might find, thought to herself, well at least the poor woman isn't dead.

Then, unexpectedly, she heard a noise downstairs. It was unclear what it was. It sounded like knocking.

I never checked the front room downstairs, she thought to herself. She crept to the top of the stairs and looked down. The menacing shadow of a tall man had been cast onto the hallway floor. His muscular body seemed to be pressing against the front door and he was calling out softly, 'Miss Moretto. Miss Moretto.'

Come on! You're a Detective Sergeant now, she told herself.

Steeling herself as best she could, she descended the stairs and slowly drew open the front door.

Standing there with a torch in his hand was that stalwart of Queensbridge police, PC Derek Underhill.

'Oh, Derek!' The words burst from her lips. 'You really had me going there for a minute.'

He frowned. 'Whatever's the matter, Sergeant? You've turned as white as a sheet.'

'Well, you did look a bit like Lurch from the Addams Family, standing there in the doorway. But I'm glad to see you.'

Underhill stepped into the hall. 'What are you doing here?'

'I could ask you the same question.'

'I asked first.'

'The Chief Inspector asked me to interview Miss Moretto. I've been trying to catch her in for days. Today I decided to take a chance and search the house.'

He looked bewildered. 'How did you get in?'

She shrugged. 'The back door was unlocked, believe it or not. I've checked all the rooms except the front room. I phoned Pam Listers earlier on, but she hasn't seen her for several days.'

On saying this, she opened the living-room door and peered inside. 'She's definitely not in the house.'

'That's strange. We received a call from her employers. She's not made any contact with them and they gave us a call. It's a shame. We've got some news about her jewellery – someone tried to pawn them up in Brum.'

Just then the pair heard a noise in the garden.

A scruffily dressed man with long grey hair and a beard approached the doorway. 'Excuse me. I saw the light was on.'

Sunita, who was standing near the stairs, was startled by his appearance. His face bore a small scar and she suspected he'd got a glass eye. But Underhill remained calm and composed.

He turned and smiled. 'Good evening, Michael. Can I help?'

The stranger stepped towards them. 'Oh it's you, Derek. You know we live next door? Well, something really strange has just happened.'

The constable glanced towards Sunita and lowered his voice. 'It's all right. It's one of our local characters, Michael Peploe.'

Underhill turned to the man. 'You'd better come in, Michael. What's happened?'

The newcomer was short of breath. 'Our cat's been out all afternoon. She just came back. She's got blood on her paws.'

Underhill shrugged. 'Perhaps she's cut herself on something.'

'No. It's on at least two of her paws.'

Sunita walked towards the doorway. 'I saw a small black cat in the street the other evening.'

'That's right. That's our Blackie. He goes in all the gardens round here. Just a short while ago he clambered over the fence between this house and ours, like he often does, and came through the cat-flap in the back door. He left red pawprints on the kitchen floor.'

Sunita looked at the hall carpet. 'Could it be red paint?'

'I suppose that's possible.'

Underhill asked if Peploe would accompany them to Angelina's back garden, where petunias, fuchsias and begonias were attempting to thrive among the weeds. As they walked, Peploe chatted constantly. 'Angelina was in the local paper, you know. Page three. It was about her burglary. My mum calls her the man magnet.'

Sunita was intrigued. 'Did Miss Moretto have a lot of male visitors?'

'You could say that.'

They approached the part of the fence where, according to Peploe, the cat often clambered up and down. But Sunita was distracted. Her eyes had noticed what seemed to be a large clump of foliage beneath a boundary hedge. She looked more closely and realised in horror that she could make out the shape of a human hand, poking skywards.

'Oh my God, Derek!' she exclaimed. 'There's a body under the hedge.'

Chapter 15

Sunita Roy clasped her hand round her mouth as she stared at the human hand in the dim light. She found herself shaking. The nails were decorated in red varnish. She also caught glimpses of a red dress. But she refrained from removing any of the leaves, plants and earth that covered the body for fear of disturbing the site.

Underhill quickly assumed charge.

'Look, Michael, I think it's best you leave. It looks like we've got a crime scene here.'

Peploe's eyes twinkled with curiosity as he was shepherded along the side path towards the front gate.

'Do you think it's Angelina?'

'You'll have to leave us to get on with our job, Michael.'

Within half an hour, the garden became a hive of activity. Underhill's uniformed colleagues cordoned off the pavement at the front of the house while a forensic team set up arc lights and took steps to protect the scene.

Sunita stood a few metres away, watching the activity. A police photographer arrived to take images of the body and an inch-by-inch search was conducted of the area round the location, but they delayed removing the body as they were aware that Home Office pathologist Dr Silas Reynolds was on his way.

Eventually, a black Mercedes E-Class convertible drew up outside and the doctor emerged. After putting on a plastic apron and rubber gloves, he removed his brown leather bag from the boot and proceeded towards the body.

'Good evening, Sergeant,' the middle-aged pathologist murmured as he passed her. 'Right. What have we here?'

He and a forensic assistant knelt and carefully removed the dead plants and leaves. Sunita could see more clearly now that it was the body of a woman, partly caked in blood.

She called out to him, 'Are you all right, sir?'

He glanced towards her. 'I'm fine, Sergeant. Which is more than can be said for this young lady. Was it you that found her?'

'Yes. We believe this could be the body of Angelina Moretto, who lives here. She's been missing. We searched the house and garden and were about to go when we found her.'

'Well, welcome to the gruesome world of pathology, my dear. Is Gavin on his way or is he leaving it all to you?'

'He's been alerted. We think this woman's got links to the man killed at Biddington.'

'Well, it looks like you're on the money there, young lady,' said Dr Reynolds. 'She appears to have been killed in the same manner. She's got a red crossbow bolt in the heart and a handkerchief's been stuffed into her mouth.'

* * *

Twenty minutes later, the chief inspector arrived at the murder scene and first spoke to the crime scene manager by the front door of Miss Moretto's house.

Sunita noticed him and was about to join him when her attention was drawn to tiny traces of white fabric that had been caught on the rough brickwork at the corner of the house. The material had become snagged at waist height. She signalled to a woman from the forensic team, who was walking past.

'Could you take a look at this?' she asked. 'Seem to be threads of material caught on the brick.'

'Certainly, Sergeant. I'll make that my next job,' the woman replied.

Roscoe stepped towards her. 'Ah, Sergeant. I gather you found the body?'

'Yes, sir. Only by chance.'

'Well done. You look a little unwell. Are you all right?'

'Yes. I'm fine. Just the shock of finding it, I suppose. I'll be OK.'

'Good. Is that Silas I can see over there?'

As he walked towards the back garden, he found lightweight anti-contamination plates made from rubber had been placed at certain points so that detectives and forensic staff could walk around without the risk of damaging potential evidence.

On approaching the pathologist, he could make out the body of a dark-haired woman. She was wearing a floral-patterned, red dress. He thought she resembled the burglary victim who'd appeared in the local newspaper, but he wasn't sure.

The pathologist stood up and placed his hands on his hips.

'Good evening, Gavin. This is a sorry business.'

'I can see that. What do you know so far?'

'Well, the poor woman's five feet six inches tall and Caucasian. She's got dark hair and she's in her late twenties, I'd say. She was lying in a supine position. There are certain similarities to the murder in Biddington. But there's one major difference. In this case, the arrow's passed right through the body. It's pierced her chest, sliced through her heart and possibly a major blood vessel and then emerged from her back. Death would have occurred five or ten minutes later.'

Roscoe frowned. 'Any idea when she died, Silas?'

'Rigor mortis has already set in, which takes twelve hours. I'd have thought some time yesterday, but we'll be taking temperatures of parts of the body and I'll carry out further tests in an effort to be more precise.'

Roscoe crouched down. 'Presumably she wasn't killed at this exact spot?'

'That's right, old fruit. The body's been dragged here. There are scuff marks on the ground. There's also been superficial attempts to conceal the body. The handkerchief that was in her mouth, again, has an embroidered letter *C* in the corner.'

A forensic assistant interrupted him, pointing to the woman's clenched right hand.

'Something else. A clothes peg in her right hand. Looks like she may've been hanging out or collecting the washing.'

Reynolds added that the victim had been wearing a Swiss-made ladies' watch and a silver necklace – probably made in Italy.

Making use of the rubber stepping-stones, Roscoe then made his way to the washing line, which stretched right across the back lawn. He examined the grass and found a large pool of blood in the middle of the lawn with further traces of blood leading to the hedge. He also found tracks in the lawn which could have been left by a pair of feet being dragged.

As Sunita approached him, Roscoe took her aside. 'It may be that the killer came upon his victim while she was pegging out the washing.' He pointed to traces of blood on the grass.

In turn, the sergeant pointed to the corner of the house. 'I found some threads on the brickwork earlier, sir. They've been bagged up by forensics, but it suggests the person with the crossbow stooped down and leaned on the wall for support.'

He patted her on the shoulder. 'That's a great find. Could prove crucial. The only thing is the house was burgled recently, wasn't it? It's possible the burglars got close to the corner and left the material you found.'

She shrugged. 'Yes, that's possible.'

Roscoe frowned. 'It looks as though the killer fired as Miss Moretto was facing him. Then he dragged her body to the hedge, pressed the handkerchief into her mouth and tried to cover the body over before making off.'

Sunita agreed. 'We need to get going with some house-to-house, sir.'

'Yes, we must make a start on that.'

The poignant words of Oliver Bufton kept sweeping through Sunita's mind. He'd known a woman for two months, he'd said, and had become 'absolutely besotted' with her. It seemed clear that the woman must have been Miss Moretto. Now she, like Bufton, was dead. Both slaughtered in the prime of their lives. Bufton had said, 'Someone's out to get me.'

Sunita made a solemn vow to herself as she stood at the scene of this second crossbow attack. She'd catch the person responsible and bring them to justice.

'That's the least I can do for this poor couple,' she declared.

Chapter 16

The chief inspector received some encouraging news when he arrived at St James Street headquarters the next morning. He answered the phone and Dr Reynolds' educated tones greeted him.

'Gavin, we've got some useful shoe prints off the body of that Martello woman.'

Gavin raised an eyebrow. 'Moretto.'

'Sorry, Moretto. Never was very good with foreign surnames, apart from Latin and Greek ones. Listen, we've got two really good impressions of shoe marks from the body.'

'I'm being a little slow this morning, Silas. These aren't her shoe prints you're talking about?'

'Good God, no. Didn't I tell you? Besides being shot with a crossbow, this lady was kicked repeatedly by her assailant in a show of great anger.'

Roscoe was annoyed with himself. 'When you mentioned shoe prints, I thought you meant marks on the ground.'

'No, there's nothing on the ground, but the killer's kicked the poor lady in the head and stomach. So we're looking at two impressions – one on the right side of the deceased's forehead, which left a gross swelling, and one to the stomach, which isn't quite so clear. People don't realise we can get shoe print patterns off clothing. In this case, it's a fairly small shoe with the sole featuring lines, circles and ellipses.'

Roscoe sat down at his desk. 'Any idea what kind of footwear, Silas?'

'I can't tell you much else, apart from the fact we believe it was a right shoe. We're checking the national database to see if the prints come from the shoes of any known offenders. I'll send pictures over to you so you can see for yourself. She doesn't appear to have been sexually assaulted though.'

There was a long pause. Roscoe wondered if the pathologist had hung up. Then his voice roared down the phone again.

'Nearly forgot to mention, old fruit. Just received a report on the fibres caught on the wall. They appear to come from some kind of cream-coloured shirt made from cheesecloth. Might be a vintage shirt sold at markets. But your forensic people haven't turned up any dabs on the shafts of the crossbow bolts. Looks like the killer could have worn gloves.'

After ending the call, Roscoe felt pleased. At any moment of the day, he dreaded a phone call from the floor above – the office of Chief Superintendent Nicola Norris. Known throughout the building as 'Niggler Norris', she kept her senior officers on a tight rein. But CID seemed to be making significant progress with the two murders and he felt she'd have no reason to berate him.

His thoughts were suddenly interrupted by a knock. DI Vickers peered round the doorway.

'Are you free for a moment, sir?'

'Yes, of course. I wanted to speak to you anyway, Tom. Come in.'

The inspector smiled as he passed his boss a list of names.

'There are around thirty crossbow users at the Wackos club and I'm gradually going through them, making inquiries about each one. I've started with a group of ten who regularly shoot with a crossbow.'

'Anything of interest turned up?'

'Not so far.'

Roscoe leaned back in his chair. 'I think we should contact Andy Chadwick at Stratford – just out of courtesy – and find out about the break-in at the club. Didn't we hear two members got banned? We need to know more about that as well.'

'Yes sir. I'll get onto that right away. And I think we should apply for the phone records of Bufton's and Moretto's phones?'

Roscoe nodded. 'I'll ask Khalid to see to that.'

He followed the inspector as he made his way to the doorway. Once Vickers had gone, he bellowed across the office, 'DS Roy, have you got a minute?'

Moments later, his sergeant tapped on the door and entered.

'Morning, sir. I've discovered a few things at Miss Moretto's house.'

'Yes, take a seat, Sergeant. Tell me about it.'

'Well, sir, the SOCO team found evidence that Olly Bufton had been at the house with Miss Moretto, but they've found no links to any other men. However, I've found some interesting material. First of all, she kept a diary. She didn't write much and what she did write was in Italian, so we're getting a translator. But I did pick up details of a man we've not come across before. He's called Ricky Stanton. He lives in Masons Road, Stratford. His name and address are not in her handwriting, so maybe she got someone to write them in her diary for her.'

'Yes. Maybe she couldn't grasp the spellings and got him to jot it down for her.'

'Yes, sir. Exactly. The same person must have written down the name of a garage, West Avon Motors as it's in the same handwriting as the name and address. That's probably where this Mr Stanton works.'

'Yes, could be a mechanic or a salesman. Good work, Sergeant.'

She stood up, ready to leave. 'Oh, I forgot to mention. I looked through a bundle of correspondence in a bedroom drawer, I also found lots of letters to her from Cristina Lorenzo.'

'Does it give the same address as the one you discovered the other day in the kitchen?'

'That's right – Cumbernauld Road.'

'All right. It looks as though the two of us will have to go to Stratford in the next day or two to see this Mr Stanton and also the Lorenzo woman. But right now, go back to Oakdale Road. Talk to the neighbours. Find out about any visitors. We might pick up some useful information from them.'

As she walked to the door, he added, 'Take a bit of time with them, Sergeant. Neighbours often know more than they first let on.'

* * *

George Roscoe rushed downstairs to greet his father the moment he arrived home from work that evening. He stood in the open doorway of the family home with a smile that could light up a street.

The chief inspector closed the garage doors and strode past the windows towards him.

'You look like a man with something important on his mind.'

George nodded. 'I've got some news, Dad.'

His father stepped into the hall and placed some documents on the small table. 'What is it, George?'

'I may as well come straight out with it, Dad. I've got an interview with Heart of England.'

'You never actually told me you were applying. I could've helped you with the application.'

'To be honest, Dad, I wanted to do it on my own. I know you could've helped me, but I suppose I wanted to prove something to myself.'

Roscoe smiled. 'Well, if that's your chosen career, good for you. The force has changed a lot since the days I was pounding the beat. Anyway, George, I'm so pleased for you.'

George stepped into the living room. 'This is only the start of the recruitment process. I've got to get through the interview. Then I'll have to go away on a course.'

'Yes, it's rigorous training, but from what I know of you, you shouldn't have any problem. Have you told your mother?'

George shook his head. 'Not yet. I want to find the right time when she's not too busy. The course is at least ten weeks. I'll have to give up my shifts at the Coach and Horses.'

'I dare say your mother and I can help you out financially. Money's the last thing you should be worrying about. Come here, son!'

The pair hugged as the sound of rain could be heard splattering on the stone path outside and tapping against the windows.

'I'm really proud of you.'

Roscoe noticed for some reason a lump had formed in his throat.

Chapter 17

Michael Peploe's home was in a dilapidated state. The cement rendering was cracked and letting in damp. The wooden frames round the windows were rotting.

As Sunita Roy entered his front garden, she found the only splash of colour was provided by yellow dandelions and mauve buddleia – the plant that often thrives on railway embankments.

The ground was choked with weeds. Some wooden boxes and a rusty bicycle had been left by the front window.

She rapped on the partly rotten grey front door and waited. After a brief moment, fifty-five-year-old Peploe dragged it open.

He frowned. 'Oh, you're the detective I saw last night.'

She held out her warrant card. 'That's right. DS Roy from Heart of England. Can I come in?'

'Yes, I suppose so. Excuse the mess. You've just missed Mother. They've picked her up and taken her to her luncheon club.'

As she walked into the dim hallway, Blackie the cat sprang out from somewhere and followed her, purring loudly.

Peploe led the sergeant into the living room where his eighty-eight-year-old mother, Violet, was accustomed to sitting by the bay window with a view of the street. The room was cluttered with piles of clothing and furniture.

Sunita smiled. 'It must've been upsetting, finding the blood on Blackie.'

'Yes, it was. I thought he might've been in a fight with a dog or a fox when I first saw him. When I realised it was our neighbour's blood, well... you can imagine... we were horrified. Mum keeps asking, "Is she dead?"'

Sunita noticed two empty chairs by the door before telling him, 'I'm afraid she *is* dead.'

She found the atmosphere unsettling. There was a musty smell – possibly cat's urine. She was eager to get the interview over quickly.

Peploe glanced at her. 'So what's all this about?'

'Don't worry. It's nothing to worry about. It's just that my guvnor wanted to know about Miss Moretto's visitors. We understand several men would turn up.'

They sat down simultaneously. Michael nodded. 'There were always men. Would you like some tea?'

Sunita wanted to decline. She feared that, if the house was dusty and untidy, the teacups might not be clean. But she also felt Michael was more likely to speak freely if she accepted his hospitality.

'Any chance of a lemon tea?'

'We don't have any lemon.'

'Just a tea with no milk and one sugar, please.'

Five minutes later, he was back with two steaming hot cups of tea.

As he handed Sunita her cup, he remarked, 'You're from India, aren't you? They're big fans of tea over there.'

She nodded. 'That's right. We love our tea.'

Michael was eager to tell her about Angelina's male friends. 'There were at least three men visiting in the last few months. We weren't really spying. We're not like that, but Mother likes to sit by the window and watch the street. I suppose you could call her a people-watcher. She called one of Angelina's visitors Flash Harry. We reckoned he might have been some kind of salesman. I heard him shout at Angelina once – real cockney he was. He often dressed up smartly in a suit and always drove a posh sports car. Gave her flowers a lot, he did.'

Sunita took out her notebook. 'When did you both first notice Flash Harry?'

'Must've been February or March. He was still knocking on her door a few days before she was murdered.'

'What did he look like?'

'Short, receding hair, average height. We didn't just see the men turning up at the front door. In the summer months, she'd be sitting out in the garden with them.'

Sunita folded her arms. 'One at a time, I take it.'

'Yes, of course, but she really liked men, did Angelina.'

'Can you describe any of the others?'

Michael thought for a moment as he sipped his tea. 'Well, there was the one Mother calls Smiler.'

'Smiler?'

'Yes, he always had a grin on his face.'

Sunita knew at once he must be referring to Oliver Bufton.

She raised her pen. 'When did Smiler start visiting Miss Moretto and when did you last see him?'

Michael looked to the wall as if seeking inspiration. 'He was new on the scene. Mother first noticed him about a month ago, but the first time I saw him was that day it rained heavily. He was made up like a trawlerman, but still with a broad smile.'

Sunita said, 'When did you last see him?'

'Sometime in April. He was out in the garden with her. I went round to get Blackie and he was there.'

'What – you went into her garden?'

'Yes. She didn't seem to mind as I needed to get the cat in. I often went round there – sometimes Angelina was in, sometimes she wasn't. Sometimes Blackie won't come when he's called.' Michael shrugged his shoulders. 'She never complained so I carried on going round there every now and then.'

Sunita decided she was glad the Peploes weren't her neighbours.

He looked into her eyes. 'They were kissing and cuddling on garden loungers.'

Sunita made a note of his remarks. 'Were there any other men?'

Michael smiled to himself. 'There was one other man. He was well-tanned as if he'd spent a lot of time in the sun. I suppose you might call him swarthy. And he'd got jet black hair. Mother called him Sun-lover.'

'When did you first see him?'

'I only saw him a couple of times in the middle of last month.'

'You obviously don't know the proper names of any of these men?'

He shook his head. 'No idea who they were – just Angelina's boyfriends.'

'What sort of ages were they?'

'Flash Harry was about forty. Smiler was about thirty. Sun-lover was mid-twenties.' Michael glanced at Sunita as she was writing. 'They were getting younger all the time. Sorry. I suppose I shouldn't joke as the poor woman's now dead.'

She slipped her notebook into her handbag. 'All right. I'd better be going.'

'Any news about the burglars who took the jewellery?'

'Sorry. Not my department.'

'We thought one of her men friends might've taken her jewellery – maybe out of spite if she played with their affections,' said Michael. 'Having different men round... well, men sometimes get upset if they're jilted.'

Sunita decided it was time to leave. 'You've been very helpful, Michael. I'm going to have to speak to some of the other neighbours as well.'

'You might get somewhere with the Woods next door. They're real gossips. If anything's going on round here, they tend to know about it.'

'Thank you,' she said.

'Don't bother with the people on the other side of Angelina's house. They keep themselves to themselves.'

Sunita stood up. 'By the way, I want to reassure you. We don't believe there's a homicidal maniac on the loose. Police think the two deaths are connected, so we're confident that will now be the end of the matter.'

Chapter 18

A key could be heard turning in the latch. Footsteps thudded onto the mat. The door in the Birmingham suburb of Hall Green slammed shut.

Sunita's flatmate Rupa Chakrabarty put her leather laptop bag down on the hall carpet. 'Sunita, are you home yet?'

'Yes, I'm in the front room.'

Rupa found her lying the full length of their grey, three-seater settee. She frowned. 'Oh there you are, Sunita. Hey, you look terrible.'

The detective tried to smile. 'I don't feel great. I'm exhausted.'

Rupa noticed a half-empty box of tissues on the coffee table and a trail of used ones on the floor.

'You've been crying. What's the matter?'

'I'm thinking of giving up my job. I don't think I can take it.'

Rupa slumped down into an armchair. 'Is this the crossbow case you were telling me about – the man killed at the thatched cottage?'

Sunita shook her head. 'I haven't seen you since Monday, have I? There's been another murder. This time it was me that found the body.'

'Oh, Sunita. That's terrible. How did you come to find it?'

'I called round at a house in Queensbridge, trying to speak to the dead man's girlfriend. It was just by chance that I found her in the garden. She was under a hedge, hidden by leaves.'

Rupa leaned towards her friend. 'Oh my God, Sunita.'

'I always wanted to be in the police. Now I'm not sure if I'm cut out for it.'

Rupa, not as tall as Sunita and with medium-length, black hair, tutted. 'We all have our bad days. You've always wanted to join the police – even before you went on your law course at uni. You must've known you'd have to deal with sudden deaths.'

'I know. I thought I could handle it. But I've had to gawp at two dead bodies in two weeks. I can still see the poor woman's face, staring at me. I'm sure I'm going to have nightmares.'

Rupa frowned. 'You're bound to react like that.'

Sunita sighed. 'I thought, after four years in the police, I'd be used to seeing dead people.'

'Maybe it takes far longer to get used to the experience. Come on. I'll make you a cup of tea.'

She stood up, intending to head for the kitchen. Then she hesitated and sat down again.

'Sunita, I don't know if this is the right time for me to mention this but, since I might not see you for a day or two, I think I'd better tell you now. I've got a new job.'

Her friend sat up. 'Oh, Rupa, that's brilliant. Where?'

'It's a full-time job, teaching Information Technology.'

'Where's the school?'

'They want me to come in for the second part of the summer term to see how the school is run and then my job will start properly in September.'

Sunita frowned. 'You seem to be avoiding the question about where the job's based.'

'That's the only problem with it. I couldn't get a job in Birmingham. It's in Stoke-on-Trent. So obviously I'm going to have to move out. Stoke's fifty miles away.'

'Was that why you were late back the other evening? You'd travelled all that way for your interview?'

'Yes.'

Sunita stood up. 'Come here,' she said.

Rupa rose from the armchair and Sunita gave her a warm hug.

'I'm so pleased for you,' said Sunita. 'But there's a sad side to this. I won't be able to see so much of you.'

Rupa shrugged her shoulders. 'You'll have to come and visit me in Stoke.'

Sunita picked up the used tissues and placed them in a pile on the table. Then she sat down again.

'You'll have to find accommodation up there, won't you?'

Rupa leaned against the arm of her chair and nodded.

'Yes. I couldn't travel all that way every day from here. Maybe you can advertise for another flatmate.'

Sunita shook her head. 'No, it's time for me to move on. I wouldn't want to share this place with a stranger. I started flat-hunting last year, as you know, and now it's time for me to get serious about it. I've already built up some savings.'

Rupa beamed at her. 'It would be good to get your foot on the property ladder. I wish I'd saved more. I'd love to be able to buy a flat.'

'Maybe this is just the push I needed.'

'Are you still thinking of moving to Warwick?'

'Yes. It's got good shops and restaurants. It's only two or three miles from the Shree Krishna Mandir.'

Rupa took to her feet. 'So maybe some good fortune will come to you as a result of my good fortune.'

Sunita grinned. 'You'll be one of the first people I'll invite round when I get my own place.'

'Only one of the first? I thought I'd be the very first.'

They laughed.

'Come on,' said Rupa. 'I'll make you that tea now.'

Chapter 19

The chief inspector's phone was ringing as he hurried to unlock his office door and answer it.

'Roscoe!' he announced as he snatched the handset from its cradle.

'Sir, it's Tom Vickers.'

'Morning, Tom.'

'Andy Chadwick in Stratford's been giving us a bit of grief. Claims we should've told him we were going to be operating on his patch.'

Roscoe frowned. 'Was he expecting some kind of advance warning? How ridiculous the man is.'

'Anyway, sir, I've found out that fifty crossbow bolts and thirty longbow arrows were stolen from the armoury at the archery club.'

'That's interesting.'

'Yes, sir. I've spoken to a DC in Stratford who investigated the burglary. It took place on Sunday, 2 April. They smashed a window at the back to get in and made off with more than a thousand pounds' worth of cigarettes from the cafe as well as the arrows. No vehicle tracks were found, but they managed to get fingerprints from the window frame which they believe could belong to the burglars.'

'Any matches on the database?'

'No, unfortunately.'

'Bloody nuisance.'

'But, sir, Stratford are looking to trace an old green Toyota Carina. They believe it may have been used in the burglary. So far the car hasn't been traced.'

Roscoe drummed with his fingers on his desk. 'What about the two men thrown out of the archery club?'

'The DC over there didn't seem to think there was a connection with the break-in. They were just a couple of drunks. Jasmine Turner, the secretary, got hold of three heavily built club members and had them ejected.'

Roscoe stood up and gazed out at the park beyond his window. 'Any idea who the men were?'

The inspector said, 'Not really. New members have to give addresses, but the details they gave don't check out. Either they moved after joining or gave false addresses. I'm not sure. The club say they can't help us any more than that.'

Roscoe scowled. 'You'd think the management of a respectable archery club would have proper membership lists with bona fide names and addresses. Don't club members have to have proposers – club members who can vouch for them?'

'Maybe they're short of funds and quietly relaxed the rules to boost membership, sir.'

'That's very poor – especially when we're dealing with an archery club whose arrows can be used as lethal weapons in the wrong hands. I may have a word with licensing when this case is finally wrapped up and put to bed.'

* * *

'Dad! Dad!' George's voice rang out around the family's home that evening.

Roscoe had spent an hour in the back garden, mowing the lawn.

As his father walked through the back door, George waved a letter and envelope.

'I've got a letter back, Dad, and I've been accepted for initial assessment.'

'That's great news, George.'

'I've got an interview at police headquarters in a week's time.'

Roscoe's mind travelled back to the 1980s. 'I was as nervous as hell when I went for assessment. But I was a few years younger than you. You'll be fine!'

'Thanks, Dad! You'll have to give me some tips.'

'The best advice I can give you is to read through everything they send you and make sure you understand it. And make sure you've got plenty of answers ready – just in case they spring a surprise question.'

George groaned. 'Oh, God. I hope they're not going to ask awkward questions.'

'No, what I mean is that you should think of everything possible that they might ask you. For instance, why didn't you apply as soon as you were eighteen?'

'Well, because I couldn't work out what I wanted to do.'

'Yes, but is that what you should tell them? It would be far better if you said something like, "I always wanted to be in the police, but I thought I needed to get some experience of life first." Do you see what I mean?'

George nodded. 'I see. Dress it up a bit – and give them what they want to hear.'

'Exactly.'

'Dad, I wanted to mention something else. You know the two guys who attacked Oliver?'

Roscoe nodded. 'Of course.'

'It occurred to me the other day they might be brothers. They both had black hair and were dark-skinned.'

His father looked thoughtful. 'That's an interesting point you make, George. I'll be frank with you. We haven't forgotten your picture of the Jeep. But we've got a number of other lines of inquiry and we're following up all the leads.'

He sat down at the kitchen table. 'Do me a favour, George, while I think of it. If I give you Tom Vickers' number, can you give him a call? I know you gave a statement at the time, but he wants to go through everything again – just in case we've missed something.'

'Sure thing, Dad.'

Later, while changing out of his gardening clothes, Roscoe's mind turned again to the investigation. Had Bufton been targeted in the car park by a gang because he owed money? Perhaps drugs were involved – they often were, he reminded himself. And what was the connection between Bufton's murder and the murder of Miss Moretto? Had they both fallen foul of the same gang?

He decided he'd later phone his old friend, Pat Clancy, who had vast knowledge of the criminal underworld in the Midlands. Roscoe was eager to discover whether a new gang was now operating. If so, perhaps they were behind the double murder.

Chapter 20

Sunita Roy leaped into the passenger seat of the chief inspector's car just after ten on Thursday morning and they swept out of the headquarters car park.

'We've chosen a nice day for it, sir.'

Roscoe, smartly dressed in a dark-blue suit, nodded as they headed towards the Warwick road.

She glanced at him. 'So we're off to West Avon Motors?'

He shook his head. 'No, we're off to Stratford. We called the company and they said Stanton had got the day off. So we're heading to Masons Road. He's got a ground-floor flat there. By the way, are you feeling all right?'

'Yes, sir. It was a hell of a shock finding the body of Miss Moretto. But I've had a couple of days off and I'm feeling a bit more cheerful.'

'That's good.'

'The break from work's done me good.'

After a journey of nearly sixteen miles, they arrived on the outskirts of the market town. Masons Road was close to the town's hospital. The street comprised a variety of styles of houses and flats. There were also several industrial premises like vehicle repair businesses, tyre firms and warehouses.

Ricky Stanton's flat – the lower floor of a red-brick, semi-detached house – proved easy to find. His gleaming yellow Lotus Evora was parked outside, along with two older sports cars.

Pink foxgloves and blue delphiniums, parading together beside an unkempt lawn, swayed in the light wind as Sunita led the way up the concrete path.

The pair could hear the sound of loud voices as Sunita pressed the doorbell. Stanton drew back the door and stood in his hallway, laughing.

'Good morning!' he said. 'Can I help?'

Sunita frowned. 'Heart of England CID. Mr Stanton?'

'Yes.'

'We need to talk to you.'

The balding Londoner, who had a round face with a ginger moustache, scowled. 'Oh God. How did you get my address?'

Sunita folded her arms. 'West Avon Motors.'

'I know why you're here. Look, this isn't the best time. I've got friends round. Can we do this another day?'

They were irritated by the man's attitude. 'This is a murder inquiry,' Sunita insisted.

One of Stanton's friends, a tall, dark-haired man in a checked shirt and jeans, emerged from the living room to the left of the front door.

'It's all right, Ricky,' the friend said. 'We can come back.'

Stanton shrugged. 'If you're sure.'

'Yes. We'll go down the road and have a coffee if you're going to be tied up. We can come back at eleven.'

The tall man and his colleague – an older man with short brown hair in a shabby T-shirt and green slacks – mumbled their goodbyes and walked off down the road.

Stanton shook his head. 'Well, you'd best come in.'

He led the detectives into a small living room with a tiled brown fireplace, a cream-coloured three-piece suite and a small dining table and chairs.

'Is this about Angelina?'

Sunita nodded. 'We found your details in her diary. Can we ask how you knew her?'

'You'd best sit down. That woman was the light of my life. I was devastated when I heard she was dead. And what a way to die – a crossbow bolt through the heart. I couldn't believe it.'

'So you were in a relationship with her?' Roscoe asked as he and Sunita sat on the two-seater settee.

'Yes, but I ain't seen her for several weeks. She met this other guy and she changed – for the worst. She became moody. I think he might've brainwashed her. Oliver Bufton, he was called.'

He sat down at the table. 'I heard this Bufton guy was a part-time actor. Maybe he tricked her. I think deep down she still loved me. Oh God...' He cradled his head in his hands.

Sunita frowned as she removed a notebook from her pocket. 'You knew Mr Bufton?'

'Not really. I only learned his name through the papers. What could she have seen in a bloody electrician like him?'

Roscoe gazed round the room before his eyes settled on the salesman. 'When did you first meet Miss Moretto?'

'Last October. It was at a dance. We got on great for eight months, but it all changed this summer. She became a bit distant, do you know what I mean? She was a flirty type and I guessed she'd got another man in tow. Then four weeks ago she said she wanted a break – time to think things over.'

Roscoe looked him in the eyes. 'Where were you on April 24th?'

'24 April? Oh, that was the day the electrician got bumped off, eh? Let me think. I'm sure I was at work that day.'

'Are you certain? If it helps, it was a Monday.'

'My working week varies. I sometimes work on Saturdays and, as a result, get a day off in the week. I don't have a set day off. It differs from week to week. Today's a bonus day off from the boss because I was salesman of the month for April.'

Sunita, who had been taking notes, interrupted. 'Mr Stanton, you sell cars for a living?'

'Yes.'

'We can easily check whether you were at work on that day. Now where were you on the first weekend of May?'

'Oh, come on. You don't think I bumped them both off, do you? Ask anyone. I'm big-hearted Ricky, the trusty trader. I'm everybody's friend – not a double murderer.'

'Just answer the question,' said Sunita.

'I'll be honest. I know this doesn't make me look too bloody clever,' he said, 'but I spent the best part of both days in the pub – the Jolly Waggoners. I was drinking and playing pool. The manager knows me well. I dare say he'll vouch for me.'

'You've mentioned you were having a break in the relationship.'

'Yes. It was her idea. She wanted things to cool down. So I ain't been anywhere near Oakdale Road since mid-April. To be honest, it's crossed my mind that I might be next. Whoever's out there with a crossbow might not stop at those two.'

The chief inspector glared at him. 'Could anyone have any reason for wanting you out of the way?'

He laughed. 'Only a small army of unhappy car buyers. No, I'm only joking. There's nobody I can think of.'

The chief inspector shook his head. 'Do you mind if we take a quick look round your flat?'

'I don't know what you expect to find. I ain't got a crossbow hidden in the spare room, if that's what you think.'

'We won't know till we've searched,' Roscoe continued. 'Of course, if you refuse, we can always come back with a warrant.'

Stanton shook his head. 'I've got nothing to hide. Carry on.'

As Roscoe rose to his feet, Sunita felt there were more matters to raise with the 'trusty trader'.

'If it's all right with you, sir, I'd just like to ask our friend a few more questions.'

'Go right ahead,' said Roscoe, as he wandered into the hall and began to explore the flat.

Sunita smiled. 'Mr Stanton, are you the member of any archery club?'

'No. Ain't never been.'

'When we arrived just now, you'd got two friends here. Can I ask who they were?'

'Just mates I've known since moving here. They're both in the motor trade. We were thinking of going to the Waggoners.'

'Tell me about your past and how you've come to be in Stratford.'

'It's a bit of a long story. I was brought up in the East End of London. Dad was a market trader. I've been mad about motors since I was a toddler and I started in sales for a firm in Canning Town.

'I got married to a Brummie girl and we moved to the Midlands in 2001. It didn't work out and I've been here ever since. Still selling the motors.'

Sunita put down her pen. 'People called Ricky are sometimes Richard and sometimes Eric. Which is it in your case?'

'It's Richard.'

She began writing again. 'Is that your full name?'

'My full name's Charles Richard Stanton. I'm Charles after my dad. But, as I grew up, people started calling me Richard or Ricky, to avoid confusion with me Dad. Eventually Ricky stuck.'

Sunita asked, 'Do you sell any Land Rovers?'

'We get all types. I sold a Chevrolet Camaro the other day. Lovely car, it was – wish we had more of them.'

'Has an American Army Jeep passed through your firm recently?' Sunita asked.

Just then, her boss called out from Stanton's bedroom, which was at the far end of the flat.

'Sergeant! Come and take a look at this.'

Sunita passed along the narrow hallway and found her colleague in a bedroom. He'd placed a large navy-blue suitcase on the bed and was examining its contents. Stanton followed close behind.

'How do you account for these, sir?' asked the chief inspector, holding up a pair of hunting knives.

Stanton shrugged his shoulders. 'I used to go deer stalking.'

'Used to?' asked Roscoe.

Sunita found herself peering inside the case at a pair of binoculars; a flashlight; a khaki shooting jacket; khaki shooting trousers; and gaiters for wearing on the ankles or lower leg in rough terrain.

She stared into his face. 'A crossbow comes in handy for deer stalking. Ideal for a silent kill.'

'I've never had a crossbow,' he muttered.

They were discovering the unsavoury side of his character. He was blithely open to killing animals, she told herself. That was just one short step away from killing human beings in her mind.

The chief inspector frowned. 'You've got the whole caboodle here, Mr Stanton. Where do you go hunting?'

'I used to go to Scotland for stags, but I ain't had time of late.'

Without shifting her gaze from the suitcase, Sunita asked, 'What weapon do you use when you're hunting?'

'I used to have a high-velocity rifle, but I sold it.'

'So you don't have one at the moment.'

'I told you. I don't do hunting no more.'

Sunita opened the doors of a double wardrobe and inspected the salesman's clothes. He had a wide selection of shirts and suits. She noticed one shirt was made from light, cream-coloured cheesecloth. She removed it and carefully placed it on the bed.

'All right, Sergeant?' Roscoe asked.

'Yes, sir. I think we should take this suitcase and shirt away.'

He nodded. 'I agree. We can get forensics to look them over.'

Stanton glared. 'You really *do* think I bumped them off, don't you!'

Roscoe shook his head. He closed the case and lifted it onto the floor. 'It's just routine. We've got to consider all possibilities.'

'When will I get them back?'

Sunita peered into his eyes. 'Don't worry. You'll be hearing from us again fairly soon, Mr Stanton.'

Chapter 21

Laurence Holland clambered off the bed and stood naked by the net curtain in the window of his hotel bedroom. The corpulent businessman could see cars driving off and fresh cars arriving in the courtyard below.

'That was terrific, sweetheart,' he said, turning his head towards the woman lying naked on top of the sheets.

He'd chosen one of the most sumptuous rooms in the building. It had magnolia walls – except by the head of the bed, where the wall was adorned with grey, horizontal wood-styled panels. A bottle of pinot noir and two glasses stood on the woman's bedside cabinet.

'I do love you,' she said.

'I know,' he said. 'I love you too.'

'Come back here,' she said.

He bent down and put his arms round her.

'It was lucky I could get the afternoon off,' he said.

'Me too,' she said. 'I got another girl to stand in for me. Larry, we must get things sorted. We should start a new life together – you and me. You've enough money to pay

Ginny off and still live in comfort. You've got a nice house, nice car, a villa in Spain...'

'I know, but these things aren't that easy,' he said. 'I'm working on it.'

'What do you mean, working on it?'

'I've had a chat with a solicitor friend. We're working out how best to arrange things.'

'Don't leave it too long. I get so bored when you're not around – as well as randy.'

'Don't I know it,' he said, walking across the beige carpet and climbing onto the white sheets beside her. He put his arm round her and kissed her.

'By the way, I'm meant to be going to an exhibition in Aberdeen at the end of the month. I've got the Bank Holiday weekend off and don't have to get to Scotland till the following Tuesday afternoon. How are you fixed that weekend?'

'I'll definitely be able to arrange something – having that much notice,' she said. 'It's short-notice dates I've got a problem with. Where do you fancy going? You could come to my place if my flatmate's at work.'

'OK, and I might have a big surprise for you,' he said.

'Ooh, you cheeky monkey!'

Half an hour later, there was a knock on the door followed by the sound of a man's voice. 'Mr Holiday? The sandwiches you ordered.'

Holland opened the door and a smartly dressed hotel waiter entered the room with two large ham salad sandwiches on a silver platter.

'You ordered them for three o'clock, sir.'

The businessman handed over a ten-pound note. 'That's right – and keep the change for yourself.'

'Thank you very much, sir,' the waiter said, closing the door.

His lover smiled at him. 'It always amuses me that you use that name, Mr Holiday.'

'Yes, that's right,' Holland said. 'It avoids any silly squabbles or unpleasantness. I always pay in cash as well. Obviously, if they insist on a credit card being shown, I have to explain myself, but they always understand. I'm told people like Beyoncé and David Beckham do a similar thing, using a false name. I've only once had a problem. I was at a London hotel and it came to the moment to pay. I handed over one of my cards and the receptionist said loudly in front of other guests, "So your name's not Mr Holiday?" After asking her to keep her voice down, I simply said, "Sorry, I'm *on* holiday. You didn't think my *surname* was Holiday, did you?"'

* * *

Later that same day, Roscoe's car drew up outside a block of modern, privately owned flats in a quiet, tree-lined close in Stratford.

Sunita got out and stretched her legs. She wondered if she'd ever get used to her boss's rather erratic style of driving, but she tried to remain upbeat. It wouldn't be long before their day was over and she'd be back at her flat in Hall Green, she thought.

Applewick House was a large, red-brick building consisting of fifteen flats on three floors. The one they sought was on the top floor with partial views over the town from its windows and front balcony.

Roscoe had phoned Cristina Lorenzo in advance and she'd been pleased to hear of their planned visit. She'd been Miss Moretto's only close relative in England and was eager to do all she could to help catch her aunt's killer.

Cristina was waiting with the front door open as the two detectives strolled up the stairs and walked along the balcony towards her flat.

'I'm devastated,' she told them as they approached. 'As you can imagine. Please come in.'

Cristina, twenty-three and slim with dark hair tied behind her head, invited them into a small hallway which led into a modest living room. Sunita was deeply moved to see how distressed the woman seemed as they took a seat on a blue, three-piece suite. Cristina was close to tears.

'I thought the world of Angelina,' she explained. 'We were more sisters than aunt and niece. I'd just returned from a holiday in Rome and had been planning to call on her. Then a policeman comes to tell me what happened, and I read about it in the paper. Now I can't even organise a funeral. The coroner of the Queen won't let the body go.'

'That's right,' said Roscoe. 'There has to be a post-mortem first and then the coroner has to investigate.'

'What does this mean?' she said.

'An autopsy is held – a medical examination of the body to find out the cause of death. The coroner also looks into all the circumstances. It can take several weeks.'

Cristina took out a small handkerchief and began to cry openly.

'What a terrible country this England is,' she said as she began to sob. 'First she lose her necklace and rings. The necklace was from my Italian great-grandmother. Then she lose her life. You won't have a surprise when I say I'm thinking of going home.'

Sunita gave a gentle smile. 'We're terribly sorry for your loss. It must be especially difficult for you when you're in a foreign country. Sometimes it might seem that England is riddled with crime. In the police, we obviously see a lot of it. But levels of crime aren't as severe as in many other countries. Our police do their utmost to bring criminals to justice and we're determined to catch your aunt's killer.'

The chief inspector wanted to move the conversation on. He gazed across at her. 'Did you know Oliver Bufton?'

'No. Who is this Oliver? I'm reading about him, but I never knew him. The only man I knew was Mr Ricky.'

'Ricky Stanton?'

'That man. He give her chocolates and vino. He take her to the theatre and the dining.'

The chief inspector frowned. 'Did you know they split up in the middle of April?'

'Split up?'

'Their relationship ended,' he added swiftly.

'Oh, no. I've no knowledge. I think she's still with Mr Ricky.'

'So Ricky treated her very well?' Roscoe asked.

'Not all the time. Angelina – she's from Italy, like me. She's a little – how do you say? A little wild sometimes.'

Sunita suggested, 'A fiery spirit?'

'Exactly. She and Mr Ricky, they fight. But, the next day, they are making it up. She damage her leg and tell me she fall on the stairs. In secret I don't believe her. But I think he love her. Oh Angelina, what's happened to you? I'm so sad she's no longer around and the whole family in Italia, they are in bits and pieces.'

Sunita leaned forward. 'Do you live here on your own?'

'No, I have boyfriend. He works in Stratford and will be back later. I don't know what'll happen to us.'

'And you're Miss Moretto's only relative in England?'

'Yes.'

'So what'll happen to her house and possessions?'

'I think her mother will get her things.'

Sunita looked down at the red patterned carpet. 'Can you think of anyone who'd have wanted to kill your aunt?'

Cristina shook her head. 'I'm thinking of nobody.'

'I got the impression Angelina had a lot of male admirers. Is that right?'

Their hostess grinned. 'I know Angelina played the game. She – she flirt. I know she flirt. She knows many men. Despite her name, she's not the angel. But I don't know of the man who would kill her.'

Roscoe stood up. 'All right,' he said, taking a card from his pocket and handing it to her. 'This is my office phone number. Please call me if you need to. I'll make sure we keep you updated of any developments – either over the burglary or over your aunt's unfortunate death. Please accept our condolences.'

Sunita offered her hand, which Cristina shook. 'If there's anything we can do to help, Cristina, please call us.'

Cristina began to sob again. 'Thank you for coming.'

As the pair travelled towards Queensbridge, Roscoe insisted on talking about Ricky Stanton.

'In my mind, he's becoming our principal suspect. I'm going to ask Tom Vickers to check out his alibis for the two murders. He's a bit of a shady character and he knew both the victims. He certainly had a motive for murder. He'd been replaced in the lady's affections by Bufton.'

But Sunita was uncertain whether Roscoe was on the right track.

'Motive isn't everything, sir. It looks to me as if he thought the world of Miss Moretto and probably doesn't have the right mindset to make him a killer.'

As she spoke these words, Roscoe's phone rang. He answered it on hands-free and found himself speaking to DI Vickers.

'Tom, I'm driving at the moment. Is it important?'

'I'll make it quick, sir. I've just been speaking to a lawyer. You wanted to know who benefitted from the death of Miss Moretto. Well, she left everything to her niece, Miss Cristina Lorenzo.'

Chapter 22

Trudy Marwood drove her silver Jaguar XK convertible through the black iron gates and drew up outside the front door. She'd visited her friend's 1930s detached house at Cranleigh Park several times before and she remained envious.

It had a medium-sized front garden filled with rose bushes. There were four bedrooms – although Larry and Ginny only needed one – and a large dual-aspect living room. But the couple were most proud of their beautiful, fully landscaped rear garden.

Ginny heard her friend's car trundle across the gravel drive. Adjusting her wavy hair in the hall mirror, she went to the front door to greet her.

Trudy, who had long, black frizzy hair, got out and embraced the woman she'd known since schooldays.

'Ginny, what a glorious day,' she said.

'Yes, I thought we could sit in the garden. It's so nice,' said Ginny, who at first led her friend into the house.

After making some cold drinks, Ginny invited Trudy into the back garden where, moments later, they were sitting out in the sun, relaxing in two of the Hollands' wicker chairs.

Trudy turned towards her friend and smiled. 'How's Larry?'

'Same as ever – moaning about money. I'm sure he'd fit a lock and chain to his wallet if he thought he could get away with it.'

They laughed.

'Your Rowan was a bit like that, you used to tell me,' said Ginny, who was thirty-six and two years older than her companion.

Trudy, a slim, attractive woman with lily-white skin, stretched out her legs. 'Yes, he could be a bit of a tightwad.'

'How have things been since you separated?'

'It was such a relief when he finally moved out. I just couldn't have coped with any more of his heavy drinking. You'd think that, after appearing in court for drink-driving, he'd have cut back a bit. If anything, he got worse and, although I haven't mentioned it before, I've had a few bruises to prove it.'

'You don't mean he was knocking you about?'

'It's happened twice when he's come back three sheets to the wind. The second time I told him I couldn't take any more. He's still staying over with his brother.'

'That's not going to work out.'

'Well, he's looking for a flat – or so he says.'

'God, I'm sorry, Trude. As you know, me and Larry have had our ups and downs. I tell you what we both need – a good night out.'

'You can say that again. You don't mean that though. Oh my God, you do! What about Larry?'

'He's going to an exhibition in Scotland at the end of the month. I was wondering if you fancied going into Stratford – to the over-thirties night you told me about.'

'What – just you and me?' said Trudy.

'Yes. I know the old Municipal Hall is a little bit run-down, but it's all right and there's a bar. We could have a great time.'

'OK. Sounds good to me. I'm always open to picking up a nice fella. I wonder if Zac Efron or Harry Styles can make it to Stratford on a Thursday?'

They laughed again.

'The night I'm thinking about is June 1st. Are you free that night?'

'Yes. Let's put it in the diary right away.'

'I'm not looking to meet anyone myself, of course.'

Trudy smiled. 'Of course. But there's no harm in window shopping, is there?'

'Exactly, and I could do with a drink and a bit of a laugh.'

After a pause in the conversation, Ginny asked, 'What happened to that man you were telling me about? The menswear salesman?'

'Oh, nothing came of that,' said Trudy, a former secretary. 'I had to end it. He was a real charmer, but I found he'd got debts. He was starting to tap me for money. In the end, he began to remind me of that factory manager from Leamington Spa who was always short of money.'

Ginny nodded. 'You don't want a man who can't stand on his own feet.' As a former estate agent, she'd been used to working among energetic, hard-working and enterprising men.

Trudy suddenly had a thought.

'Hey, I tell you what,' she said. 'Jane would probably like to come with us.'

'Jane Perks, who lives near you?'

'Yes. She mentioned a few weeks ago she was bored and was asking if I was having an evening out. She's divorced and gets a bit lonely sometimes.'

'Didn't she buy a dog and a cat?'

Trudy grinned. 'Yes, but I've heard there are a few things you still need a man for.'

'Sex and money perhaps?'

'Or fixing the toilet and the TV.'

Ginny scowled. 'Mine isn't much good at those sorts of jobs. Come to think of it, he's not much good at the other two either. I think I'm going to wear the new summer dress I bought at Andersons. It's a light-green summer dress.'

Trudy shook her head. 'I'm not sure what I'm going to wear. I'll have to have a think about it. I've got a new sleeveless purple dress that looks very nice and I've got some new black, high-heeled shoes. But they might be awkward for dancing.'

* * *

The next morning Roscoe arrived late for work. He'd been delayed by an accident near Redditch, but still managed to retain a smile. Tom Vickers caught his attention as he turned the key in his office door.

'Morning, sir! The chief super wanted to speak to you.'

Roscoe's smile quickly faded. 'Oh, God. What does she want now?'

The inspector shook his head. 'She didn't say, sir.'

'Do you know if DS Roy handed Stanton's suitcase and shirt to forensics?'

'Yes, sir. She did.'

'Any other developments?'

'The only thing is that I've had a call from Derek Underhill in Queensbridge. They've got a partial description of a lad trying to flog a gold necklace to a jeweller. Looks like it was the one belonging to Angelina Moretto. He's slim, light-brown hair, mid-twenties. He told the jeweller he lived on the Troutbeck estate. Don't know if that's kosher.'

Roscoe said, 'Could you look at that as a matter of priority? Also, I'd like you to call in at West Avon Motors and see if there are Land Rovers and Jeeps on their forecourt. And see if they'll give you a list of vehicles bought and sold over the past few weeks. Maybe that green Toyota Carina linked to the archery club raid will be on their books. Can we also check Ricky Stanton's alibis for the two murders? Meanwhile I'd better go and see Norris.'

The chief inspector climbed the stairs to Chief Superintendent Norris's second-floor office. After knocking, he entered to find her sitting in her usual place in her wheelchair behind her desk.

The grey-haired, sixty-year-old police chief had been seriously injured in a horse-riding accident and was expected to retire at any time.

She smiled. 'Ah, Gavin. Just going in to see the Assistant Chief Constable. We were both wondering how you're getting on with Operation Promenade.'

Roscoe always felt uncomfortable in her presence.

'The crossbow murders? Quite well, ma'am. We've got a number of leads. I should mention I've got a personal connection with the Bufton murder.'

She moved her wheelchair round to the front of her desk. 'How do you mean?'

'My son witnessed Bufton being stabbed in Queensbridge three weeks before he was murdered. Because I thought George might be called as a witness to the stabbing, I took a decision to send DS Roy round to see Bufton instead of going myself. We set up random patrols, but he was killed shortly after they began. So I feel responsible in a small way.'

She smiled at him. 'You mean, you wish you'd done more?'

He nodded. 'Yes, I wish now we'd moved him from his cottage straight away. That would've given us time to look into his situation more closely.'

'No sense beating yourself up over it. What's done is done. We've got to find the perpetrators.'

'Yes, ma'am. Thank you for allowing Tom Vickers to be seconded to us. He's been invaluable, as has DS Roy.'

'Have you got any suspects in mind?'

'Well, there's the delivery man who reported Bufton's murder. There's a question mark about him and there's an eccentric neighbour of the dead woman. He seems to wander in and out of her garden as he pleases. But right now our main suspect's just come onto our radar. He's a car salesman who goes deer hunting. He's Moretto's ex-boyfriend, who was replaced in her affections by Bufton.'

The chief superintendent raised her eyebrows. 'That sounds promising. Good. Let's get cracking.'

Chapter 23

Inspector Vickers made an anonymous call on Monday morning to West Avon Motors. He wanted to establish when Ricky Stanton, their highly regarded salesman, would be taking his next day off.

On finding Stanton was due to be away from work the following day, he decided he would wait twenty-four hours before paying the firm a visit. He was keen to ask questions of staff at the showroom in Marina Gardens, Queensbridge while out of earshot of the salesman and free from any possible interference by him.

As he arrived at the premises on Tuesday morning, he noticed three Land Rovers on the forecourt and examined their tyres, but there was no sign their tread was worn on any of the inner edges.

There was no green Carina, but he was not surprised at that. Somehow he'd not seriously expected to find the car associated with the archery club break-in standing on a used car lot in Queensbridge. Life was rarely that simple.

'Can I help?' said a young salesman who had been watching Vickers gazing at the vehicles and had strolled out from behind two large showroom windows.

'I was wondering if your boss is around today?' the inspector asked.

'I'll see if Mr Lumley is available. Who shall I say's asking?'

Vickers showed his warrant card. 'DI Vickers, Heart of England CID,' he said before peering through a window at a car's mileage.

He didn't have long to wait. Within minutes, a company executive appeared in the half-open glass doorway.

'Inspector Vickers,' said the overweight but smartly dressed businessman. 'I'm Jett Lumley. Can we help you? I hope one of our vehicles hasn't been flagged up.'

The inspector walked up the slight incline towards the doorway and shook Mr Lumley's hand.

'No, sir. I'm making inquiries relating to a murder.'

'You'd better come inside, Inspector. Tea? Coffee?'

'I'd like a tea with milk and two sugars, please.'

'Ann, could we have a tea with two sugars and a coffee for me, please? In my office? Thanks.'

The balding businessman led Vickers into a back office and closed the door behind them. The two men then sat down either side of Mr Lumley's desk.

'Now, a murder inquiry, is it?'

'Yes, sir. Actually it's a double murder.'

'Oh, you must mean the crossbow deaths that have been on the news. How are we meant to be connected?'

'One of the victims, Miss Moretto, was until recently the girlfriend of one of your salesmen, Ricky Stanton.'

Lumley looked shocked and appeared lost for words. The silence was broken because his secretary, Ann, chose that moment to arrive with the hot drinks.

He managed to blurt out, 'Thank you, Ann,' before she left, closing the door.

Vickers grinned. 'We're just in the initial stages of the investigation at the moment. These are routine inquiries.'

'Well, you're out of luck today, I'm afraid. Mr Stanton isn't available. He's got the day off.'

'To be honest, sir, I didn't need to see him. He's already been interviewed. We need to know more about him from the company's point of view. To start with, do you keep a careful record of staff days off? We need to know whether he was at work on April 24th.'

Lumley asked, 'What day of the week would that have been?'

'A Monday.'

'Let's have a look at the diary. Yes, he was at work that day, but he wasn't here at the showroom all the time. There were a few customers who wanted to test-drive cars and he went out with them.'

'Do you know which vehicles he'd have taken?'

'No, we don't keep a record of that. If we had to monitor people and vehicles to that extent, I'd have to employ an extra member of staff just for that. I could ask Ann, but I don't think she'd remember.'

'Could I take a look at a list of vehicles bought and sold over the past three months?' Vickers asked as he took out a small notebook.

Lumley nodded. 'Yes, we can arrange that.'

'Now, can you tell me about Mr Stanton. When did he start working here?'

'Let me think. It must've been two years ago. He was with a company in Stratford before that. Came with good references and, I've got to say, he's been brilliant. He nearly always hits his sales targets. I know he's a bit of a rough diamond, but he's always extremely helpful. He'll go that extra mile to clinch a sale.'

'Have you got his personal file?'

'Yes. Let's have a look,' said Lumley, rummaging through a drawer in his desk. 'Here we are. Charles Richard Eustace Stanton. Date of birth – do you want that? – 12 January 1977, Tower Hamlets. Address: 6A Hodley Close, Masons Road, Stratford.'

Vickers made a note of the details. 'Thank you. Now was he at work during the first weekend of May?'

'Well, we're always closed on a Sunday, so that sorts out 7 May. Let's look at the diary again. 6 May... 6 May. He was off that day.'

The inspector nodded. 'Just one more thing. I notice you've got a Jeep on the forecourt. I think it's an American Army Jeep.'

'Yes, that's right, Inspector. We don't normally sell that kind of vehicle, but I'm selling it as a favour for a friend. It's sparked a bit of interest and I nearly sold it yesterday.'

'Who's the friend, sir?'

'A man named Harding. He's an old pal from the Rotary Club.'

'Well, a similar vehicle's cropped up during our inquiries. There's probably no connection, but I think we ought to check it out. Would you mind holding onto it for a day or two? I need to bring a witness round to take a look at it.'

'Yes, that's no problem.'

'We need to eliminate it from inquiries.'

Lumley beamed at him. 'We've a good relationship with the police in this town and are only too happy to help.'

After leaving West Avon Motors, Vickers made a series of phone calls, trying to track down the whereabouts of the chief inspector's son, George. Eventually, he found him working behind the bar of the Coach and Horses pub in the nearby village of Norton Prior.

The landlord granted George a half-hour break and Vickers drove him to the showroom. But immediately George knew it was not the Jeep he'd seen in April as the khaki canvas was less faded, and, despondently, Vickers had to drive him back.

* * *

As lunchtime approached, the inspector headed into Stratford, trying to remember where the Jolly Waggoners was located. He eventually found the large, red-brick pub on a street corner, a short distance from Ricky Stanton's flat.

Hanging baskets outside overflowed with red and purple flowers – geraniums, fuchsias and busy lizzies. For a few minutes, he smoked a cigarette while admiring the flowers and considering the questions he would be asking. Then he ventured inside.

Mark Withers, the manager, was a tall, stout man with short, black hair. He'd just finished serving a customer when Vickers walked in. He told the inspector he'd been trying to make a stand against loutish behaviour and appreciated visits from police.

The detective lowered his voice. 'Can I have a quiet word? You've got a regular customer, Ricky Stanton. Would you say he comes in here a lot?'

'Balding? Ginger moustache? Yes, I know who you mean. Tricky Ricky, some of the lads call him. Has he done something he shouldn't have done?'

'Just routine inquiries, sir. He says he was here, drinking and playing pool over the first weekend of this month. Just needed to clarify that.'

Mr Withers stood back from the bar and peered across the huge, all-in-one bar. The three pool tables were seeing heavy use.

'I think that was the weekend we had a pool competition,' he said. Then turning to one of the drinkers, who was sitting on a stool chatting to two friends, he called out, 'Dan!'

The customer, who had straggly brown hair, approached the bar clutching a half-empty glass of lager. 'What's up, Mark?' he said.

The manager frowned. 'Do you remember the weekend of the pool competition? It was the first Saturday of the month, wasn't it?'

Dan thought for a moment. 'That's right, because my missus was away. I don't like to talk about it.'

'Why's that?'

'The other team won.'

'Do you remember if Ricky came in on the Saturday or the Sunday?'

'I don't know. It's nearly three weeks ago. I remember having a chat with him at some point in early May because I'm after another motor. He's not on the pool team at the moment, so I don't know if he was here or not. Is it important?'

The manager said, 'This gentleman is...'

Vickers shrugged. 'It doesn't matter. It's often difficult to remember things that may seem insignificant at the time.'

Dan looked blank. 'Oh, OK,' he said before wandering back to his pool table.

'So you don't recall him being here either?' Vickers asked the manager. 'He insisted he was here that weekend.'

'He does come in here from time to time. I know he plays darts a lot. He's on our darts team. But I've got to be honest. Personally I don't recall seeing him for a while.'

Chapter 24

Dark clouds wafted ominously across the North Warwickshire skies as George Roscoe arrived for his interview at St James Street police headquarters. A light rain began to fall. But nothing would shake his confidence as he mounted the entrance steps that his father had climbed so many times over the past twenty or more years and pushed his way through the glass door.

A constable at reception peered over his glasses at the visitor in his smart blue suit and navy-blue tie. 'Assessment?'

George nodded. 'Yes, that's right.'

'I thought so. Along the passageway, through the double doors and join your colleagues.'

George walked briskly along the corridor until he saw five young men and a woman sitting on benches in a waiting area.

'Assessment?' he asked, as if mimicking the receptionist.

'Yes,' they chorused. As he found a seat, he pointed to a door at the end of the corridor. 'It's that room, is it?'

The young man beside him nodded. 'Two guys have gone in so far. I think I'm probably next. What time were you given?'

George sighed. 'Half past nine.'

'Oh, you've got heaps of time. It's only just gone quarter past. You must be keen.'

'I guess so.'

The young man smiled. 'I'm Sean. Sean Munro.'

George shook his hand. 'George Roscoe.'

Sean explained his father had been a uniformed officer with the Metropolitan Police in London. 'Have you got any family in the job?'

The other candidates stared at him as George revealed, 'My dad works up on the first floor. He's the DCI here.'

Sean grinned. 'Should give you a head start.'

'I don't know about that. Depends whether they rate my dad or not.'

A young man with ginger hair sitting opposite decided to join in the conversation.

'Has your dad been involved with the crossbow murders?' he asked.

'He's the guy in charge,' George admitted.

'That's interesting. That poor chap killed at the thatched cottage was a member of my skittles team and I knew him quite well.'

George sat back and folded his arms. 'Oliver Bufton?'

'Yeah. I'm Tommy, by the way. Tommy O'Sullivan.'

George and Sean shook hands with him. The corridor became quiet apart from the sound of traffic passing along the street outside.

'How long have you known Oliver?'

'Must be two years. My brother knew him better. We all used to share a few jars after skittles.'

Sean leaned forward. 'What team did he play for?'

'Crown and Sceptre in Queensbridge.'

At that moment, the door opened. A fresh-faced young man in a light-brown suit emerged and walked past them towards reception. He was followed by a solemn-looking police sergeant with a clipboard who held the door open and announced loudly, 'Miss Butler.'

The young woman, sitting in a white, short-sleeved shirt and dark trousers, rose and followed the sergeant through the door.

'So it must have been quite a shock for you then,' said George, 'when you realised it was him?'

'Yeah. I know a few things about old Olly. He was a bit of a ladies' man and used to keep us up to date with his conquests. Do you know, about a year ago, he was having a fling with a florist for several weeks? His fiancée, a chubby girl with long, blonde hair, came home unexpectedly and found them romping on the bed.'

Sean laughed. 'Caught in flagrante delicto.'

George looked blank, so Sean quickly added, 'It's Latin. It means to get caught with your pants down.'

Tommy continued, 'The girl left him and broke off the engagement soon after that. Poor kid. She just popped her head round the corner of the room to ask if he'd had a good day at work. There's this florist – stark naked as the day she was born – riding on top of him, waving her arms wildly in the air.'

'I bet that guy's fiancée didn't get her hydrangeas there anymore,' joked Sean.

George shrugged. 'I suppose we shouldn't laugh about the poor guy – seeing as he's just died.'

Half an hour later – fifteen minutes after his appointed time – it was George's turn to be grilled by the interview panel. He felt slightly self-conscious as he entered the force boardroom, which was being used for the interviews. He crossed the light-grey carpet and greeted the two interviewers, who were sitting behind a long wooden table, with a cheery 'Good morning!'

As he sat in front of them, he noticed a picture of the Queen on the pale-yellow wall behind the panel members. Various police flags and framed photographs of senior officers were displayed on other walls.

The sergeant put his clipboard down on the edge of table. 'This is George Roscoe, aged twenty-one, from Queensbridge.'

The officer on the right grinned broadly. 'Ah, young Roscoe. I was looking forward to meeting you. I used to work with your father. I'm Inspector Kenneth Dugmore and chairman of the assessment panel. My colleague here is Sergeant Michael Williams, our training officer.

'Can I say what a pleasure it was to work with your father? I'll never forget how he tackled an affray outside a pub single-handedly. If your application succeeds and you're anything like him, you'll have a great career with Heart of England Police. Now your application form was excellent. You meet all the criteria and you're of good character. I want to ask you why you didn't follow your father's example and apply at seventeen or eighteen?'

George was well prepared for this question. 'I wanted to gain some experience of life outside the police. My mother runs tearooms and I've often helped out there, preparing food and dealing with customers. This allowed me to learn about running a business, communicating with the public, handling difficult situations. I've also gained experience as a barman, working in a village pub.'

Dugmore beamed at him. 'That's good.'

Sergeant Williams frowned. 'May I ask the young man a question? I'm concerned about his level of fitness. You say on your application form you played cricket and rugby at school, but you've not continued with either of them since leaving school. Is that correct?'

George shrugged. 'I go to the gym occasionally and do a lot of walking and running.'

The sergeant was unimpressed. 'We need young men and women who can achieve high fitness levels. Spending time working in a pub – no doubt drinking beer, playing lots of darts and skittles – isn't going to cut the mustard.'

Dugmore dismissed his colleague's remarks. 'We shouldn't worry too much about that. There will be lots of opportunities to test this young man's agility. He'll face a fitness test like all the other candidates. Now, looking at your application form, it seems you've got the necessary school exams. We've got to give you a complete medical check, of course, including eyesight. You'll be notified about the date for that.

'I see you can't drive. That isn't a problem at the moment, but if your application were to be successful, I always recommend recruits should consider learning to drive. It means more opportunities are open to you once you've passed your two-year probationary period. I'm pleased to see you've got no criminal convictions and you're not a member of a notorious crime family.'

Mr Williams interrupted. 'Mr Roscoe, has anyone explained exactly what'll be happening later today? We're going to set you a brief numeracy test, examine your verbal reasoning and your English. This won't take too long, and you should be free to go home later on this afternoon. Is that all understood?'

'Yes, sir,' said George. 'Perfectly.'

Inspector Dugmore captured his attention again. 'I must warn you there's no guarantee you'll be accepted into the police. As you can see, there are numerous hurdles. I expect your father's explained how the system works.'

Sergeant Williams nodded. 'That's right. Nothing is guaranteed at this stage. I remember your father as well and he was a bit of a slacker when it came to physical exercise. I hope you're made of a different mould.'

Then he seemed to peer at George in a slightly menacing way as if to say, 'I'm going to be watching you, sonny.'

George was inwardly amused by the sergeant's manner and he'd look forward to teasing his father about his weakness at sport when he next saw him. He glanced at Dugmore again, who was staring at him intently.

'Police work is challenging but it's also rewarding,' the inspector was saying. 'You'll learn a lot if you become a constable. You'll meet a lot of people and, as your career progresses, you'll find every day will be different. You'll play a vital role in preventing crime and at the same time protecting the public.'

George nodded. 'Yes, sir. I understand that. Thank you.'

'Right, the sergeant will show you where to go now. Could we have the next candidate, please?'

Chapter 25

Bright sunshine streamed through the windows of his private room the next morning as Gavin Roscoe turned the key and opened his door. The time had just turned eight o'clock, a time when he was usually at home having breakfast with his wife. But he'd enjoyed little sleep during the night because of the humid weather. By six o'clock, he'd given up trying to doze and instead decided to make an early start at CID.

He removed his navy-blue jacket and placed it on the back of his chair. Then he walked into the main office to see if anyone else was around. To his surprise, he found DI Vickers hard at work.

'Morning, Tom! Couldn't you sleep either?' he said.

Vickers shook his head. 'I received a call last night which could lead to a breakthrough in the case, sir. It looks as though Tricky Ricky's got form under his first name of Charles. I've been talking to the Met and I've just got a printout of his convictions.'

Roscoe studied the list and drew a quick breath. 'Well done, Tom. We might go and feel his collar sometime this week.'

Then he spotted Sunita talking to another female detective by the coffee machine. 'Sergeant, have you got a moment?' he yelled.

As she joined him in his room, he could tell she was in a brighter mood.

'This warm weather seems to suit you, Sergeant.'

'Yes, sir. I'm feeling a lot better, sir. Finding Miss Moretto's body the other day was upsetting, but I think I'm over it now and I've been out looking for a flat.'

Roscoe raised an eyebrow. 'You're thinking of moving?'

'Yes, I'm looking at places in Warwick.'

'Beautiful town. Listen, you'd better sit down. There have been some developments. Ricky Stanton's got form – including one count of violence. So, what with his access to Land Rovers and shaky alibis, I'm thinking of bringing him in.'

He went on to detail the convictions. 'He's been in trouble for poaching game and dishonesty and for turning back the mileage on cars. He's also got a conviction for an assault following a pub fight. Although we couldn't find a crossbow at his flat, he's got hunting equipment. He hasn't got a firm alibi for the date of the first murder, and he seems to have been lying about his whereabouts at the time of the second one. He's also a man with a motive.'

Sunita nodded. She picked up the list of convictions and studied them. 'Of course, there's no harm in bringing Mr Stanton in for questioning, sir, but the evidence seems rather circumstantial and I suspect the case against him will gradually crumble away.'

Roscoe frowned. 'Why do you seem so sure that Stanton isn't our man?'

Sunita shrugged. 'Well, sir, as you say, he hasn't got a crossbow. We've no knowledge as to whether he's skilled in firing one. Most of these convictions happened before he was twenty-five and, since his marriage, he seems to have calmed down. The assault charge was a minor one involving a drunken brawl. On top of that, there's no evidence of a vehicle linked to him having tyre wear on the inner edge.'

Roscoe nodded. 'There's some truth in what you say.'

'There's another thing – how could Mr Stanton have got hold of the distinctive bolts?'

Roscoe leaned back on his chair. 'Perhaps he was behind the break-in at the club.'

'Unlikely, sir. He himself couldn't have got through the window, so he'd have had to find someone who could. Anyway, what about the two burglars seen at Miss Moretto's house? Shouldn't they be in the frame as well?'

Roscoe shrugged. 'They were just a couple of lads who nicked some jewellery. We've caught one of them. He was interviewed under caution and he's due in court on Friday. But there's nothing to link him to the deaths and he's an extremely unlikely murder suspect – unlike our Mr Stanton.'

Roscoe was quietly annoyed by his sergeant's objections to the notion of arresting the salesman. 'What about the letter *C* on the two handkerchiefs? Stanton's first name is Charles. So that seems to fit.'

Sunita placed the list of convictions back on his desk. 'Sir, there are several people in the case whose names begin with the letter *C*. Off the top of my head, I can think of Cristina Lorenzo and Moretto's ex-husband Carlo .'

Roscoe shook his head. 'I'm sorry, Sergeant. We're just going to have to differ on this. I plan to arrest Stanton later this week and go over his flat with a fine-tooth comb. I'm going to apply for a search warrant later today.'

* * *

That afternoon Sunita hummed to herself as she drove through the pretty village of Knowle with DI Vickers sitting beside her. They were on their way to Warwick.

She smiled at him. 'It's lucky we both managed to get the afternoon off.'

Vickers glanced across. 'I haven't got the afternoon off. I told the guvnor I had to go back to the Jolly Waggoners, which isn't an out-and-out lie because I'm going over there later on.'

Sunita laughed. 'What for?'

'To chat to some of the regulars. I've spoken to lunchtime drinkers. I now want to catch some of the evening customers.'

She smiled. 'I think I might've upset the boss. He's convinced Ricky Stanton carried out the murders and I expressed my doubts.'

Vickers shrugged his shoulders. 'I'm not sure at the moment. It might be too early in the investigation to draw any conclusions.'

After another twenty minutes, they arrived on the outskirts of the county town. Although they were delayed there in the traffic, she soon found Meadow Drive and cut the engine. Reaching over to the back seat, she grabbed the property details.

She showed them to Vickers. 'Superb ground-floor apartment, it says. Within a popular development. Moments from the historic town centre.'

'Sounds a real peach. What's the catch?'

'They're asking for a hundred and sixty thousand.'

'That's the catch. I like the way the living room has a "sunny double aspect". How does that work for cloudy days?'

She laughed. 'Come on. I can see the estate agent waiting for us outside.'

Amir Khan, from Royal County Properties, smiled broadly and waved his sheaf of property details as the pair approached the flat – one of four in the building. It had a narrow strip of grass and a parking area to the right.

'Miss Roy, delighted to meet you. This must be the friend you mentioned.'

'Tom Vickers. Pleased to meet you,' said the inspector, shaking the man's hand.

As Mr Khan was about to invite them in, a black-and-tan dog scampered across the grass towards them. He jumped up at the two newcomers, craving attention.

'Oh dear, I think I might have left the back door open when I came earlier,' said Mr Khan. 'He must have slipped out.'

After Sunita had stroked the German shepherd puppy, Mr Khan scooped him up awkwardly and they all stepped into the flat.

Sunita liked the large living room and medium-sized bedroom, but the kitchen was too small and she was unhappy about the lack of cupboard space.

Mr Khan rolled his eyes. 'It's very good value for the money, but not to worry. There are plenty of other wonderful flats on our books.'

After he'd locked the dog safely inside and ensured both the main doors were locked, he set off for nearby Crompton Gardens.

Vickers studied the property details as Sunita did her best to keep up with Mr Khan, who was driving a black BMW. He mumbled, 'This one's on the first floor. It says it's a modern apartment close to Warwick racecourse and golf course.'

Sunita smiled. 'In a break from the traffic noise, maybe I'll be able to hear the galloping horses.'

She was captivated by the second property. Although it was no larger than the previous one, she was pleased it was on the first floor. The décor was immaculate and some of the white goods were remaining. It was also slightly cheaper than the previous flat.

'I like this one, Mr Khan,' she said. 'Do you know how long the lease is?'

'You'd like to make an offer?'

'I think so.'

'That's cool. If you follow me back to the office, I'll have a peek at our files and find out what I can.'

Vickers was delighted. 'Sunita, that's amazing. You've found your dream home in just a couple of hours.'

She shook her head as they sped off behind the BMW again. 'This is the third time this month I've been out flat-hunting.'

After Mr Khan made a few phone calls, Sunita managed to secure the flat for a hundred and fifty-five thousand pounds. As Vickers pointed out, it was at the lower end of the market, where competition among first-time buyers was fierce, and it had only been on sale for a week.

'You saw it at just the right time,' he said. 'If you hadn't offered close to the asking price, I think you might've lost it.'

Mr Khan smiled across at her. 'Have you got your mortgage arranged?'

She was about to reply that her loan with her building society had been approved in principle when his phone rang.

Mr Khan's smile vanished as quickly as a snuffed-out flame. 'What do you mean it's not your dog? I was sure he came out of your back door. It's your *neighbour's* dog?... Well, he seemed to know the run of your flat very well... I'm sorry? What did you say? He pooped on your kitchen floor? Well, I'm very sorry, Miss Pickering.'

As soon as they left the estate agency, the pair burst out laughing.

Vickers looked into her sultry, dark eyes. 'Well done, Sunita, on buying your first home.' Then he kissed her.

At first she was taken aback. Then she smiled, clasped his hand and pulled him in the direction of her car.

'Come on, Tom. Let's go and celebrate.'

Chapter 26

A convoy of police cars drew up outside the car showroom at three o'clock on Thursday afternoon.

Gavin Roscoe climbed out of his car and marched up to the main door, accompanied by six uniformed constables. There he was confronted by the stout, smartly dressed business owner.

Roscoe folded his arms. 'It's Jett Lumley, isn't it?'

'Yes, and I seem to know your face.'

'DCI Roscoe, Heart of England CID. Is your Mr Stanton around?'

Lumley nodded. 'I'll just fetch him for you. I hope he's not in any trouble.'

Moments later, the bewildered salesman was frogmarched out forcibly as he shouted, 'You've got the wrong guy. You've got the wrong guy.'

He continued ranting and struggling with the officers before he was handcuffed and bundled into the back of one of the cars. Then all the vehicles drove away.

Now resigned to having to account for his conduct, Ricky Stanton tried to keep himself cheerful as he and the two constables in the car with him travelled the short distance to Queensbridge police station. But no matter how hard he tried, he couldn't erase the memory of the various events that had led to this predicament – his excitement on first meeting Angelina, the realisation she was seeing another man, their break-up and then the two deaths.

Only a month before, he'd been in a close relationship with Angelina, whom he considered the most beautiful woman he'd ever met. He'd hoped to marry her. But then a gawky electrician had inveigled his way into her affections.

Now, inexplicably, the police believed he might be responsible for both murders and, despite his efforts to dissuade them when they visited his flat, they still seemed to suspect his involvement.

After emptying his pockets at the charge desk, he was locked in a small cell with a high window and a narrow couch, where he tried to make himself comfortable.

An hour later there was a knock on the door and tall, bespectacled duty solicitor Roger Sims walked in, clutching a chair.

He gave a weak smile. 'Mr Stanton, I've been assigned to look into your case. I don't know if you want me to represent you?'

'I'm in no position to turn you down, mate.'

Sims sat down on his chair. 'That's what I thought.'

After spending ten minutes listening to Stanton's story, Sims advised him to make no comment until they could assess the strength of the police case.

Stanton gazed at him. 'They showed me a search warrant. They're probably going over my flat right now.'

Mr Sims nodded.

'OK, Mr Lawyer. What d'you think my chances are of getting bail?'

'I'll be frank with you, Mr Stanton. I wouldn't have thought they were very strong just now. These are serious charges, although I must admit, from what you've been saying, their case doesn't appear too strong. The problem is we don't know exactly what they've got. The phrase "pulling rabbits out of hats" sometimes springs to mind in cases like this.'

Stanton believed it might be wiser to put up at least some defence.

'I feel I need to give it to them straight, Mr Sims,' he said. 'If I hold back, it might make me look guilty. I'm in a hell of a jam. I need to tell it like it is and get home.'

'If that's the way you want to play it, fair enough,' said the lawyer. 'But if you find a problem with any of their questions, simply say you don't want to comment at the moment. I'll listen carefully and, if any of their questions are contentious, I'll intervene.'

Later, two constables led Stanton up to the first-floor interview room, where he took a seat at a small table beside Mr Sims. For a while, all he could hear were the whispered comments from the two constables standing guard at the back. Then Roscoe and Sunita Roy came in.

Roscoe greeted them both with a smile. 'I'm sorry it's a bit stuffy in here. Sergeant, could you see if we can open the window a bit more?'

The chief inspector switched on the recording equipment on the cabinet behind his chair.

'Right, this is DCI Roscoe at 6 p.m. on Thursday, 25 May. Interview with Charles Richard Stanton. Also present: DS Roy and Mr Stanton's legal representative, Mr Roger Sims. Everything in this room is being audio recorded and video recorded.'

He sat down on a hard wooden chair, facing the salesman.

'Just to remind you, you're still under caution. Mr Stanton, let's get a few things straight. Why did you change your name – was it for a new identity after you left prison?'

Stanton shook his head. 'No, I was christened Charles Richard, but it caused confusion because me dad was also Charles. From the age of about four, everyone's known me as Ricky. You obviously found out I've done a turn inside. I got done for clocking motors. But I've been straight for the past fifteen years or more.'

Sunita, sitting opposite Mr Sims, glanced across. 'You've also got convictions for poaching and assault.'

'Yes. I got caught on an estate hunting rabbits and the assault charge was after a pub fight that got out of hand. I'm not proud of what I've done, but I was young.'

Roscoe gave him a disapproving look.

'You told us you spent a lot of time at the Jolly Waggoners the first weekend of this month. One of our team has spoken to the manager, Mark Withers, and one of the pub regulars. They don't remember seeing you the whole weekend. So where were you?'

Stanton shrugged his shoulders. He looked at his lawyer. 'I'm not going to comment on that.'

Roscoe frowned. 'Do I have to remind you that we're investigating two murders? You told us the manager would vouch for you. Now your alibi's collapsed. I can't tell you how bad this would look in front of a jury, so I ask you again. Where were you on May 6th and 7th?'

The salesman tutted. 'All right. I was seeing a woman.'

The two detectives exchanged glances but said nothing.

'I know it doesn't look good, but I'd been so depressed at the break-up of my relationship with Angelina. So I spent a bit of time with her. She's married. That's why I didn't tell you before. We spent most of the weekend in bed at her home. Her husband was away. It was a distraction for me.'

Sunita frowned. 'So you lied about where you were.'

Roscoe shook his head. 'I've heard sleeping with a married woman called a few things in my time – calling it a "distraction" is a new twist on it. Obviously, we'll have to speak to this lady. We'd need her name and address.'

'All right but be discreet. Her husband don't know about it.'

'You should've given us this explanation before.'

'I didn't want to get the lady into any bother.'

Roscoe was annoyed that the salesman had lied. But for some reason he decided Stanton's story had begun to sound a little more convincing. However, he'd not finished with the man yet.

'Now, as you know, we got a search warrant and searched your flat. One of our officers made an interesting discovery. She found two letters you've written which give an insight into your attitude towards Mr Bufton and Miss Moretto.'

He looked aghast. 'How did you get your hands on them?'

'Calm down. She found them in a cupboard.'

'I was never going to send them. Them was just thoughts. Writing them was like letting off a pressure valve.'

Roscoe shrugged his shoulders. 'Well, they make very interesting reading.'

Mr Sims interrupted. 'May we see them, Chief Inspector?'

'Yes. In good time. They're being examined by our forensics team. One was obviously to the murdered woman because it starts off, "Dearest Ange," and it describes your hopes of a reconciliation. The other is more sinister. It comes with an envelope addressed simply to "Olly". The letter consists of various letters cut from newspapers and pasted onto the page. It says, "Keep away from Oakdale Road or else."'

Mr Sims said, 'Until we've seen these letters, I'm going to advise my client to say nothing.'

'Mr Stanton?'

'I'd better heed the advice of my brief.'

Roscoe stood up. 'I'm ending this interview here. We'll speak to the married lady concerned and will no doubt need to interview you again after that. For the moment, you'll be remaining in custody.'

Chapter 27

It was the evening Ginny Holland had been anticipating with a rising level of excitement. It was Thursday, 1 June and this was the night she would be heading out on the town with her two friends.

It was a night when separated, widowed and divorced men and women – and, undoubtedly, a few married ones – could let their hair down and enjoy themselves at the over-thirties night.

Ginny believed the event was held on a Thursday because this was the day when the majority of people in this part of England got paid.

In a sense, she felt a little guilty. She was a married lady and could not be classed as unattached like most of the guests. However, she saw her role as accompanying her single friends, Trudy and Jane, and giving them moral support while having a good time herself.

Ginny conceded she might have a dance if a man approached her, but in a few days her husband would return from his trip to Aberdeen. She'd then happily resume her role as a dutiful wife. But for now, she was determined to enjoy a few drinks and soak in the atmosphere.

Just to get herself into the mood for an evening out, she spent an hour before the taxi was due sipping glasses of a semi-sweet German wine that Trudy had introduced her to the year before.

Just before eight o'clock, as requested, her taxi drew up on the gravel outside her front door and she emerged in her new, light-green, loose-wrap dress with white sandals.

'We're going to Stratford?' asked the driver. 'Is that right?'

'Yes. We're stopping to collect two people in the Warwick Road area and then going to the Municipal Hall.'

Already feeling light-headed from the wine she'd drunk, Ginny made herself comfortable in the back of the black Ford Mondeo and proclaimed, 'Let's go.'

After seven miles of travelling past open fields, hedgerows and woods, the grey-haired driver called out, 'You'll have to let me know when we get to your friend's house.'

Ginny nodded. 'Any minute now. There's a turning on the left.'

Moments later, they reached the side turning and stopped outside Trudy Marwood's large, four-bedroom, 1930s detached house. It stood out from the others because it was encased with scaffolding. Trudy's husband, Rowan, had been forced to spend money on a new roof.

Both Trudy and their friend Jane Perks were standing by the open front door, laughing and joking. Trudy was wearing a sleeveless purple dress with leopard-print flats, while blonde Jane had a white summer frock with tiny pink and blue flowers and white shoes. All three looked stunning, as they set off towards the town centre.

Trudy was talking excitedly. 'Ginny, Ginny, Ginny. We're going to have a terrific time. You remember Jane, don't you?'

Ginny nodded. 'Yes, of course. How are you, Jane? Nice to see you.'

Jane beamed. 'Fine, thank you. But we've been a little naughty. We've shared a bottle of wine and had a few shorts.'

'Just to get us in the right mood,' Trudy explained.

On arrival in the town centre, the taxi became ensnared in heavy traffic. Although they were only a short distance from their destination, the vehicle took several minutes to move a few metres.

The driver turned his head. 'I think it might be a good idea for you to walk the rest of the way. There are so many people in town tonight spending their wages. There's also a funfair.'

Trudy glared at him. 'Walk?'

'Come on,' said Ginny. 'It'll be a lot quicker. It's only up thc road now.'

She paid the driver and asked him to meet them outside the venue at midnight for the return journey. Then the three friends set off along the street. Their pretty feminine outfits attracted a few glances, but they took it all in their stride. The alcohol they'd already consumed gave them added confidence.

Within a few minutes, they reached the entrance of the dance venue. A banner above the archway declared, 'Over-Thirties Night'. Then, in smaller letters beneath, it said, 'Dance party every Thursday until midnight'.

After paying at the door and leaving coats in the cloakroom, they strolled to the carpeted area at the far end of the dance floor and chose a table with three chairs. They discovered they were early.

Only around twenty men and women had arrived before them. Trudy immediately seemed to become involved in an argument with a man near the entrance. He was a tall, broad-shouldered man in a dark suit whom the other two women had at first assumed was one of the security staff. Jane leaned her head in the direction of the conversation. All she could hear from the man were the words, 'You promised.' From Trudy, all she could hear was, 'Just leave me alone.'

Jane looked concerned as their friend returned.

'Are you all right?'

Trudy nodded. 'Yes, it's fine! He's an idiot I met on a night out last month. Some men won't take no for an answer.'

She immediately offered to buy the first round of drinks – two white wine spritzers and a rum and Coke for Jane.

'Not too much soda!' Ginny called as her friend departed for the bar.

The dance hall had a lavishly decorated stucco ceiling and impressive red and gold walls with Victorian lighting and mirrors. It had a large, wooden parquet floor for dancing. The disc jockey on his podium at the far end was making final adjustments to his speakers and decks.

As disco sounds began to blare out, Ginny's feet began tapping.

She touched Jane's arm and smiled. 'What are you doing with yourself these days?'

'I've got myself a little part-time job in a shop. But I don't really need to work. I got a pretty good deal in my divorce. I got the house because our two sons are still living at home.'

Ginny's smiled faded. 'I never had children. Don't suppose I ever will now.'

As Trudy returned to the table, the pair noticed their tray of drinks was being carried by a handsome-looking man with black hair in a dark suit.

Good God, Trudy doesn't waste much time, thought Ginny.

'This is Den,' she announced. 'We got chatting at the bar. He kindly offered to bring our drinks over for me.'

After the women murmured their thanks, Den expressed hope he'd see his new acquaintance later and disappeared.

As Trudy sipped her spritzer, she explained Den had arrived early and had been spending some time chatting with a couple of his friends.

She chuckled. 'He wants a dance with me later.'

'You could be in there,' said Jane.

Trudy shrugged. 'He seems very nice. Quite the gentleman.'

Ginny scoffed. 'Not all the men you meet in these places are like that.'

More revellers kept arriving at the hall as the evening went on. Eventually the number of men began to outnumber the women. Then, at around nine o'clock, the disc jockey began playing music with a stronger beat and turned up the volume. It was a clear sign that it was time for dancing to begin in earnest.

Trudy and Jane needed no further prompting and ventured out onto the floor, gently swaying in time to the rhythm. They were joined moments later by Ginny, and then by dozens of other women. After a quarter of an hour, the trio returned to their table, where they had left their handbags and cardigans.

'Can I join you?' said a voice. It was Den again, smiling at Trudy and drawing a chair over from a nearby table.

Trudy nodded. 'Of course. Is this your first time here?'

'I've been to one or two nights here,' he said.

Just then, the strains of Diana Ross's fourth number one single, *Love Hangover*, came pulsating over the air.

'Shall we?' asked Trudy, taking his hand and leading him onto the floor. 'What d'you do for work?' she yelled as the pair gyrated to the music.

'I'm in transport,' he said.

'What kind of transport. You're a lorry driver?'

'I work on trains,' he said. 'I do all sorts. I take money, clean carriages and run operations.'

'Where – round here?' she asked, noticing he'd got tattoos on both forearms.

'All over the place. I made sure I was on a day shift today – so I could come here tonight.'

'You don't drive trains?' said Trudy as the American soul group Rose Royce began belting out their disco classic *Car Wash*.

He laughed. 'No, I don't sit at the front with a hat on. The job keeps me out of trouble. What d'you do?'

She grinned. 'That would be telling.'

While they flirted, her other two friends were attracting attention from several men.

Eventually, Jane accepted an invitation to dance from a well-dressed man with spiky dark hair. The man, debonair with an Irish lilt to his voice, was in his forties. He told her his name was Hugh and he worked for an electrical company.

Clearly, Jane had earlier noticed him laughing and joking with Den, although he insisted the pair had only met for the first time that evening. She spent the rest of the night dancing and drinking with him.

At around eleven o'clock, Trudy went to the ladies' toilet for fifteen minutes to adjust her make-up. During this time, Den asked Ginny for a dance. She'd clearly been closely following her personal rules. She was there to have a good time and support her friends. She was not there to begin a relationship. She'd got a husband and, although their marriage had lost some of its sparkle, she believed it was a union for life.

However, she'd become slightly beguiled by Den's attractive looks. She particularly liked his smile and his twinkling eyes. He reminded her faintly of the footballer Cristiano Ronaldo. She took to the floor with him and had several dances before Trudy returned. She caught Ginny laughing as Den was whispering in her right ear.

'Hey, what's going on?' she demanded to the intense embarrassment of her friend. Trudy then grabbed Den's hand and tugged him into the melee of dancers.

As the end of the evening approached, the disc jockey turned the lights down. 'Please take your partners for the last dance.'

The slow, melodic tones of the American soul favourite *I'm Stone In Love With You* began to play. Den led Trudy onto the floor. Within moments, they were clasping each other tightly as they rocked slowly together to the beat.

Jane and Hugh also held each other closely for the final dance while Ginny watched from the sidelines. Several men stopped at her table to ask if she wished to dance, but she turned them all down.

At last the smooching was over. The lights came on fully. The guests said their goodbyes and queued for the exit.

Den kissed Trudy on the cheek. 'Can I see you again, like?'

'Of course,' said Trudy. 'I'll key my number into your phone.'

After she'd entered it in his handset, the group of friends stepped outside and felt at last the cool night air on their faces.

'Give us a call sometime, Den.'

He nodded. 'I will. It's been lovely meeting you.' He kissed her again and then walked off up the road with Hugh and another man.

The black Ford Mondeo taxi drew up across the street and the women got in.

Jane stared at Trudy admiringly. 'Wow, what a good-looking guy you were with. Are you seeing him again?'

She nodded. 'I hope so. We'll have to see if he phones me. You were getting on all right yourself, Jane.'

'Yes, I was, wasn't I? Hugh wants to take me for a meal. We exchanged phone numbers.'

They both leaned forward to see how Ginny was. She was sitting in the front seat next to the driver and complaining she was feeling unwell.

As the car travelled along the Warwick Road towards Trudy's house, Ginny began moaning. 'Could we stop for a moment? I think I'm going to be sick.'

She managed to restrain herself while in the car. But no sooner had she stepped out than they heard the sound of her retching by the grass verge.

Then she resumed her place in the front seat. 'How embarrassing. I'm so sorry.'

'Maybe it was something you drank,' said Trudy.

The driver scowled. 'There's no "maybe" about it.'

Chapter 28

Brett Dawson smiled at his older colleague, Omar Khalid, as they queued up at the bar of the Golden Fleece on Friday lunchtime.

'It's kind of the guvnor to buy us all drinks,' said Dawson.

The fellow constable nodded. 'How much did he give you to get the round in?'

'Thirty pounds.'

Khalid, a shy, thoughtful man of average height who was popular with his colleagues, grinned as he tried to remember the list of drinks.

'It would be cool if we could make this a regular Friday tradition,' said Khalid.

A few minutes later, Roscoe and his team were sipping their drinks in a corner of the modern, open-plan bar, beside white walls adorned with colourful paintings of rural scenes.

It was a quarter past one and more and more drinkers were trooping into the pub, which was a short distance from the headquarters building and run by an ex-policeman.

Sunita, who was sitting beside Tom Vickers on the opposite side of the table from the chief inspector, put her orange juice down and whispered in her colleague's ear. 'Even though he bought the round, the boss has been in a bad mood all morning.'

Vickers nodded. 'Do you know why?'

'Yes. He's still annoyed at having to let Stanton go. But we had no choice as the married woman backed up the man's story.'

Vickers smiled after sipping his lager. 'The evidence from the neighbours was probably crucial – saying they'd seen a balding man visiting her. They probably remembered him because of his flash car.'

Sunita sipped her drink. 'Dr Ling in forensics says Stanton's shirt didn't match with the fibres on the brickwork. The boss still clings to the hope we may find a flaw in his alibi. The married woman slipped out to visit her mother for a couple of hours, so she can't account for his movements for that time. Now Dawson, Khalid and two others have been asked to keep a watch on his flat. So first thing tomorrow morning...'

The chief inspector, who'd been talking to Dawson, switched seats so he could talk to Sunita.

'Well, Sergeant, congratulations. You've been proved right. I'm not sure where we go from here.'

Sunita nodded. 'Nor me, sir.'

'I don't understand why anyone would want to use a crossbow, sir,' said Vickers. 'Bloody awkward thing. Why not a gun or a knife?'

Sunita gazed into his eyes and smiled. 'A crossbow's quiet and doesn't draw attention. The killer's more likely to flee the scene unnoticed.'

'Let's hope we get more leads soon – before anyone else loses their life,' said Vickers.

Their boss leaned back on his seat. 'I shouldn't worry about that. I firmly believe these attacks were all about Bufton and the Italian woman. We can be fairly certain there won't be any further incidents.'

After half an hour, Sunita rose from her seat and made her way towards the ladies' toilet.

As she stepped past the bar, twenty-two-year-old Dawson grabbed her arm. 'Sunita, I've been meaning to catch a word with you.'

'Hi, Brett. How are you getting on?'

'I'm fine, Sarge, but I'm concerned about you.'

'What d'you mean?'

'Well, I've noticed you seem to be around Tom Vickers a lot.'

She glared. 'What's that got to do with you?'

'Well, nothing really. I guess I'm just a little put out you were too busy to spend time with me but you're clearly not too busy to spend time with him.'

'How I spend my time's nothing to do with you.'

He was silent for a moment. Then he grinned. 'I'm surprised at you really. Carrying on with a married man who's still living at home with his wife.'

A shocked expression flashed across her face. Dawson was swift enough to notice it.

'You didn't know, did you? I'm surprised no one told you. I thought everyone in the building knew. Anyway I've done my good deed for the day, Sarge.'

Then he marched out of the pub.

* * *

During her volatile ten-year marriage, Trudy Marwood had never had to worry about car maintenance. If her husband Rowan had been well-disposed towards her – and sober – he would inspect the oil and water levels in her Jaguar convertible.

He would also dutifully check the tyres and book it in at the nearby garage for its annual service. SA Autos was run by Rowan's friend and he regularly used the garage, both for the Jaguar and his own car, when he was not banned from driving it.

This time was different. Her car was misfiring, but Rowan had moved out and it was up to her to get the problem resolved. Since SA Autos was the only repair firm she'd ever dealt with, she vowed to take it there.

So at 2.30 p.m., after making some tea for the builders who were working on her roof, she set off for the garage.

Two mechanics were working beneath a VW Polo on a ramp when she drew up outside.

'Hello, my darling!' said the older of the two men, Phil Davies. 'You got a problem?'

Trudy got out and walked over. 'Yes. It's misfiring a bit.'

Phil drew in his breath. 'That sounds costly.'

Trudy frowned. 'God, I hope not. I'd like you to bear in mind we've been loyal customers for years.'

'I was only joking, love. We'll have a look at it for you – probably later this week. Do you want to book it in with the chap in the office? Nice motor anyway. I tell you what. I'll leave my mate working on the Polo. Let's have a look.'

After raising the bonnet, he examined the engine from a variety of different angles. 'Your husband no good with cars then?'

She shook her head. 'He's moved out.' Then she immediately regretted what she'd said.

He stood back with his hands on his hips.

'Can't see anything immediately. Could be something simple like a short circuit. How old is it? Six years?'

He opened the driver's door and inspected the milometer, which recorded more than twenty-seven thousand miles. He shook his head as he glanced at her.

'I tell you what, darling – I reckon the clock's been turned back. How many miles do you do a year?'

She became embarrassed at her minimal knowledge of cars. 'How many miles do I do? I've really no idea, but we bought it last year and the milometer read just under twenty-five thousand miles.'

He stared at her. 'If the average mileage in England is about seven thousand miles a year, you'd think a car like this would've travelled at least thirty-five thousand miles – and probably a lot more.'

She walked towards the office. 'I'll just book it in and leave the keys in the office.'

'Yeah, you do that.'

'I'll need it back for Friday.'

Phil grinned. 'Going anywhere nice?'

'Just to a friend's house.'

'I bet a lovely lady like you's got loads of friends.'

'A few.'

'You live on the Warwick Road, don't you? I'm not far from there. I could drive it back for you on Friday – after we've repaired it, like.'

Trudy was concerned at the way the conversation was developing. Cutting him short, she said, 'No, that won't be necessary. I'll pick it up. Anyway, I'd better get it booked in.'

An hour later, when she arrived home, she made some more tea for the builders and then received a surprise phone call from her new acquaintance, Den.

'Wasn't sure if you'd be in,' he told her.

She was slightly disconcerted to hear his voice clearly for the first time since they had had to yell at each other at the hall. He was rather roughly spoken with a strong Midlands accent. But she was pleased he'd been motivated enough to call.

'Yes, I work from home,' she lied, unwilling to reveal she was financially secure and not currently having to work.

The pair chatted for a few minutes before Den came to the point. 'I was wondering if you'd like to go out somewhere.'

Trudy smiled. 'That would be cool. I'm free next Wednesday evening. I tell you what – why don't we go out for a meal in a foursome? I'm thinking of you, me, Jane and Hugh.'

Trudy detected a hint of disappointment in his voice at the suggestion the other couple should join them, but she ignored it.

'All right. If you like,' he said.

'Good. I'll have a word with Jane and get back to you.'

Chapter 29

Gavin Roscoe tapped gently on the diamond-paned windows of the Apollo Tearooms and waved at his nineteen-year-old daughter, Melody, as he spotted her short, mousy brown hair through the window.

She'd just served tea to a middle-aged couple sitting at a window table, who were briefly startled. The waitress broke into a smile and waved back.

'Sorry. It's my dad,' she explained.

She stepped towards the open doorway. 'Hi, Dad.'

Roscoe, who was clutching flowers, kissed her. 'Thought I'd give your mother a surprise, dear. Where is she?'

'In the kitchen, I expect.'

As Helen emerged, wiping her hands on a white teacloth, her eyes twinkled in delight. 'Flowers? For me?'

Roscoe beamed at her as he handed her the bouquet consisting of pink and white peonies, yellow roses and mauve stock. 'Thought it was about time.'

She kissed him. 'They're gorgeous, darling. I'll take most of them home, but this place could do with brightening up a little. Thanks, darling. I suppose this makes up for us not having our holiday.'

Melody walked past carrying some dirty plates and cups. 'Wasn't there talk of you both going to Bournemouth?'

His smile faded. 'Yes, that's had to go by the by. Maybe we can book the Royal George when my current case is dealt with.'

All three went into the kitchen, where Helen filled two vases with water for the flowers. 'No more progress then, darling?'

'No. The case has got us beat,' he said. 'Our number one suspect is RUI.'

'What's that?'

'Released under investigation. He's not out of the woods, but he's unlikely to be charged for the moment.'

'Have you spoken to George?' Helen asked. 'He's been trying to get hold of you. He wouldn't tell me what it was, but it sounded important.'

'No. I'll give him a call now.'

Roscoe found a quiet corner of the restaurant and called his son, who answered promptly.

'Dad, where are you?'

'At the tearooms. Everything all right?' asked Roscoe.

'Yes. Dad, I've had some brilliant news this morning. I've been accepted by Heart of England and I'll be based in Warwick to start with. I've got an email from the course directors.'

Roscoe smiled broadly. 'That's terrific.'

'Yes, I've got to visit the main town police station for a meeting with the senior officer. Then I'm due to go for six weeks' training in Ryton on July 24th. I passed my medical and security checks. I scraped through the fitness test as well.'

'Have you got your accommodation sorted out?' his father asked.

'Not yet. I've only just heard.'

'Do you know who's going to be in charge on a day-to-day basis?'

'I don't know, but I've got to report to Sergeant Michael Williams.'

Roscoe's face fell. 'He's one of the guys I didn't get on with.'

'I know. He was at the interview. He claimed you were a bit of a slacker when it came to physical exercise.'

'Did he? He was always a bit of a pain in the backside. Doesn't sound like he's changed. George, I'm so proud of you. Don't expect it to be a doddle because it won't. I don't want you going to Ryton with any idea it's going to be like sixth form college. When I was there, the heating kept breaking down and I'd get into trouble, being late for classes.'

George laughed. 'It sounds like boarding school.'

'Don't be put off. It's only for six weeks. The police is partly modelled on the army and a lot of it's to do with discipline. But it'll make a man of you.'

'Dad, do you want me to tell Mum or will you?'

Roscoe deliberated. 'I think it would be best coming from you,' he said as he ended the call.

He sat on his corner chair quietly contemplating George's news as Helen and Melody rushed around preparing tea and scones for the final customers of the day.

He realised he was feeling emotional, thinking of how his son would be following his footsteps. He withdrew a paper tissue from his pocket to wipe a tear that had formed in his eye.

* * *

As she began to climb into her car, Sunita Roy heard a voice calling her name. She glanced towards the headquarters entrance. Tom Vickers was running towards her. 'Sunita, wait!'

The sergeant got behind the wheel and closed the door.

He knocked on the glass. 'I need to talk to you.'

She wound down the window. 'What d'you want?'

'You've been ignoring me all afternoon. What's the matter? What have I done?'

'I've just been busy. That's all.'

'Too busy to talk to me?'

'I've heard your life is also extremely busy. I've heard you've got a wife who keeps you on your toes.'

The inspector rolled his eyes. 'Is that what this is about?'

She started the Peugeot. 'I think you should sort out your domestic situation before you embark on a new relationship, don't you?'

He shook his head. 'Sunita, you've got it all wrong. Who've you been talking to?'

'Brett Dawson. He says everyone in the office knew except me.'

'You're joking. Brett Dawson's fancied you since you arrived in the office and you both worked on the Oxford Lane murder case last year. He'd say anything to try and get round you. What did he actually say?'

She turned the engine off again. He could tell she was close to tears.

'He just said I was carrying on with a married man who's still living at home with his wife.'

Vickers rested his hand on the car door. 'My wife left me two months ago, but the marriage had been shaky for more than a year.'

'Why didn't you tell me, instead of allowing me to look an idiot in front of Dawson?'

'I thought you knew. There've been stories flying around for a year about how I often sleep at the office. I know I've joked about working late and not having time to get home, but sometimes I just couldn't bear being in the house with her.

'I thought you knew my marriage was on the rocks and didn't think it would be an issue. As far as I was concerned, I was a free agent. I know the wife and I haven't got round to making things official with a divorce, but I think she's found someone else and I'm trying to move on with my life too.'

She stepped out of the car and gazed into his kind, brown eyes. 'Tom, I'm sorry.'

She wrapped her arms around him. He was such a warm-hearted man. He had such a reassuring smile. She cared for him so deeply.

'Now you've explained, Tom, everything makes sense.'

His moustache brushed against her face as he kissed her.

'I've felt terrible today,' he murmured. 'I've felt so far away from you, even though we're in the same office.'

'I'm sorry, Tom. I should've spoken to you about it straight away – as soon as Dawson spoke out.'

'Yes, that Dawson needs to be put in his place.'

Sunita shook her head. 'Don't do anything, Tom. Promise. It'll only make matters worse. We should just ignore him.'

'Listen, are you hungry? There's a fab new Italian restaurant in Solihull. I think it's called Luigi's.'

Sunita smiled. 'Sounds cool. If you jump in, you can guide us there.'

Chapter 30

It was a sultry summer's night when Trudy Marwood and Jane Perks arrived at the White Swan in Shawley Green. The sun was slowly fading from the sky, leaving an orange blaze on the horizon.

They parked at the far end of the car park and stepped out of the Jaguar. Trudy, who looked dazzling in a medium-length blue, patterned dress, sighed. 'Looks like we're the first here.'

Jane, who looked equally alluring in a pink dress, nodded. 'I'm glad we decided to meet this way. It's safer in a group until we know the guys better. You did tell them eight o'clock?'

'Yes.'

Jane smiled. 'This place does a good range of food. I had a look at the menu online.'

The pair spent a few minutes waiting outside the main entrance, wondering whether the two men would appear. But, at about a quarter past eight, a green Toyota Carina with a noisy exhaust roared along the road towards them. The women's spirits rose and they smiled at each other.

'We're not late, are we?' said Den as he stepped from the driver's seat.

Trudy laughed. 'Only by quarter of an hour.'

Den shrugged. 'Weren't sure of the way.'

'Why have you got an old car like that?'

'I'll have you know it's on the way to becoming a classic.'

The White Swan was a small roadside pub with a somewhat dark interior which required updating. Its new owners had boosted trade by offering food at competitive prices, which meant the pub was rather crowded.

Although Den and Hugh were eager to begin with a round of drinks, the women were hungry and insisted they should immediately take their seats in the dining area.

A barmaid showed them a table by an open window. The men sat with their backs to it and the women sat opposite.

While they studied the menus, Trudy noticed the men were very casually dressed. Den had an open-necked, white sweatshirt and dark jeans, while Hugh had a short-sleeved fawn shirt with faded blue jeans. She could see the tattoos on Den's arms more clearly than in the poor light of the dance hall. He had a full-length skeleton on his left forearm and the figure of a cartoon ghost on his right forearm.

They could've made more of an effort, she thought to herself.

Jane was also making a mental note of aspects of the men's dress and conduct. She thought she could quickly become exasperated if she had to endure a long period of listening to Den's rasping voice.

Trudy and Jane drank white wine and the two men cider while waiting for their meals to arrive. Trudy was shocked to watch as Den downed his pint in one go and immediately asked the waitress for another. He drank the second more slowly but was nonetheless halfway through it when their meals arrived.

He and Hugh had opted for ham, egg and chips, while Trudy had chosen beef Wellington and Jane coq au vin.

In the middle of the meal, a wasp flew in through the window and seemed to acquire an interest in Trudy's wine. She became flustered. She was terrified of wasps since being stung as a child. She dropped her knife and fork on the table and jumped out of her chair.

'Never you worry!' said Hugh.

He sprang up from his seat opposite Jane, scurried round the table and crushed the offending insect with a menu. Then, as the wasp continued to show signs of life, he dropped it onto a spare plate in the centre of the table and slowly antagonised it with a table fork. Not wishing to be left out, Den reached across and tortured the wasp's writhing body with a lit match.

'Stop! Don't do that!' cried Jane, an animal lover who possessed two cats and a goldfish. She picked up a spoon from the empty table next to them and ended its misery.

'I hate wasps,' said Trudy.

'Me too,' said Den, as they resumed their meal.

'You know where they go on their holidays, don't you?' asked Hugh. 'Sting-a-pore!'

Den slouched over the table. 'Did you hear about this man who went into a pet shop. He wanted to buy a wasp, didn't he? The bloke said, "We don't sell them." So the customer says, "But you got one in the window!"'

The women smiled out of politeness. Not only had Trudy heard the joke before, she was also dismayed at the men's poor table manners.

After their meal, the group left the table and continued drinking in the main bar.

Den grinned at Trudy as he bought her a second gin and tonic. 'So you haven't got a steady job then?'

'I'm a lady of leisure. I told you.'

'I reckon I could find you a job.'

'I'm used to office work.'

Den picked up his pint of lager from the bar and took a mouthful. 'That might be tricky.'

As he replaced it on the edge of the bar counter, Trudy splashed some tonic onto her gin and took a sip.

'What rail firm do you work for? West Midlands Railway, Network Rail, HS2?'

'No. It's not a big outfit like that.'

Just then Den's pint slipped off the bar top, splashing lager all over Trudy's dress.

'You, clumsy idiot,' she cried before rushing off to the ladies.

Trudy had stripped off her dress and was dangling it under the drier when Jane caught up with her in the ladies' toilets.

'You all right, Trude?'

'I'll be OK, but it's no thanks to Den. It should be a lot drier in five or ten minutes and I'll be able to walk out of here with my dignity intact.'

'What a muppet,' Jane muttered.

By the end of the evening, Trudy had severe doubts as to whether she wished to see Den again. In a few days, she'd have forgotten about the drink spillage. Maybe it was an accident. But there were aspects of both men's behaviour she disliked.

And as they eventually returned to their cars, she realised her initial feelings of affection towards Den had begun to wane.

Chapter 31

A noise like a gunshot resonated around the street outside, but Ginny Holland was unperturbed. She guessed at once that her friend Trudy had arrived – and her Jaguar's backfiring problem remained unresolved.

She strolled from the dining room into the front sitting room and gazed out through a gap in the blinds. Good old Trudy, as timely as ever – even though many of the neighbours were also peering from their windows to see what had caused the disturbance.

Then she became concerned. She realised some of the paintwork on Trudy's cream-coloured Jaguar was no longer in pristine condition. Somehow, some of it had peeled off.

'What on earth's happened to your car?' asked Ginny, stepping onto the gravel and kissing her friend.

'Some swine's thrown acid or paint stripper over it while it was outside my house last night. Probably teenage vandals. There are a lot in Stratford. It's going to cost me hundreds.'

'That's a nuisance. Shall we sit in the garden? I've made a nice salad for lunch,' said Ginny, who looked comfortable in a loose-fitting, white summer dress. 'I've got some Pimm's, some gin, or Martini.'

Trudy smiled. 'Could I have a gin and tonic?'

'I can manage gin and soda.'

'Brilliant.'

Five minutes later, they were relaxing in the sun in Ginny's white wicker garden chairs.

Ginny grinned at her. 'How've you been, Trudy?'

‘Oh, don’t ask,’ she said. ‘I’m finding it harder than I thought I would, living on my own. There always seems so much to do in the house – even though Rowan never did much himself. I took the car into the garage the other day, but do you think they could find out what’s causing it to backfire? The best they can offer is having another look at it next week.’

‘Oh dear, you’re having a bad time,’ said her friend.

‘Yes. On top of that, the roofers seem to be taking forever.’

‘That’s a nuisance.’

‘And then last night I had a flaming row with Den.’

‘What about?’

‘Well, he knocked beer over me after our meal. I reckon he was drunk. Then later he had his paws all over me and wanted to go back to my place. Luckily, I don’t think he knows where I live because I’ve decided he’s not my type.’

Ginny nodded. ‘You don’t want another boozer like Rowan.’

‘No, definitely not.’

‘So have you finished with him?’

‘Yes. I told him on the phone this morning I wouldn’t be seeing him again. The cheeky bugger said, “It’s not over.” I said, “I don’t think we’re compatible.” He screamed at me, “You’ll regret this!” But I won’t, Ginny. There are plenty more fellows around. How have you been, anyway?’

She poured herself a glass of Pimm’s and added some lemonade, cucumber and ice. ‘More rows with Larry,’ she said. ‘I feel a bit trapped because he doesn’t want me to spend anything. I’m not sure how long I can go on like that.’

‘I’ll let you into a little secret,’ said Trudy, who sipped her drink and was careful not to spill any onto her green dress. ‘You know that man I had a row with at the start of our night out?’

'Broad-shouldered? Built like a stack of bricks?'

'That's the one. Well, I've got to tell you. He's great in bed.'

'Trudy!' said Ginny. 'I'm surprised at you. Are you planning to get back with him then?'

'Probably not. I shouldn't have slept with him in the first place. But anyway, plenty more pebbles on the beach.'

Ginny laughed. 'You scoop them up, admire their shine and then hurl them back onto the shore.'

'I've just got to find the right pebble. Oh, I forgot to tell you I've had problems with the mechanic at my garage – you know, the place where Rowan always takes his cars? He's quite good-looking but he can't be more than twenty-eight. He says he lives near me and that he'll call round to have a proper look at the car. I'm a bit worried about him. He looks at me in a strange way.'

Ginny shrugged. 'Some men are just a bit too forward.'

'Anyway, there are builders at my place most of the time, so I feel quite safe.'

Ginny poured her friend another gin as their conversation seemed to reach a natural pause. She was thinking about how, that very morning, she herself had received a surprise phone call from Den.

At first she'd demanded to know how he'd obtained her phone number. However, as the call had gone on, she began to feel sorry for him. He was devastated that Trudy had finished with him.

He spoke to Ginny as though his whole world had come crashing down. Then he surprised Ginny by saying, 'I don't suppose you'd cheer me up and go on a date with me yourself?'

'I'm a married lady,' she'd told him.

'What's that got to do with it?' he'd said. 'I could be your secret boyfriend.'

'I don't mean to upset you. You're very nice, but I think I'll have to decline.'

'Why? Is there something wrong with me? Don't I come from the right stock?' he'd demanded.

'No, it's not that.'

Although flattered by his interest, Ginny was aware of the age gap between them. Deep inside, she recognised he was from a different background and that a relationship with him wouldn't work. In any case, she genuinely wished to give her marriage another chance.

'There's nothing wrong with you,' she had insisted. 'It's just that I'm married and that's an end to it. But I'm very flattered by you asking.'

Den had then shouted down the handset in a slightly threatening manner, 'You'll be sorry!' before ending the call.

Now she wondered if she should mention this to Trudy. Then she answered her own question. No. Trudy might misunderstand and think she'd been making a play for Den behind her back. It was best to say nothing rather than put their lifelong friendship at risk. She might tell Trudy about it at a later time, but, for now, she'd remain silent.

Chapter 32

'I hope you've got good news,' the chief inspector moaned as he saw Sunita Roy approaching his room on the morning of Friday, 16 June.

'Fraid not, sir,' she said. 'We've had a round-the-clock watch on Stanton's flat but he hasn't been seen since he was released from custody more than a week ago.'

He sat down at his desk with his head in his hands. 'So now he's bloody disappeared.'

Sunita, clutching a copy of the *Queensbridge Gazette*, settled down on a chair after shutting the door. 'Not exactly, sir. I've made a call to West Avon Motors. He's been given compassionate leave because of his arrest and the death of his ex-girlfriend. He's told them he's visiting his sick mother in East London.'

'We need to check that out,' he said. 'Can you contact the Met? We can find the mother's address and they can send someone round to ascertain whether our man's with his mum or not. I don't know, Sergeant. If he's been upset over the death of Miss Moretto, that's news to me. He didn't seem to be shedding too many tears for her when we brought him in for questioning. He only seemed concerned about saving his own neck.'

Sunita held up the local paper. 'Have you seen this week's *Gazette*, sir?'

Roscoe shook his head. 'Helen bought one, but I haven't had a chance to read it yet.'

'One of the DCs left it lying around and, as I was flicking through, I noticed this headline on page three: "Break-in clue to crossbow murders".'

She opened the paper and spread it out on her boss's desk.

'It's about crimson bolts being among property stolen from the archery club,' she said. 'They've spoken to the secretary, Jasmine Turner.'

Roscoe frowned. 'I thought we were going to ask the club not to tell the press about the bolts.'

'We did. Either Miss Turner's ignored us or the press have found out by some other means.'

He read to the end of the report. 'Well, at least there's no mention of the handkerchiefs. We've got to keep that out of the public arena until we've got this crossbow maniac under lock and key.'

The sergeant stood up to leave. Then she turned back to face him. 'Sir, were you aware the Queensbridge jewellery thief's been sent down for six months?'

'No, that's passed me by.'

'His name's Frank Baker.'

'Oh, I remember that name. There was a time when he was behind nearly every burglary in West Warwickshire.'

'Well, he was back in court yesterday. He admitted two burglary charges.'

'He'll be back on the streets in six months' time, doing the same thing again.'

'Sir, did you know he'd been receiving archery lessons as part of a community scheme to deter him from anti-social behaviour?'

'Yes, I seem to remember something about that.'

'I was wondering if we should make some inquiries about him and some of the other club members.'

'Very good idea, Sergeant. I'll flag this up at the next team briefing. I take it you'll be away this afternoon?'

'Yes, sir. I took your advice and I'm using the solicitor in Queensbridge you recommended to do my conveyancing. I've got to go down there to sign the mortgage documents.'

'So the move to Warwick's going ahead?'

'Yes, sir. Looks like it. It'll be strange at first leaving Birmingham.'

'Yes, you studied at the law school in Edgbaston, didn't you?'

'That's right, sir.'

'Used to know that area well. Anyway, you'll be closer to work from now on.'

'Yes. By a few miles.'

'We'll be able to call you in at short notice.'

She frowned. 'I'm sure people have made worst suggestions to me in the past, sir, but at the moment I can't think of one.'

He smiled. 'It's all right, Sergeant. I was only joking. I hope the move goes smoothly for you.'

* * *

That afternoon, Sunita spent more than an hour at her solicitor's office in Queensbridge, signing papers and gathering information about her flat.

Afterwards, she gazed in the High Street shop windows at some of the goods on display. She was minded to buy a gift for her father, businessman Ranendra Roy. Perhaps a personalised pen? Perhaps a watch?

The pair had become estranged for a while, but, after a reconciliation last year, she'd become close again to both him and her mother, Bina. He was providing part of the deposit for her new home, so she wanted to show her gratitude.

She couldn't find anything impressive enough to warrant her parting with money and was on the point of returning to her car. Then, at the last minute, she spotted a gift shop called Keepsakes.

It was a small shop with a dark green façade sandwiched between a chemist and a menswear shop. Her spirits rose.

After browsing for only a few minutes, she chose an elegant quartz mantel clock, priced at sixty-five pounds.

But as she was queuing to pay at the counter, she noticed boxes of handkerchiefs piled up in a huge display in a corner.

After buying the clock with her credit card and allowing the young assistant to place it in a carrier bag for her, she walked over to take a closer look.

To her amazement, the handkerchiefs were exactly like those that had featured in the case. Each box contained a set of three.

Sunita called the assistant over. 'Do all these handkerchiefs have an embroidered capital letter in the corner?'

'That's right, madam. They're from our supplier in Ireland. They're unisex. We've got most letters of the alphabet in three colours: red, blue and silver. But I know we've run out of some. Which letter were you looking for, madam?'

'Well, I was wondering about the letter *C* in silver.'

The assistant rummaged around the shelves and fished out three boxes, which were each priced at nineteen pounds ninety-nine pence.

She smiled at Sunita. 'These are the ones with the letter *C*.'

Trying to control her excitement, Sunita took them from the assistant's hands. 'May I open one?'

The assistant nodded. 'Sure. Go ahead.'

As she raised the white cardboard lid, she was delighted to find the three white handkerchiefs inside seemed a precise match with those found at the murder scenes. The floral script monograms in silver thread were identical, as was the linen's weave. Each handkerchief had a narrow, rolled hem.

'Right, is the manager around?'

'I think she's rather busy, madam.'

Sunita removed her warrant card from her pocket and showed it to the girl. 'Would you kindly interrupt her and tell her it's police business? I'm from Heart of England CID.'

The assistant gave an astonished look. 'Goodness. I'll fetch her at once, madam.'

A few minutes later, an austere-looking, overweight woman in her fifties with tortoiseshell glasses came waddling towards the sergeant. She was frowning. 'Good afternoon. Is there a problem?'

Sunita smiled. 'DS Roy, Heart of England CID. I'm interested in the handkerchiefs you've got here with monogrammed initials in the corner. Similar ones have cropped up in a recent criminal case. I'd like to take one of these boxes with the letter *C* away for our purposes. In return, I'll give you a receipt.'

The manager shrugged. 'All right. Do you want us to wrap one up?'

The sergeant shook her head. 'No, I'll put it in the same bag as the clock I've just paid for.'

As she walked back to the counter, she noticed a CCTV camera trained on the till.

'Is that the only camera in the store?' she asked the manager.

'There's one by the door as well.'

'We'll want to view the footage. I'll ask one of my colleagues to come and see you about that.'

The original assistant handed her a box of handkerchiefs under the manager's watchful eye. Then the sergeant wrote a receipt on a page torn from her notebook and passed it over.

She glanced up at the manager. 'Could you give me the name of the firm that supplies them to you?'

'Yes, madam. I'll go and find the details.'

'Oh and do any other shops around here sell them?'

'I really couldn't tell you, madam,' she said. 'I've only been here a few months. As far as I'm aware, we're the only local retailers.'

'One other thing – have you got the names of the customers who have purchased these handkerchiefs since they first went on sale?'

'I'm afraid that would be asking too much, madam. Many paid in cash since they went on sale six months ago and we don't have details.'

Sunita sighed. 'Very well,' she said.

The manager then wandered away, muttering to herself.

Sunita was jubilant as she left the shop and returned to the car park after establishing the killer might well have bought the linen items in the town.

Did this point to the killer coming from Queensbridge? Were they regular customers of the gift shop? Were Keepsakes the only local stockist? And would these new inquiries lead them to the killer's door?

As soon as she returned to her car, Sunita took out her mobile phone and called the chief inspector to tell him of her discovery.

Chapter 33

It was Thursday, 22 June, exactly three weeks after Trudy Marwood and her two friends had attended the night out at the Municipal Hall. A line of smartly dressed men and women would no doubt that evening be taking to the floor again.

Trudy could visualise the scene in her mind, but she couldn't decide whether to join them. Jane Perks was free to go dancing with her, while Ginny had declined, explaining that her attendance on 1 June would not be repeated for a while – if ever.

The minutes ticked by. Finally, at around eight o'clock, Trudy phoned Jane. 'I'm sorry,' she said. 'I don't think I'm going to go this evening. I think I'm going to have an early night, unless you can think of a good reason why I should go.'

It was a humid night, the kind insomniacs fear. Anyone intent on sleep could cover themselves with a single cotton sheet and still find it hard to doze.

A few hours passed. A vehicle glided along the main road towards the Marwoods' detached house. It parked a short distance from the front door. Then its driver stepped silently along the pavement and crept through the open garden gates.

The intruder, dressed from head to foot in an army-style camouflage jacket and trousers, walked along the side of the house clutching a crossbow fitted with a bright torch beam. A ladder left behind by the builders was quickly placed upright against the side of the scaffolding. It was almost as if the figure had known it would be there. Wearing black leather gloves and balaclava, the intruder clambered up until reaching first-floor level.

In the back bedroom, the wooden-framed casement window had been opened to let air in, but the dark-haired woman inside lay slumbering in her bed.

Just a dim nightlight was glowing in a corner close to the door – a lamp provided to assist during night-time trips to the bathroom. Then the sleeper woke with a start.

What was the creaking sound she could hear? It seemed to come from just outside. Could there be someone moving along the scaffolding boards? How could that be?

She lay there in the stillness of the night, hardly daring to breathe. More creaking. Now it was sounding more like a clattering. It was coming closer. It was close to her window.

She got up, sat on the edge of the bed and stared out into the pitch-black night. Was her vision deceiving her? In the partial moonlight, could she detect the silhouette of a figure peering in?

'Who is it? What d'you want?' she demanded as she saw the outline of the blue balaclava.

A beam of light streamed over the waking woman's startled face. She screamed as a crossbow bolt tore through the air, piercing her chest. She slumped back, dying.

The stranger climbed nimbly in. By now the victim lay almost motionless on the bed. Several strands of her long, black, frizzy tresses of hair clung with perspiration to her lily-white face.

Blood seeped onto her nightgown and trickled onto her bedsheet. The final tragic moments of her life were ebbing away. Her naked legs lay apart where she'd clumsily fallen back. Her mouth lay open.

The figure pulled a white handkerchief from a trouser pocket and forced it into the victim's gaping mouth until she was close to taking her final breath.

The visitor stood back to admire their handiwork. Then, with a satisfied smile, returned to the window, scrambled out and clambered down from the scaffolding before disappearing into the night.

* * *

Much later that same morning, detectives involved in Operation Promenade were working with renewed enthusiasm. For several days, they'd been making inquiries about the monogrammed handkerchiefs that Sunita Roy found on sale.

Just after ten o'clock, Roscoe ventured into the CID office. 'Tom, have you got a moment?'

DI Vickers nodded. He rose from his desk and joined the chief inspector in his room.

'Tom, I want you to talk to me about the handkerchiefs.'

The inspector watched as Roscoe installed himself behind his desk.

'Sir, there were altogether a hundred and eighty boxes of handkerchiefs on sale at Keepsakes. They were sold to the shop by a firm called Craft Logo Linens.'

'Just tell me about the ones with the monogrammed *C*.'

'There were originally twelve boxes of those when they first went on sale. DS Roy bought one box and they now have four left. So my schoolboy maths tells me the shop have sold seven sets to customers over the past few weeks.'

'If only we could find out who those customers were,' said Roscoe as his colleague closed the door. He leaned back in his chair. 'By the way, don't leave the sergeant's box around. People will be blowing their bloody noses on them.'

'No, sir. I've locked them in a drawer.' As he drew his chair closer, the inspector continued, 'Forensics have finally come back to say the ones DS Roy bought are a perfect match for the handkerchiefs used in the murders.'

'So there's a good chance the killer bought them at that gift shop?'

'Yes, sir.'

'Do we have any names and addresses so far for the customers who bought them?'

'Sadly, not. The manager's got no sales details. All the handkerchiefs – no matter what letter was embroidered on them – have been listed in the sales ledger simply as "monogrammed handkerchiefs". There's no letter-by-letter breakdown. On top of that, they've got lots of part-time staff and the manager cannot find anyone who specifically remembers selling ones with the letter *C*.'

Roscoe shook his head. 'Damn! I might've known it. We're thwarted at every turn. I can't recall an investigation in which we've faced so many obstacles.'

Just then, there was a knock.

'Not at the moment. We're tied up.'

Sunita opened his door a few centimetres and peered round.

'Sir, I'm sorry to interrupt.'

Roscoe glared at her. 'Can't you see I'm busy, Sergeant?'

'Sorry, sir, but there's been another murder. A woman in Stratford's just been found dead in her bedroom with a crimson bolt in her chest.'

The chief inspector folded his arms. 'That's all we need. What do we know, Sergeant?'

She took a few steps into the office. 'Some builders have been working on the roof of a four-bedroom house in Warwick Road. They turned up for work this morning and no one seemed at home.'

She glanced at some scribblings in her notebook. 'The householder, a Mrs Trudy Marwood, usually comes out to greet them and make them an early-morning cup of tea, but she was nowhere around. They thought she'd perhaps gone to the shops and they started work. After a few minutes, they noticed a back bedroom window was wide open. Becoming concerned, one of them climbed up on the ladder and was horrified to find her lying on the bed.'

Roscoe rolled his eyes. 'Don't tell me – there was a white handkerchief in her mouth?'

'Yes, sir. One of the builders got into the room to check on her, but there was no pulse. She was stone cold.'

The chief inspector frowned. 'God. It must've been frightening for them. Right, Tom, alert the SOCOs and get straight down there.'

He glanced at the sergeant waiting by the door. 'Sergeant, see if that fellow Stanton is still in London. After that, we'd both better head to Stratford.'

Chapter 34

DI Vickers arrived at Trudy Marwood's house nearly an hour after the first 999 call had been received. Although the imposing house stood close to a major road, he could tell at once that its location could be appealing for any intruder.

There were open fields to the left of the house, which was the first in a row of detached houses. Trees and bushes sheltered the rear of the building from the eyes of neighbours. There was just a two-metre-high fence standing between the Marwoods' home and the fields – offering any criminal an easy escape route if required.

An access road, partly obscured from passing traffic by a line of trees, lay between the row of properties and the main road.

He found it difficult to park near the house. Three police cars and two unmarked cars had already claimed spaces. He had to drive for thirty metres along before he could find a place.

As he walked back, he noticed a silver Jaguar with damaged paintwork parked outside the Marwoods' home. Two men who looked like builders were standing on the front lawn. A male and female constable were interviewing them.

His attention was then drawn to the familiar face of a police colleague standing by the garden gates.

DI Andy Chadwick smiled broadly. 'Good morning, Tom.'

'Morning, Andy.' Vickers tried to smile, but it dawned on him an argument over jurisdiction might develop. 'That's the last thing we need today,' he muttered to himself.

Chadwick was a fifty-two-year-old policeman, whose main role was running the small CID department in Stratford. He was a quick-tempered, overweight man with receding grey hair.

'How are you keeping, Tom?' he asked as Vickers reached the gateway. 'How's your bullying boss, Gavin Roscoe?'

Vickers at once leaped to his DCI's defence. 'The guvnor's no bully – just a hard grafter. We're both fine. You all right?'

'Yes. Too much work like everybody. Is Roscoe on his way down?'

'Yes.'

Chadwick grinned. 'Well, anyway, let me show you round the back where it all happened.'

A concrete path running along the side of the house beside a narrow patch of grass led to the rear garden. The whole area had been taped off, but detectives and forensic staff could reach the back by stepping on anti-contamination plates.

As he looked up at the scaffolding cocooning the whole of the back of the building, the inspector could see two forensics staff at first-floor level, examining an open window frame for fingerprints. He was told a police photographer was inside the bedroom, taking pictures of the body.

Vickers tapped Chadwick on the shoulder. 'Have you seen the body?'

'Yes, not pretty.'

'According to our records, a woman called Trudy Marwood lives here.'

'Yes. The builder who found Mrs Marwood was devastated. He said she was incredibly kind and a stunning-looking woman as well. Ah, here's Dr Reynolds.'

Vickers had always held a fascination for the pathologist. If he was available, Reynolds arrived promptly and was always well prepared. He sauntered round the corner of the building in his waterproof apron and rubber gloves, clutching his brown leather bag. He was accompanied by his assistant, David.

Dr Reynolds gazed round jovially at the row of expectant faces. 'Is this the right address for the Townswomen's Guild summer picnic?'

Vickers enjoyed his humorous banter, despite the gravity of the occasion. 'Yes. We'll be round with the vol-au-vents in a moment.'

'Right, let's have a look at the body,' Dr Reynolds said. 'Up there, is she?'

Vickers noticed Chadwick scowling after the doctor's jesting.

'You need gallows humour in his job,' he remarked to Chadwick as the pathologist looked up towards the first-floor window and watched the forensic work taking place. 'Silas must see so many examples of what the poet Robert Burns called man's inhumanity to man.'

Chadwick's mood lightened. 'I suppose so.'

The forensic team had earlier removed the builders' ladder for closer examination. It had been replaced by a police ladder, which officers had been using to reach the upstairs window.

Dr Reynolds glanced at the two detectives. 'I'd better use the stairs,' he mumbled before gingerly entering the house through the back door. At the same time, Vickers walked round to the front of the house, searching for the very first officers to arrive at the scene.

* * *

An hour later, Gavin Roscoe and Sunita Roy arrived at the house in separate cars. By then, Trudy Marwood's husband had been notified and had travelled there. He was being comforted by officers who were providing him with tea in the front room.

Roscoe and the sergeant were keen to speak to the builders first. The workmen's burly fifty-two-year-old foreman, who hailed from Coventry, explained he and his two workmates had arrived at around eight o'clock to resume their work on the roof.

The foreman tutted. 'We knew something strange had happened as soon as we got here. The ladder were resting on the scaffold. We'd left it on the ground.

'And when we went up, oh Lord! You've never seen such a sight. Mrs Marwood's body were covered in blood and there were this arrow poking out of her chest. We didn't know what to do. We thought we'd better check she were dead. I sent in one of the others – I could never have got through the window, on account of my size. We just wanted to see if she were alive and if there were anything we could do. But we were too late.'

Sunita gazed into his eyes. 'You said "Mrs Marwood's body". It was definitely her, was it?'

The foreman nodded. 'Fraid so. We've been here a few weeks. She's been making us tea every day. We knew it was her. She'd also told us she were the only one living here. She split from her husband, see.'

The sergeant asked if they could see the man who first saw the body.

'No, I sent Ted home. He were too shaken up.'

Sunita shrugged. 'What did Ted tell you he did when he entered the room?'

'We were watching him. He checked the pulse, but there were nothing. The body were cold. He just wanted to get out of there as quick as he could. Then we phoned 999.'

At that moment, Roscoe caught sight of Chadwick out of the corner of his eye. He left his sergeant with the builder and strolled across to the centre of the lawn, where the inspector was standing with his hands on his hips, gazing up at the casement window.

The chief inspector gave a weak smile. 'We're not going to waste resources doubling up on this one, are we, Andy?'

Chadwick shrugged his shoulders. 'Well, this is clearly my patch. We're already handling calls from the press and public.'

Roscoe frowned. 'It seems obvious this must be linked to Operation Promenade.'

'All right. I thought you'd take that attitude. I won't make a fuss about it. I'll let you handle the case, but I'd like to be kept informed.'

The chief inspector nodded. 'Yes, of course. I'll get Vickers or Roy to liaise with your team.'

To his relief, Chadwick waved and began walking off towards his car.

But the arrogant inspector had one final message for his superior. As he reached the corner of the house, he turned back.

'Good luck with this one, Gavin. The first guys on the scene have already spoken to neighbours. No one saw or heard anything. See you!'

'Bloody smarmy prat,' Roscoe muttered.

Sunita had meanwhile stepped round to the front of the house and was negotiating with the crime scene manager to be allowed upstairs.

It seemed clear that the dead woman was Trudy Marwood, a former secretary in her thirties who owned the Jaguar parked outside.

But as she passed into the hallway and headed towards the stairs, she wondered what the connection could be between Mrs Marwood and the two previous victims. She felt certain there must be one. She hesitated at the foot of the stairs, waiting for her boss to join her.

Then, moments later, Roscoe's face appeared in the doorway and the pair went up to the first-floor landing. They found the doctor in the back bedroom.

Although the smallest of the four bedrooms, it was nonetheless an adequate size with light-blue patterned wallpaper and a fairly new beige carpet. The only furniture was a single bed, a dressing table and mirror, a single wardrobe and a small bedside cabinet. Dr Reynolds was completing his examination of the body, which remained on the bed.

Dr Reynolds stood up as they entered. 'It's exactly the same MO as before, folks. It's a clean shot to the heart. A classic case of penetrating projectile trauma with a rear exit wound.'

The pair peered across at the blood-spattered corpse, lying still with her mouth open and an anguished expression on her face.

Roscoe folded his arms. 'Poor woman. Is there anything to suggest this is the same killer as in Biddington and Oakdale Road?'

'Yes, old fruit, I'd say so. The handkerchief's been removed now, but it had the letter *C* in the corner – just as before. Whoever did this has obviously shot her from the window and then walked in here. There were dabs on the window and ledge, but they could be from the men who found the body. There are traces of mud on the floor which we're preserving with covers, as you can see,' Reynolds said.

He added that it would be necessary to confiscate all the workmen's boots so their impressions could be eliminated from the investigation.

'If we're lucky, we could have the shoe mark of the killer again. If so, we'll have to see if it matches the marks on poor Angelina's body, where the brute kicked her.'

Roscoe immediately left the room. He went downstairs to make sure the builders' boots were being impounded. But Sunita remained upstairs. She had more questions.

'Any idea about the time of death?'

'As far as we can ascertain, between midnight and 5.00 a.m.'

She gazed around. 'What's really puzzling me is how the bowman could see into the room. Surely, at that time, it would've been extremely dark. I see there's a dim nightlight by the bedroom door which is still on. But that hardly gives out enough light for someone aiming a weapon.'

The pathologist grinned. 'How about this then? He fits a torch to the underside of the crossbow and Geronimo! You've got a bowman's nightlight.'

She nodded. 'Yes, that makes sense.'

The pathologist picked up an evidence bag containing items a forensic officer had recovered. 'Thought you might be interested in this. Looks like the woman's bag.'

He led her from the room, fearful of contaminating the scene. Sunita knelt down as the doctor removed a black leather handbag. Then, after handing her a pair of gloves to wear, he watched as she removed the items and examined them one by one: a purse containing three pounds and some loose coins; three partly torn tickets for a night out; a receipt for two hundred and ninety-five pounds from SA Autos in Stratford; and a small, brown address book containing dozens of phone numbers.

Flicking through the book's pages, Sunita noticed a variety of men's names beside phone numbers: Steve, Kirk, Mark, Den, Hugh, and Phil. She also recognised the names of Warwickshire pubs – including the Jolly Waggoners in Stratford and the White Swan in Shawley Green. She quickly took photographs of the key addresses and the tickets on her mobile phone.

'Sarge!' a voice called. 'You're wanted downstairs.'

She stood up. 'Sounds like the DCI needs me. I'd better let you get on, Dr Reynolds. But a quick question – any sexual interference?'

He shook his head. 'Not that we can see on initial inspection.'

Sunita carefully put the handbag and its contents back in the evidence pouch and then passed it back to the pathologist.

'Thanks for all your help,' she mumbled as she rushed off down the stairs.

Chapter 35

As Sunita Roy made her way down the oak staircase, she discovered the chief inspector was standing in the hallway, beckoning her.

'Where've you been?' he demanded.

'I've found a list of addresses that could prove vital, sir.'

Roscoe tutted. 'We can look at those later. Mr Marwood's here.'

He introduced her to a man sitting on a cream leather settee in the front room. 'Here's my sergeant now,' he explained.

She approached Marwood and stooped to shake his hand. 'DS Roy. Pleased to meet you, sir. I'm so sorry it's in these circumstances.'

'So am I,' moaned the visitor, dabbing his eyes from time to time with a paper tissue.

Roscoe strode to the centre of the oak-panelled room. 'Are you feeling up to talking about your wife?'

'As good as I'll ever be,' he remarked. 'Oh God, she was such a wonderful woman. Who could do this to her, inspector? Who could do this?'

Roscoe shrugged. 'We don't know, sir. But we'll move heaven and earth to find out. May I ask when you last saw your wife?'

'I'll be honest with you. We split up a few months ago. I saw her last month, but only to exchange a few words. The separation was her idea. I'm staying with my brother *pro tem*. God, I can't believe anyone could do this to poor Trudy.'

While Sunita took a seat close to Marwood, Roscoe noticed his teacup was empty and suggested they might be able to arrange a fresh cup for him.

The man shook his head. 'No, I'm fine, thank you. Oh, God. This has come as a total shock. I just never expected anything like this.'

Sunita nodded. 'We can see that, sir. Take as long as you like to answer our questions.'

'Mr Marwood, a young constable showed you round the house a few minutes ago. Are you absolutely certain nothing's been stolen?' Roscoe asked.

The tearful man muttered that he could not be entirely certain because his wife had shifted objects round since he'd moved out. But there seemed nothing missing, as far as he could tell. Poignantly, he'd positively identified the murdered woman as his wife when he first arrived.

As there was a pause in the conversation, Sunita glanced towards Marwood. 'I'd like to ask something which may not seem strictly relevant. Mr Marwood, you're a builder, as we understand it. Yet you brought in a firm of builders to replace the roof. Why was that?'

'Yes, I've spent my whole life in the building game. But I don't get my hands dirty anymore. I'm in management and property development now.'

'I see.'

'Did Mrs Marwood have any men friends and did she go out socially a lot? I found some tickets for a night out in her handbag for an event that took place on June 1st.'

'I'm afraid my wife's recent life is a closed book, as far as I'm concerned. I don't believe she'd got any men friends. Certainly, I've had no one tell me about her seeing anyone. I don't know anything about a night out. I know she took the car to the garage a few days ago to get it repaired because I was talking to one of the mechanics.'

The chief inspector asked, 'Which car is that, sir?'

Marwood pointed to the window. 'The Jag that's out the front. It's been backfiring, apparently. It's also got damaged paintwork, which I'm mystified about.'

'Right, sir. I wanted to fire a few names at you to see if they mean anything to you,' Roscoe said. 'Oliver Bufton, the electrician?'

'Never heard the name.'

'A fashion photographer called Angelina Moretto?'

'No. Means nothing.'

'A car salesman called Stanton? Ricky Stanton?'

Again Marwood shook his head. 'The last name sounds familiar, but I can't place him.'

'In what way is his name familiar? Did you buy a car from him?'

'Possibly. It might come to me later.'

Sunita, who had been listening to the questions, turned her head towards Marwood. 'Can we ask whether your wife enjoyed a drink, sir?'

He dabbed his right eye. 'She liked a drop now and again, like most of us, but I'd describe her as more of a social drinker.'

'What did she drink?' asked Sunita, who believed you could tell a lot about a person from their choice of drink.

'She likes white wine spritzers – and Martinis, but I can't see how that matters.'

She was developing a theory as she gazed absent-mindedly at the room's light-grey wallpaper. It was only an initial feeling, but she sensed Mrs Marwood was a rather mysterious woman, intellectual and cunning but also likely to capture men's attention in a social setting.

Marwood was still talking. He was finding it a struggle to cope with his loss. He stared at the chief inspector.

'Look, can you tell me why my wife's dead? Was this a burglary that went wrong? Was it mistaken identity? Was he meant to kill someone else? Or did my dear wife become mixed up with some bad people?'

Roscoe leaned forward in his armchair. 'These are all questions in the forefront of our minds as well, sir. It's very early days, but we already have a lot of information and there are several lines of inquiry we'll be pursuing later today and tomorrow. Well, Sergeant, do you think we can let Mr Marwood go for now?'

'I just have one more question, if I may. Mr Marwood, why do you suppose your wife had three tickets for a night out in her bag, each with a different serial number?'

His face was blank.

She went on, 'They were partly torn – suggesting a doorman checked them after purchase, ripping the tickets slightly as they entered the venue.'

'You've put me on the spot there, officer,' he said. 'I don't know about a night out or about any of my wife's current friends. I think she's got an old school friend in Warwick, but I've forgotten her name.'

Sunita signalled to the chief inspector that she had no further questions.

Roscoe folded his arms, then said, 'You made a written statement with the help of one of the constables earlier, so you're free to leave whenever you like, sir.'

Marwood stood up. 'You'll catch the bastard, won't you? Because if you don't, I bloody will. I've been trying to get back with my wife and this has ripped my future plans apart.'

'We wouldn't recommend that you consider taking things into your own hands in any way, but don't worry, sir. We promise to keep you up to date with any developments.'

After Marwood left, Roscoe stepped into the front garden, where DI Vickers was speaking to the builders.

'Tom, can we make sure we've got the names of all the builders who've worked on the house over the past few months – including the people who erected the scaffolding?'

'Yes, sir.'

'Can you also do some house-to-house?' he asked. 'Get hold of DC Khalid and get him to help you.'

As he returned to the living room, Roscoe found Sunita engrossed in her thoughts. He sat down beside her on the settee.

'Why were you so interested in the night out in Stratford?'

'Because we need to probe Trudy Marwood's social life,' she said. 'I believe the clue as to why she was murdered could lie there. She had some tickets in her handbag. I don't know if they're of any importance.'

She added, 'We need to know who her friends were and what happened at the event. One assumes that either one of them drove or that they took a taxi. The event was at the Municipal Hall, according to the tickets. That's far too far to walk from here. If there were three or more of them, it would've made economic sense for them to hire a taxi. That would also have meant they could all drink alcohol.'

Roscoe nodded. 'Yes, that's got the ring of truth about it.'

The pair stepped out of the house and headed down the access road towards their cars. As they walked, Sunita wondered how this attractive woman with lily-white skin and black hair could have become the third crossbow victim.

What was the connection between her death and those of Bufton and Moretto? Were they friends? One fact was now certain. The detectives' previous belief that the murders of Bufton and Moretto would be the last had been very wide of the mark. The killer had shown they were ready to kill again.

'At least this proves one thing, if nothing else, sir,' Sunita said. 'This business wasn't just about Bufton and Moretto and their relationship. This maniac – whoever they are – has wider issues.'

* * *

DI Vickers knew that around midday on a Friday was not the best time to conduct house-to-house inquiries. Most householders fortunate enough to have a job would be out at work.

However, it was a task that had to be done. So somewhat reluctantly, after he'd taken a five-minute cigarette break, he and twenty-five-year-old DC Khalid began their series of visits, taking it in turns to press the bell or rap the knocker at each of the large, detached houses in the row.

There was no reply when they tried the home of the Marwoods' immediate neighbours. It was a similar story at the next two.

But they had more luck at the fifth house, which was newly painted at the front and appeared well maintained. Vickers rang the doorbell and a cheerful middle-aged man came to the door in a light-coloured business suit.

'Heart of England Police,' said the inspector, showing his warrant card. 'DI Vickers. This is DC Khalid. We're investigating an incident a few doors away.'

The householder nodded. 'Yes, I've heard. Terrible business.'

'How well did you know the Marwoods, sir?'

'Not really well enough to have a long conversation,' he said. 'I see Mr and Mrs Marwood from time to time. We sometimes say hello. That's about all.'

Khalid pointed at the access road in front of the row of houses. 'Have you seen anything unusual happening out here in the past twelve hours?' he said. 'For instance, early in the morning, were there any strange vehicles parked here?'

He shook his head. 'Me and my wife, we were sleeping. The only strange thing was seeing all the police cars this morning. We saw and heard nothing at night. But I'm telling you something, Mr Inspector, sir. If you come back in two hours, my son will be out of bed. He's a night worker and he may've seen something.'

Vickers folded his arms. 'What time does he arrive home in the morning?'

The householder glanced at the sky as if seeking inspiration. 'Around three o'clock. I've not seen him since he got in. There's a chance he might've seen something. I can't promise.'

'All right,' said Vickers. 'What's your son called?'

'Vijay. His full name's Vijay Shah.'

'Well, thank you for your time, sir. We'll call back, if that's all right.'

'Yes, that's no problem, Inspector.'

The two detectives continued making their inquiries along the street. But they made little more headway. Only two other householders opened their front doors to speak to them. Both explained they'd been asleep in the early hours and had no information that could help.

At that point, Vickers decided to return to St James Street headquarters, asking his colleague to remain at the scene and visit Vijay Shah when he woke up.

Chapter 36

As soon as Sunita Roy arrived back in CID, she became determined to find the taxi driver who took the three women to the over-thirties night.

So while the chief inspector was summoned to the second floor to see Chief Superintendent Norris, she immediately set to work.

She first found the names and phone numbers of all the taxi and private hire firms in the Stratford area. There were more than she'd ever have guessed – fifteen based in the town itself and thirty-five in the nearby areas of Queensbridge, Warwick, Shipston-on-Stour and Leamington Spa.

Then she set to work, phoning the first few companies on her list, asking if they recalled taking three ladies in their mid-thirties from Warwick Road, Stratford to the Municipal Hall between the hours of seven and ten on Thursday, 1 June.

PC Dawson strolled over, looking contrite. 'Sarge,' he said. 'I'd like to apologise for some of the things I've said. I'd got no right to assume...'

Sunita put her desk phone down and smiled at him. 'You're all right, Brett.'

'I hope you'll accept my apology.'

'Of course.'

He sat down at a desk opposite her. 'I've overheard what you're saying to the taxi firms. Do you want me to help?'

'Yes, that would be cool. There's a lot to get through.'

She photocopied the list she'd made and marked six of the firms for him to call.

After they'd both spent nearly half an hour making calls, Sunita saw how challenging their task was proving to be. There had been thousands of tourists in the town on that first night of the month for a theatre production, two cinema screenings and a funfair, she had discovered.

Thousands of revellers had packed into the pubs while restaurants had been full of diners. Dozens of separated and divorced people had descended on the Municipal Hall – and many of them had requested taxis.

One taxi phone operator tried very hard to assist her. 'Haven't you got the customer's name, darling? We're stuck without that.'

Sunita frowned. 'The only name I've got is Marwood and the cab may not have been ordered in that name.'

The woman apologised. 'Nothing for Marwood that night and I've been right through the records, darling.'

She and Dawson received a similar response from many other companies. Eventually, they found they'd made calls to all fifteen firms that traded in the town and began calling those located further away.

After three hours, Sunita was thinking of giving up when one of the first companies she'd tried, Aardvark Radio Cars, called her back.

'Was you the lady who called me about a booking earlier this month to the Municipal Hall?' a woman's voice asked.

'That's right!' Sunita replied amid rising excitement.

Dawson looked up from his desk.

'It was ordered in the name of Holland,' the woman revealed. 'It was booked for eight o'clock for an address in Cranleigh Park, Warwick. Then there was a pick-up in Warwick Road, Stratford. Our driver, Mr Marley, took them to the Municipal Hall for an over-thirties night.'

'Thanks ever so much for getting back to me,' said Sunita, grinning and nodding at Dawson.'We'll need to speak to your Mr Marley. Could you arrange for him to be at your office in an hour's time so we can have a chat? That would be great. Thank you so much.'

As she ended the call, she turned to Dawson. 'Do you fancy a trip to Stratford to see this driver?'

'Yes, sounds like a good lead, doesn't it?'

Sunita nodded. 'I'll have to square it with the boss, but this looks really promising.'

* * *

Aardvark Radio Cars was run from a former tobacconist's shop. The premises had been skilfully converted to provide a desk with phones behind a wood partition and a two-by-three-metre waiting area for drivers and passengers.

Joe Marley, the driver who took three ladies to the over-thirties night, was waiting to speak to DS Roy and DC Dawson when they arrived just over an hour later.

Mr Marley was sitting by the door, studying his smart phone.

'Shall we talk outside?' he said, as the pair introduced themselves to him.

Once in the street, he explained how, on the night in question, he'd first travelled to Warwick to collect a Mrs Virginia Holland from a house in Cranleigh Park at about eight o'clock. He'd then driven her to a house in Warwick Road, where he collected two further women passengers. Because of traffic gridlock in the town, he'd left them in the street, a short distance from the hall.

Sunita nodded. 'We believe one of the women in Warwick Road was a Mrs Marwood. What was the exact time you dropped them off?'

He thought for a moment. 'Must've been about twenty-five to nine. Then I picked them up at just after midnight and took them back to the two addresses.'

Dawson frowned. 'Did you see any men with them?'

'I saw three men walking away from them and waving back to them as I arrived to collect them,' he said.

Sunita's eyes lit up. 'How were the men dressed?'

'Just dark suits is all I remember. I immediately thought, they've been out on the pull. Don't ask me what they looked like. It was dark and I was more concerned I shouldn't run over any of the ladies as I parked up. They were in a bit of a state.'

Sunita raised an eyebrow. 'They were drunk?'

'Too right. I think they'd been drinking before I even picked them up. One of them, Mrs Holland, was nearly sick in my car on the way back. Luckily, she got out of it in time.'

'Did you know the names of the other two women?'

'I think one might've been called Jane. But the car was booked in Mrs Holland's name. I didn't need no other names. I gathered from the way they talked that Jane and the third woman, who had black, curly hair, lived near each other in the Warwick Road area.'

Sunita instantly remembered seeing the name 'Jane Perks' in the address book. 'Is there anything else you think we should be aware of?'

'No, not really. I only remembered them because they were so tiddly. What's all this about anyway?'

Dawson frowned. 'I'm afraid one of the women's been murdered.'

'Which one?'

'Mrs Marwood.'

'Oh God. That sounds like the woman with black hair. She was the most attractive one. What a pity. So you think they might've met her killer that night?'

Sunita nodded. 'It's possible.'

'How did she die?'

She shrugged. 'I'm sorry. We're not really at liberty to discuss the case in detail, but thank you so much for your help, Mr Marley.'

'You're welcome.'

As they drove away from the minicab office, Sunita was keen to interview both Mrs Virginia Holland and the second woman, Jane Perks.

Since they were just a few miles away from Warwick Road, they decided to focus their attention on the latter. One of her phone images of the address book pages showed Jane Perks as living in Sunderland Drive.

Within a few minutes, Sunita's Peugeot reached the address, which was just three streets from the Marwoods' home.

Jane lived in a modest but well-kept semi-detached house. There was a green Ford Fiesta in the drive, next to a neatly kept lawn and flower borders, containing mainly orange and yellow marigolds. A teenage boy answered the door.

He looked the pair up and down. 'I think my mum's at the shops.'

But immediately afterwards a woman called out, 'No, I'm not. I'm in the kitchen. Who is it?'

Sunita raised her voice. 'It's the police.'

The embarrassed boy, who appeared to be in his late teens, muttered, 'Sorry. I didn't know she was home.' Then he ran up the stairs.

Jane Perks emerged flustered in the hallway. 'Forgive my son. His mind's always on his computer games.'

Sunita produced her warrant card. 'We're from Heart of England CID,' she said. 'DI Roy. This is DC Dawson. Are you Jane Perks?'

'Yes. What's happened?' she said. 'What's this all about?'

Sunita lowered her voice. 'I think we need to come in. We've got some rather upsetting news.'

'Oh dear. You'd better come into the lounge.'

Jane led them into a large room with cream-coloured wallpaper, a beige carpet and a light-grey three-piece suite.

'Do you know a woman called Trudy Marwood?'

'Yes, she's a close friend.'

Sunita continued. 'I think you'd better sit down.'

'Oh my God. What's happened?' said Jane, sinking onto her settee.

Sunita frowned as she stepped into the centre of the room. 'I'm afraid she's been murdered.'

'Murdered? Where? When?'

'At her home in the early hours of this morning.'

Jane scoffed. 'That's ridiculous. She was standing at the very spot where you're standing five minutes ago. You've just missed her.'

Chapter 37

Sunita Roy had encountered a few surprises during her twenty-six-year life. She'd nearly been killed at the age of six when she was struck by a car that came from nowhere. She'd nearly been stabbed on a plane when tackling a drunken passenger.

But none of her experiences – including events that happened during her three-year spell at law school and four years in the police – could have prepared her for the shock of hearing that the murdered woman believed to be Trudy Marwood was still alive.

Dawson was equally astonished to hear Mrs Marwood had, after all, escaped the crossbow's lethal shaft. For hadn't the woman's husband been shown the body by Dr Reynolds and identified it as his wife's just a few hours earlier?

The detectives exchanged mystified glances. Sunita shook her head as Dawson's complexion turned pale.

'I think it's us that need to sit down – not you, Mrs Perks,' she said.

Jane shifted in her seat. 'Why on earth would you think she's been murdered?'

Sunita was the first to respond. 'We were at Mrs Marwood's house earlier after reports of a woman being found dead. The body was identified as hers by Rowan Marwood four hours ago. I don't understand how she could have been here a short while ago.'

Jane shrugged. 'She hasn't been home since yesterday evening, so any body that's turned up can't have been hers. Look, it's quite simple. Trudy was humming and hawing yesterday about whether to go to the Municipal Hall again. She at one stage phoned to say she wasn't going. Then, at the last minute, she phoned me back and said she'd changed her mind.

'We hired a cab and got there for half past nine. We had a great time. But, afterwards, she was very tired, so I made up a bed for her on the settee. Before I went up to bed myself, I taped a message on the lounge door to warn my teenage sons, who are sixteen and eighteen, not to disturb her when they got up.'

Sunita was writing in her notebook while listening intently. 'But you got to know somehow that someone had been murdered at your friend's house, did you? The fact a body was found doesn't seem to have surprised you?'

'We just saw it on the news. Trudy was devastated to see her house on the telly. She's gone off there now to try to find out what's going on.'

Dawson walked across the room and sat on a dining chair. 'I'm puzzled. So whose body could it be at your friend's house?'

Jane put her hand to her mouth. 'Oh my God. I've just realised. She told me her niece Coral was staying with her for the week.'

Sunita frowned. 'Coral? Her niece?'

Jane nodded. 'On the news, they believed someone was killed with a crossbow. Is that right?'

Sunita sighed. 'I'm afraid during the night someone climbed up some scaffolding at the Marwoods' house. They went to a first-floor window at the back of the house with a crossbow and killed a lady sleeping there.'

'Oh my God,' said Jane. 'Maybe that was Coral. That's terrible. I had no chance to talk to Trudy when she rushed off.'

Sunita stopped writing. 'Do you know the woman's full name?'

'Yes, Coral Devon. She's a singer and that's her performing name, but her real name's Coral Lewis. I think we all need some tea.'

As Jane slipped out to the kitchen to put the kettle on, Dawson seemed to recover his composure.

'They're all going to be thunderstruck when Mrs Marwood turns up at the house,' he said. 'I don't suppose old Silas will still be there, but there will still be several officers there and all the SOCOs. I'd like to see the look on Rowan Marwood's face when he finds out.'

'You're right,' said Sunita. 'Brett, quickly put a call into CID and let the boss know what's happened.'

He stepped into the garden to make the call and returned a few minutes later, telling her he'd left a message with DC Wendy Hopkirk.

Sunita leaned back on the settee. 'What a tragedy for the niece's family. She goes to stay with her aunt for some reason and gets killed. I wonder if this Coral's got links with Bufton and Moretto.'

Dawson sat down. 'Yes, was the niece killed by mistake by someone targeting Mrs Marwood? Or was the niece the intended victim?'

Sunita was engrossed in thought. Then she said, 'Another possibility is that the husband was the target.'

Dawson shook his head. 'Don't think so. He moved out of there quite a while ago.'

'Yes,' said Sunita. 'But did the killer know that? And something to bear in mind is, if the killer blundered and killed the wrong person by mistake, he could make a fresh attempt upon Mrs Marwood's life.'

Jane Perks overheard these final words as she emerged from the kitchen with a tray containing three cups of tea, a sugar bowl and a spoon. She placed the tray on a small table by the settee.

'You think the person was trying to kill Trudy?' she asked.

Sunita put a spoonful of sugar into her cup and stirred it. 'We're not absolutely sure. Police inquiries are obviously at an early stage. A woman's been killed. We don't know yet whether she was the intended victim or whether she was killed in error. But I think it's fair to assume Mrs Marwood may well have been the target and there's a risk of a second attempt being made on her life.'

Jane was dismayed. 'Poor Coral. Is it possible her death is connected with the two other crossbow murders?'

Dawson shrugged. 'We just don't know.'

'Oh my God. There's a maniac at large. Are any of us safe?'

'Don't worry,' said Sunita, without much conviction. 'The police are working hard to bring whoever it is to justice.'

'But are they?' Jane said. 'You didn't even seem to know who the latest victim was five minutes ago.'

Sunita sipped her tea. 'I can assure you we'll do our utmost to catch the perpetrator quickly. Mrs Perks, can you tell us where Mrs Marwood went when she left here just now? Was she definitely going to her home in Warwick Road?'

Jane nodded. 'Yes, she wanted to know what the hell had happened at her house.'

Dawson was stirring his tea vigorously. 'We saw Mrs Marwood's car outside her place a short while ago. So how did she travel home from here? Did she walk?'

'Yes. It's only round the corner,' said Jane. As she spoke, the germ of an idea developed in her mind.

'Oh. I've just had a terrible thought,' she said. 'If Trudy was meant to be the victim, there's a chance I could be next.'

'I don't think you need to worry, Mrs Perks. But it would be sensible to take precautions – look around carefully when you arrive home or leave home. Change your patterns of behaviour. Contact the police if you've got any concerns. They may be able to set up regular patrols if there was a real threat.'

As she dispensed this advice, a worrying thought occurred to Sunita as well. She remembered that the last time she'd been involved in giving personal safety advice, she and Roscoe had been speaking to Oliver Bufton. Surely there was no threat to Jane's life, was there? The sergeant couldn't be sure in her own mind. They were seeking a serial killer who seemed to strike at random.

Chapter 38

Sunita Roy and Brett Dawson were unprepared for the reception they received when they returned together to the Marwoods' house in the late afternoon.

The atmosphere at the house had been as sombre as a mortuary waiting room earlier in the day. Mr Marwood had been weeping and a police welfare officer had been on hand to offer counselling. Now, dramatically, the mood had changed.

'My prayers have been answered,' Rowan Marwood cried as the sergeant pushed against the partly open front door and entered the house. 'My Trudy's returned to me.'

Sunita nodded as she glanced at the lady standing next to him in the centre of the front room. She had long, frizzy, black hair and lily-white skin – exactly like the corpse she'd seen earlier in the day.

'You must be Mrs Marwood,' said Sunita, striding across the grey carpet and shaking her hand.

Her husband was bewildered. 'You don't seem at all surprised to see her.'

'We're not. We've just seen Mrs Perks. She explained everything.'

He shrugged. 'I see. One of your colleagues came round a short while ago. I was speaking about my wonderful fortune in having Trudy back. He behaved very strangely. I think he wondered if I'd been drinking because I was so happy. Then he peered at my wife and must've thought he'd seen a ghost.'

He paused before adding, 'Of course, we mustn't forget the shocking murder of our beloved Coral. It's not really a time for celebrating.'

'One of our colleagues?' said Sunita. 'Oh, that must have been DC Khalid. He's been spending some time talking to neighbours. Yes, it's been a shock to all of us, Mrs Marwood, discovering your remarkable resurrection. Of course, as your husband says, there's also a sad side to all this – the apparent death of your niece.'

The conversation in the room had had a dramatic effect upon Trudy. She still had to face up to the shocking reality of her niece Coral's death. Emotions were shifting like a roller-coaster.

'They've taken the body away in a van,' she admitted as her smile vanished. 'Oh my God. How am I going to tell Moira? She's lost her only daughter – and it's probably my fault. If I'd been here, I might have been able to save her.'

She broke down in tears and sat on the leather settee where her husband had been racked with grief a few hours earlier.

After Mr Marwood made some excuses and left for his brother's house, Sunita introduced herself properly to Trudy.

'We need to talk, Mrs Marwood,' she said. 'I'm one of the main officers involved in the hunt for this crossbow killer and you may have important information for us.'

They sat on the settee while Trudy fetched a dining chair for herself.

'Firstly, can you explain why you weren't at home last night?' Sunita asked as she took out her notebook.

Trudy shrugged. 'Coral had been staying with me for the week – that's my niece, she's twenty-five. When she came back with some shopping at around six on Thursday evening, I told her I might be going out. Jane had been pestering me to go to the over-thirties night. Coral insisted she'd be all right on her own. She was going to read a book in her room. I couldn't make my mind up, but, in the end, I went to the hall with Jane.'

'Why did Coral choose to stay with you?'

'Her mother had gone on holiday to Tenerife. She invited her along, but Coral didn't want to go. She felt she was too old to go away with her mother. So she's been staying with me for a bit of company. But, to be honest, she spent most of her time on her phone or tablet in the back bedroom.'

Sunita was writing notes. 'I can understand how the killer might've thought the sleeping woman was you. You look very similar.'

Dawson nodded. 'Yes, the same black frizzy hair. You could say the same looks, the same locks.'

Trudy smiled. 'Everyone says we look alike.'

Sunita glanced up from writing. 'Even your husband thought it was your body. Mrs Marwood, we'll need you to go to the mortuary as soon as you can to identify the body properly.'

'Yes, of course.'

'When did you last see Coral?' Sunita asked.

'It was about quarter past eight last night. The last words I spoke to her were, "Go to bed. Don't wait up for me."'

'You had an inkling you'd be staying away all night?' Dawson asked.

'No, not really. I thought I'd be getting in sometime between one and two in the morning. As it was, we were pretty exhausted after leaving the hall. I was on the dance floor most of the time. Jane kept going on about me staying over, so I slept on her couch. I never dreamed something like this would happen.'

Sunita had been carefully watching Trudy's demeanour. The homeowner was nervously playing with her hands.

'So do you think the crossbow bolt was meant for you, Mrs Marwood?'

'Of course I do. No one apart from me and Moira, my sister, knew Coral was here.'

'Unless she was followed to this address,' Dawson suggested.

'No one could have any kind of grievance against our Coral. She was the kindest soul you could meet. No, this was something to do with me.'

Sunita looked her in the eyes. 'Have you got any idea who might have wanted to kill you?'

'Not at the moment.'

'We've noticed your car's damaged. Are you being targeted by someone?'

'I think that was just vandals. There are a lot of feral teenagers around here.'

'We're obviously aware you're separated from Mr Marwood and have been socialising quite a bit,' said Sunita. 'Is it possible you've met someone who's formed a bad opinion of you or has developed some grievance?'

'I can't think of anyone.'

'By the way, we found your handbag upstairs. I'm assuming you took a different one when you went out last night?'

'Yes, I took my pink clutch bag. Why? I suppose you've been through it.'

'The pathologist, Dr Reynolds, took a quick look this morning. At that time, we thought we were looking at the contents of a murdered woman's bag.'

Trudy stood up. 'I must have left my main handbag upstairs when I was tidying the rooms. Coral's bag would only have contained money and a few cosmetics. I'll go and get it for you. I put it in a drawer for her. I'd better check it's still there.'

She left the room for a few minutes. When she returned, she was holding a small grey handbag, which she passed to the sergeant.

Sunita placed it on the carpet beside her. 'Thank you. Mrs Marwood, I wanted to ask you about the various men listed in your address book.'

Dawson felt embarrassed and sensed his sergeant would appreciate some time alone with Mrs Marwood. 'I'll just go and have a word with the crime scene manager,' he said, slipping out of the room.

Mrs Marwood leaned back on the settee. 'What would you like to know, Sergeant?'

'Can you tell me about each one in turn, please? Steve?'

'Is this really necessary? Steve was a guy I met a few weeks ago at the hall in town. I had a fling with him. Big, broad-shouldered man from a mining family in Wales. We went out for a few weeks and then it petered out. He was too controlling – and too drunk, most of the time, like my ex-husband.'

'What about Kirk?' asked Sunita, as she noted down Trudy's remarks regarding Steve.

'I met him at the Jolly Waggoners during a skittles match. He took me for a meal. We're still friends, but that's as far as it goes.'

'Then there's Mark.'

'Mark's the manager of the Jolly Waggoners. I went out with him for a few weeks, then found out he was married. He's separated from his wife, but not divorced.'

'What about Den?'

'Another loser,' she said. 'Met him at the Municipal Hall. He told me he worked on the trains. He was a heavy drinker with wandering hand trouble. Finished with him.'

'How about Hugh?'

'He's just a friend of Den's who's been dating Jane. I once had to phone him when I couldn't get hold of Den.'

'Then we've got Phil,' said Sunita.

Laughing, she said, 'He's just the mechanic who looks after my car. Nothing romantic there – although he's been pestering me for a date.'

'One more name for you. This one doesn't seem to appear in your book: Ricky Stanton.'

Trudy became pensive. 'I can't place him. Stanton, Stanton. No, don't seem to know him.'

Sunita took to her feet. 'Mrs Marwood, where are you proposing to stay tonight?'

'Why? Here, of course.'

'I wouldn't recommend that.'

'Whyever not?'

'Whoever's on this killing spree may try and strike again. If you were his target, and he discovers you're still alive, he may be back for you.'

She placed her hand on her mouth. 'Good God! I never thought of that. You're right. I wonder if I should stay round at Jane's for a while?'

'Let us know what you decide, because, obviously, we'll be wanting to talk to you over the next week or two. In the meantime, I'll have a word with our boss – DCI Gavin Roscoe. He's the senior investigating officer. We'll see if we can get you some police protection.'

'Jesus, do you think the situation's that serious?'

Sunita looked solemn. 'Yes, I do... unless your niece had some secret that made her a target.'

Chapter 39

As the sky darkened overhead, Sunita Roy found a parking space for her car at around midday on Sunday, 25 June. Then, as a light rain began to fall, she and Tom Vickers crossed the street and hurried inside the well-lit cafe, Ali's Pantry, on the outskirts of Queensbridge.

She paused to catch her breath. 'I suppose we could have called in at the tearooms. It's only up the road.'

'I'm fairly certain they're closed on a Sunday,' he replied, as they sat down at a table in the window.

'Thanks so much for coming today, Tom,' she said with a smile as she glanced past the range of more than a dozen other tables.

She could see a woman whom she believed to be the cafe owner, Alison Ford, chatting on the phone behind a counter crammed with enticing cakes and pastries.

'Well, I think we've got a good vehicle there,' he said. 'They say a Luton is big enough to move the contents of a two-bed flat or a small house. As you're only going into a one-bed place, there should be ample room for your furniture and white goods.'

Alison approached them with a broad grin.

'Two teas, please,' said Vickers.

Sunita sat up and smiled. 'Could you make mine a lemon tea?'

'Would you like any cake or biscuits, Sunita?' he asked.

'A slice of carrot cake would be nice.'

'Good idea,' he said. 'Two slices of carrot cake, please.'

Moments after placing their order, two figures in motorcycle gear, dripping with rainwater, entered the cafe, speaking to each other in excited voices while clutching crash helmets. They chose a table on the opposite side of the room and, while water trickled to the floor from their leggings and boots, began peeling off their wet leather jackets and placing them on the backs of their chairs. Then they sat down.

Alison darted from behind the counter seconds later with a mop in her hand.

'Look at the mess you've made,' she fumed, swabbing the puddles as they formed upon the floor.

'It's not our fault. It's the bloody rain,' insisted the woman sitting furthest from the door, who was wearing dark glasses.

The inspector at once thought she resembled Lucy McKie, whom he'd met at Warwick & Queensbridge Company of Archers in Shawley Green.

As Alison took their order for two teas and disappeared to the kitchen, McKie muttered loud enough for the two detectives to hear, 'What a stuck-up cow.'

Vickers beamed at her. 'Lucy, isn't it? I met you at the Wackos clubhouse at the start of May. Do you remember? You showed me how to fire a crossbow.'

The young woman waggled a finger at him. 'You're the cop who paid us a visit. I'm sorry. I don't remember your name.'

'No problem. Tom – Tom Vickers.'

Her companion turned round and he recognised her as Charlene Jones, who helped with the demonstration.

'I remember you, too,' he said. 'This is Sunita, one of my colleagues.'

All three women nodded at one another.

'So what brings you here? You're not just sheltering from the rain?' he asked as the frowning owner served their tea and cakes.

'We've just been out for a ride to try out my new bike,' Lucy explained. 'We were heading for Evesham, but then the skies opened and it began to bucket down.'

Vickers seemed impressed. 'What kind of bike have you got?'

'A Bonneville T100.'

Sunita smiled at Lucy while slicing into her carrot cake. 'So you live round here?'

'Yeah. Just up the road.'

'How's your target practice going?' asked Vickers, as he sipped his tea and cut his cake in half.

'Fine, but I've left the Wackos.'

'How come?'

Charlene answered on her friend's behalf. 'She had a bust-up with the club secretary.'

'Jasmine Turner?'

'Yeah. She's a control freak,' Lucy explained. 'She's got rules about who has access to the range, who's allowed in the armoury, how long the sessions are. She decided a few weeks ago to close the whole place half an hour early. There was uproar. People had paid for up to nine o'clock and she started sending them home at quarter past eight.'

'Lucy went mad,' Charlene informed him in a low voice.

'Too right I went mad,' Lucy shouted. 'You don't get to the top level unless you're managing between a hundred and a hundred and twenty arrows a day.'

'She refused to go home and ignored the instruction,' Charlene added.

'Yes, I just carried on with my bow while everyone else left. After ten minutes, Jasmine came to me with a face like thunder and ordered me to stop firing. I refused and I'm afraid it got a bit out of hand after that.'

'Voices were raised, you could say,' Charlene whispered.

'Yes, and, after that, the cheeky mare banned me from the club, which she's got absolutely no right to do under the rules.'

Alison brought their drinks with a scowl on her face. 'Can you please try and keep your voices down,' she implored them before walking back to the counter.

'Bloody hell!' said Lucy. 'Can't even have a bloody conversation in here now. I don't think we'll be coming back here, Charlie, do you?'

Her friend turned towards Vickers and pulled a face. 'No, not very friendly in here, are they?'

Sunita shrugged her shoulders. 'The lady was all right with us, wasn't she, Tom?'

Vickers nodded as he ate his cake. 'So you haven't been back to Shawley Green for a while?'

Lucy shook her head. 'Not for six weeks.'

'I'm still going to the club,' said Charlene, 'but I don't know for how much longer. Jasmine can be a real bitch. She's upset two of her regulars. Anyway, when the weather's fine, we can go up to Biddington Woods and practise there.'

'I've only been there a couple of times,' said Lucy. 'Jasmine's not worried. There's been a surge in new members since the crossbow murders have been in the news. Hey, Charlie, my tea isn't very hot. Is yours all right?'

'Not really. You expect it to be piping hot when it comes, don't you?'

'Excuse me!' Lucy shouted towards Alison, who was tidying up behind the counter. 'Our teas aren't hot enough. We'd like fresh ones.'

'I'll tell you what. You've been nothing but trouble since you came in here,' said the proprietor, marching towards the women's table. 'Dripping water on the floor, shouting your head off and now you're moaning about the tea. You can both clear off.'

Sunita turned round to face Alison. 'To be fair, it's been raining quite hard. They didn't mean to get the floor wet.'

'Yes,' said Vickers, 'and they were explaining to me about an upsetting incident and the lady only raised her voice to express her feelings.'

'I don't care. They can both leave,' said Alison. 'I've been thinking of shutting for the day anyway. We never get many customers on a Sunday.'

'All right. Keep your hair on,' Lucy said as she slipped on her jacket and picked up her helmet from the floor. 'We've leaving anyway. But don't expect us to pay for lukewarm tea.'

Chapter 40

Gavin Roscoe rarely embarked upon police work on a Sunday. He seldom attended church either. For him, the sabbath meant family time.

However, he was forced to abandon this principle on the day his two colleagues were searching for a van to rent. Although two uniformed officers had already broken the news to Moira Lewis that her beloved daughter, Coral, had died, he felt the poor woman deserved more.

He'd always felt the constabulary could improve the way it treated next-of-kin. He believed it was incumbent upon him, as the senior officer, to visit her and offer her any help that was within his powers.

He also recognised that the newly returned holidaymaker might have information that could assist with their investigation. So just before midday – after obtaining the full address from her sister, Trudy Marwood – he set off for the village of Smerton Heath, near Solihull, to see Moira.

Her house was a three-bedroom detached cottage with a thatched roof that overlooked the village green. As it was nearly lunchtime, players were arriving to prepare for a cricket match. If he'd been curious enough to inquire of passers-by, he'd have discovered Smerton Heath Cricket Club were hosting a team from Biddington.

The chief inspector parked in a side road. He was wary in case any cricket ball might strike his pride and joy, his BMW. By the time he'd walked round the corner to the cottage, men dressed in their freshly laundered white flannels had taken to the field and play was about to begin.

Roscoe pushed open the small, white wooden gate before walking up the stone path to the front door. As he knocked, he noticed blinds had been drawn over the front windows. It appeared as if the house might be deserted. But after a few minutes, he heard a voice, demanding to know what he wanted.

'Heart of England Police,' he said. 'DCI Roscoe.'

A small, dark-haired woman in a white floral blouse and dark-green skirt opened the door timidly.

The chief inspector smiled sympathetically. 'Mrs Lewis? Your sister's identified the body. I wanted to pass on my condolences after the loss of your daughter.'

'Yes, well, nothing will bring her back. You'd better come in,' she said.

He bowed his head to enter the dim hallway while showing his warrant card.

Moira, who was forty-five, lived alone after splitting up with her husband seven years earlier. As she led him into a cosy front room with dark, wooden beams, he at once noticed photographs of a small young woman with black frizzy hair and alabaster skin upon the oak mantelpiece. They were images of Coral. In several of the pictures, she was holding a microphone in her right hand.

'I only just got back from Tenerife last night,' she said.

Her visitor was intrigued by the photographs. 'Your daughter was a singer?' His sergeant had mentioned the fact to him, but it had slipped his mind.

'Yes, she was blessed with a beautiful voice.'

The pair sat down on a brown leather settee beneath the leaded-light front windows. Moira opened the blinds, flooding the room with light.

'I'm the senior officer investigating the death. I wanted to meet you and express our sympathy. I also wanted to assure you we'll do everything we can to catch the killer. Is there any information about Coral's life you think we ought to know?'

Moira shook her head. 'Not really. I'll tell you briefly about her life, if you like. She messed about at school. The only lesson she ever took an interest in was music. After school, she got a lucky break and met someone in the music business. She talked herself into believing she was going to be a star. But her career failed, she got into drugs in a minor way and her life went off the rails. She had several boyfriends, but nothing worked out and she spent years battling depression. Over the past two years, she's been living here with me and started to become a bit reclusive.'

Roscoe shrugged his shoulders. 'I'm sorry if her life had become unhappy, but she certainly didn't deserve to die in such a gruesome way. Did she have any enemies?'

Moira shook her head. 'She didn't have an enemy in the world.'

'So she didn't work and was having to live off the proceeds of her music royalties?'

'She had a job last year. I was really worried about the way her life was going, so last summer I got her some work in my friend's flower shop in Queensbridge. It was only part-time, but it got her out of the house and it kept her mind occupied for a while.'

'Was she working there right up until she died?'

'No, she gave up the job in December. She complained the shop was too cold for her to work in.'

Roscoe needed to inquire into the events of Coral's final days. 'Mrs Lewis, who knew your daughter was staying at the Marwoods' house last Thursday night?'

'No one, as far as I know – except me and Trudy,' she said.

She began to relax a little. Roscoe's eyes followed her as she walked to a corner of the room and began searching through some CDs.

'When did she travel to your sister's house?'

'Last Tuesday. She took a bus from the village to Solihull and then caught the train to Stratford railway station. She walked from the station. It's only a couple of miles to my sister's house.'

'What was she wearing?'

'She told me a pretty white floral dress. She'd have been carrying her red overnight bag.'

'What time did she leave here and what time would she have arrived at your sister's house?'

'She texted me to say she would be leaving here at about half-past three and aimed to arrive at Trudy's by five o'clock. Would you like to hear one of Coral's songs?'

The chief inspector nodded. 'I'd be delighted to, if it's not too upsetting for you.'

Moira began fiddling with a CD player, which was on a shelf beneath her widescreen television. She pressed a button and a tuneful young woman's voice burst out of two speakers.

'Here you are,' said Moira.

Roscoe listened intently as the words filled the room. *We've got plenty to do and we haven't much time. Come up and look around. It's Christmas in Chinatown.*

'Very beautiful,' said Roscoe after the three-minute track finished. 'You must've been very proud of her.'

'We were,' she said. 'She had a Top Fifty hit with that track, *Christmas In Chinatown*, three years ago. Then her follow-up release, *Girl In Disguises*, got to number forty-seven before slipping out of the charts. After that I'm afraid the right song never came along.'

Roscoe leaned forward and peered into her face.

'Look, I'm sorry to ask you this,' he said. 'But getting back to Coral's decision to stay at your sister's house, is it conceivable that anyone else could've had knowledge she was staying there?'

'I can't see how.'

'Could she have been followed when she travelled there?'

'Who'd have wanted to follow her?'

'Well, I'm not sure. It's possible your daughter wasn't the killer's intended target and that she was killed in error by someone aiming to kill your sister. But we mustn't discount the possibility that she might've been the target. So we must consider who could've known she was staying in the Warwick Road house. Did anything strange happen to her recently?'

'No, life here is usually quiet and uneventful. She led a very sheltered life.' Moira removed a tissue from a box on the table and wiped her eyes.

'Please try and think hard about these questions I've asked and let me know if anything comes to you,' the chief inspector continued. 'Finding out how the killer knew your daughter was at the house could be key to our investigation. Now I need to ask you about your ex-husband, Mr Lewis. Where is he now?'

'In America,' she said. 'We divorced six years ago. Coral was very upset about it.'

'Did she still see her father?'

'Yes, but it was difficult – with him being so far away.'

'I should like to speak to him. Have you got a phone number?'

'Yes, of course. I'll get it for you now. But you'll have to take what he tells you with a pinch of salt. He's an alcoholic and... well, let's just say he tends to lose his temper very quickly and can be a little irrational at times.'

'I understand. Mrs Lewis, I've been thinking of holding an informal press briefing in police headquarters. Would you feel up to taking part?'

'What would I have to do?'

'Well, just come along and say a few words.'

'I'll have a think about it.'

'All right. This is the phone number for our incident room. We'll send a car to collect you if you feel able to help. And, Mrs Lewis, please call us if there's anything else we can do for you.'

'Thank you very much. What's your name again? Oh, it's on the card – Mr Roscoe.'

Chapter 41

The next morning, the chief inspector was in the CID office organising the press briefing when he received a call from Dr Reynolds.

'Morning, Gavin. I've just been informed that the body in Warwick Road wasn't Trudy Marwood,' said the pathologist.

'That's right, Silas,' said Roscoe, leaning back in his chair and gazing across at the park. 'I got one of our people to call you about it. What a shock. Mr Marwood had identified her as his wife as well.'

The doctor tutted. 'I'm a little annoyed with him. I asked if he was sure and he said he was. Now it turns out it was the woman's twenty-five-year-old niece.'

'She's a spitting image of the older woman.'

'So I gather.'

'But you'd think a man would recognise his own wife. Didn't he get a clear view when shown the body?'

The pathologist tutted again.

'There were strands of hair on her face, some of which I'd removed,' said Dr Reynolds. 'He took a casual glance and looked away sharply. Sometimes it's like that with relatives or partners. They can't bear to look too closely.'

'Perhaps I should've been more insistent Mr Marwood should take time to study the face, but he seemed so positive on his first glance. Still we can't be too hard on the man, old fruit. He was so upset at the time. Anyway, here's some good news. It looks as if the partial shoe print found at the scene of Coral Devon's death matches the kick marks left on the Italian woman's body – so there's a clear link between murder two and murder three.'

'Well, that's progress, Silas.'

'The bolt matches the other two as well, which again indicates one killer was responsible for the whole run of murders. If I get any more information, I'll let you know.'

'Thanks, Silas.'

Later DI Vickers arrived back at the office. He'd made a return visit to the Shah family in Warwick Road – and he'd finally made some headway. He related how twenty-two-year-old Vijay Shah had been very helpful.

The inspector was beaming. 'The young man's just left university and he's taken a temporary job working nights in a canning factory. He usually gets home between 2.30 and 3.30 a.m. Well, last Friday, as he got back, he spotted an unusual vehicle in the access road in front of the row of houses. It was parked in the place where he usually parks his Skoda Fabia.'

'What kind of vehicle was it?'

'It was an American Army Jeep – just like the one George spotted in Queensbridge in early April.'

'No one in it, presumably?'

'No. The Shah boy thought nothing more of it at the time. He was eager to get inside the house and get his head down.'

'Sharp-eyed young man. Did he have any idea as to the exact time?'

'He thought it might've been quarter to three in the morning, but he can't be sure. He also said he thought it was in a poor state. There was some mud on the jeep.'

'Was there a canvas hood on it?'

'No. It was an open vehicle.'

'I don't suppose he took the registration number?'

'No.'

Roscoe smiled. 'This is a vital lead.'

He and Sunita had discussed the Jeep several times since the murder of Oliver Bufton. However, its significance had been downplayed because the track found at Biddington had suggested the electrician's killer had used a Land Rover and no Jeep had featured in the murder of Miss Moretto either.

But since a Jeep featured in the street attack on Bufton and was now linked to the third killing, it was essential to trace it, as well as the Land Rover connected to the crime scene in Biddington.

After a brief pause in their conversation, Roscoe turned to Vickers. 'I need you to go back to Warwick Road this evening, when residents are likely to be around. Take a whole team. We need to find out if the Jeep belongs to any of them or their visitors. We must establish that first.

'If we draw a complete blank, then we know there's a good chance it's linked to the killer. It could be a case of find the Jeep and we find the killer.

'Then tomorrow, as a priority, we must start work on tracing all the local registered owners of Willys-Overland Jeeps.'

* * *

On the day of the press conference, Sunita was given the unenviable task of disclosing to a group of journalists that Moira Lewis, the mother of the murdered pop star, would not be appearing before them.

'We were hoping Mrs Lewis might be here this morning to explain how devastating the family's loss has been,' she admitted as the press briefing at headquarters was about to start. 'But we've just received a phone call, saying she's too upset. So you'll have to manage with the Chief Inspector and myself.'

She knew Roscoe would be pleased that more than thirty reporters and photographers and several TV crews had gathered in the ground-floor press room. But she could tell from their faces they were annoyed at Moira's absence. Her words could have given the publicity campaign added impetus.

After ten minutes, Roscoe weaved his way through the gaggle of journalists to the front. He glanced at the three posters on display on the wall behind him, each showing a victim's face along with the image of a crossbow. 'Murder. Ten-thousand-pound reward' was the message at the top of each poster. Phone numbers for the incident room and Crimestoppers appeared underneath.

'Our major investigation team has made some substantial progress over the past few days,' he told them. 'I can now reveal the murder of Miss Devon early on Friday in Stratford has been positively linked to the two murders in Queensbridge.'

Murmurings circulated among his audience at these words.

'So we're looking for a serial killer, ladies and gentlemen. We've strong evidence that this individual may be driving a highly unusual vehicle and we'd like members of the public to look out for it.

'It's a Willys-Overland American Army Jeep – a vehicle that found fame during the Second World War. It's possible the owner or keeper may be a military vehicle enthusiast. We'd be grateful for any information. Sergeant, do you have anything to say?'

Sunita nodded. 'Yes, sir. We need anyone who saw anything suspicious in the northern outskirts of Stratford – in particular, in the Warwick Road area – in the early hours of Friday to come forward.' She handed out printed biographical details of the three victims. 'I'd urge any witnesses who believe they may have important information – no matter how trivial – to call the incident room.'

'Are there any questions?' Roscoe asked.

A man near the back raised his hand. 'John Singleton, Midlands TV. Chief Inspector, can you tell us more about the vehicle you're interested in tracing?'

'Yes, John. There are a few around in the UK – left over from the time when GIs were based in England during the war. I've just been told that, believe it or not, there are around a hundred in this part of the Midlands. A witness saw one like it in Queensbridge High Street at the start of April and one was observed near the scene of Miss Devon's murder. We think it's the same one. We don't have its registration, unfortunately–'

Sunita interrupted. 'It's in a rather shoddy condition.'

'That's right.'

Singleton raised his hand again. What was the matter with these people? thought Sunita. Didn't anyone else have any questions?

'It's been nearly eight weeks since Oliver Bufton was killed,' Singleton declared. 'Since then two more innocent people have died. Why is it taking police so long to find the killer?'

'Thank you, John. I can assure you we've not been idle. We've made one arrest already. This person's now been released on police bail pending further inquiries. But we need more help from the public. That's why it's so crucial we get information about this Jeep and from anyone who saw anything suspicious on Thursday night into Friday morning in Warwick Road.'

Then Adam Bunyon, the *Queensbridge Gazette*'s chief reporter, spoke up. He asked why police were so convinced all three deaths were linked. 'Mr Bufton and Miss Moretto had been in a relationship together, but Miss Devon seems to have no connection with them,' he said.

Roscoe shrugged. 'For operational reasons, I don't want to go into the reasons why we believe this, Adam. All I'll say is there are irrefutable links between the deaths.'

Chapter 42

Dark clouds gathered in the sky, gliding menacingly towards her as Sunita Roy waited outside Warwick railway station on Wednesday, 12 July.

Two days of storms had been forecast by meteorologists after the long spell of hot, dry weather. But while it was expected, she hoped desperately the heavy rain would hold off for a few hours more.

The slender, dark-haired law graduate had made an effort to dress more smartly as she waited for the chief inspector to collect her in his car. She was wearing a light-blue trouser suit as she stood reading a newspaper near the station entrance. She smiled as her boss drew up.

'Looks like rain,' he said. 'I hope you've got an umbrella. I've forgotten mine.'

'Yes, sir. I've got a small umbrella,' she said, climbing into the passenger seat beside him.

They drove out of the station along a tree-lined avenue and past a small park. Within a few minutes, they reached a detached house belonging to Virginia and Larry Holland in prestigious Cranleigh Park. Roscoe drove past the gates into the driveway and turned the ignition off.

'Someone spends a bit of time gardening,' he remarked, gazing at the red, yellow and white roses on display.

Ginny Holland, who had heard the car arrive, came out to greet the detectives. She briefly inspected Sunita's warrant card before inviting them into her dining room.

The slim blonde was secretary of a ramblers' society and on the committee of Cranleigh Park Residents' Association. She'd been heavily occupied by meetings for most of the previous two days.

But it had been mutually agreed the detectives should call round at a quarter past ten on Wednesday morning. Ginny invited them into her dining room and opened the patio doors to let in some air as the atmosphere remained humid.

After asking permission to sit on a dining chair, Roscoe smiled and said, 'You realise, of course, why we wanted to see you?'

'Yes. I'm still in shock. To think someone would go up that scaffolding in the pitch black and kill a woman. They must be a mental case. Trudy is my best friend and it looks very much as if the crossbow arrow had been meant for her. But I can't get my head round why anyone would target her.'

Sunita, who had removed a small notebook and pen from her pocket, sat at the table near her boss.

'Your husband's called Larry?' she asked.

'Yes, his full name's Simon Laurence, but he prefers to be known as Larry. He's at work, but he wouldn't have been able to help you anyway. He doesn't really know Trudy.'

Sunita nodded. 'We need to ask you if you can think of anyone who might've done this to your friend?'

'No, not all.'

'We've got a list of men's names here that we've compiled after speaking to Mrs Marwood. Could you take a look and tell us about the ones you know?'

Sunita handed her a typewritten list. Next to each name was a potted biography based on comments made by Trudy.

'There are only three names here that mean anything to me – Steve, Den and Hugh,' she said.

Roscoe smiled. 'Can you tell us as much as you know about these three? Don't miss anything out. Even the most seemingly insignificant detail could be of tremendous help.'

Ginny sat down and peered at the list. 'Well, Steve's a Welshman. Trudy met him on a night out a few weeks ago. She got to know him quite well. Very well, actually.'

Roscoe raised an eyebrow. 'She obviously slept with him.'

'She didn't go into detail, but yes and it was definitely more than once.'

The chief inspector glanced at his sergeant. 'What about Den and Hugh?'

'We met those two at the Municipal Hall in June. I'm pretty certain it was June 1st, but I can check my kitchen calendar in a moment.'

'You and Mrs Marwood conversed with them?'

'What actually happened was she met Den for the first time at the bar. We took turns to dance with him. Our friend Jane, who was with us, danced with Hugh. You've got to understand that I'm in a different position from them. Trudy's separated and Jane's divorced, so they were free to meet someone. However, I'm a married woman and was really only there to accompany my friends.'

Roscoe found this final part of her account difficult to believe, but he let her remarks pass without comment.

Sunita looked up from her notetaking. 'Who's this Den that you both danced with? What sort of age would he be?'

Ginny thought for a moment. 'He'd be somewhere between twenty-three and twenty-eight. He's a gentleman, but a bit of a Jack the Lad. He's swarthy and a little taller than you – I'd say about five feet nine inches tall. Curly, black hair. Quite good-looking actually. He led us to believe he was a rail manager, but you know what men are like. Us girls always take everything we get told on a night out with a pinch of salt. Trudy told me she's met so many jet pilots, brain surgeons and football managers. A guy once told her he was an environmental protection awareness officer. We found out he was a binman.'

The detectives laughed before the chief inspector asked his next question.

'Any idea of Den's surname and where he lives?'

'No idea. He was fairly secretive.'

Sunita then asked about the man named Hugh. She suspected that Mrs Marwood and Mrs Perks might know more, but she felt someone on the periphery of events – such as Ginny Holland – often spotted details that could be missed by those more closely involved.

'All I know is he's an electrician from Leamington Spa. He, Den, Trudy and Jane went for a meal in Shawley Green a few weeks ago.'

Roscoe was interested to hear what kind of vehicle the men arrived in. 'They didn't turn up in a Jeep?'

'Trudy told me the boys had an old banger – a Carina with a faulty exhaust–'

Sunita interrupted to ask, 'Do you know what colour it was?'

'No, but Trudy or Jane would know.'

Just then, an old man in work clothes knocked on the patio door from outside.

'I've finished for the day, Mrs Holland,' said the man. 'Oh sorry. I didn't know you'd got company.'

Ginny smiled at him. 'That's all right, Bob. It's the police. They're here about that terrible business at my friend's house.' Then, turning to Roscoe, she added, 'This is Bob Hopkinson, our gardener.'

The two detectives nodded towards the newcomer. He was wearing a pale-green peaked cap, blue shirt and dark trousers. Both of his hands were caked in soil.

'Oh God, yes. When you catch that bugger, you want to lock him up and throw the key away. It's just not safe for folk at the moment – not while William Tell's out there.' He turned towards Ginny. 'If it's all right, Mrs H, I'll see you Friday.'

'All right, Bob. Thanks for all you've done.'

Roscoe and Sunita watched as the gardener, who suffered from a slight stoop, wandered away across the patio in the direction of the side gate.

Ginny grinned and nodded towards her visitors. 'He's a wonderful old boy. Do you know he's seventy-six?'

They smiled before Roscoe stood up and Sunita realised he wanted to go. But as they both moved towards the door, Ginny had a question for them.

'I'll be honest. I'm worried,' she said. 'My friend Trudy had a close escape. Do you think I could be next?'

Roscoe shook his head. 'The police are working hard on this case to ensure that the perpetrator is caught as quickly as possible. Everyone should take sensible precautions, but I don't think you've any cause for worry. For one thing, you don't seem to be out and about meeting people as much as your two friends.'

'That's true. I don't have much of a social life. Thanks for rubbing it in.'

Sunita, who was struggling to place her notebook in her pocket, looked directly at Ginny. 'Can you think of any connection between your friend Mrs Marwood and the first two victims – Mr Bufton and Miss Moretto?'

Ginny shook her head. 'No, not at all. I don't know anything about the first two victims, although I've been reading about them in the press. I'm sure Trudy doesn't either.'

Roscoe handed her one of his cards. 'Please call me if you remember anything else that might be important or if you've got any concerns.'

As they drove away from Cranleigh Park, the chief inspector suggested they should make for a cafe and mull over what Mrs Holland had told them.

'That's a brilliant idea, sir,' she said as they travelled. 'Things often make more sense over a cup of tea or coffee.'

But as they approached one of the town's cafes, the skies darkened and rain began to fall. It seemed at first to be a light shower. Then it became a deluge. They would have been drenched within minutes of stepping out of the car.

The chief inspector watched a pedestrian running like fury along the pavement. They resigned themselves to staying in the car for a while.

'It's vital now to discover the link between the lives of Bufton, Moretto and Devon,' he said.

Sunita nodded. 'Tangled love lives are at the heart of this.'

'Do you think so? I'm not sure. Let's consider what we know of the killer. They're pretty mobile. The first death was near Worcester. The second in Queensbridge. Now they've struck in Stratford – something like thirty miles from the scene of the first murder.'

'Whoever he is has got access to vehicles.'

Roscoe became silent. Then he said, 'What do you make of the three women who enjoyed a night out together – Mrs Perks, Mrs Marwood and Mrs Holland? You've met them all now.'

She shrugged her shoulders. 'The first two seem to be lonely women trying to make a new life for themselves.'

'I agree. As a result, they're vulnerable and prone to meeting men from diverse backgrounds.'

'Yes, sir. They're more at risk than, for example, the lady we saw today. Mrs Holland seems to be trying to make her marriage work.'

Roscoe nodded. 'I think we should take a look at two of the men, Den and Hugh.'

'Yes, sir. We need to know more about them.'

'Then there's the Jeep. We've spent weeks trying to find it. Tom and Omar did well finding Vijay Shah, but on tracing the Jeep, they've got absolutely nowhere. I think I need to have words with Tom,' Roscoe said.

This touched a nerve with Sunita. 'I think that's a bit unfair of you, sir, if you don't mind me saying. Tom is a very hard-working, loyal and efficient officer. I know because I've worked with him a lot recently.'

'Well, if I'd been assigned to it, I'd have had a list of Midlands Jeep owners by now.'

'If you don't mind me saying, you're being unfair. He works twelve-hour days. It's not for me to question anything, but perhaps the blame lies elsewhere.'

The pair sat in silence for the next five minutes as the rain continued to cascade down onto the street. Was her boss beginning to realise she had a soft spot for the inspector? She'd been so vociferous in her defence of him. Was he aware of how close they were becoming? she wondered.

The rain abated. Sunita unrolled her umbrella. She was thinking of making a dash for the cafe entrance. Then a sudden thought crept into her head. She opened one of the pages of her notebook and reminded herself what she'd written.

'Sir,' she said. 'There was a remark Mrs Holland made that caught my attention. She used an interesting word to describe the man called Den. According to my notes, she described him as "swarthy". It's a word you don't often hear. But I'm sure I've heard it used by someone else over the past few weeks.'

'Well, have a good hard think,' said Roscoe. 'Let me know when you remember who said it and about whom.'

'Yes, I will, sir.'

Chapter 43

Chief Superintendent Norris looked up from her desk. 'Ah, Gavin. Come in. I need to talk to you.'

Roscoe forced a smile. 'It's not often we see you in work on a Saturday, ma'am. Such a hot day's been forecast as well.'

'You're right. I'm not often in the office on a Saturday and this hot weather certainly doesn't help, now I'm stuck here. How's Helen? How are the family?'

'All very well. We're holding a farewell party for George this evening.'

'I heard he's off to Ryton soon for his training. Good. He has the makings of a fine officer. Listen, Gavin, the ACC was in a foul mood yesterday. He's anxious about these murders. Are you making any progress?'

The chief inspector drew up a chair. 'Worcester traffic stopped a Jeep on the outskirts of the city this week being driven recklessly. The driver also owns a Land Rover, so DI Vickers is following it up. DS Roy is investigating the private life of Trudy Marwood. DC Khalid is looking into suggestions that Coral Devon was buying drugs.'

'There seems to be a lot going on, Gavin.'

'The whole team are working flat out.'

'Nothing helpful came out of your press briefing?'

He shook his head. 'No. Lots of calls came in, but nothing of great interest so far.'

Norris frowned as she handed him the latest issue of the *Queensbridge Gazette*. 'Have you seen this?'

'No, ma'am.'

'Have a good look.'

The headline read, 'Police slated over crossbow failings. The story began:

> *Heart of England Police were under fire yesterday for failing to stop the Queensbridge crossbow maniac who has killed three times so far. The latest victim has been revealed as twenty-five-year-old pop star Coral Devon, who stormed into the charts three years ago with the song Christmas in Chinatown...*

'God, that's all we need,' he murmured.

'You'll see Miss Moretto's niece, Cristina Lorenzo, is also kicking up a fuss in the same article, complaining about the lack of police action.'

Norris manoeuvred her wheelchair round the desk until she was barely a metre away from the chief inspector.

'This case has become too much for you, hasn't it, Gavin?'

'I wouldn't say so, ma'am. We're continuing to make progress.'

She frowned. 'It doesn't look like it from where I'm sitting.'

'You've said, ma'am, in the past that you don't pay attention to press criticism.'

'Well, largely not, Gavin. We plough our own furrow, of course. But this case has wider implications. There have been stories in the national papers and on national TV. We've the reputation of the whole force to consider. You made one arrest, didn't you?'

'Yes, but we had to let him go, as I told you. There was no cast-iron evidence against him.'

'We've decided to give you just a few more days, Gavin. If by then there's no breakthrough, we're going to switch you onto another case and hand the job to someone else. Is that understood?'

'Yes, ma'am. Well, I suppose I don't have any choice in the matter.'

'I'm afraid you don't, Gavin.'

* * *

The sound of clinking glasses, laughter and noisy conversation filled the air as Sunita arrived that evening at the Apollo Tearooms. The entrance was festooned with bunting. The strains of a song from *The Sound Of Music*, 'So Long, Farewell', reached her ears from somewhere in the building.

Helen Roscoe, who looked alluring with curled hair and an off-the-shoulder dress, grabbed her hand as she passed through the door.

'I'm so glad you could make it. We're just about to start.'

The Roscoes' son George, who had spent two weeks on an induction course, was dressed in his uniform for the first time.

'The helmet takes a bit of getting used to,' he told Sunita with a grin. 'I've already knocked it on the beams twice.'

The chief inspector picked up a spoon and tapped it on the edge of a glass as he prepared to propose a toast.

'To the finest son a man could wish for,' he said. 'Good luck in your career.'

'Good luck!' everyone chorused, raising their glasses.

Gavin Roscoe handed his son a cylindrical parcel wrapped in shiny gold paper. George tore off the wrapping like an eager child at Christmas to reveal a sturdy chrome torch.

'I'm not joining the boy scouts, Dad,' he said.

Everyone laughed.

'Believe me. Where you're going, you'll need that,' his father said.

Melody kissed her brother and handed him a gift-wrapped china mug. On opening it, he discovered the words 'Mind how you go!' printed on the side. His mother presented him with an expensive pair of black leather gloves.

'I'd been thinking of getting you a pocketknife,' she said. 'But I decided it might be confiscated.'

'Yes,' said George. 'It wouldn't look too good getting arrested on my way to class for having an offensive weapon. By the way, I've now seen the bedroom where I'm going to be staying.'

His father smiled. 'Don't tell me. It's not big enough to swing a cat?'

'You'd be hard-pressed to swing a grasshopper.'

Sunita handed George a 'Good luck!' card. 'I hope you enjoy your course and I look forward to seeing you in St James Street in a few years.'

George laughed. 'Me and Dad working in the same building? Probably not a good idea.'

Sunita was delighted to have been invited. Apart from the chief inspector, she was the only member of Heart of England Police who was present.

They're such a lovely family, she thought to herself, recalling the joyful family gatherings and festivals she experienced while growing up in Leicester.

In the middle of the proceedings, Roscoe's phone rang.

'Yes? What is it?'

'Sir, it's the operator at St James Street. There's a gentleman from America who's keen to speak to you. Claims he's Coral Devon's father. I thought it might be important.'

Roscoe rushed out into the high street so he could hear better. 'You did the right thing.'

'I've got the gentleman on the line. Shall I put him through to you, sir?'

'Yes, please.'

The man who came onto the line possessed a strong New York accent.

'Am I talking to the boss man?' he asked.

'This is Detective Chief Inspector Roscoe. I'm in charge of the Coral Devon murder investigation. Can I help?'

'I'd like to string up the goddam bastard who killed my little girl,' said the gruff-voiced man.

'I'm sure you would, but we no longer have the death penalty. Could you confirm your name, sir?

'I'm Wesley Lewis, Coral's father.'

Roscoe moved out of the way to let two pedestrians pass. 'So you've got some information?'

'Yeah. I know who did it. Makes life easy for you guys, eh? He's a drug dealer that Coral helped put behind bars. He's been stalking her since he came out a few months ago.'

'These are very serious allegations.'

'I know. All you guys have got to do is go along to his flat and arrest him.'

'Look, I know you're trying to be helpful, Mr Lewis, and of course we pass on our sympathies to you over the loss of your daughter. But we believe your daughter was killed in a case of mistaken identity and that your wife's sister, Trudy, was the intended victim.'

'I don't want to tell you guys how to do your job, but I've got the killer's name and address here.'

He gave the chief inspector details of a man from Walsall, which Roscoe jotted down on the back of a shopping receipt. He promised the caller he would pass on the information to the drugs squad.

'I need to ask you something, sir. How could this fellow know your daughter was staying in Stratford? It was a last-minute decision. Only Coral's mother and aunt knew.'

Mr Lewis laughed. 'Don't you believe it. If this fellow didn't know, he's got ways of finding out.'

Roscoe shook his head. He was convinced the man in Walsall was unconnected to the case.

The American added, 'You see, what happened is that Coral managed to get herself off drugs, but it took a monumental effort. He kept contacting her. In the end, she shopped him. You can look up the court reports if you like. It's all there. And now he's finally got his revenge.'

Chapter 44

Ginny Holland realised immediately that her friend's car looked different as Trudy drew up outside her house in Cranleigh Park.

'You've had it resprayed,' she said as Trudy got out.

'Yes, not done a bad job, have they? It was a specialist body shop recommended by Rowan.'

'You're not getting back with him, are you?'

She grinned. 'No chance. But he does know a lot more than I do about cars.'

Ginny held out her arms as her friend approached. She gave her a brief hug before they went inside.

'Thank God you're all right,' Ginny whispered.

Trudy nodded. 'It's definitely thanks to God that I'm here. But I feel so bad about Coral. She didn't deserve to die at twenty-five. Only a quarter of her life had passed.'

'Come through anyway,' said Ginny. 'I've got a salmon salad for lunch.'

It was a mild day, but there was a cold wind and it suited them to sit and talk in the dining room.

'How do you feel in yourself?' asked Ginny.

Trudy shrugged her shoulders. 'I'm meant to be having police protection, but it doesn't amount to much. I'm still staying with Jane. We get regular patrols driving past every few hours and I decided to let them know I was visiting you today.'

'It doesn't sound too brilliant.'

'I imagine laying on patrols is all they can afford.'

'Have you been back to the house?'

'I call round every few days to pick up post and check everything's OK. I don't know if I'll ever be able to live there again – at least, not until the killer's caught.'

Ginny asked how Trudy's sister was taking the death of Coral.

'Very badly indeed. Moira's not talking to me. She says it's my fault. She blames my lifestyle and says I was attracting the wrong kind of men. The cheek!'

Ginny shook her head. 'Did I tell you I saw my sister the other day?'

'Did you? I'd forgotten you had a sister.'

'I sometimes forget too. Do you know, I hadn't seen her for something like ten years, but she hasn't changed much.'

'Where did you see her?'

'She was just coming out of a cycle shop in Stratford.'

'Did you talk to her?'

'She didn't have time. She was in a hurry.'

'I remember you telling me you're like strangers.'

'Yes. So do you think one of your boyfriends could be behind the murders? Den or Hugh? I remember you telling me about the way they tortured the wasp at the pub. It sounded very cruel.'

'I don't know. I gave the police all the details I could. It's down to them.'

'They don't seem to be making much headway. By the way, I haven't shown you the work Bob's done in the garden. Come and have a look.'

Ginny led her friend through the patio doors. The gardener had pruned back many of the rose bushes and added some autumn flowering plants to the borders. He'd also been making adjustments to the rose arch, which shielded the patio area from the prying eyes of her neighbour, retired architect Gilbert Stout.

Trudy wandered into the middle of the lawn.

'Yours is always like a show garden. I wish I'd got green fingers. Who's that over there?'

They stood together on the grass, staring towards the trees on the left-hand boundary of the Hollands' garden. They caught glimpses of a pale-yellow shirt and blue jeans through gaps in the hedge and shrubs.

'It's that damn neighbour of ours, Gilbert,' said Ginny as her floral-patterned dress billowed in the wind. 'He probably noticed your car and he's very inquisitive. I sometimes suspect he might be spying on me.'

'Oh God.'

'Yes, I wonder if he's lonely. I must see if Bob can repair that gap in the hedge. That might solve the problem.'

They returned to the dining room, where Ginny served her friend a gin and soda.

'Oh, I didn't tell you. Coral's dad is planning to visit England. He doesn't trust the British police. He's become obsessed with the idea that a drug dealer was stalking Coral and went on to kill her.'

'Do you think someone that Coral knew is behind the murder, Trudy?'

'I don't know what to think. I find it hard to believe anyone knew where Coral was – apart from Coral, her mother and me.'

Ginny thought for a moment. 'I've had the police round here. I'm not sure I was of much help. I told them what I knew about the men you and Jane met. They kept asking whether I knew the first two people killed. I told them honestly that I knew absolutely nothing about them.'

Trudy nodded. 'Same here.'

* * *

'You know there's been a third murder involving a crossbow arrow, don't you?'

The voice echoed round the hotel bedroom. The question was met with silence. The woman admiring herself in the mirror was trying to decide whether she should wear a blue or a mauve dress that evening.

'What's that, darling?' she said.

'I knew you weren't listening,' said Laurence Holland. 'I was talking about the arrows. Another one's turned up.'

'How do you mean "turned up"?'

He tutted. 'It was used to shoot a pop singer called Coral Devon. I've been reading about it in the paper. It was a crimson one, apparently.'

She nodded. 'That's terrible someone else has been killed. I hope this hasn't all started because of the bolts stolen from the club.'

Holland was lying naked in bed with just a sheet to preserve his modesty.

'More and more people are taking up archery. I think the government should crack down on crossbows. Why should guns be licensed but bows which can kill just as easily be spared from regulation?'

'That's a good point. I was reading a news report on my tablet that, in a future Britain, the economy will require people to do less work and, as a result, there will be more leisure time – and archery is a great leisure pursuit.'

He sighed. 'There's definitely going to be less work in the future. There are more and more redundancies. I'm having to lay a few people off this month.'

'It's fair to say that when there's a lot of news about crossbows, more people want to take it up as a hobby.'

'You'd have thought it might've had the opposite effect. I wouldn't touch one myself.'

'That's only your personal feeling,' she said. 'The reality is very different.' She was holding the mauve dress in front of her as she peered into the mirror. 'Whoever is behind the murders must be someone totally unstable – mentally ill. Don't you think?'

'Yes. Someone totally unstable who's a really skilful bowman. By the way, did you hear whether the police caught the burglars who stole the cigarettes and arrows?'

'No, I'd have thought they'd have more chance of finding a turnip in a cabbage patch. Burglaries are two a penny these days. Do you think I look better in the blue or the mauve?' She held up the dresses, one in each hand.

'The mauve,' said Holland, without looking up. 'It's definitely more your colour.'

'Well, Mr Holiday, I'll let that be the final word. Mauve it is. Come on. We'd better hurry up. They'll be serving dinner shortly.'

Chapter 45

Tom Vickers was feeling pleased. The traffic officer in Worcester he'd been trying to track down for two weeks had returned to work that day and was ready to speak to him.

'Do you remember me?' Vickers asked at the start of their conversation. 'I was asking about an incident in April near Worcester. A reckless driving case.'

There was a pause and the sound of fingers tapping on a computer keyboard.

'Yes, here we are, Inspector Vickers. Yes, the Jeep is currently registered to an Elijah Jonas Slack.'

'This is the fellow who also owns a Land Rover. Is that right?'

'Yes. His registered office is in King's Heath. Do you want the address?'

'Yes, please.'

Vickers scribbled the information down before hurrying into Roscoe's office.

The chief inspector was pleased by his progress. 'You're going round there now, are you?'

The inspector nodded. 'Yes, but don't expect too much straight away. The traffic officer says Slack's never there.'

'Is he due to appear in court over his driving?'

'Yes, but not for a few weeks.'

'That's a nuisance. We might've grabbed him at the court.'

Roscoe became distracted by a call on his desk phone.

'Yes, I'm his father ... When did this happen? ... Which hospital is he in? ... The injury's not life-threatening, is it? ... So you can't be certain? ... All right. I'll be there as soon as I can.'

He turned to Vickers. 'George has been injured.'

'Oh God. Is he all right?'

The chief inspector stood up and swept his jacket off the back of his chair. 'They don't know. He's been stabbed and he's drifting in and out of consciousness. He's in the University Hospital in Coventry. I'm going over there now.'

'Very well, sir. I'll head over to King's Heath on my own and report back. I hope the lad's all right, sir.'

'So do I.'

* * *

It took Vickers more than half an hour through heavy traffic to reach the Birmingham suburb of King's Heath. He quickly found Cuckmere House, one of four blocks of flats in a quiet street opposite some woods.

But, as he'd been warned, there was no one at home when he knocked at Mr Slack's ground-floor council flat.

He tried peering through the window to see if there was furniture inside, but he couldn't see clearly through the net curtains.

He was further disappointed when he gazed through the letterbox. He found mail scattered over the hallway. The inspector knocked on all the other downstairs flats in the block, but only one tenant was in – the grey-haired, middle-aged man who lived next door. He laughed when Vickers asked about his neighbour.

'I've only seen the old guy twice since he took the flat on two years ago. Someone told me he only uses it as a registered address for his business and lives somewhere else.'

Vickers thanked him for his help and drove back to the office dejectedly.

* * *

Meanwhile Roscoe arrived at the modern hospital, four miles north of Coventry, to find his son had been placed on a general ward on the first floor. The anxious father was directed to the Fairfield Ward.

He found George sitting up in a side ward chatting to a young woman that Roscoe guessed was his son's girlfriend. Two nurses were attending to nearby patients in the six-bed ward. Someone had filled a clear vase by his bedside with pink roses, purple carnations and yellow chrysanthemums. George appeared to be in a cheerful mood, despite having a bandage across his chest.

'Hello, Dad. This is Amanda. Amanda, this is my dad.'

Roscoe shook Amanda's hand. 'Pleased to meet you. George, your mother's been frantic with worry but I must say you look fine.'

'Still in a bit of pain, but it looks like I'm going to be all right.'

'What are the doctors saying?'

'They're doing their rounds now. They'll be assessing me in a moment.'

Roscoe was about to sit down on the edge of the bed when a nurse tapped him on the shoulder. 'George's dad? The doctor would like a word.'

She led him out to the ward's reception desk, where a middle-aged doctor in a white coat was peering over his glasses at some notes. He looked up.

'Mr Roscoe? I just wanted a word about your son.'

'He looks all right. We were told he was losing consciousness.'

'He wasn't too good when they brought him in, but he's shown amazing resilience. He's been receiving painkillers and antibiotics and we're optimistic he'll make a full recovery.'

'That's good.'

'Luckily, the fibrous membranes around the heart and lungs haven't been affected. Thc X-ray's found a slight problem around the heart – air in the pericardial cavity. But this should disappear in time. Because of that, we probably need to keep your son in for a few days for observation. He's very lucky the wound wasn't closer to the heart. People often die from a single stab wound in that area of the body.'

When the chief inspector returned to the ward, he found himself a chair and sat down.

'So what actually happened?'

'George's friend Sean's got a car and we went for a drive,' explained twenty-year-old Amanda, who was tall with brown hair, a delicate nose and mouth and a gentle smile. 'Sean only stopped at a newsagent's for cigarettes. But it was just our luck, wasn't it? Some guy was robbing the till. Sean warned George the man had a blade but George went forward to grab it–'

George interrupted. 'I didn't hesitate, Dad. I remembered how slow I was when Olly Bufton got attacked. I ran forward and grabbed him by the arm.'

'Were you in uniform?' asked Roscoe.

Amanda shook her head. 'No, none of us was. Anyway, the guy slashed about wildly with his knife. He stabbed George in the shoulder but we managed to hold the man on the floor till the real police arrived.'

George smiled. 'Dad, it was funny...'

Roscoe frowned. 'I'm glad you think it was funny. Your mother's in pieces.'

'No, Dad. It's funny what Sean said, "We're meant to be doing robbery training next week, not this week." Afterwards the cops said we'd done a good job.'

His father shook his head. 'You did a great job, but you all put yourselves at risk. There are moments when it's right to step in and moments to hold back. That's only something you learn in time.'

George laughed. 'The robber didn't get it all his own way, Dad. I hit him with the torch, which I'd been carrying in my pocket.'

'I told you it would come in useful,' said Roscoe.

Chapter 46

It was a cold, cloudy day as Sunita Roy parked her car outside police headquarters and entered the building. She was disappointed. She'd been hoping to enjoy some warmer weather, especially as it was the first day of August.

As soon as she reached the CID office, she headed for the photocopying machine and produced some printouts. Then she stuffed them into the pocket of her jacket and rushed to the chief inspector's room. He was on the phone to someone, but beckoned her in.

'Yes, we think so,' he was saying. 'Nasty wound, but the doctor thinks he'll make a full recovery ... Yes ... Thanks for your concern.'

He glanced up at his sergeant as he ended the call. 'Just one of the relatives inquiring about George.'

Sunita nodded as she took a chair. 'So he's on the mend, sir?'

'Yes. He can't wait to get back to his course. He's worried about missing classes. You seem in a hurry this morning, young lady?'

'Yes, sir. I've had some ideas about the case. I began thinking about what you said about the killer being mobile. It struck me we're not looking for an office worker with a nine-to-five job or a factory worker who's tied to one place.'

Roscoe looked up. 'That's true.'

'It got me wondering whether the killer could be an itinerant worker or a shift worker – someone travelling from place to place. I wondered whether they could be someone moving round the Midlands, taking part in archery events. I considered gipsies; people with campervans or motorhomes; fruit pickers travelling from farm to farm; road workers or navvies; delivery drivers; and sales staff who go from place to place. I thought to myself, what do we know about the killer? My theory is they journey from place to place, forming relationships and then ending them in a brutal fashion.'

Roscoe nodded. 'This is making a lot of sense. Go on.'

'I've been looking at the calendar and I've noticed something interesting.'

She handed him a printout which was headed 'Events and dates'. Sunita started reading from her copy of the document.

'2 April: theft of bolts from Shawley Green club; 5 April: street attack on Bufton in Queensbridge; 24 April: murder of Bufton in Biddington; first weekend in May: murder of Miss Moretto in Queensbridge; 23 June: murder of Coral Devon in Stratford.'

'I don't understand. We know all this. What's the point you're making, Sergeant?'

'All right. Before I explain further, take a look at this second list as well.'

She handed Roscoe a printout headed 'Travelling Fair.' It said, 'Worcester, 13–25 April; Queensbridge, 28 April–7 May; Shawley Green, 12–20 May; Redditch, 24–29 May; Stratford, 1–24 June; Warwick, 30 June–15 July; Kenilworth, 19 July–5 August.'

'What's all this mean, Sergeant?'

She smiled. 'I remembered that this summer, for the first time in a few years, there's been a travelling fair. I wondered if there might be some connection between this fair and the events we're investigating. The first murder, for instance, happened in Biddington during the week that the fair was in nearby Worcester. The fair was in Queensbridge at the time Miss Moretto was murdered. When Coral Devon was killed, the fair was in Stratford.'

The chief inspector shrugged. 'It's an ingenious idea. But folk have vehicles – and this guy seems to have his pick. He can travel wherever he wants and claim his victim.'

'Yes, but don't you think this is a bit more than just a coincidence? It suggests to me that maybe – just maybe – the killer works at the fair. These fairs travel all over the Heart of England force area. You mentioned your daughter Mel went along when the fair was held in Queensbridge. All I've been able to find out is the fair's registered office is in Birmingham.'

'All right,' said Roscoe. 'I'll examine these two lists when I get a moment. By the way, what's the name of this fair?'

Sunita looked down at a note she'd made. 'The operators go under the name of Elijah Slack's Family Funfair.'

Roscoe leaped from his chair on hearing the name of Elijah Slack.

'Good God, Sergeant,' he shouted. 'That's the name of the Jeep owner that Tom's been trying to track down – Elijah Slack!'

He felt as if they'd been trapped for months in a dark tunnel and only now emerged into the daylight.

'If he works for a travelling fair, that explains why he's never at his council flat in King's Heath – he's on the road all the time,' he said. 'DS Roy, once again, you've got to the heart of the case.'

She smiled. 'It's just that I've spent a few days reflecting on everything and trying to make sense of it. If I'm right, I've just been lucky, sir.'

'You make your own luck,' said Roscoe as he sat down again. 'This is an important lead and we must get working on it right away. Let's see your list. Where's the fair this week?'

'Deacons Park in Kenilworth.'

'I'll send Tom over there straight away and he can get the lie of the land. I'll also put in some calls to my Birmingham contact Pat Clancy, who's got knowledge of gangs and see what we can unearth about this guy Slack. We must also check on whether he's got any form.'

Roscoe emerged from his room, clapping his hands. Members of his CID staff turned their faces in his direction.

'Right, listen, everyone. We've got a great new lead for Operation Promenade. I want you all joining in. Find out as much as you can about a guy called Elijah Slack and his travelling fair. DC Khalid, has Slack got any form? DC Dawson, find out about his family and any phones.'

The team were hard at work on this new lead the following morning when a call came in that meant all inquiries about the Slack family had to be shelved. Someone in Warwick had made an emergency call to report a woman had been found dead in suspicious circumstances in the town's Cranleigh Park.

Chapter 47

The first report of the Cranleigh Park death lodged at force control gave few details. A Mrs Holland had collapsed and was found on the patio by her husband, Laurence, at approximately one o'clock in the afternoon. She'd stopped breathing. Uniformed officers from

Stratford were at the scene and SOCOs had also been alerted.

Detective Constables Khalid and Dawson set off immediately on the sixteen-mile journey, followed shortly afterwards by Roscoe and Sunita, all in separate cars.

Sunita was beginning to perspire in the heat as she drew up in the long, tree-lined street of detached houses just after three. There were several police cars, two ambulances and various other vehicles – including Dr Reynolds' black Mercedes – parked outside the Hollands' home. Larry Holland's Porsche 911 was on the gravel forecourt.

The front of the house had been cordoned off with blue-and-white tape saying, 'Police – don't cross'. A young constable was standing by the black iron gates, scrutinising visitors. Most of the front garden was filled with rose bushes, sheltered by a lime tree which stood proudly on the pavement outside.

The sergeant gazed around. How could a horrific crime have occurred at such an idyllic spot, she wondered, and in the middle of such a glorious, sunny day?

She and the chief inspector walked round the right-hand side of the house, unwilling to disturb a forensic team who were busy in the hallway. On the rear patio, they found Dawson trying to question Larry Holland, the dead woman's husband, while attempting to offer words of comfort.

A large white tent had been erected in the middle of the patio, a few metres from the house. Dr Reynolds emerged from beneath the canvas to greet them, peering at them over his horn-rimmed glasses.

'Dear, oh dear,' he muttered. 'I didn't expect to see you two again so soon.'

'What's the size of it then, Silas?' the chief inspector asked.

'Crossbow bolt in the heart – same as before, crimson in colour. It appears the lady was sitting in her wicker chair, relaxing in the sun and reading some local council agendas. Then a bolt penetrates her pericardium – the tissue surrounding the heart. Death appears to have been caused by cardiac tamponade. This is pressure on the heart caused by a leakage of blood from the ventricular lumen – the hollow area in the heart chamber. She's fallen from her chair onto the patio and this is where it gets interesting. She's remained alive long enough to write something on the ground in her blood. Look, over here.'

He explained that the victim's husband had dialled 999. The first ambulance had arrived within ten minutes, but the two paramedics had been unable to save her.

Roscoe and Sunita took turns to venture into the tent and gaze at the blood-splattered body of Ginny Holland. She was lying exactly as she'd been found by the first police officers on the scene – on her left side with her right arm outstretched.

She was dressed in the same pink blouse and black trousers she'd worn on the day the two detectives had interviewed her three weeks earlier. Red-stained planning documents lay scattered to the left of the body. What disturbed Sunita most was the look of abject horror upon the victim's face.

One by one, the two detectives also inspected the symbols in blood on the patio. They appeared to have been made by the victim in a desperate attempt to identify her killer.

According to how one chose to interpret them, the letters, which were eight centimetres high, appeared to say, 'SI'. Sunita concluded they were alphabetic letters while Dr Reynolds suggested they might be digits representing the number 51.

The pathologist frowned. 'In her last action on earth, she obviously wanted to help police nail her killer. But, sadly, she ran out of time.'

He explained the police photographer had arrived earlier and taken images of the two scrawled characters.

Sunita folded her arms. 'It's possible she left the second letter incomplete. For instance, she may've intended to create a letter *T* for Tango but in her dying moments was too weak to cross it.'

Dr Reynolds and the detectives stood together in quiet contemplation for a moment.

Then Sunita looked the pathologist in the eye. 'Could they just be random smears of blood that accidentally resemble letters or numbers?'

He shook his head. 'Well, if you want my opinion, they seem to be deliberately written. I don't believe they're just random smears of blood.'

Sunita thought hard for a moment. 'Have you any idea of the time of death, Dr Reynolds?'

'I should say between eleven o'clock and midday, but we'll be carrying out further tests. Don't take that as Gospel.'

He paused before continuing. 'Of course, there's one essential difference between this death and the other three.'

Roscoe looked puzzled. 'What do you mean, Silas?'

'Well, this victim didn't have a monogrammed handkerchief in her mouth.'

Sunita nodded. 'Yes, that's strange. No attempt by the killer to claim the victim as theirs with their hallmark sign.'

The chief inspector shrugged. 'Perhaps they ran out of time.'

'Or perhaps they ran out of handkerchiefs,' said the doctor. 'You know they usually sell them three to a box.'

Sunita stared across at the red markings. 'Perhaps they simply forgot to bring one. But it's strange that, with the other murders, the killer left us a message and this time it's the victim who's left the message.'

The chief inspector walked off towards DC Dawson and Larry Holland, who were standing at the edge of the patio. He was keen to speak to the grief-stricken husband himself.

Once he'd gone, Sunita crouched down and inspected the area around the tent.

'Dr Reynolds, what's this broken glass?' she asked, pointing to some fine fragments on the ground beside a small trail of liquid.

'I didn't notice that,' he said. 'Looks like the lady was enjoying a drink outside and it tumbled over at some stage during the attack.'

Reynolds dipped his finger in the dark-brown liquid, which had a reddish tint. 'Tastes like Pimm's Number One,' he said. 'I'll get my assistant, David, to carry out tests on the liquid to be certain. I'll also get him to examine the shards of glass.'

He called out for his assistant. 'David, I want you to have a look at this glass and liquid. It appears the lady may've been having a drink on the patio and it tumbled to the ground.'

Sunita's attention remained focussed on the two letters written in blood. She glanced across to where Dr Reynolds was standing.

'Presumably you'll find samples of Mrs Holland's fingerprints and check she wrote the two letters or numbers herself?' she said. 'You know, just in case they were written by the killer as a diversionary tactic?'

'Don't worry, my dear. We've already taken sample prints and have been carefully examining the letters made in the blood. All the signs are that they were daubed there in her hand, but we're looking into all the possibilities, of course.'

The sergeant was aware of past criminal cases where murderers had attempted to lay a false trail – although never before involving symbols in blood. She wondered if the bowman had been trying to do exactly that.

* * *

Larry Holland was sitting on a wooden bench on his own when Roscoe approached. 'Your guy's very kindly gone to fetch me some water,' he explained.

Roscoe smiled sympathetically at Holland, who appeared downcast and disorientated.

'We'd like a statement from you, sir, when you've gathered your thoughts.'

Holland nodded. 'Yes, of course.'

When Dawson had presented the businessman with his water, the chief inspector took the constable aside.

'Can you get a full account from him when he's in a fit state? Stay with him and see what he says. Don't rush him.'

'He's a little confused, sir. He keeps asking me why anyone would target his wife.'

'He's bound to be in a state of shock.'

'Sir, I need to mention they've got a gardener, an old boy called Bob Hopkinson, who usually comes round on a Wednesday morning.'

'Yes, I met him three weeks ago. Did he come this morning?'

'Mr Holland's not sure. He got here at one o'clock to find his wife dead and dialled 999. He says the gardener works for a couple of hours on a Wednesday morning – usually between 8.30 and 10.30 a.m., although these times vary a bit. He lives two miles away.'

'Could be an important witness.'

Dawson handed him a page torn from his notebook. 'Here's the gardener's address, sir.'

'Thanks. With any luck, he should be home now after finishing his lunch.'

While heading back to his car, Roscoe met up with DC Khalid, who'd been making house-to-house inquiries.

'Sir, the guy next door was the only person of any help.'

'Gilbert Stout, a retired architect?'

'That's right, sir. The only person he noticed visiting the house was the Hollands' gardener. He believes he's called Bob.'

'That's right. That's the guy I'm off to see.'

Khalid glanced at his notebook. 'Mr Stout said, "It must've been about quarter past eleven. I'd just finished listening to the news. Bob was just leaving through the side gate." He recalls this Bob was wearing what he always wears – a peaked cap, blue shirt and dark trousers.'

'Right. Let's see what Bob's got to say for himself.'

Chapter 48

As soon as Tom Vickers parked his car close to Kenilworth's leafy Deacons Park, he could hear the deafening cacophony of sounds that's emitted from any fairground. Long-forgotten pop songs, chimes, jingles, bangs, the drone of the generators and the shouts and whoops of revellers.

A banner stretched above the black iron entrance gates proclaiming, 'Elijah Slack's Family Funfair'. Beneath, in smaller lettering, it said, 'The best rides and the most fun'.

The atmosphere was filled with the gleeful cries of children and the sound of the clattering rides. The smell of fried potato chips and onions used to garnish hotdogs wafted through the air. Eager youths ran hither and thither among the crowds, searching for adventure among the stalls.

The inspector was implored by one stallholder to throw three hoops and win a goldfish, but he declined as he walked steadfastly ahead. He also ignored the entreaties of a stallholder offering him the chance to win a teddy bear on the throw of three darts.

'They're just after our money,' he moaned to himself as the late American singer Bobby Vee begged anyone listening to *Take Good Care Of My Baby*.

Dazzling lights drew his eyes towards a children's roundabout, the dodgem cars, a candyfloss stand and a coconut shy. He spent a few minutes staring at the Lost Jungle Fun House before peering across at the Ghost Train, where for three pounds a customer could travel through the dark, encountering illuminated skeletons and headless phantoms, listening to blood-curdling sounds and being brushed by imitation cobwebs.

Then he remembered the urgency of his mission. He began to explore the areas behind the stalls and amusements, searching for the operator's office.

Eventually he came upon a section at the back of the fairground that had been reserved for the homes of the crew. Caravans of all shapes and sizes were parked so closely together you could barely pass between them.

But he threaded his way through the labyrinth of passageways and eventually reached the edge of the compound, where a large caravan was parked. A sign saying 'Office' was hanging above the doorway.

This must be it, he thought to himself.

The chief inspector had advised him not to venture in. He was simply on a scouting mission. So he lit a cigarette and stood unobtrusively in a passage between two vans, keeping an eye for any comings and goings.

He watched as two men – probably staff – entered the office and left a few minutes later. But despite his efforts, he sensed his presence might be arousing suspicion.

Then, without warning, a voice behind him demanded, 'What you up to, mate?'

Vickers turned to see a six-foot-tall, dark-skinned, muscular man with black hair tied in a ponytail. The man was staring aggressively at him.

'Just having a quiet smoke,' said the inspector.

'You're up to no good,' the man snarled. 'You're snooping.'

He lunged forward, grabbing Vickers' shoulders with both hands, slamming him against a van. The inspector, slightly shorter than his attacker, vowed to remain calm. He dared not reveal his identity at this stage. His boss was likely to mount a police raid on the fair at any time.

'Who you with, mate?' the man demanded. 'Taxman, insurance company, the law?'

He shook his head. 'Just wanted somewhere quiet for a fag, mate. Leave me alone.'

'I'll send you somewhere quiet – somewhere really quiet, like a bloody graveyard,' said the man.

A woman's voice called from the office. 'What's the matter, Toby?'

Vickers noticed an anxious-looking woman with a sun-tanned face standing in the doorway. He guessed she was in her late forties.

'Caught this geezer snooping, Ma,' he said. 'He won't tell me who he's with.'

Within seconds, a gruff-voiced man could be heard saying, 'What's the matter, Ma? Move out of the way.'

The woman stood back, allowing a giant of a man to show his face in the doorway. He squeezed his way out and clambered down the three wooden steps. He was at least six feet six inches tall, Vickers thought, heavily overweight and had a fierce look on his face.

The inspector had been in terrifying situations before, but nothing had prepared him for this confrontation. The man who had pinned him to the side of the caravan still maintained a stubborn grip on him. He seemed ready to beat him to a pulp. His captor just needed the older man – presumably his father and funfair owner Elijah Slack – to give him the word.

The older man appeared to be in an equally belligerent mood, but the inspector could not decide whether this anger was directed at himself or the man who held him in his grip.

Inexplicably, the older man, who had a Black County accent not unlike the inspector's own, seemed to calm down as he waddled towards him. 'What d'you want, mate? This here's out of bounds to the public.'

'Just having a fag, honest. Wanted to get away from the noise.'

Elijah Slack relented. 'Let him go, Toby. But make sure he leaves the area and don't come back.' Then he waddled back to his office.

No sooner had his father spoken than Toby released his grip on Vickers, who slipped away and followed a passageway that led round the side of the office. Toby followed closely behind, ensuring the intruder obeyed his father's instructions.

The inspector felt relieved he'd been allowed to leave without having to divulge his identity nor become the victim of a serious assault.

So that was the Slack family, he thought to himself. Wouldn't want to meet those two in a dark backstreet on a wet Wednesday in Wolverhampton.

He passed another caravan before reaching a makeshift car park where he thought Slack and his entourage must park their vehicles.

It was then that Vickers made a breathtaking discovery. For standing before him were two of the exact make of vehicles he'd been searching for: a Willys-Overland Jeep and a light-blue Land Rover. Next to them was a green Carina. All had featured in Operation Promenade.

At the far end of the parking area stood the strangest vehicle of all, a Humber Pig – one of a range of armoured personnel carriers once used by the British Army.

Vickers was aware he'd made a major breakthrough. But he could see from the corner of his eye tough-guy Toby was watching from a distance.

It was imperative he leave without risking any further encounter. Then he had to call the chief inspector so they could mount a raid and impound the vehicles. There was no time to lose.

Chapter 49

Bob Hopkinson was at home, relaxing after his lunch, when the chief inspector called round. The Hollands' amiable gardener lived in a ground-floor council flat near Warwick Station with his wife Muriel and their ginger cat, Lucifer.

Hopkinson hadn't had time to change out of his work clothes – a blue check shirt and dark trousers – which he always wore while tending his clients' gardens.

'Who's this?' he muttered to himself as he opened the door. Then out loud, he declared, 'You're police, aren't you?'

Roscoe gave a weak smile as he waved his warrant card. The gardener seemed to sense he was about to receive bad news.

'What's happened?'

'Heart of England Police. I met you the other day at the Hollands' house. Do you mind if I come in?'

Hopkinson led the detective into his modest hallway, decorated in light-green flock wallpaper.

'Yes, I think I remember you.'

Roscoe frowned. 'Did you do some work for the Hollands this morning?'

'Yes. Are they all right?'

'What time did you leave?'

'I don't know. About a quarter to eleven, I suppose. What's happened?'

Roscoe sighed. 'I'm afraid it's my sad duty to inform you there's been an incident at the Hollands' home. Mrs Holland's been found dead.'

'There must be some mistake. I was talking to her just a few hours ago.'

'I wish it was a mistake,' the chief inspector said solemnly.

Hopkinson shook his head as he led Roscoe into his small rear kitchen. 'Good gracious! This is terrible! She's such a kind lady.' He looked as if he would collapse from the shock at any moment.

'Can I ask about your movements today? What time did you arrive there this morning?'

Hopkinson sat down at his kitchen table. 'About a quarter to nine.'

'You say you left at a quarter to eleven. Are you quite sure about that?'

'Well, I make sure I do a full two hours, so the Hollands can't claim I'm not fulfilling my hours. Mrs Holland was sitting on the patio. I imagine she was drinking her usual drink, Pimm's. I asked her what the time was. She said it had just gone quarter to eleven. I told her what I'd done and she said, "Good. Thanks for all you've done. I'll see you Friday" – and that was that. So what's actually happened?'

Roscoe frowned. 'It appears Mrs Holland was murdered this morning – we think between eleven and midday. It looks as if you were the last person to speak to her before she died.'

'Oh, good God.'

'Can you tell us what happened when you left? Did you use the side gate?'

'Yes, I left by the side gate. I think I fastened it behind me, but now I come to think of it, I can't be sure if I did because I had some small tools. Anyway I collected my bike from where I'd left it, leaning against the wall of the house, and cycled off home.'

'Did you see anyone in the street as you left? Was there anyone hanging around outside the house, for example?'

'I don't recall seeing anyone. There may have been someone around. I really couldn't say. I was just focussed on getting home.'

'All right, thank you for your time, sir. I think that's all for now. We'll be back in touch.'

Hopkinson followed the chief inspector into the hallway. 'Oh, that's terrible news you've brought. She was such a lovely lady. I feel so sorry for Mr Holland.'

Just as he was walking away down the short path to the garden gate, the chief inspector's mobile phone rang. It was DI Vickers.

'The sergeant's theory about the fair's proved spot on, sir,' the inspector said. 'Just behind the Slack family's office there's an American Jeep, a Land Rover and a green Carina. But I nearly got beaten up for my trouble.'

Roscoe noticed the gardener peering out at him through his front door. He gave him a casual wave.

'Great work, Tom!' he said. 'We'll have to move on this quickly in case the family try to shift any of those vehicles. Stay there while I make some calls.'

* * *

Two hours later, revellers stood and stared as sirens blared and grew louder. Startled toddlers scurried for their mothers as dozens of police on foot stormed into Deacons Park.

The chief inspector had at first considered closing the whole fairground and sending the punters home. But, after discussions with his sergeant, she had convinced him that that would cause huge disruption and might even impede the investigation.

Instead he'd followed her suggestion of mounting a smaller-scale operation which involved cordoning off only the area around the Slacks' office and the family car park. Officers from CID, members of the traffic department, the sniffer dog team and forensic officers had all been drafted in.

Tom Vickers was slightly aggrieved at having to forego lunch. But he carried out his boss's instructions to the letter, maintaining a watch over the Slacks' vehicles from a safe distance to ensure no one attempted to move them. So he was relieved when the sirens sounded at 5.00 p.m. and he knew the raid had begun.

Roscoe and Sunita, accompanied by five constables in uniform, marched past the rides and sideshows towards the Slacks' office, attracting the attention of inquisitive fairgoers as they passed.

Sunita was intrigued to see a crossbow stall was operating at a red-and-white striped booth. A customer was being handed a primitive bow and urged to shoot at one of two targets in the hope of winning a prize. Next to the booth was one of the fair's most popular attractions, the Ghost Train.

As she watched a couple emerging into the daylight from the train with laughing faces, a thought crossed her mind. What was it that Trudy Marwood had said to her when running through the list of her male friends? 'Den. Met him at the over-thirties night. Worked on the trains.' When the man mentioned trains to her, she wondered, could he have meant...? No, surely not.

But gradually, in the same way the sun slowly rises over the hills, came a realisation that Den, Trudy Marwood's acquaintance, could be the man at the heart of their investigation. No one had known his surname. Could he be a member of the Slack family?

Eventually, Vickers met up with the team and led them to the Slacks' office, a shabby, cream-coloured caravan containing two desks, four office chairs, three filing cabinets and two phones. As Vickers and two constables went round the back and officially inspected the Slacks' vehicles, Roscoe and Sunita climbed inside.

Elijah Slack and his wife Rebecca were sitting behind separate desks. A man with curly, black hair was settled quietly on a chair in the corner.

Sunita was startled as Elijah erupted in anger.

'What the hell d'you want? This is a private area. Toby!'

Roscoe waved his police identification. 'Heart of England Police. We need to search your premises. We're making inquiries about some vehicles believed to have been involved in serious crime.'

Elijah's twenty-stone frame was clothed in a tight-fitting white shirt and badly creased dark-brown trousers.

'That's nothing to do with us,' he sneered. 'Where's your warrant? If you're carrying out a search, you need a warrant.'

The chief inspector shook his head. 'We don't need a warrant in this case because it's a murder inquiry.'

Rebecca appeared visibly shaken by his words.

'Murder?' asked the woman, whose voice betrayed a faint Scottish accent. 'You've made some mistake.'

'No mistake, madam,' Sunita said. 'There's an American Jeep and a Land Rover behind this caravan we believe may be linked to a series of murders.'

The chief inspector peered across at the third member of the family skulking in the corner, while he removed a notebook from his pocket.

'Now, we want your names and those of anyone who's driven those vehicles.'

Chapter 50

Sunita Roy sensed Elijah Slack was an argumentative man who had almost certainly had many dealings with police in the past. But, for some reason, he decided to cooperate on this occasion.

'All right. The name's Elijah Slack. I run the fair. This is my wife Rebecca, and that lazy good-for-nothing over there's my younger son, Den.'

Roscoe was writing in his book. 'You called out the name Toby when we first arrived.'

'Yes. He's my older boy, Tobias. He's around here somewhere.'

Sunita smiled. 'He's probably keeping out of the way, sir.'

'Show me the vehicle documents,' Roscoe demanded.

As the fair owner searched through drawers, Sunita turned her attention to the man in the corner. So this was Den Slack. As she peered at the strong, clear bone structure of his face and his athletic body beneath the artificial light, she could see why some women might be attracted to him.

Could their weeks of work on Operation Promenade finally be drawing to a close?

Roscoe was also peering at the young man, aware his description matched the man who stabbed Oliver Bufton in the arm.

Vickers' face appeared in the doorway. 'Sir, could I have a word?'

Roscoe clambered down the caravan steps, accompanied by his sergeant.

'Yes, Tom?'

Vickers lowered his voice. 'The vehicles are all registered in Elijah Slack's name. We're taking them all away on lorries and they should be off the park in the next couple of hours. But at some point the personnel carrier's gone missing. I don't know how that happened.'

'Don't worry about that one. Thanks, Tom.'

'Oh, one more thing. It looks like the tyre on the Land Rover could've left the marks in the mud at Biddington.'

The pair returned to the office. Roscoe decided to tackle the father.

'Mr Slack, there's a green Toyota Carina behind your office. It's not taxed or insured. Neither is the Land Rover.'

'I know. I've been meaning to sort it out. The point is they're not used. They're nearly always off-road.'

'You've got to alert the authorities if they're off-road. I'm going to ask you to accompany me to police headquarters for further questioning.'

Elijah, who had a tattoo of a rampant lion on his right forearm and a prowling tiger on his left, was striving to control his temper. The fair had been founded in the 1930s by his grandfather and he'd been fighting a constant battle since taking it over in 1992 to keep the enterprise afloat. He stood up and moved round his desk.

'You're going to completely disrupt our business.'

'May not take too long, sir,' said Sunita. 'The sooner we get this sorted out, the sooner you can get back to work.'

Roscoe turned towards Den Slack, who was pretending to show no interest in the police questioning but was, in reality, hanging on every word. 'What's your job at the fair, young man?'

Elijah answered for him. 'Den runs the ghost train.'

Sunita recalled Trudy Marwood's remarks about Den running trains. She now knew why he'd been so reticent.

'So you don't have anything to do with shooting crossbows?' said Roscoe.

Den shook his head.

His mother turned to face her son. 'You dinnae use a crossbow anymore, dae you, Den?'

'No, Ma. I'm not even sure where it is now.'

Elijah glanced at his wife. 'As I say, Den runs the ghost train. Toby runs the crossbow stall. Now you know the whole set-up.'

Sunita frowned at Den. 'Where were you on Monday, 24 April and the first weekend of May?'

'He's always here, working at the fair,' said Elijah.

'I'd like him to answer,' Sunita insisted.

'Like me dad said, I was at the fair,' said Den.

'How about the early hours of Friday, 23 June and just before lunch this morning?'

'At the fair,' said Den.

Turning to Rebecca, the sergeant asked, 'Has he been here all day today?'

'Aye. The train stopped working and he had to call in the fitter. He was tied up with that all morning.'

Sunita glanced at her boss in a manner suggesting she wanted a private word. The two detectives stepped outside and moved a short distance from the office, nodding at the constables outside who were waiting for instructions.

'I've had an idea, sir. It's possible this Den Slack could be behind the murders, don't you think?'

'Wouldn't put it past any of them. I've half a mind to arrest the whole family. Den Slack certainly sounds like the fellow Trudy Marwood and Virginia Holland met up with.'

She agreed. 'Once you've taken the father away, I'm going to station myself behind the office. I might be able to eavesdrop through the window and record their conversation. I might even get a confession.'

'If you're prepared to try it, let's do it,' said Roscoe. 'The forensics people will soon be searching the other two caravans used by the Slacks. I can hold them back from searching the office until later.'

The two detectives stepped back inside and Roscoe glared at Elijah. 'Right, if you'd like to accompany us, sir. One of the constables will caution you.'

The fair owner begrudgingly climbed down the steps and was formally arrested. All eyes were focussed upon him as he was escorted away.

Sunita waited until all the officers had gone. Then she walked round the side of the caravan and crouched down on the grass, beneath the open window.

At first, after switching her phone to 'Record' and holding it close to the window, all she could hear was forty-nine-year-old Rebecca denouncing her husband's arrest. The ranting went on and on for more than fifteen minutes. Den would interrupt his mother from time to time, but he was also highly critical of the police action.

She was trying to make herself as comfortable as possible between the office and the next caravan along. But she wasn't used to squatting for long periods and her knees were soon aching.

Then, after a few more minutes, as luck would have it, a row began to erupt between mother and son. Angry words were exchanged. Angry words that could be clearly heard by Sunita and would, she hoped, be clearly audible on the recording.

'Den, be honest now. Have you been up tae nae good?' the mother demanded.

'No, Ma. Of course not.'

'You have, haven't you? Some nights you dinnae gae to bed till four. Toby's told me. The last Thursday we were in Stratford you were out all night and Toby couldn't find your crossbow.'

'I just took the Jeep for a run and went to bed late. I was in bed by two. Toby got it wrong.'

'Dinnae lie to your mother! I can tell when you're lying, Den. It's mother's intuition. You've been to see that woman, Trudy, haven't you? Your attitude fair scunners me.'

'So what if I went to see my girlfriend? That's my business. I'm not going to hang around here being spoken to like this,' he shouted. 'I'm going to the train.'

'Come here, Den!' his mother yelled.

Sunita heard the door slam shut and the sound of someone storming out. Now she had to sneak away unobserved. She crept from the narrow passageway between the vans and reached a wider alley that led to the family's car park. But as she emerged, brushing wisps of grass from her trousers, a burly man with black hair in a ponytail was walking towards the office – Toby Slack.

'Oy, what're you playing at?' he demanded. 'Ma! There's another trespasser. It's a gal. She's been right outside the office – snooping, I shouldn't wonder.'

He charged towards Sunita and grabbed her round the throat. Then he thrust her hard against the side of the office, causing her head to strike against the rigid surface.

'Heart of England Police!' she shouted. 'You're obstructing an officer.'

'D'you think I care?'

He punched her in the face, causing her to wince with pain. But this only spurred her into retaliating.

Toby had his right hand on the sergeant's left shoulder, close to her neck. She suddenly reached across with her own right hand and grabbed her assailant's hand.

Then, taking a step back, she twisted her opponent's arm, using both hands to inflict maximum pressure on Toby's middle knuckle.

'Have some of that, you bully,' she shouted.

She'd learnt the move as part of her martial arts training and knew how effective it could be if you could exert control over that particular joint.

Then, as Toby was bent over, she kicked him in the face with force, sending the thug reeling back in shock. She finally head-butted Toby on the nose. This was followed by the hammer blow of a right fist to the face.

Toby recognised when he was beaten and, as blood began pouring from his nostrils, limped away to the office, leaving Sunita free to continue on her way.

After putting some distance between herself and the Slacks' office, she stopped for a moment to regain her breath. Then she resumed her walk towards the main car park. As she went, she played back her recording and was relieved to find she'd captured both voices perfectly.

Then, although her head was throbbing, she tried to call her boss. At first there was no reply. But, after trying several times, he picked up.

'I've only just got back to the office. How did you get on?'

Sunita laughed despite her discomfort. 'I've got Den being accused by his mother of "being up to no good". She accuses him of being out for the whole night at the time Coral Devon was murdered. He looks like our man. But we'll have to move quickly or there's a risk he may go on the run.'

'You're right, Sergeant. We must arrest him immediately. I'll send Tom Vickers over with some back-up. You sound a bit breathless. Are you all right?'

She shrugged. 'I'll be fine. Just had a bit of a tussle with Toby. He banged my head against the caravan and I think he's bruised my cheek.'

Roscoe sighed. 'He's a bit fiery, that one. He and his brother are clearly the guys who stabbed Oliver in April.'

She nodded. 'Yes. Sir, if it's all right with you, I'd like to stay down here and link up with DI Vickers.'

'Well, if you feel up to it. I admire your enthusiasm.'

'We've come this far, sir. It would be a shame to miss the final stages.'

Chapter 51

Sunita Roy was experiencing mixed emotions as she awaited her colleagues' arrival at Deacons Park. She was exhausted after a long day. Her face was smarting from the blow struck by Toby Slack. But she was also excited since they were on the point of making a key arrest.

Vickers arrived at around seven thirty. The numbers of thrill-seekers enjoying the fair seemed to have soared by then. The revelry seemed louder and more boisterous as the detectives waited to be joined by four constables in uniform.

Then, amid the flashing lights and the clamour, the team began to thread their way through the throng.

Several metres ahead of her, Sunita recognised the entrance to the ghost train, which Den Slack was supposed to supervise. She at once tried to recall a poem she'd learnt at school. How did it go? *Who's in charge of the clattering train? The axles creak and the couplings strain.*

The only other lines she could remember were, *And signals flash through the night in vain, Death is in charge of the clattering train.* She'd always been fond of poetry and, for some reason, could not rid her mind of these words.

Vickers, walking beside her, noticed a bruise on her face and was concerned when she related how Toby Slack had assaulted her.

'Don't worry. I got the best of it in the end,' she insisted.

Vickers sighed. 'Both the brothers look like trouble.'

If the evening turned out badly, she was sure he would do his best to save her from harm.

But where was Den? In one of the caravans? Running the ghost train? Or had he fled the fairground already, sensing his reign of fear as the crossbow killer was about to be exposed?

The six-strong team gathered outside the ghost train, gazing up at a huge, white, illuminated skull on the left of the façade and the face of Dracula with blood spurting from his fangs on the right.

A group of young people were queuing for rides, but no one appeared to be in charge.

Then they saw him, the man with jet-black hair and a sallow complexion that Sunita had questioned earlier. He was collecting money in an open-necked, red-and-blue check shirt and black jeans.

She now recalled it was Angelina Moretto's neighbour, Michael Peploe, who had some time before described Miss

Moretto's dark-haired visitor as 'swarthy'. He was right, of course. And so had been Virginia Holland. Den Slack was swarthy.

Vickers stepped forward, easing his way past the youths queuing beside the wooden platform.

'Den Slack?' he said. 'You're under arrest.'

But hardly had the words slipped from his mouth than Den turned and fled inside the attraction.

The inspector pointed at two constables. 'You guys get round the back quickly to block him.' Then he ran to a nearby stall, desperately wondering how to turn off the power for the trains.

The remaining two constables declared the attraction closed and ushered would-be customers away. But Sunita was determined to go after Den Slack.

Although aware the power remained on, she slipped a small torch from her pocket and switched it on. Then she ventured onto the rail track, pushed her way through the wooden double doors and vanished into the darkness.

She realised it would be a near-impossible challenge to find Den amid the maze of scary sounds and special effects. He was the master of this domain. He must know how and where to hide. Death was in charge of the clattering train.

Alone in the gloom, she flashed the torch beam around. The sideshow was no more than a huge room with boards and doors bearing ghostly figures and images. The running track for trains swept around the enclosure in a figure of eight.

She thought she heard a noise beside her. Was it Den? She held her breath in case the sound of her breathing would alert him to her presence. More than a minute passed. Just silence around her.

All at once she heard a shout from outside, 'Stop that man!' Perhaps Den had been caught fleeing through a rear exit. Perhaps the danger had passed.

Sunita manoeuvred her way towards the gleam of light behind her, hoping it would lead her back to the attraction's entrance. Sure enough, within a few moments, she emerged, rubbing her eyes in the humid evening air.

'He's got away!' Vickers told her between gritted teeth. 'He got out through an emergency exit and our team weren't quick enough.'

'Well, let's go after him, Tom.'

The pair raced to the end of the park and sprinted past the war memorial, past a row of whitewashed Victorian cottages, past the clock tower. They were heading in the direction of the town centre. They could see the dark-blue uniforms of the four constables ahead of them, weaving among the crowds of revellers and late-evening shoppers.

At first, they could distinguish Den Slack's curly hair bobbing along, above the pavement, in the distance. He was carrying something in his hand. But after a few minutes, they lost sight of him.

Sunita wondered if he'd darted into a doorway, dashed down a side road or taken refuge inside a pub or cafe. It seemed a hopeless task – like trying to find Blackie the cat in a coal cellar, she thought. However, the pair were determined to catch him since they feared he might try and kill again.

Two of the constables raised objections, but Vickers insisted the search should go on. He glanced through the doorway of a pub, while Sunita peered inside a cafe. They spent time at the junctions of several side roads, staring down them in the hope their eyes would catch sight of the fugitive. But Den Slack couldn't be found.

Vickers ordered the constables back to Deacons Park in case Slack tried to double back. He urged them to inspect the office, the man's personal caravan and the staff car park.

He raised his voice as they left. 'Turn the place upside down if you have to. The sergeant and I will carry on here.'

Vickers entered a second pub and ambled through the bars, looking left and right for any sign of the wanted man. Sunita was checking premises next door.

She glanced down an alley between a supermarket and a dry-cleaner's. Was that the flicker of a shadow, the faint suggestion of a figure?

She stood still beneath the orange glow of the streetlight. There was no sound except the roar of occasional traffic, the chatter of shoppers and the rowdy shouts of the distant fairgoers.

Sunita's heart was in her mouth. She took her torch from her jacket pocket again. She switched it on. Its beam lit up the alley. A few cardboard boxes, some sweet wrappers – nothing of interest.

Step by step, metre by metre, she made her way down the passageway. She'd gone more than halfway when she suddenly came upon a recessed exit door and someone or something leaped out. Was it Slack? The terrified sergeant felt a man's hand round her mouth and an arm round the middle of her torso, dragging her into the doorway.

She struggled and tried to remember her self-defence moves. It was all too late. The man had her fully under control. She felt his hot, stinking breath on the back of her neck. After this energetic pursuit on a warm summer's evening, she also became aware of his noxious body odour.

'You're a pretty one, aren't you?' he declared, his reptilian voice sending a shiver through her body. He undid the top two buttons of her white blouse with his right hand and fondled her breasts.

She struggled, but he was powerful, and she felt helpless. Then, to her relief, she heard a shout. It was Vickers yelling her name. His cries met with silence. Slack's right hand was clamped round her face.

'Is that your boyfriend, looking for you?' he sneered.

She lowered her jaw, in the expectation that one or two of his fingers might slip into her mouth. She'd anticipated correctly. One of his fingers inadvertently slid between her teeth. She at once bit into the flesh as ferociously as she could. He hollered in pain.

'You little bastard,' he cried, hurling her into the alley.

Then, stooping only to pick up the crossbow that he'd left on the ground, he raced off towards the car park.

Sunita lay sprawling on the concrete. 'Tom!' she screamed. 'I'm down the alley. Tom!'

Within seconds, the breathless inspector found her struggling to get to her feet after her encounter.

'He grabbed me. The toerag grabbed me through my clothing.'

Then she bravely set off down the alley in the direction Slack had taken, closely followed by the inspector.

They found a car park at the end of the alley which was half-full of shoppers' cars.

The pair looked hopefully across the dimly lit scene for any glimpse of a man with curly, black hair, but in vain. Den Slack was nowhere to be seen. By then, it was nearly nine o'clock and they were forced to admit defeat.

'Damn it!' said Vickers. 'We'll have to arrange a round-the-clock watch on the Slacks' caravans now and arrest him when he returns.'

Sunita shrugged. 'If he returns, Tom.'

The inspector gazed anxiously into her eyes. 'Are you all right, Sunita?'

She nodded. 'I'll be OK.'

He smiled. 'You're a tough girl, we know that. But it can't have been very pleasant down that gully with a man like that scumbag Den Slack.'

'Tom, I was in my school's netball team. I've seen the dark side of life.'

As they returned to the main street, Vickers turned his head towards the darkening sky.

'For now, we've got a problem. The bird has flown the coop. What on earth are we going to tell the guvnor? He's going to be livid. Slack could be anywhere right now and he's armed with his crossbow.'

Chapter 52

Sunita Roy greeted DI Vickers warmly as she arrived in CID on Thursday, 3 August.

'Good morning, Tom. How's Elijah Slack today?'

The inspector glanced round at her and smiled. 'The guvnor's not too happy. He said interviewing the old codger had been as much fun as spending a cold Sunday trapped in a flooded car park.'

She grinned as she took a chair beside him. 'He wasn't very helpful then?'

'No.'

'Have you told him about last night?'

'Yes. I thought he took the news surprisingly well.'

'I'd better say hello.'

She strolled over to Roscoe's door and tapped gently before opening it.

The chief inspector looked dejected.

Sunita gave a weak smile. 'Sir, I'm really sorry we messed up the arrest.'

Roscoe sighed. 'Don't worry. These things happen. We've got officers stationed around the fairground. He's bound to show up eventually.'

She slipped inside and drew up a chair. 'I hear the interview with the father didn't go well.'

'Didn't really get anywhere and we've granted him bail until 14 September while further inquiries are made. He blamed his older son, Toby, for failing to tax and insure the vehicles.'

Vickers knocked and came inside, taking a chair beside Sunita. The chief inspector glanced up before continuing.

'The old man claimed both sons were brought up as honest, God-fearing lads and insisted neither of them would commit murder. They'd been taught life is sacred.'

Vickers shook his head. 'Always the same with the criminal underclasses. It's never them. Always someone else.'

'Right, let's hear what Den Slack and the old woman had to say.'

Sunita fetched her mobile phone and searched for the recording. Moments later, the heated words exchanged the previous afternoon between Den Slack and his mother were echoing round the room.

The chief inspector slurped some coffee as he listened to the mother accusing her son.

After Sunita had switched off the recording, Roscoe leaned back in his seat. 'We've got plenty of evidence against Den Slack now. This just adds to it, Sergeant. Well done!'

She beamed at him. 'There's something else I've discovered. Den isn't his proper first name. I contacted our family researcher. We know Den is twenty-five years old, which means he should've been born in about 1992. But the researcher couldn't find any babies born in that year with the name Denis or Dennis Slack. Then I suggested he should look for the brother, Tobias, born in 1989. That gave us the mother's maiden name of Macdonald. Then he searched Den's birth year for a Slack-Macdonald baby and found the right one.'

Roscoe smiled. 'Come on then, Sergeant. Don't keep us in suspense.'

'His full name's Culloden Jonas Slack, registered in Birmingham in March 1992.'

'Culloden?'

'Yes. Since Culloden's a bit of a mouthful, the family have obviously shortened it to Den. Maybe this explains the letter *C* on the handkerchiefs.'

'Well, that's astonishing, Sergeant.'

Vickers nodded in agreement. 'Still I suppose it could've been worse. They could've called him Bannockburn or Killiecrankie. How's your face now, by the way?'

She grinned. 'Much better now, thank you.'

'It looks much better.'

Roscoe looked up. 'Did you want to press assault charges against Toby Slack?'

'No, we've got more important matters to deal with, sir.'

'Very well.'

Roscoe had been distracted for a moment. He'd been reminded about the handkerchiefs. 'So why did Den Slack want to advertise his dastardly deeds with initialled handkerchiefs?'

Sunita shrugged. 'Maybe he was proud of his actions, sir, and wanted to mark his territory.'

The chief inspector leaned forward and gazed at the pair.

'I've a few things to tell you both as well. DC Dawson's been talking to staff at the funfair. Apparently, Den became fascinated as a child with the crossbow booth and he's become something of a marksman, though his family might deny it. In Den's caravan, the forensic team have uncovered a cheese-cloth shirt with a tear on the right arm which they're examining.'

Vickers wondered if he'd heard back about the vehicle inspections.

'All I've heard, Tom, is that the Carina matches the description of the one stolen just before the archery club break-in. The evidence is building up against young Slack.'

Sunita frowned. 'I don't know if we can pin all four murders on him, sir.'

'Whyever not?'

'Well I've been wondering if Ginny Holland's murder was a copycat killing.'

'Why do you think that?'

'Well, there was no handkerchief in the mouth. We'd carefully kept details of the handkerchiefs out of the public arena. It's occurred to me someone who wanted Mrs Holland out of the way might have killed her with a crossbow bolt to try to blame the serial killer.'

Roscoe tutted. 'I don't think we should let a little thing like a missed handkerchief stop us from tying in the Holland murder with the other three. The Holland murder's got all the same hallmarks.'

Sunita shook her head. 'I'm sorry. I don't agree, sir. And what do you consider the letters written in blood meant?'

The chief inspector made a wide gesture with his hands. 'She was probably trying to write "Slack". That's the most obvious explanation, although his motive for the murders escapes me entirely.'

'I believe Den Slack may have formed an obsessive attachment to the Italian woman, Angelina Moretto. This led him to harass and kill the man he perceived as his main rival for her affections.

'Then, when the Italian woman spurned him, he couldn't accept it and killed her. He also couldn't take rejection from the Marwood woman, so he attempted to kill her too – and failed. It appears Coral was shot by mistake because she had the misfortune to resemble her aunt. It reminds me of a legal case I studied at university. A man murdered his own brother and his brother's girlfriend. The judge said the killer had "abnormal personality traits". I can see Den Slack might well have similar traits,' Sunita said.

Roscoe was becoming agitated. 'Forget university. That's all theory. This is real life, Sergeant. It's our job to show Den Slack was criminally responsible for these murders and we don't want to open the doors to any potential defence that he might have been mentally ill at the time.'

'I wasn't suggesting that at all, but the man obviously reacts extremely aggressively to being rejected. He could be suffering from a narcissistic personality disorder.'

Suddenly she became silent. Roscoe noticed an excited expression spreading across her face. She was clenching and unclenching her right hand repeatedly. Vickers detected the change in her demeanour.

'What is it, Sunita? What's the matter?'

Her eyes lit up. 'I've had the glimmer of an idea. I think I know how we might be able to catch Den Slack.'

The chief inspector shrugged. 'I know as well. We'll launch a manhunt with all the forces at our disposal – sniffer dogs, helicopters, the works. This guy's dangerous. He's killed four people and he's on the run.'

She nodded. 'But launching a large-scale hunt may not be the answer. We don't want the embarrassment of it leaking out, sir, that we had him in the palm of our hands and bungled the operation – which is what it may appear. Just give me twenty-four hours. I'm sure I can catch him.'

'In twenty-four hours, we could have another poor victim with an arrow through the heart.'

'Hear me out,' she insisted. 'I think we've begun to understand how this man's mind works. There's a good chance he's going to head for Trudy Marwood's place in Stratford.'

Roscoe stroked his chin. 'Good God, you're right. We need to give Trudy Marwood top-rate protection.'

'It's Thursday and tonight the over-thirties event is being held in Stratford. He may well expect Trudy to go. He may try and see her there or go to her house with murder on his mind.'

'So what are you suggesting?'

'I'm suggesting the inspector and I go down there and put pay to his plans.'

'What about Trudy Marwood? We can't put her life in danger.'

'We give her the choice. She can stay at her house or stay elsewhere. But if he senses she's not going to be around, he may remain in hiding.'

'Sergeant, it sounds a risky operation.'

'Don't you think we owe it to Oliver Bufton and the other victims to give this plan a chance?'

Roscoe nodded. 'All right. Tom can go down to Stratford with you. Sergeant, you've got your twenty-four hours – but be bloody careful.'

Chapter 53

The air was humid as Sunita Roy set off alone for Stratford just after eleven o'clock that same morning. Scattered showers were forecast, but for the moment the rain was holding off.

She'd expected to see Trudy Marwood's Jaguar outside Jane Perks' semi-detached house in Sunderland Drive as she drew up outside, but there was no sign of it in the street. She discovered later Trudy had left the car at her own home and walked round to Jane's.

It was Trudy who opened the door to the sergeant. As Jane made them tea in the living room, Sunita explained to Trudy, as gently as she could, that police believed Den Slack was the serial killer. She also outlined her plan for catching him.

Trudy sat on her friend's grey settee with her head in her hands. Sunita guessed she was wondering how she could have been so blinkered, so misguided to become infatuated – albeit briefly – with such a man as Den Slack. How could she have been so reckless to put her life – and that of others – in so much danger? She wept inconsolably. Jane heard her crying and rushed to her side, trying to comfort her.

'They think Den might be the killer, Jane – the man the press are calling the crossbow stalker,' Trudy mumbled before the tears resumed.

Sunita frowned. 'I'm sorry to be the one to break the news to you. But I haven't told you the worst of it. He's at large and I fear he may make a fresh attempt on your life, Mrs Marwood. As it's a Thursday, there's every likelihood he'll assume you're going to the Municipal Hall tonight.'

Trudy broke off from crying. She glanced at the detective. 'Yes, he probably will. But doesn't he believe he's killed me? Doesn't he believe the woman in the back bedroom was me?'

Sunita shook her head. 'No, it's been on the news and in the papers, hasn't it? He knows Coral's the woman he killed – not you.'

Sunita paused for a moment while Trudy wiped her eyes. Then she went on, 'I'm sure Den's now determined to kill you once and for all.'

Trudy, casually dressed in a white T-shirt and jeans, looked aghast as Jane brought in the tea and set it out on a small table.

'You don't mince your words, do you?' said Trudy.

'It's only fair that you should be aware of how much danger your life could be in. It's important for us to be honest with you. But I'm not here to frighten you. I'm here to catch the killer. My colleague, DI Vickers, will be here shortly. We'll have a recce of the area and see if we can find any signs of Den Slack being about. But, if we can't, I have to ask you this: are you willing to help us trap him?'

Trudy glanced towards Jane as though seeking moral support. 'Look, I owe it to Coral and my sister Moira to get this man stopped. Yes, Sergeant Roy, I'll help you, of course.'

'It's my personal belief he just can't take rejection,' said Sunita. 'When he starts dating a woman, he believes he's an Adonis who cannot fail to win her affection. When her interest wanes, the emotional effect upon him is devastating. He simply can't accept it and something inside him spurs him into killing the person who jilted him.'

Inspector Vickers arrived just before half past twelve. Sunita took him into the living room and introduced him to Jane Perks, whom he hadn't met before. He nodded towards Trudy.

'Have you explained everything, Sarge?' he asked Sunita.

'Yes, and Mrs Marwood's bravely agreed to help us.'

Vickers stood by the door to the room, frowning. 'I'm afraid Den Slack is already in the area.'

Trudy and Jane cried out in unison. Jane sat down beside her friend. They both seemed shocked.

'How do you know that?' Sunita asked.

'The missing personnel carrier, the Humber Pig, is parked in the next street.'

Jane looked blank. 'What's a Humber Pig?'

'It's nothing to do with farm animals from the East Riding,' Vickers explained. 'It's a heavily armoured British Army vehicle. One of the fairground workers told me the two Slack brothers are vehicle fanatics and picked one up cheaply.'

'But what's it doing round here?' asked Jane.

'After the police raided the fair at Kenilworth yesterday, Den got away. He must've taken this vehicle, because all their other forms of transport are accounted for.'

Sunita suggested that she and Vickers should take Trudy's door keys and go round to inspect the Warwick Road house. They promised the women they'd also examine the personnel carrier and search surrounding streets.

Sunita spoke to them sternly. 'Promise me you won't leave this house.'

The two women nodded. They exchanged glances. They were petrified and it was clear they wouldn't open the door to any visitors after the detectives had departed.

'Where did you see the Humber Pig?' Sunita asked once they were back out on the street.

'It's just round the corner. Come on. I'll show you.'

The pair turned right at the top of Sunderland Drive and found themselves in Marchant Street, a side road which led directly into Warwick Road. Exactly as Vickers had described, there was a khaki-coloured personnel carrier parked near the junction. Armoured shutters shrouded the firing ports and blocked any side view of the interior. The front and rear openings were likewise covered.

'Does it have the right number plate and markings?'

'Yes, it's the same one I saw at the fairground yesterday,' he assured her.

Sunita smiled. 'It just looks so out-of-place round here. It belongs somewhere like the Bogside.'

He knocked on the side of the vehicle loudly. There was no response. 'So where's chummy boy?'

'Maybe he's gone to the Marwoods' house.'

They strolled to the top of Marchant Street and turned into the main Warwick Road.

'I still can't get over his name – Culloden,' he said. 'Who'd want to be named after an eighteenth-century battle?'

As they entered Trudy's front garden, Vickers studied the lock on the front door. 'Looks like someone's had a go at this. Someone's used a screwdriver or chisel to try to force it. I definitely didn't see those marks before.'

He slowly turned the key in the lock and the door swung open. No sound could be heard except for passing traffic. The house was as quiet as a temple at prayer.

They stepped into the hallway and entered the living room. Then they climbed the oak stairs, stopping every few seconds to listen for any noise. There was none. They inspected the two large bedrooms and two smaller bedrooms. Everything seemed in order.

'Let's see if any attempt's been made to break in through the back of the house,' Sunita suggested.

They left through the front door, carefully closing it firmly behind them, and then followed the concrete path round to the rear of the house. As they did so, they passed the narrow patch of grass which stood between the path and the light-brown timber fence, which bordered a field.

'It doesn't look as if there's been any attempt to force the back door,' said Vickers. 'But it's not very secure. All anyone's got to do is smash one of the two glass panes, put a hand through and turn the key, which someone's helpfully left in the inside lock.'

The two detectives gazed round the garden, which was mainly laid to lawn. The wealth of colour produced by this glorious summer was sadly fading from the narrow borders at each side. Yet there remained an appealing array of hues with daisy-like mauve asters and nodding blue clematis flowers. Blooms of pink phlox, offering a light scent, tossed their heads in the breeze.

While the inspector returned to the front of the house, Sunita ventured into the left-hand corner of the rear garden, where a small wooden shed stood.

She found it was unlocked. The door creaked open. She peered in. At first the contents were all she'd have expected – spades, forks, rakes and hoes; containers of weedkiller and pest killer; rubber gardening gloves; cans of paint; and a variety of other tools.

But as she ventured further inside, she stopped in her tracks. A green sleeping bag, partly zipped, was lying in the middle of the dusty concrete floor. Two cans of lager stood beside it.

Had Rowan Marwood slept there one night after a row with Trudy and failed to dispose of his empties? Unlikely, Sunita thought. She slipped her right hand inside one of the gloves and carefully picked up each of the cans, in turn. One still retained half its contents. Someone must have spent the night sleeping in the shed, she decided.

Could that someone have been the fugitive, Den Slack? She closed the door and walked slowly back towards the front garden to join the inspector.

'I've just been looking round the field next door,' he said. 'It looks as if someone's been there recently. There are footmarks in the long grass.'

'No sign of an arrow dropped by mistake then?' added Sunita, half-jokingly.

He smiled. 'No.'

'Well, there's a sleeping bag and some lager in the shed, so it looks like maybe Den slept there last night.'

His smile faded. 'That guy's got some brass neck, sleeping in her shed.'

'I know, but I don't think we should tell Trudy. That would really unnerve her.'

'So where is he right now?'

'We can't see him. We don't know where he is. But I've no doubt he's out there, and he's watching.'

* * *

Over the course of the next few hours, the pair sat in Trudy's living room, adding finishing touches to their plan. Then Vickers returned to Jane Perks' house so he could explain how they visualised the operation proceeding.

Sunita remained at the house, examining doors and windows. She wanted to familiarise herself with any method an intruder might use to gain access. When she was satisfied with this private research, she too walked back to the house in Sunderland Drive.

She was just metres from the personnel carrier when a police patrol car roared round the corner and screeched to a halt beside her, its blue light flashing.

Two uniformed constables leaped out and ordered her to lean against the side of a house with her hands on the wall and her legs parted. They then searched her in a rough manner as she attempted to explain herself.

'I'm DS Roy from CID...' she began, at a loss to recall where she'd put her warrant card.

'Yeah, yeah,' said the first constable, a tall, overweight man with striking ginger hair. 'The reason we've stopped you is there's a dangerous suspect at large in this area and we decided you were behaving suspiciously. Open your bag.'

Sunita was embarrassed to reveal to them her cosmetics, purse, credit cards, comb, a pen and a Swiss Army knife, the keys to her flat and Mrs Marwood's door keys. Her police pass was missing.

'Got a lot of keys, haven't you?' said the second constable, a more reserved man with a softer voice. 'But no ID.'

Then Sunita remembered. She'd slipped it into a side pocket of her fawn jacket after the fairground raid. She quickly located it and brandished it in front of them, whereupon the officers' conduct changed.

'Oh, sorry, Sarge,' said the ginger-haired constable. 'We're on a special operation which involves stopping lots of people. There's meant to be a man with a crossbow on the loose.'

Sunita nodded. 'Yes, I know. That's why I'm down here. Glad you're keeping on the ball.'

'A circus hand, isn't he?'

'A fairground worker,' said Sunita. 'Listen, boys. There's a good chance he'll make an attempt on Mrs Marwood's life tonight. So it would be helpful if you were around later.'

At that moment, alerted by the police car's flashing light, Vickers had stepped out of Mrs Perks' house and was approaching them. He waved his warrant card just as the sergeant was inviting them to help at the Marwoods' house.

'I think we should also call in the firearms team,' Vickers muttered.

She nodded. 'Yes, cool idea.'

Turning to the constables, she said, 'We believe this guy could strike between eight and nine tonight when his target is preparing for a night out. So it would be handy if you were available then – without being too noticeable, if you know what I mean.'

'You mean: no car, no lights, no siren?' said the ginger-haired constable.

'Exactly. We'll let you know when we want you.'

He nodded. 'It won't be us. It'll be the later shift, but we'll pass on the details to them.'

Chapter 54

At eight o'clock that evening, Trudy Marwood returned to her house, conscious that the man she'd met a couple of months earlier now seemed, according to the police, hell-bent on snuffing out her life.

She'd had personal reservations about the detectives' plan to trap Den Slack, but she'd bravely decided to set aside her fears. She knew she had to support their efforts to catch him – if only for her niece's sake.

Sunita had earlier prepared Trudy's sleeveless purple dress and leopard-print flats, so that they would be ready for her to put on before Slack arrived, as both women were convinced he would.

Sunita and Vickers wanted Den Slack to believe, if he were watching, that Trudy was only returning to the house briefly and that she'd shortly be leaving for her over-thirties night in town.

With trepidation, Trudy went upstairs and got dressed. Then she took a seat in the bay window at the front, where she spent a while applying her make-up. She was close enough to the glass to be noticeable, but far enough away to avoid any bolt that might come crashing through the pane.

The two detectives took up position in the kitchen at the rear of the house. As Slack had already tried – and failed – to gain entry at the front, Sunita suspected he was far more likely to attempt any break-in through the back.

They didn't have long to wait. Just after eight fifteen, they heard a scraping noise and a thump. Sunita guessed that Slack had clambered onto the wooden fence from the field next door and jumped into the Marwoods' back garden.

Vickers, armed with a taser and a truncheon, pressed himself against the wall next to the back door. Sunita sat at the kitchen table in the fading light ready to meet their expected visitor face to face.

Footsteps thudded along the concrete path. Sunita had left the door unlocked, saving any intruder the need to smash one of its glass panes. The knob turned. The door creaked open. A man's black boot stepped onto the black-tiled kitchen floor. Sunita waited until Slack had taken a second step. Then she called out a greeting.

'Come in, Mr Slack,' she said.

The visitor's olive-skinned face was etched with shock and surprise, but, seconds later, so were the faces of the two detectives.

For instead of a crossbow in his hands, their visitor was clutching... a bouquet of flowers. Den Slack may've considered turning on his heels, but the inspector was too quick. As soon as their visitor was clear of the threshold, he slammed the door shut and stood against it.

'What's this all about?' Slack demanded, as he stood in the middle of the kitchen between the two detectives. 'I've come to see Trudy.'

Vickers tapped his shoulder. 'Last time we spoke to you was half past seven last night, when you were warned you were under arrest. Then you ran off and, while down an alley, laid your filthy hands on the sergeant here.'

Slack slumped down onto a chair. 'I shouldn't have run off. I realise that now. I should've waited to see why you wanted to talk to me. I'm sorry I touched you, miss.'

Sunita frowned at him as she stood up and approached him.

'Oh you're full of apologies now we've cornered you. But try and get out of this one. You're under arrest on suspicion of murder.'

The stallholder lost his temper on hearing these words. He hurled his bouquet of yellow lilies and blue irises onto the tabletop.

Then he jumped up and punched the sergeant in the stomach, leaving her winded.

Vickers, a fraction taller than the intruder and physically fitter, grabbed him from behind and knocked him to the floor. He then held him down as he screamed and shouted abuse. Slowly recovering from the assault, Sunita managed to make a call to the force control room so the local patrol could be alerted.

Trudy had all the while been ordered to remain in the living room by the detectives. But, alarmed at hearing the commotion, she rushed to the kitchen.

She stood in the doorway, trembling. 'Have you caught him?'

Sunita nodded. 'Yes, it's all under control,' she muttered as she regained her breath.

While gazing across the kitchen, Trudy recognised Slack's hair and face as he lay crushed upon the floor.

'Why did you kill Coral, you bastard?' she screamed. 'And why were you after me? What have we done to you?'

Slack lay motionless with the weight of Vickers' body still pressing upon him. He struggled to speak. 'I ain't killed no one. I came here with a peace offering.'

Sunita pointed out the flowers spread across the table.

'These blooms here – they're for you. I thought I'd give you a surprise, so I came round the back. I've come to take you to the over-thirties night.'

Trudy harrumphed. 'I told you it was over between us,' she said before marching off into the house.

Vickers pressed his knee into the small of Slack's back, causing the unwelcome visitor to cry out.

'That's enough from you. That's for Oliver and the women.'

Sunita tutted. 'No more of that, please, Tom,' she murmured. 'We want a nice, clean arrest. I know he probably deserves a good thrashing, but we've got to keep our reputation for fair play.'

Just then the doorbell rang and two armed policemen marched in and burst into the kitchen. They were bewildered at first on seeing the flowers but Sunita quickly explained what had happened.

Then, as Slack was handcuffed, Vickers recited the caution, 'Culloden Slack, I'm arresting you on suspicion of the murder of Oliver Bufton, Angelina Moretto, Coral Devon and Virginia Holland. You may also face other charges. You don't have to say anything unless you wish to do so, but what you say may be given in evidence.'

Sunita ordered the constables to turn out Slack's pockets. In doing so, they found the key that operated the Humber Pig, which Vickers seized.

Slack shouted, swore and struggled with the officers as he was led from the kitchen and out through the front door.

The two detectives strolled into the living room, where Trudy had now settled on the settee. Sunita smiled at her before turning to the inspector.

'Tom, there's something that doesn't add up here.'

'How d'you mean, Sunita?

'If he came to kill Trudy, where's his crossbow? And why bring flowers?'

Vickers sat down on the settee. 'The crossbow. That's a thought. I wonder what he's done with it.'

She shrugged. 'Maybe it's in the armoured carrier.'

'Yes, maybe. Well, I've got the keys so I can go and have a look. But there's no way I'm going to attempt to drive that thing. I'll get onto transport and arrange for them to take it back to St James Street. After that, since I'm the arresting officer, I guess I should head that way myself.'

Sunita nodded. 'I've tried to let the boss know what's happened but his phone must be off.'

He grinned. 'Keep trying him. The guvnor will be well pleased we've finally caught the guy. He was talking about a Midlands manhunt. We've saved him all that bother.'

After he left, Sunita sat in the living room, talking to Trudy and trying to comfort her. The past few days had been an ordeal.

'Never mind. It's all over,' the sergeant told her. 'We've got a wealth of evidence and Den Slack's going to go to jail for a very long time.'

But, as they spoke, the nagging thoughts kept creeping into Sunita's mind. Den Slack hadn't arrived there like a crazed attacker lusting for the blood of a woman who'd spurned him. He'd arrived like a penitent suitor who, although stung by rejection, was striving to win back a woman's affection.

Had Den Slack, the fairground man, been misjudged? Or were the flowers just part of a preliminary move to inveigle his way into Trudy's house? Would he have coaxed her into relaxing her guard so he could attack her when she least suspected?

She was unable to rid her mind of the worrying possibility that he might, after all, be innocent of murder.

Chapter 55

Gavin Roscoe thumbed through the national newspapers on his desk the next morning. The Israeli Prime Minister was battling corruption allegations. A panda had given birth to twins at a French zoo. And, closer to home, three of the tabloids carried reports on how police hunting for a West Midlands serial killer had carried out a raid on a travelling fair.

He stood up and gazed out of his window at the young mothers and children in the park. He was anxiously waiting to hear whether DS Roy's scheme to trap Den Slack had proved successful.

Several times he'd come close to phoning her or DI Vickers. But each time he'd stopped himself. It was only half past eight. They'd both been working ceaselessly for the past two days. They needed their sleep. They were both highly reliable and he would hear from them as soon as they had any news.

Then his desk phone rang and Chief Superintendent Norris's voice roared out of the handset.

'Is that you, Gavin? My office. Right now, please.'

The apprehensive chief inspector climbed the stairs to the second floor and then stepped along the corridor to her office.

'Ah Gavin,' she said as he knocked and entered.

She'd manoeuvred her wheelchair into the middle of the room while waiting for him. She'd been spending the last few minutes peering at portraits of former police chiefs on the wall. The latest issue of the *Queensbridge Gazette* was on her desk.

'I'm not happy about some of these headlines,' she moaned. 'Did you read the report in the *Gazette* about the pop star's father in America?'

'Yes, ma'am. One of the reporters did some research and found the singer was a witness in court against a drug dealer using her real name, Coral Lewis.'

'The father's suggesting there may be a drugs cartel operating in the region involving people in the electrical industry and believes this is connected with the murders. He says he told you about it, but you showed no interest.'

'That's not completely fair, ma'am. This man's got a bee in his bonnet about his daughter being targeted because she got involved with drugs. But our inquiries strongly suggest she was killed by mistake and Mrs Marwood was the intended victim.'

She wheeled herself across the carpet towards him while he found himself a chair.

'I'm sorry, Gavin. The ACC and myself are in agreement on this. You've had your chance. You've made no real progress on this case. From the middle of next week, all the files from Operation Promenade are being handed over to DCI Ainslie Hill and you'll be switched to other cases.'

The chief inspector felt as shocked as a rabbit in a snake-pit. He realised she'd been concerned over his lack of success in finding the killer. But hearing he was being replaced came as a blow to both his pride and his authority.

'That's a bit harsh, ma'am. We were just beginning to move forward with the investigation. We've got a fresh suspect on our radar.'

'I can't see any signs of headway being made at all,' she muttered as she wheeled herself back behind her desk.

Roscoe frowned. 'I'm surprised you're giving so much credence to a man in America obsessed with the notion his daughter's been killed by a drug dealer. While I'm sure Mr Lewis's information was intended to be helpful, I didn't find it relevant to our inquiry. His information hasn't been ignored altogether. It's been passed to the drugs squad.'

'So who's this suspect you've got?'

'Thanks mainly to DS Roy, our main suspect's turned out to be a fairground worker from Birmingham.'

'Good, so you've got this man in custody, have you?'

The chief inspector knew he'd have to choose his words carefully. 'No, ma'am. I'm afraid I've got to report that, when two of our team went to arrest him, he managed to escape.'

'Gavin, are you telling me you believe you know the killer's identity but that he's still at large after a bungled arrest?'

'Well, I wouldn't put it quite like that.'

'How the devil would you put it then?'

'I'd say strenuous efforts are being made to secure his arrest, believed imminent.'

Roscoe wished now he'd acted on his own instincts and launched a major manhunt the moment he learned Slack had fled the fairground, instead of leaving the task to his colleagues.

I shouldn't have listened to my sergeant, he thought to himself.

The chief superintendent leaned forward across her desk. 'Why haven't you got dozens of officers scouring the region? Where's the armed response team, sniffer dogs and so on?'

'We didn't want to go to all that trouble and expense when we believed we could trap our suspect with a low-key operation.'

'A low-key operation?'

The chief inspector was about to answer her when there was a knock on the door.

Norris glared. 'We're busy!' she shouted.

The door opened a fraction. Brett Dawson's anxious face appeared in the opening.

'What is it, Dawson?' Roscoe snapped.

'So sorry to bother you, Chief Superintendent, but it's important. Wanted to let the DCI know Den Slack was arrested in Stratford last night.'

The chief inspector felt like a condemned man saved from the gallows at the eleventh hour. Just as the hangman's noose was being tightened over his head, a young knight on a white charger had arrived with a reprieve.

He smiled. 'Thanks for letting me know, Dawson,' he told the constable as he closed the door.

'This is the fairground man that's been arrested, Gavin?'

'Yes, ma'am.'

'How do you believe he's connected with the case?'

'We're confident he's the man that stabbed Oliver Bufton in early April. There's evidence he was associating with Miss Moretto and he befriended Mrs Marwood. As regards his arrest, I put my faith in the sergeant and inspector and it looks as though we've been rewarded.'

When Roscoe returned to CID, Tom Vickers was sitting on a desk outside his door, drinking coffee and talking to Brett Dawson.

Roscoe sighed. 'Right, Tom. We've got just a few days to crack this case before Ainslie Hill takes over.'

The inspector drew a quick breath. 'Ainslie Hill? That's unbelievable.'

'So quickly tell me what happened last night.'

'Just as DS Roy predicted, Den Slack came to the Marwoods' place. He came to the back door and we tackled him, but he wasn't armed. He was carrying a bunch of flowers.'

'A bunch of flowers?'

'Sir, it appears he was trying to get Mrs Marwood to go out on another date. But he became violent when we told him he was being arrested and punched the sergeant in the stomach.'

'Is she all right?'

'I spoke to her this morning. She's fine. I think she's been to see the prisoner, Slack. He's been causing problems overnight. He's been banging on his cell door and shouting constantly.'

* * *

Just after ten o'clock, struggling and mouthing obscenities, Den Slack was brought up from his basement cell to the ground-floor interview room at St James Street.

Roscoe and Vickers arrived a few minutes later, accompanied by Slack's solicitor, Roger Sims. Roscoe glared at Slack across the oblong table after cautioning him.

'Now, before we go any further, what size footwear do you take?'

Slack looked astonished. 'Footwear? I take size-nines. Why? Are you going to buy me a new pair of shoes for my birthday?'

'Examine his shoes, Inspector, and check they're size-nines.'

Vickers stepped round the table, crouched on the floor and studied the suspect's shoes.

'Yes, sir. I'd say they're size-nines, same as mine.'

Roscoe nodded as the inspector returned to his seat. 'As you know, we're investigating the deaths of four people. All were killed by crossbow bolts stolen from the Shawley Green archery club. The green Carina found at Deacons Park was used in that burglary.'

'No comment.'

'You were one of two men with a Jeep who stabbed Oliver Bufton in Queensbridge on 5 April and a man matching your description was seen at Angelina Moretto's home on 18 April.'

'No comment.'

'You befriended Trudy Marwood after meeting her at an over-thirties event. An eye-witness saw your Jeep near

Mrs Marwood's house on the night her niece was murdered.'

'No comment.'

'That bring us to this week. Virginia Holland – whom you met at the same event– was found murdered by a similar bolt.'

'No comment.'

Mr Sims interrupted. 'I'm confused about the vehicles, Chief Inspector. Could you clarify what vehicles are involved and what connection they have to my client? Couldn't someone else working for the funfair have had access to them?'

Roscoe sighed. 'There are four vehicles – the Carina, the Jeep, a Land Rover and a military vehicle. Mr Slack had access to them all.'

The solicitor smiled. 'The evidence doesn't seem very strong. I can't see why you arrested Mr Slack.'

Roscoe frowned. 'He has connections with the murders of four people. His stolen Toyota car was used in a burglary at an archery club. The bolts taken in that burglary are the same kind that were used in the murders. We also believe he was planning to murder Trudy Marwood, after he was spurned by her.'

'That's a lie!' screamed Slack. 'I'd never hurt her. We were made for each other.'

The lawyer tutted. 'I strongly recommend you remain silent for the moment, Mr Slack. Chief Inspector, my information is that my client was invited into Mrs Marwood's house by the lady herself last night.'

Vickers scowled. 'Hardly. Mr Slack came in uninvited through the back door and, when we told him he was under arrest, he assaulted our colleague, DS Roy.'

Roscoe glanced at Slack. 'Would you care to say anything about that?'

Slack shook his head. 'No comment.'

After a whispered conversation between Slack and the solicitor, Mr Sims requested a brief adjournment. When the interview resumed later, he informed the detectives Slack wished to make a short statement and read it to them.

> *I admit knowing Mr Bufton, Miss Moretto and Mrs Holland. But I have no knowledge of Coral Devon and deny killing any of them. In the early hours of 23 June, I couldn't sleep and drove to Mrs Marwood's house just before three o'clock in the morning in the hope of seeing her arrive back from her night out. I wanted to talk to her and assure her of my best intentions towards her. I couldn't make any contact with her and drove away.*

'That's the end of the statement and, if I'm allowed to make a personal observation, it looks as if the police have been clutching at straws to find someone – anyone – who could've been responsible for these deaths.'

'Complete twaddle,' Roscoe retorted. 'We plan to keep your client in custody a little longer as I'm certain we'll need to discuss these deaths with him again. We also have other matters to deal with – evading arrest and assaulting my sergeant being just two of them.'

After Slack had been returned to his cell, Roscoe and Vickers continued discussing the case in the chief inspector's room.

'Very uncouth individual that Den Slack,' Roscoe muttered. 'I fancy he may've gone to the same charm school as Gordon Ramsay and Liam Gallagher.'

'Are we taking action against other members of the Slack family, sir?'

Roscoe nodded. 'We may charge Tobias Slack with common assault on you and DS Roy and his brother with indecent assault on her. There's also the archery club burglary, the stolen car, the untaxed vehicles and the little matter of some poaching.'

Vickers raised an eyebrow. 'Poaching, sir?'

'Yes. We've found traces of deer entrails in the back of the military vehicle. A stag was slaughtered with a crossbow bolt by poachers on the Bickleigh Estate in the second week of June. The Slacks had been using it to shoot illegal game.'

Chapter 56

Seeds of doubt had been planted in Gavin Roscoe's mind about Den Slack's culpability. The evidence against him was circumstantial, just as it had been with Ricky Stanton. There were a multitude of questions in his mind that the pathologist Dr Reynolds might have helped to answer. But he was somewhere in Wales, examining a body.

After several failed attempts to reach him, he called senior forensic scientist Dr Alice Ling, an expert on textile fibres.

Roscoe began by asking about the white threads found snagged on the brickwork at Miss Moretto's house.

'Well,' she said, 'we carefully examined them. We decided it was muslin, which is a slightly different material from the cheesecloth it was first assumed to be. It's used in fashion, baby blankets, photography backdrops and many other things. We also carefully examined Mr Den Slack's shirt that CID brought in. It was produced from a finely woven cloth, but the fibres were different and there was no sign of any brick dust. So it's unlikely the fibres on the wall were left by Slack.'

Roscoe frowned. 'You're sure about that?'

'Ninety-nine per cent.'

He shrugged. 'OK. What about the tyre track at Biddington? Could any of the Slacks' vehicles have left that impression in the mud?'

Her voice was apologetic. 'Our vehicle expert has examined the tread on all the family's vehicles. None of the tyre treads match the imprint left in the mud.'

Roscoe felt as powerless as a child who'd spent all day building the finest sandcastle on the beach only for it to be swept away by the advancing tide.

'Perhaps the tyres have been switched,' he grumbled.

'That's possible, sir. If you find any previous tyres, we'd of course be happy to examine them.'

He had one more chance to revive the case against the fairground worker. The shoe marks.

'Dr Ling, can I ask you about the shoe prints on Miss Moretto's body?'

'Yes. I was just coming to that. We've checked the impressions on the national database of shoe imprints and we couldn't find any matches. As your DI Vickers discovered, Mr Slack takes a size-nine shoe. The impressions left were either a man's size-seven shoe or a woman's size eight and a half.'

The chief inspector groaned. He'd been confident he was holding some promising cards in his hands. He'd planned to play them at his next interview with Slack. Now, one by one, they were slipping from his grasp.

The forensic officer mumbled an apology. 'Sorry. This isn't what you were wishing to hear, Chief Inspector.'

Roscoe sighed. 'You're right. Our case is sinking fast.'

'Very sorry, sir. My mother was a wise woman. In situations like this, she'd say, "Don't hang out washing when the pegs are broken."'

'Your mother was a wise woman, Dr Ling,' he murmured as he ended the call.

He partly blamed DS Roy for his predicament. It was she who'd first suggested the killer might be a fairground worker.

At the same time, DI Vickers had come across Elijah Slack – a man found driving near Worcester in an

American Jeep – and the Slacks' fair had been thrust into the case.

Sunita Roy was in a light-hearted mood when he called her mobile and she answered almost at once with a cheerful, 'Good morning, sir.'

'No, it's not, Sergeant,' he told her. 'The whole case against Den Slack's at a point of collapse.' He explained what Dr Ling had told him.

'Well, it was a hunch that, initially, looked like paying off. I'm very sorry it hasn't worked out, sir.'

Roscoe sighed. 'I suppose there isn't much either of us can say. Ainslie Hill is taking over the case in a few days and I suppose it'll be down to him whether you continue as part of the Promenade team. As for me, I'll probably get switched to burglaries and bag snatches.'

Sunita laughed. 'Don't be too harsh on yourself, sir. We gave it our best shot. It just didn't turn out the way we'd hoped. Sir, while we're still running the case, a thought has just occurred to me. Who did we get to check the CCTV cameras for Warwick Road? Was it Omar Khalid?'

'No. Brett Dawson. He's spent some time trawling through the footage for Biddington and Oakdale Road and he's also done some work on the Warwick Road cameras.'

'I think we need to focus on Warwick Road. I've found out there are more cameras there and there's a good chance we might get some luck.'

'I wish I could be as optimistic as you. By the way, if you've got time, we're having a small gathering at the tearooms to welcome my son back from hospital. It would be good to see you, if you can make it.'

'That's kind of you, sir. I'll do my best to come.'

* * *

Two hours later, Roscoe was just about to leave the office when he received a call from Dr Reynolds.

His voice boomed down the phone. 'Gavin, old fruit. I'm sorry I haven't called earlier. Been stuck in a quarry with a corpse.'

'Not to worry, Silas. What d'you know?'

'Gavin, this lady from Cranleigh Park, Mrs Holland, wasn't killed by the bolt we extricated from her body.'

'Of course she was killed by it. I saw the bloody thing poking out of her chest as sure as I'm sitting here now.'

'Yes, that's what you saw. But, when we carried out the post-mortem this morning, we realised the wound was unlike those of the first three victims.'

The chief inspector got up and started pacing round the office. 'But there was a bolt embedded in the woman's chest, Silas.'

'Yes, I know, old fruit. Your forensic people are examining it for dabs as we speak. But she was stabbed with a knife first and then the bolt was implanted in the wound.'

'How can you be so certain she was stabbed?'

'It's all down to the shape and size of the slash. The wounds on the other victims had a cross shape. This injury was caused by a long-bladed knife. Afterwards, the bolt was inserted to give the impression the victim had been shot with it. The cause of death was a stab wound to the heart.'

Roscoe was stunned to find the style of the fourth murder was so different from the previous three. DS Roy might be right, he thought. They could be dealing with two killers: the crossbow maniac and a copycat killer.

'Silas, if I understand you correctly, you seem to be suggesting that the person who struck in Cranleigh Park has tried to disguise the crime as a crossbow killing? That they're trying to put the bowman in the frame for it?'

'I deal in facts, Gavin – not hypotheses. Do you remember what Isaac Newton said? *Hypotheses non fingo* – I make no hypotheses. In the Cranleigh Park murder, we believe Mrs Holland remained alive long enough to start daubing out a word or number. The killer may well have stood watching her dying moments before thrusting the bolt into her chest.'

The chief inspector sat down at his desk. 'Silas, what kind of knife could have inflicted the wound?'

'I'd think we could be talking about a sturdy kitchen knife with a single cutting edge. The approximate depth of the wound track was thirteen centimetres, and the blade was directed downwards at a forty-five-degree angle.'

He went on to explain that the injury caused a massive haemorrhage in Mrs Holland's left chest cavity and her left lung had collapsed. Her pancreas and abdominal aorta – the human body's main blood vessel – had been pierced.

'There were no signs she put up a struggle. There were no traces of drugs or alcohol in the body either. It looks as if she'd just prepared her Pimm's and hadn't had a chance to take a single sip.'

* * *

George Roscoe was surprised how bright the afternoon seemed and how cold and fresh the air was as he squeezed into the front passenger seat of his friend Sean Munro's ten-year-old Astra. George's new girlfriend, Amanda, clambered into the back.

'This is so kind of you, Sean,' said George as they set off for Queensbridge.

'Think nothing of it,' said Sean as he grinned broadly. 'It's what mates are for. How're you getting on anyway? How's your chest?'

'Getting better every day,' said George. 'The nurses have given me some painkillers to take.'

'You look a little fragile still.'

Amanda smiled. 'He is. But the doctors needed his bed.'

George glanced across at Sean. 'Have I missed much of the course? Amanda says I haven't.'

'Not much. We had a mock trial yesterday, didn't we, Amanda? I had to question Tommy O'Sullivan, who was playing the part of a witness to a road accident. I didn't ask enough questions and the tutor lost his rag with me a bit.'

'I can't wait to get back,' said George. 'I've got to see my GP, but after that I'm hoping I'll be well enough.'

There was a pause as Sean negotiated a roundabout.

'That yob who stabbed you has appeared in court and denied attempted robbery and assault. We'll be asked to appear as witnesses.'

'I know. The officer in the case saw me in the ward,' said George.

After forty-five minutes, the car drew up outside the Apollo Tearooms, where George's mother had arranged a light tea to mark his release from hospital.

Helen and Melody dashed onto the pavement and helped him out of the car.

'Welcome back, George!' said his mother, wrapping her arms around him.

'I've only been gone two weeks. Mind my shoulder!' he said. Then he kissed his sister lightly on the cheek.

'Mum, Mel – this is Sean. He's very kindly brought me back. And you know Amanda.'

'Hello, Sean,' said Helen. 'Thank you so much for bringing him. Hello, Amanda. Come in and I'll get you all some tea.'

Within half an hour, the three trainee constables were tucking into sandwiches and cakes at a reserved table set for twelve people.

Gavin Roscoe arrived when most of the cakes had gone. He hugged his son.

'Those nurses seem to have been looking after you rather well,' he murmured.

George grinned. 'How's the case going, Dad?'

'Don't ask. Why I do believe my young sergeant's just arrived. This is a nice surprise.'

Sunita Roy smiled as she pushed open the door.

He hurried to greet her. 'So you found time to drop in?'

'Yes, sir. But I can't stay long. I promised Derek Underhill I'd collect Miss Moretto's jewellery and take it to her niece in Stratford.'

'Come and sit down,' Helen said. 'You like lemon tea, don't you?'

Sunita nodded. 'If it's not too much trouble.'

She exchanged a few words with George before joining them at the table.

Roscoe sat down opposite her. 'Your face is looking a lot better,' he said. He then explained Dr Reynolds' revelation that Virginia Holland had been stabbed and a bolt placed in the wound.

She took the news in her stride. 'As soon as I arrived in Cranleigh Park just after the murder, I sensed Mrs Holland's murder was different from the others. Listen, sir. I've had a useful tip. On my way here, I bumped into Susan from the *Gazette*.'

'Oh, I know. Susan Ellis-Jones.'

'Yes. I met her for the first time at Cranleigh Park. A few minutes ago, she stopped me in the High Street and we had a quick chat. Well, during our conversation, she let something rather important slip. Sir, with your permission, I'd like to spend a few days making some inquiries on my own. I've got a feeling they might lead us to the door of the copycat killer.'

Chapter 57

It was a warm but cloudy day as the white Luton van trundled into Warwick's Crompton Gardens and stopped halfway along the street early on Saturday.

Tom Vickers cut the engine. 'We couldn't have asked for a better journey, Sunita.'

The sergeant nodded as she gazed at the three-storey block, which was about to become her home.

'There was just that small hold-up on the Stratford Road.'

She delved in her handbag for the keys and walked briskly up the path, stopping only to admire the solitary red rose bush close to the ground-floor flat, which was in full bloom.

Vickers had trouble keeping up with her as she ran up the stairs to the first floor of the building, which altogether contained six flats. As she proudly opened the door to her own flat for the first time, they both noticed a musty smell and a pile of mail on the doormat. Without stopping for a second, she headed into the living room.

She clutched his arm. 'It's just as I remember it.'

Tom kissed her. 'I hope you're very happy here, Sunita.'

'I'm sure I will be. Before we start unloading, shall I make some tea? I'll just get the kettle and cups out of the van.'

Fifteen minutes later, the pair were sitting on two of Sunita's newly purchased dining chairs, drinking tea out of two china mugs.

She glanced at him and smiled. 'So were there any conditions attached to Den Slack's release?'

'Yes. He's got to report to a police station once a week until our inquiries are finished. But, between you and me, he's out of the picture now. There's no strong evidence against him regarding any of the deaths. Witnesses at the fair confirmed he was at the ghost train when Bufton, Miss Moretto and Mrs Holland were killed.'

Sunita nodded. 'I'm intrigued by the Holland murder.'

'Maybe because it's so fresh in our minds.'

'Maybe. But I think it's more because of the message she tried to daub on the patio. You do realise, Tom, that only the husband and gardener were seen at the property around the time of the murder? We've no eye-witness accounts of anyone else. And we've no description of any unaccounted vehicles in Cranleigh Park at the time.'

Vickers took a sip of his tea. 'We can probably rule out the gardener. He's a most unlikely suspect. He's nearly seventy-seven and hobbles as he walks. He seems to be wilting and shrivelling up even more quickly than his flowers.'

She laughed. 'So we're left with the husband as the only real suspect, Tom.'

He put his cup down. 'If I was a betting man, I'd put money on it being Larry Holland,' he said. 'Marital partners are always high up on the lists of suspects. Did you realise around a third of female murder victims are killed by close partners? That was in a magazine last week. I know Mrs Holland just wrote SI, but she might have been trying to write SL.'

Sunita shook her head. 'It's unlikely she was trying to suggest her husband.'

'Why do you say that? His initials are SL – Simon Laurence. Or maybe it's SI and she was intending to write Simon.'

'If she'd been trying to blame him, she'd have surely written LA for Larry or even HU for husband. It's clear Mrs Holland never called him by his first name of Simon.'

He smiled. 'We'll have to agree to differ on this one,' he said.

'The boss thought she was trying to write SLACK,' said Sunita after a pause. 'But it's unlikely she knew that was his surname.'

'We were having a chat in the office. All sorts of suggestions came up. Dawson said maybe we should look for the owner of a Mercedes SL while Omar wondered if the killer came from Sri Lanka or Slough.'

'The possibilities are endless. Come on. We'd better get the furniture out of the van.'

He glanced at his watch. 'Yes. I've got to get the van back. We'd better get moving. Will you be all right here after I've gone?'

She nodded. 'Yes. I've got heaps to do here. But later on, I'm going to take a trip over to Cranleigh Park. I've got an idea why Mrs Holland was targeted. But I've got a few questions to ask first.'

* * *

Gilbert Stout didn't receive many visitors. He was therefore surprised when he heard someone crunching their way across his gravel drive and knocking loudly on his front door on Saturday afternoon.

That's strange, I'm not expecting anyone, he thought. He crept into the lounge and peered out from behind his blinds.

His visitor was an attractive woman with long, dark hair, hanging loosely over her shoulders. She was slim, in her mid-twenties, Asian and wearing a smart grey trouser suit.

He scowled. 'Hope it's not the bloody police again.' Reluctantly, he ventured to the door and opened it cautiously.

Sunita gave a pleasant smile. 'Mr Stout? I'm making inquiries about the sad death of your neighbour.'

He glared as she produced her warrant card. 'What are you – police or press?'

'DS Roy, Heart of England CID.'

'Did you know you're the third person the police have sent? I suppose you'd better come in.'

Sunita recalled reading previous statements taken by colleagues. But she'd not been entirely satisfied with the answers he'd given.

As she was led through the drab hall with its blue patterned wallpaper, she felt he might be holding back some crucial information. He brought her to a halt in his back room, where French doors led to the rear garden.

'Mr Stout, do you mind if we go outside? I want to understand the layout of the Hollands' garden.'

The homeowner nodded. 'By all means. I'm really surprised to see you. I thought the investigation had finished. I heard on the news a man had been arrested.'

'Unfortunately, we've had to let that guy go and our investigation's by no means over.'

She walked slowly to the side of Stout's home, casting her eyes around as she went. A hedge which was a metre and a half tall marked the boundary between the two front gardens. It stopped close to the centre of Stout's land where the border was then defined by a two-metre-high fence which continued until the bottom of the garden.

She realised the neighbour's view of the Hollands' patio – either through or above the hedge – was obscured by the rose arch, situated at least four metres from the boundary with Stout's garden. The two-metre-high metal arch had been created from railings which were intertwined with red and yellow roses.

However, Stout had a partial view of the side of the house and the Hollands' side gate through occasional gaps in the hedge – perhaps the result of disease or a lack of watering.

Sunita thanked Stout for allowing her to view his garden. 'Shall we return inside?'

The pair sat down at an oval dining table.

'I'd offer you some tea but I ran out of milk this morning,' Stout said.

'That's all right, sir. There are more important things on my mind than tea. Mr Stout, you've told our team you noticed Bob Hopkinson, the gardener, leaving through the side gate at somewhere between quarter past eleven and half-past eleven on the day of the murder. You're absolutely positive about that time?'

'Yes, definitely. I'd just finished listening to the eleven o'clock news on the radio.'

'And you're sure it wasn't the half-past-ten news?'

'There's no half-past-ten news on the station I listen to.'

She nodded. 'The reason I'm questioning you about this is that the gardener claims he left at a quarter to eleven – half an hour earlier.'

'I can only tell you what I recall. I'm sure he was going through the gate at a quarter past eleven or shortly afterwards.'

'You stand by that?'

'Look, you're the third person to question me about this, and I'm getting sick of it. It's upsetting enough poor Mrs Holland got murdered and there seems to be this lunatic with a crossbow on the loose. It was definitely a quarter past eleven or thereafter. I remember it because old Bob was walking differently.'

She raised an eyebrow. 'What do you mean?'

'Well, when I've seen him before, he always seemed to have rounded shoulders. This time he didn't seem to be bent over quite so much. It struck me as strange. I thought that perhaps he'd had some kind of medical procedure.'

Sunita shrugged her shoulders. 'All right. I don't think I need to take up your time anymore, Mr Stout. I'm sorry you've been bothered again, but, as you can appreciate, this is a serious crime we're investigating.'

'I know. You've got your job to do,' said Stout as he opened the front door for his visitor.

She stepped onto the drive. 'You're not going on holiday, are you?'

'No, I'm not. Why?'

'You may be called to give evidence. Please let us know if your plans change.'

'All right. I will,' said Stout. 'But I can't see how you could've learnt anything of any value from me.'

When she returned to her car, Sunita called the genealogist in Birmingham that the force used for family history research.

'Yes, that's right, Holland,' she said. 'That's the lady's married name. Unfortunately, I don't know her maiden name, but her date of birth is 17 May 1981 and the birth was registered in Warwickshire. You'll find out as much as you can? That's cool.'

Chapter 58

Sunita Roy watched over her shoulder as Tom Vickers removed Den Slack's picture from the whiteboard and pinned up a photograph of Larry Holland.

The inspector glanced behind him. 'Isn't the briefing due to start round about now?'

'Any minute now.'

Sunita and Vickers seated themselves next to the board. Dawson and Khalid were sitting on chairs behind, along with twenty-four-year-old DC Wendy Hopkirk. And soon after Roscoe joined them.

'Right, this afternoon we're going to question Larry Holland again. It's exactly a week since his wife's murder. As it's a Wednesday, I think we can assume he should have the afternoon off and be at home.

'It'll be good if we can take the managing director of Sheldon Lifts by surprise. I'd like DS Roy and DI Vickers to come with me. Dawson, how are you getting on?'

'We've started going through the CCTV for Warwick Road for a second time,' Dawson replied, 'but it's a long process, sir.'

'All right. Stick at it. DC Hopkirk, I want you to phone companies that manufacture, supply and sell crossbows. We need to find out customer details. I know it's a tall order but it might turn up something. Khalid, I want you to look into Bufton's and Miss Moretto's personal relationships. I know we've done it before. We've got to go back over old ground until we unearth something, I'm afraid.'

Three hours later, Roscoe, Sunita and Vickers travelled in separate cars to Larry Holland's house. The sergeant tried the front door, but there was no reply.

Roscoe tutted. 'Strange that – seeing as it's a Wednesday afternoon when he's often at home, according to neighbours.'

'Don't worry,' said Sunita. 'I've got an idea he'll be in Stratford.'

'Have you? How's that?'

'I'll explain later. For the moment, sir, why don't you follow me?'

The chief inspector was puzzled that Sunita had a second address for Larry Holland. As he set off behind her Peugeot for the ten-mile journey with the inspector following on behind, he muttered to himself, 'She knows a lot more than she's letting on.'

After around twenty minutes passing through open country, the cars reached the Stratford suburbs and the two men followed Sunita into Dorchester Avenue. She stopped on the right, across the street from a row of buildings. The two others parked behind.

The chief inspector got out and stretched as she walked towards him. 'Do you mind telling us whose place this is, Sergeant?'

She nodded and pointed to some flats on the left. 'Holland's girlfriend lives in the first-floor flat here.'

'Girlfriend? How did you find that out?'

'It's a long story, sir.'

'I knew you'd got something up your sleeve. Look, you should really have mentioned this to me before.'

'I'm sorry, sir,' she replied. 'I have been working on some theories of my own. I wasn't convinced they were right and didn't want to waste anyone's time simply because of a hunch.'

She glanced at a silver Porsche 911 which was parked beside the building, next to a red Mini Countryman.

'That, sir, if I'm not mistaken, is Holland's car.'

With the sergeant leading the way, the three detectives climbed the external staircase that led to Jasmine Turner's door. She pressed the doorbell and they waited.

Within seconds, the door was opened by the archery club secretary in a striking yellow top and blue jeans. She was shocked to see the three visitors gathered at the top of her staircase.

Roscoe showed her his warrant card. 'Sorry to bother you, madam. Heart of England Police. Mr Holland here?'

Jasmine Turner, whose long blonde hair was brushing against her shoulders, hesitated for a moment. 'Um, no. No, he's not.'

The chief inspector was beginning to lose his patience. 'Come on. His car's outside.'

'Is it? Maybe he's here then. I'll go and look.'

Less than a minute later, she reappeared. 'You'd better come in.'

The three guests followed her across the beige carpet into the living room, where newspapers, books and magazines were strewn across her fawn-coloured settee. Sunita noticed a photomontage of Midlands archers arranged above the brick fireplace.

'You'd better sit down. I'll call Larry,' she said.

Roscoe found himself a place on the settee. 'Not the biggest living room I've ever been in,' he moaned.

Sunita sat beside him while Vickers made himself comfortable in an armchair.

Larry Holland emerged sheepishly from his mistress's bedroom. He appeared to have dressed hurriedly in a white T-shirt and jeans. Jasmine remained behind him.

He attempted a smile. 'Good afternoon. You wished to see me?'

Roscoe frowned. 'Yes. Those tears you shed after your wife's demise were just part of a charade, weren't they?'

The businessman glared. 'How do you mean?'

'We've come here today to ask more questions about the death. Only two people could have ended her life – you or the gardener. We've had a whole team of people visiting neighbours and we're now convinced that nobody else visited the house in the narrow time frame between eleven and midday last Wednesday when the death is believed to have occurred. As the gardener is a doddery old man with no possible motive, we're inclined to rule him out of our inquiry. That just leaves you. And now we can see you're in a relationship with this lady, it appears to me you've got a strong motive for wanting your wife out of the way.'

Holland scowled as he stepped into the middle of the room. 'These are lies. I won't try and deny I've grown close to Jasmine here, but there's no way I'd have killed my wife with a crossbow – or any other weapon, for that matter. It would look mighty suspicious in any case, wouldn't it? A husband brutally slaughtering his wife just after he's arrived home? Surely I'd have arranged some comfortable alibi for myself if I'd wanted to dispose of her, wouldn't I?'

Sunita had been sitting quietly, listening to the conversation from her seat at the end of the sofa. She stood up.

'I'm afraid, sir, we're making a mistake in accusing Mr Holland.'

The chief inspector frowned. 'Pardon?'

She walked over to the fireplace. 'It wasn't Mr Holland who murdered Virginia. Let me explain. The Hollands' neighbour, Gilbert Stout, saw a figure that he assumed to be the gardener leaving through the side gate at the time of the murder. The person he saw was wearing a pale-green peaked cap, a blue check shirt and dark trousers. He naturally assumed this person to be Bob Hopkinson because that was the outfit Mr Hopkinson always wore. But this figure he spotted through a gap in the hedge wasn't Bob Hopkinson the gardener, was it, Miss Turner? It was you, wasn't it?'

All eyes in the room focussed upon Jasmine, who raised her hands in the air in protest.

'Don't be so ridiculous,' she said as she stood in the doorway.

Sunita leaned back against the mantelpiece. 'I've been making inquiries over the past few days. Mr Hopkinson had tended the garden that morning, but he left at around a quarter to eleven – long before the murder was committed. Gilbert Stout is a sound witness and quite rightly recalled seeing this figure that he took to be Hopkinson shortly after he'd listened to the eleven o'clock news on the radio.

'It was a very clever idea of yours, Miss Turner, to carry out the murder while dressed as the gardener. But you made a crucial mistake in your attempt to impersonate Hopkinson. He walks with a pronounced stoop, which the chief inspector and I noticed when we visited the house before Mrs Holland's death. The figure leaving through the side gate walked in an upright manner. Mr Stout had been puzzled by this and, when I questioned him in depth, he revealed this fact and said this was one reason why he'd remembered the incident.

'This set me on a path of thought that led me to conclude that Mrs Holland's killer had disguised themselves in order to carry out the murder–'

The chief inspector interrupted. 'That all sounds feasible. But how was the murder committed, Sergeant?'

Sunita nodded. 'This is what I believe happened. Miss Turner arrives at Cranleigh Park – possibly by bicycle, as this was the gardener's normal mode of transport. She brings with her some form of bag. She waits until she sees Hopkinson collect his bicycle from the side of the house and cycle off. Then she unfastens the side gate and enters the rear garden.

'Mrs Holland is sitting in her wicker chair engrossed in reading council agendas. She doesn't hear the intruder. The killer creeps up on her with a long-bladed knife which she'd been carrying in her bag. With all her might, she thrusts it into the victim's chest. Mrs Holland tumbles backwards on the chair. The murderess then takes a crimson bolt from her bag – from the same supply she'd herself ordered from the firm in Derbyshire. She finds the centre of the stab wound and drives its head deeply into the victim's chest.'

'This is absolutely monstrous!' screamed Jasmine. 'It was obviously the crossbow killer who did her in. Anyone can see that. She was sitting in the open with a drink and she was a sitting target. He shoots her. It's an easy job for him.'

Sunita shook her head. 'No. Our pathologist has told us Mrs Holland died from a stabbing and the bolt was inserted in the wound afterwards.'

Jasmine sneered. 'You're trying to frame me because you found out about me and Larry.'

Holland was looking despondent. He'd begun to feel that the sergeant's words had a certain ring of truth about them.

'So the killer then escapes, still dressed as the gardener, Sunita?' asked Vickers.

Sunita nodded. 'Miss Turner places the bloodstained knife in her bag. She may have brought with her a towel or cloth to wipe away traces of blood that must've splattered onto her hands and clothing and possibly a set of clothes to change into. She pulls her cap forward in order to hide her face and leaves – watched as she passes through the side gate by the inquisitive neighbour.'

Jasmine glared at her. 'A load of nonsense!'

Sunita ignored her. 'Mr Stout was unable to witness the actual murder because the Hollands had erected a substantial rose arch and various bushes, protecting their privacy on the patio. The murderess firmly believes she's committed the perfect crime. All the blame for it would be laid at the door of the crossbow killer.'

'So what was the significance of the letters written in blood?' asked Roscoe.

His sergeant smiled. 'Perhaps you're not aware of this, Miss Turner, but in her dying moments, Mrs Holland summoned up enough strength to haul herself onto her left side and wrote two letters on a patio stone in her own blood. We were uncertain to begin with what they meant, and the main consensus of opinion seemed to be that Mrs Holland was trying to write the letters SL. I've spent the past few days mulling this over and I'm convinced the letters were SI – the first two letters of the word SISTER. Because Mrs Holland was your sister, wasn't she, Miss Turner?'

The sergeant was surrounded by a set of shocked faces.

'What?' cried Holland. 'Have you taken leave of your senses?'

Although Jasmine Turner was shaking her head and muttering about 'damned lies', Sunita was determined to continue with her account.

Sunita stared directly at Jasmine. 'Mrs Holland recognised you as her killer, didn't she? And, as her life was ebbing away, she did her best to have you identified as the culprit.'

Roscoe was shaking his head. 'How did you work all this out, Sergeant?'

'Well, I made use of our family history researcher. I won't bore you with the full family tree, but suffice it to say, while Miss Turner's father was away at sea with the Royal Navy in the early 1980s, her mother, Daphne, had a romance with a man named Matthew Saunders. Mrs Holland – Virginia – was born as a result of that relationship.

'When news of the affair became public, it caused a scandal. Daphne divorced Jasmine's father, Michael Turner, and married Matthew. Jasmine was then placed in council care along with her brother while Virginia went on to enjoy a very comfortable life with her mother. These circumstances led to bitter resentment that continued throughout the two women's lives. Ultimately, Jasmine stole the heart of Virginia's husband and then stole Virginia's life.'

Jasmine glared at Sunita and waggled her right index finger in her face menacingly. 'You're a liar. I didn't murder her. It must've been the crossbow killer.'

But no one in the room was convinced by her entreaties. Even her lover, Holland, recognised her words were sounding hollow.

Sunita's explanation about Jasmine's family seemed compelling. The room briefly fell silent.

Then, as the woman continued to protest, Roscoe announced, 'Jasmine Turner, I'm arresting you on suspicion of the murder of Virginia Holland. You don't have to say anything unless you wish to do so, but what you say may be given in evidence.'

'It's all lies. Tell them, Larry!' Turner howled. 'I was working at the club when Ginny was murdered. I'm not the kind of person who'd do such a thing. It must've been that man Den Slack that's been in the news.'

Holland slumped down onto one of the dining chairs. He was shaking his head and crying.

'Why, oh why did you do it?' he asked his lover. 'You knew I was planning to divorce her. Why do something so foolish – so callous?'

Vickers handcuffed Jasmine. He and Sunita then led her down the external staircase and out into the street.

Chapter 59

Larry Holland travelled back to his home in Cranleigh Park on his own. To the detectives, he appeared a broken man.

Within the space of a week, his wife of fourteen years had been murdered and his long-term mistress had been unmasked as the killer.

His feelings towards Jasmine had instantly changed. He'd once showered her with love, warmth and passion, and he'd believed she reciprocated those feelings. Now, in a single horrific act which the police had been bound to uncover, she'd destroyed any future happiness they'd hoped to share. He wanted nothing more to do with her.

He didn't pause to consider the effects of his own behaviour on events. All he could think about was his lover's depravity. He couldn't rid his mind of the detective sergeant's words, 'Jasmine stole the heart of Virginia's husband and then stole Virginia's life.'

Was it possible Jasmine had pursued a relationship with him as part of a vendetta against her half-sister? Every time they kissed or made love were her feelings genuine? Or was she malevolently notching up points against her sister?

Jasmine had worked as his secretary for several years before leaving to take up her position at the archery club. He now began to wonder whether she'd applied for the post at Sheldon Lifts in the first place simply because he was Ginny's husband. He shook his head. No, that was far too implausible.

He couldn't recall Virginia ever mentioning a family feud. Perhaps the only animosity had come from Jasmine.

The woman had allowed her life to be overtaken by an obsession. A dangerous obsession that had led to murder.

As his car glided onto the drive of his home, he thought of phoning the local vicar about the funeral arrangements. But then he remembered the police had advised him Virginia's funeral could only go ahead with the coroner's permission – and that could be some weeks away. He felt overcome by depression. His life felt as out of control as a runaway train that was at risk of hurtling off the rails.

* * *

An indignant Jasmine Turner was driven to police headquarters, where she was booked in by the custody sergeant. She was photographed and fingerprinted and then placed in the same basement cell where, a few days earlier, Den Slack had been languishing.

DI Vickers smiled afterwards as he and Sunita climbed the stairs from the custody suite. 'The guvnor's going to be so pleased with you. That was a shock – killed by her own sister. Who'd have believed it?'

'Half-sister, to be precise. I got lucky, Tom. On Friday, I ran into a reporter from the *Gazette* who'd noticed Holland's Porsche at Cranleigh Park. She remembered seeing the same car outside Turner's flat when she interviewed her for an article. She also caught a glimpse of Holland coming out of her bedroom and passed that information to me. So, you see, the press have their uses.'

'So that's how you knew they'd been having an affair? Well done.'

'There was a bit of work involved too. I had to grill Gilbert Stout and put our family history guy to work.'

'She's going to need a good solicitor.'

'I overheard her requesting one as she was booked in.' She glanced out of the window. 'Anyway, Tom, I've just seen the DCI arriving. I guess he'll need me for the interview.'

'Sure. I'm going to see how Dawson's getting on with the CCTV. Do you fancy a drink in the Fleece when you're finished?'

'Cool. I'll catch you later.'

Just before six o'clock, Jasmine Turner was escorted into the ground-floor interview room by two policewomen. Her anger had dissipated. She looked pale and nervous.

She took a seat at the table and stared towards the window opposite, which offered an uninspiring view of the car park.

A few minutes later, she was joined by Roscoe and his sergeant, who were followed by solicitor Salman Siddiqui, a short, plump man of fifty-five in a dark grey suit.

The chief inspector turned on the recording equipment before taking his seat beside Sunita. He glanced at Turner.

'Just to remind you, you're under caution and everything is being audio recorded and video recorded. Now, Miss Turner, you mentioned this afternoon you were working at the archery club at the time Mrs Holland was murdered in Cranleigh Park a week ago today.'

She nodded. 'That's right.'

'Well, one of our detectives has been to the club and studied the work sheets. You're marked down as absent for last Wednesday.'

'Must be some mistake. I was definitely there.'

'Not according to the receptionist who'd been anxious to reach you for some reason. She remembers the day well.'

'Perhaps that was the day I went shopping in Stratford then. You can't seriously think I had anything to do with this woman's death in Cranleigh Park.'

'Very well. We'll leave that there for the moment. We've just been speaking to one of our colleagues at Queensbridge police station. He told us that a few days ago, a man was fishing in the lake next to your club and discovered a plastic bag about six metres from the water's edge. He hooked it to the shore and discovered bloodstained clothing inside. He called the police. Inside was a green cap, two shirts and a pair of black trousers. They're being examined right now. We also found a partial fingerprint on the shaft of the crossbow bolt, which matched one of your prints.'

Mr Siddiqui frowned. 'Goodness me. Are you sure you can pick up a fingerprint from such an item?'

Sunita nodded. 'I'm afraid we can.'

Roscoe continued, 'It's just one more piece of evidence that links your client to the murder of Virginia Holland.'

Turner stared up at the ceiling. 'Of course it's got my fingerprint on. I probably handled it at the club before it was stolen.'

'Oh, did I forget to mention the bloodstained knife with the clothing? That had your print on as well.'

Sunita detected a change in their suspect's mood. Was it exasperation at the questioning? Was it a realisation that attempts to blame the crossbow killer for the death were failing?

Turner glared at the detectives. 'Can you imagine what it's like?'

Roscoe frowned. 'How do you mean?'

'Can you imagine what it's like being dumped by your own mother when you're still young? Not knowing where she's gone?'

Sunita felt a little sympathy for the suspect as tears trickled down the woman's cheeks. 'It must have been very difficult.'

'Very difficult? You haven't got the first idea. Finding out your mother's got a new child that she loves instead of you. Some bastard child of her fancy fella. You won't have an inkling what it's like being placed in care – dumped in a building with unknown children and strangers giving you orders.'

'You've had a tough start to your life,' Roscoe admitted.

'You bet. But she didn't. Virginia didn't. She had all the best things money can buy and never cared a damn about me. The stupid bitch deserved to die. My only regret is I didn't do it sooner.'

She lowered her head and when she glanced up, a few seconds later, her eyes were red and moist with tears.

Mr Siddiqui gazed across at the chief inspector. 'I think this might be an appropriate moment.'

Roscoe nodded. 'Yes. If my sergeant here can take a brief statement, we can leave things there and adjourn until the morning. It's been a long day.'

Chapter 60

It was a warm, cloudy night as Sunita Roy and Tom Vickers left St James Street and strolled along the pavement towards the Golden Fleece. She clasped his hand as they walked.

The chief inspector was sitting in his favourite corner in the main bar when they stepped inside just before seven. He was surrounded by some of their other colleagues. She thought their boss looked disenchanted.

Vickers discovered the reason later. The pub had run out of his favourite beer, QB Bitter, a medium-strength bitter produced by the Queensbridge Brewery Company. Instead he was having to content himself with a pint of Ansells Bitter, which had never suited his palate.

He rose from his seat with a broad smile as the pair sat down. 'Well done, Sergeant!' he said. 'Let me get you both a drink.'

After returning from the bar with a pint of lager for the inspector and an orange juice for Sunita, he took a sip from his glass and pulled a face. Then he observed she and the inspector were holding hands. He decided not to embarrass them by passing comment.

'That interview with the archery club woman went well, Sergeant,' he said.

Sunita lowered her voice. 'I know a little more that I didn't tell you before. She worked for about seven years as Larry Holland's secretary at Shendon Lifts in Aston. Before that she was a nurse at the old Queen Elizabeth Hospital in Edgbaston.'

Roscoe nodded, but made no comment.

Vickers sipped his lager and then put his glass down. 'I know what I was going to ask you, Sunita. How do we know Larry Holland didn't play a role in his wife's murder? Until you spoke up, I was becoming convinced he was involved.'

She shrugged. 'I think because of his reaction when I was outlining what I thought happened. He was visibly shocked. I don't think you can fake shock like that. It seemed to me a very natural reaction from him.'

'Yes, you're right,' Roscoe said. 'As you spoke out at the flat, it occurred to me that, if he'd been involved, they'd have disposed of the body in some way. She wouldn't have needed to dress up either. Talking of which, how did she know what the gardener wore?'

Sunita smiled. 'She knew Hopkinson from six years ago. He'd done some landscaping work at the archery club. She was just an ordinary club member then. She recommended him to Larry. That's how Hopkinson began working for the Hollands. She got to know the way he dressed. Pity for her sake she forgot about his stoop or she might've got away with it.'

Roscoe grinned at her. Although he'd once had reservations about her abilities, he now fully accepted her as a key member of his team.

'Of course, we still have to find our serial killer,' he said, as he downed the rest of his pint.

Vickers had noticed the chief inspector gazing in his direction from time to time. Was he hinting that it was his turn to buy a round? Or had he just realised for the first time his two colleagues had become close? He decided to eliminate the first of the two options.

'It must be my turn to get a round in,' he said. He released Sunita's hand and stood up.

Roscoe shook his head. 'Not for me, Tom. I've got to get back.' Then, while he was leaving, he turned and whispered, 'I'm delighted with your work today, Sergeant. Keep it up.'

Vickers smiled and clutched her hand again as he sipped his second pint. 'Shall we take a stroll back too when we've finished these drinks? I was chatting to Brett Dawson just then about the CCTV. I'd like to see how he's getting on before I go home.'

* * *

As they approached the grey, four-storey building, Vickers noticed the light was off in the first-floor window where Dawson had been working.

Sunita glanced at him. 'Looks like he's gone. Perhaps we'd better leave it. Dawson won't be happy if we interfere with his work when he's not there.'

Vickers scoffed. 'I'm not worried about upsetting Brett. Finding our mystery bowman comes first, surely?'

After turning on Dawson's computer, Vickers sat down and discovered his colleague had been studying programme disks covering Warwick Road, Stratford in the early evening of 22 June.

He stood up and shook his head. 'I don't know why Dawson's focusing on the period up to 9.00 p.m. It's the early hours of the morning we should be homing in on.'

Sunita wasn't listening. She had taken his seat and was trawling through the footage, studying hazy images of the black-and-white street scene. 'Have a look at this, Tom.'

He leaned over her shoulder and peered into the monitor. He could just make out the shape of a figure in black clothing walking slowly along the pavement.

Sunita glanced up at him. 'We know Coral Devon arrived at the Marwoods' house with some shopping at about four o'clock that day. Look at this, Tom.'

She ran the disk back to some footage she'd been examining a few minutes before.

'Here's a young woman walking along the same stretch just before the figure in black. The time's given as two minutes past four. She's wearing a light-coloured dress. I'm certain it must be Coral Devon.'

The inspector squinted. The pedestrian appeared to have a mop of black hair.

'You're right, Sunita, and it looks as though the other person is stalking her.'

'Yes.'

'Interesting. Sadly, the dark figure doesn't show their face. Sunita, I think we need to show this to the guvnor.'

She nodded. 'But, like you said, we should really be examining the footage covering the early hours. Now I've been checking the recording from the same camera at around three in the morning on Friday, 23 June. Watch this, Tom.'

A Jeep was seen turning into the access road and parking.

'This looks like Den Slack making his appearance. The time given is 2.51 a.m. He drives off a few minutes later. But look at this.'

She wound the footage on. A green Land Rover could then be seen travelling away from the town. The vehicle slowed down as it approached the Marwoods' house and then parked in the access road. The time shown on the screen was 3.04 a.m. on Friday.

'Tom, can we zoom in on that number plate?'

'Of course. We can use the region of interest filter. Let me sit there.'

Taking her place, he pressed some keys to enhance the image. As he zoomed in on the registration, he spun round in his chair excitedly.

'Good God! I know this vehicle, Sunita!' he yelled. 'You know I've been checking out a load of Land Rover plates? I'm sure this one's on my list.'

He rushed through into the main CID office and returned with a sheet of paper. 'Here we are. This one's registered to a woman called McKie.'

Sunita's eyes lit up. 'Tom, that must be Lucy McKie from the archery club. You know, the woman who showed you how to fire a crossbow. We met her at the cafe.'

'Oh my God, yes. Now you mention it, I think I've got a press cutting about her on my computer. I'll just get it.'

A few minutes later, he returned from the main CID office, this time with a printout.

'Here we are,' he said. 'It's from the *Queensbridge Gazette* earlier this year.'

Sunita peered at the full-page inside story from Thursday, 16 March. It showed the smiling face of a woman with short, black, spiky hair clutching a silver trophy. The headline read, 'Woman sets new Midlands archery record'.

Sunita nodded her head as she placed the photograph on her desk and studied it. Then her facial expression changed. Vickers noticed the fingers of her right hand were twitching. Then she began to clench and unclench her right fist. She drew a quick breath.

'I've seen this woman before. I recognise the freckles on her face. But she wasn't called Lucy McKie then. Now, let me think.'

Vickers shrugged his shoulders. 'A lot of people have freckles, Sunita.'

She nodded. 'Yes, but look either side of the girl's nose. She's mainly got freckles beneath her right eye. Far fewer under the left eye. That's pretty distinctive. Freckles are as unique as snowflakes and never lie.'

Chapter 61

Two days later, on Friday, 11 August, an early morning phone call roused Sunita Roy from her bed. As she fumbled for her handset on her bedside cabinet, she could see the chief inspector's solemn face on the screen.

'Good morning, sir.'

His voice sounded agitated. 'Sergeant, we've got a major job on. You know we had an undercover team outside Lucy McKie's place? Well, late last night they realised she's done a runner.'

Sunita glanced at her watch. It was half past seven. 'What do you suggest, sir?'

'Listen. We've issued an all-ports warning so that staff at seaports and airports would keep a lookout. Then just now we had a tip-off from someone at Gatwick that a woman matching her description was booked on a flight to Spain. Her plane's due to leave just after midday. So we've got to get down there.'

'I'll get dressed straight away, sir.'

'Good. I'll pick you up in half an hour.'

'Do you know Crompton Gardens, sir?'

'Don't worry. I'll find it.'

At a quarter past eight, Sunita was waiting on the kerb outside her flat when Gavin Roscoe's car drew up. He fitted a blue beacon on top of the car and they then set off for the Sussex airport.

'What a brilliant job you've done, Sergeant, recognising that Lucy McKie from the archery club and Bufton's ex-fiancée, Lucinda Thomson, were one and the same person.'

She smiled as they joined the M40 motorway. 'It was all down to the freckles, sir. I remembered that, when we visited Lucinda's brother in Stratford, Lucinda's photo was on the mantlepiece. She'd got far more freckles under her right eye. So when Tom showed me the press picture of Lucy McKie, the similarity was quite striking.'

He nodded. 'I sent DC Khalid over to Robert Bray's flat yesterday to borrow that picture. When they were both blown up and examined carefully, the pattern of the freckles was a perfect match. Then it was mainly down to forensics. After we raided her flat yesterday, we found the sole of one of McKie's sports shoes matched up with the scuffmarks on Miss Moretto's body. The vehicle track at Biddington was caused by one of her tyres. The white thread at Oakdale Road came from her white top. Did you know she had a previous conviction for wounding an ex-boyfriend?'

She shook her head. 'I'm not surprised. Sir, I'm so glad we found the killer.'

'Yes, you've done well, Sergeant, but there's no time to celebrate. We've got to stop her getting on that plane.'

'Did you say that DC Khalid's on the way?'

'Yes. He should be there by now. I've put in a request for the plane to be held and asked Sussex Police to arrest her at the North Terminal.'

When they arrived, Roscoe parked near the passenger drop-off point.

They both jumped out and hurried up the escalator into the terminal building. Roscoe immediately spotted Khalid waiting for them.

His eyes lit up when he saw the chief inspector.

'Oh, sir. The sergeant from Sussex Police has been trying to call you. We believe the McKie woman may have been spooked when she found out the flight was delayed and saw police speaking to airline staff. She hasn't checked in for her flight. I'm afraid we don't know where she is.'

Roscoe shook his head and groaned. 'Goddammit! What a bloody nuisance.'

Sunita shrugged. 'I suppose we'll just have to search for her as best we can. Omar, are Sussex still looking for her?'

'Well, there's only Sergeant Murrell and a couple of lads. They've been roaming round, trying to spot her, but it's very busy here. The CCTV operators are also looking for her.'

'Do we know how she got here originally? Did she come by train?'

He nodded. 'I've had a word with the transport police. Someone matching her description was seen getting off the Gatwick Express.'

'If she knows we're onto her, she's unlikely to leave by plane or train,' said Sunita. 'I think there's a good chance she might try and hire a car.'

Roscoe's expression was blank. 'To go where?'

'Well, it's anyone's guess, but she might head to Dover, which is about eighty miles away. Then she could take one of the ferries over to France and make her way to Spain from there.'

Roscoe turned to Khalid. 'How's she dressed?'

'A khaki jacket and blue jeans.' Then he smiled. 'It's not a complete disaster, sir. Her suitcase has just been found by one of the cleaners. She'd left it on a trolley in a disabled toilet.'

'Why would she leave her luggage behind?'

Khalid shrugged. 'It was unzipped. Looks as though she might have removed something from it.'

Roscoe tutted as he glanced at his two Heart of England colleagues. 'Small consolation that her luggage has turned up. Come on, you two. We'd better start hunting for her. As we're in plain clothes, we might have more luck than Sergeant Murrell. Now remember, she's slim, mid-twenties and with short, black, spiky hair and might be wearing glasses.'

As Khalid was despatched to the far side of the terminal, Roscoe and his sergeant began searching around the shops. But they quickly appreciated the immensity of their task.

The hall was the size of several football pitches. Thousands of passengers were queuing, walking, running, chatting, shopping or just milling around as the pair embarked on their search.

Sunita focussed her mind on finding a woman dressed in a khaki jacket and blue jeans. But she was surprised how many passengers were dressed like that – she counted six in the first ten minutes. Sadly, none had spiky, black hair.

She glanced at Roscoe. 'Sir, this is a waste of time.'

Then suddenly his phone rang. It was Khalid. He'd spotted a woman in a khaki jacket running with hand luggage through the exit doors. He'd followed her down the escalator and watched as she ran to the drop-off point.

'I'm sure it's the McKie woman, sir!' he insisted. 'A minicab driver was loading luggage into his vehicle. She simply jumped behind the wheel and sped off with the tailgate still open. The driver was shouting.'

Roscoe yelled to Sunita, 'Quick! She's snatched a minicab!' before the pair dashed down the escalator.

The chief inspector, still on the phone to his constable, nearly knocked a holidaymaker over as he raced across the pavement. 'Khalid, what kind of car was it?'

'It looked like a black VW Passat. I think she may have taken a passenger with her.'

'You two, my car now. And, Omar, you'd better let Murrell know.'

They all clambered into Roscoe's car and raced out of the terminal. But when they reached the first roundabout, they had no idea which way to turn.

'Quick, sir, turn right,' said Sunita. 'I bet she's going north on the M23 so she can reach the M25.'

Roscoe followed the traffic towards the nearby motorway slip road. 'Well, we've nothing to lose.'

No sooner had they joined the northbound carriageway than Roscoe's phone rang. He switched to hands-free.

'Sir, it's Sergeant Murrell. We've picked up the Passat on camera travelling at high speed up the motorway towards London. But one of our motorcycle team are right on her tail. So she won't be getting far.'

Roscoe ended the call and sped on in pursuit of the minicab, determined to catch McKie. He switched on the blue light on his roof. At times, he reached speeds of more than a hundred miles an hour.

After ten minutes, just a short distance before the M25 junction to the south of Croydon, they noticed a blue flashing light on the hard shoulder ahead. As they approached, they recognised a Sussex Police motorcycle patrolman had stopped on the hard shoulder, just behind the pursuit vehicle.

They were about eight miles north of Gatwick, at a point where the motorway rose over surrounding terrain. Behind the metal crash barrier, there was a windbreak of trees before the land sloped gently away. Beyond lay fields. They were in the Low Weald, a lightly wooded landscape with the Surrey Hills in the distance.

Roscoe switched on his amber warning lights and drew up behind the Passat, which still had its tailgate open. All three detectives jumped out and rushed to the vehicle, but there was no sign of Lucy McKie. There was just a bewildered Far Eastern businessman sitting alone on the back seat, clasping his suitcase.

'Lady gone!' he exclaimed. 'Look! Look!' He pointed over the top of the barrier.

Sunita, Roscoe and Khalid peered through gaps in the curtain of trees. A figure in khaki and blue could be seen running across an open field, clasping a black canvas bag. All the while, the sun shone brightly overhead in a cloudless sky.

The chief inspector glanced at the patrolman, who was clutching his helmet while engrossed in a phone conversation.

'What do you know, officer?' he yelled.

The patrolman ended his call, dismounted and waddled towards the group in his heavy, black, waterproof motorcycle gear.

'Sorry, sir. I'm PC Abdul Malik. Somehow she managed to get away. I brought her to a stop and was just walking back to speak to her when she jumped out of the passenger door and high-tailed it down the slope.'

Roscoe frowned while stepping over the barricade. 'Come on, you two. We can't let her get away.'

He began scrambling down the grassy bank, occasionally clinging onto saplings and tree branches for support. Khalid quickly passed him and reached the bottom of the slope first.

'It's all right for Omar,' Sunita muttered to herself as she set off down the bank. 'He's been a cross-country finalist for Warwickshire three years running.'

She'd nearly reached an area where the ground levelled out when she heard PC Malik's voice. 'I'll just get out of these leggings and catch you up,' he bellowed.

After they had all hurried across the lush green meadow, dense woods stretched before them. The wanted woman was nowhere to be seen as they followed a westerly track through the trees created over time by dog walkers and ramblers.

After a few minutes, Roscoe began lagging behind. At forty-nine, he was by far the oldest of the group and least fit. The warmth of the day didn't help matters as he trudged along the shaded path, past conifers, birches and oak trees. His pace was now reduced to little more than a steady trot and he was beginning to perspire profusely.

Then, after they had trudged along the path for more than five minutes, the other officers suddenly heard his voice calling out from a short distance behind them. It was a troubled voice, the voice of a man in pain or distress.

'Give us a hand, you two!' he yelled.

The trio ran back to find the chief inspector sitting on the ground beneath an oak tree. He'd removed his jacket and was struggling to take off his shirt. A crossbow bolt was jutting out of the oak's trunk. Blood was seeping from his right shoulder.

'The bastard woman's shot me!' he declared.

Chapter 62

Sunita Roy glanced about her before examining the chief inspector's grazed shoulder. It was clear the woman they sought was now close by. She might even fire again.

'Never saw it coming. It just came whizzing through the trees.'

Sunita stood up and turned to her colleagues. 'You carry on,' she urged them. 'We'll catch you up.'

Sunita stooped down to help her boss unbutton his white shirt. Blood was trickling from his injury.

'You're lucky,' she said. 'A few centimetres further over and it could've done some real damage.'

'Don't just hang around me, playing nursemaid!' he snapped. 'Get after the bloody woman!'

She took to her feet again. 'Are you sure you're all right, sir?'

'Yes, you go on! It's only a surface wound. I'll be fine.'

She raced off after the others, only glancing back once through concern for him.

Within minutes, she spotted her two colleagues twenty metres ahead. They had taken refuge behind some bushes.

Every now and then, one of them would peer out towards a clump of trees.

Khalid noticed her approaching. 'She's holed up over there, Sarge.'

Sunita peered through the maze of trees until she caught sight of a woman in blue jeans with black, spiky hair. She was trying to hide behind some bushes.

The team were only a short distance away, but they faced an impasse. The lady was a crack-shot with her weapon. One of their number had already been harmed. They had no firearms support. Unless she ran out of bolts, arresting her could prove extremely challenging.

Then Sunita raised her forefinger in the air. 'We could try a diversionary tactic. One of us could dash off to the right and attract her fire. While she's focussed on that, the others could tackle her from behind.'

Just then Roscoe caught up with them and overhead her suggestion as he clutched his painful shoulder. 'Who's going to volunteer to be our decoy?' he asked.

After a moment's silence, Sunita turned to him. 'I'll have a crack at it, if you like.'

The chief inspector shook his head. 'Wouldn't it be wiser to let one of the lads perform that role?'

'I've got my jacket on, sir. It should help protect me.'

He shrugged. 'Very well. If you want to play the heroine. You two, wait for the sergeant to set off. Then, as quietly as you can, make your way towards McKie. And, Khalid, have your taser ready.'

Taking advantage of whatever cover she could find amid the trees and bushes, Sunita sprinted further into the woods. She made sure she rustled leaves and made as much noise as she could in order to attract McKie's attention.

Almost at once, a crossbow bolt flew through the air towards her. It skimmed past so close it struck a tree close behind her with a thud.

Sunita was reminded of the intense fear she'd felt when Den Slack had confronted her in the alley near Deacons Park and when the same man crept into Trudy Marwood's kitchen. The kitchen incident had included the offer of a bunch of flowers. There would be no flowers here. This woman was hell-bent on fighting.

'I could make a good case for arming the police on days like this,' she muttered.

A second bolt hurtled past her as she stumbled on until she was out of range. She then sat on a fallen trunk to catch her breath. She listened out for her colleagues. The woods were silent. In spite of a faint memory of hearing shouts midway through her run, it seemed she was alone.

Sunita retraced her steps, collecting one of the spent crossbow bolts from its resting place on the ground as she passed. Perhaps later it might serve as some kind of trophy or souvenir. Perhaps she'd place it on show in a glass case in CID.

Finally, she found herself close to the bushes where McKie had briefly found sanctuary. At first, there was no sign of her colleagues. Then she detected some sounds further to the west.

Willing herself on, despite her exhaustion, she followed in the direction of the shouting. Unexpectedly, she began to find the trees on either side of the track were more spaced out. Then, without warning, she reached the end of the wood and found, stretched out before her in a disused sand quarry, a vast lake.

The rippling blue water was surrounded on all sides by trees and scrubland. Fifty metres to her right, a short distance along the shore, and close to a wooden jetty, were Roscoe and Malik.

The chief inspector, still gripping his injured shoulder, was crouching at the lake's edge. He was shouting instructions to someone swimming.

A few seconds passed before Sunita realised the swimmer was Khalid, who had stripped off his outer clothing and was propelling himself towards an object floating in the middle of the lake.

Malik was hovering over Roscoe, calling out words of encouragement to the swimmer. Lucy McKie's jacket was lying discarded on the foreshore along with her crossbow. But where was its owner? Then it dawned on her. She must have plunged into the water in a final, desperate bid for freedom.

Abruptly, Khalid turned round and began swimming back towards the bank.

Sunita hurried along the side of the lake to join her colleagues, but the shore was slippery, sloping and uneven. It took her several minutes.

Roscoe shouted as she stumbled towards them. 'She's gone on the jetty and it collapsed. Must've been rotten.'

Sunita yelled, 'She's gone in the water?'

He nodded. 'Yes. She's tried to swim across. Your little ruse just then didn't work, by the way. She spotted us coming.'

As Sunita reached them, Malik waded in and helped the dripping Khalid from the murky water.

'She's gone under,' Khalid panted. 'Couldn't find her.'

Sunita raised her hands in concern. 'What the hell are we going to do? I can't swim. But she's going to drown if we don't pull her out.'

Without being asked, Malik stripped off what remained of his motorcycle clothing and waded in. After a few steps, he began swimming until he neared the spot where Khalid had been searching. Several times he dived down in a desperate effort to find the missing woman.

'He's a better swimmer than me,' muttered Khalid.

Sunita frowned. 'Is the water really cold?'

He nodded. 'It's absolutely freezing. It takes your breath away and it's very deep.'

Roscoe shook his head. 'Cold water shock. I've seen it before. She was at least a hundred metres from the edge. I reckon she's just given up.'

Sunita and her colleagues watched as Malik dived twice more, making a supreme effort to locate McKie. Each time he surfaced, he would take a gulp of air and then descend again. Finally, he too returned to the bank.

'It's no good,' he gasped as he struggled ashore, assisted by Sunita. 'You can't see anything in there. I'm guessing she must be near the bottom.'

The men stood in a group on the shore for a few minutes, staring out across the water. Nobody spoke. Then Roscoe broke the silence.

He looked solemn. 'Well, you've done your best, PC Malik, and you, Khalid. We can't do more than that.'

Malik glanced at the chief inspector. 'I don't know if you realise, but we're at Draper's Country Park. It stretches for forty acres and it's meant to be a water sports paradise. There are warning signs about swimming but not around this part of the lake.'

Sunita kicked some loose stones from beneath her feet. She continued staring at the water. Then she turned to Roscoe, who was inspecting his wound again.

'She deserved to stand trial for what she did,' she said quietly. 'But, right now, I can't help feeling sorry for her.'

Chapter 63

Rain clouds had been gathering in the sky for several hours before Oliver Bufton's funeral the following morning.

Sunita Roy was sitting beside the chief inspector as he found a parking space beside the crematorium in north Worcestershire and cut the engine. As she peered out of her window, rain began to fall in torrents.

The pair had no choice but to remain in the car as the distant strains of orchestral music were eclipsed by the roar of the storm.

He glanced at his sergeant. 'I suppose we'd better get ready to pay our last respects to Oliver.'

'Yes, sir.'

'I've been meaning to ask. How did it go with Cristina Lorenzo the other day when you took Miss Moretto's personal effects round?'

'She was in tears, sir. She slowly unwrapped the white tissue paper around the jewellery. Then she cried as she touched the gold necklace with her fingers.'

'I've heard the house in Oakdale Road is up for sale.'

'Yes, she's going to use the money to buy a place in Stratford with her boyfriend. She's made an appointment next week with her MP. She wants the law changed to make it harder to buy a crossbow.'

Roscoe was wearing his best dark-blue suit with a black tie for the service being held within an idyllic riverside park. He opened his window a fraction since the windscreen was steaming up. 'I still don't really understand what brought Lucy McKie to kill three people.'

She nodded. 'Intense jealousy and wounded pride must be part of the answer. After catching her fiancé cheating on her so brazenly, I think her love quickly turned to hatred. She must have become obsessed with revenge, leading her to kill him; his new girlfriend, Miss Moretto; and, finally, Coral Devon – the woman that McKie found him in bed with.'

Roscoe glared. 'Hell hath no fury, eh?' he muttered.

'Sorry, sir?'

'It doesn't matter, Sergeant. So the newspaper photograph was key to you linking Lucy with Lucinda?'

'Yes, as soon as I recalled seeing the same face at Robert Bray's house, I checked with our police contact in Spain. He went round to the address on the Costa del Sol we had for Lucinda Thomson. He revealed she'd moved out in the spring and was believed to be in Warwickshire.'

He frowned. 'That woman had a remarkable talent with the crossbow.'

'She'd taught herself to use it in Spain, sir. She'd also joined a cult and fallen under the spell of a Svengali figure who rebuilt her confidence and encouraged her to act on her feelings.'

'So why change her identity?'

'She thought she was more likely to get away with her murderous plan with a new persona. She used a childhood friend's name, McKie, and shortened her first name to Lucy. But she didn't let on to friends and family she was back in England. She moved into a studio flat in Queensbridge after changing her appearance as much as she could by wearing black-framed glasses, darkening her eyebrows and cutting her blonde hair, which she dyed black. She also lost several stones in weight by strict dieting.'

Roscoe was engrossed in thought. 'What baffles me is how she knew Coral Devon would be staying at Trudy Marwood's house. How do you explain that?'

Sunita shrugged her shoulders. 'I'm not certain, but McKie may have gleaned a clue as to the singer's whereabouts from Coral's Facebook page. Her ex-boss, the florist, was publicising her new Stratford premises and Coral posted a comment, "Can't wait to see your new shop Friday lunchtime."'

'So you reckon McKie waited for Coral to leave the shop and followed her to Warwick Road?'

'Exactly. Coral led her right to the front door. In the early hours of the next morning, under cover of darkness, she turned up in her Land Rover and killed her.'

Roscoe frowned. 'McKie obviously had mental health issues.'

She nodded. 'Yes, sir. A GP had referred her to a specialist in mental health, but she kept missing the date for her psychiatric assessment.'

They watched in silence as dozens of mourners passed through the car park on their way to the chapel. It appeared the service was about to begin.

'Any more news about McKie's body, sir?'

'Yes. Didn't I tell you? A rescue team arrived at the country park shortly after we failed to find her. But it was two hours before divers recovered her body. She was six metres down on the lakebed.'

'Good God! No wonder our two guys couldn't find her.'

'McKie's cheated justice. We can't say the same for Jasmine Turner, of course. Now she's admitted the murder of Mrs Holland, she can expect a life sentence when it goes to court.'

Sunita nodded. 'Sir, I think we should make a dash for it.'

He opened his door and peered out. 'Yes.' He turned up his collar and sprinted to the brick entrance porch.

Sunita, wearing her freshly pressed grey trouser suit, ran in behind him.

Gazing round the modern chapel with its pine seating and stained-glass windows, Roscoe pointed out marina owner Tyler Brown and the *Gazette* chief reporter, Adam Bunyon, sitting in the second row from the front. They were both members of Oliver's skittles team.

He and his sergeant found seats near the back as the quiver and trill of violins playing Vaughan Williams' *The Lark Ascending* filled the hall.

For a moment, Sunita's mind returned to that April day at Woodlands Cottage when she had offered Oliver advice about the campaign of harassment. Then she recalled the scene of the murder in the quiet country lane. She thought of the barbarity and inhumanity of the man's passing. She imagined a lark slowly rising amid the trees in a magical forest and gliding majestically into the skies.

She could almost see poor Oliver's soul travelling with the bird, glancing back at the world for a final time.

Roscoe was studying the order of service. He glanced at her. 'You look thoughtful, Sergeant.'

'Yes, we've been so focussed on the murders and McKie's death I'd almost forgotten about Oliver. I know he probably treated McKie badly, but he didn't deserve to be slaughtered like that.'

Roscoe nodded. 'He also didn't deserve to be stabbed and intimidated by Den Slack, trying to put a stop to his relationship with Miss Moretto.'

She looked down at the wooden floor. 'Seeing all these people here's brought the sadness of Oliver's passing back to me.' A tear was forming in her left eye.

The chief inspector was surprised to find her becoming so emotional. The service had not yet begun. He tried to lighten the mood.

'Isn't this music *The Lark Ascending*, Sergeant?'

She had a lump in her throat but managed to mumble, 'Yes.'

Roscoe shook his head. 'I don't think the poor old lark would be ascending today, given the state of the weather.'

But his feeble attempt at humour failed to raise her spirits.

The celebrant, who led the humanist service, described Oliver as a hard-working man whose career was cut short by tragedy.

'He'd harboured ambitions to be an actor and had shone in his role of King Lear in an amateur drama production. He was also close to his brother Leonard, his sister Sarah and her two children.'

American singer James Taylor's *Fire and Rain* was played to the congregation. Sunita was deeply moved as the poignant lyrics echoed round the chapel about the prospect of not seeing someone again.

After the committal, in which the coffin slid away behind curtains, the mourners drifted out into the damp morning to the strains of Simon and Garfunkel's *Bridge Over Troubled Water*. The heavy rain had eased to a light drizzle. Roscoe and Sunita stopped briefly to speak with Leonard Bufton and his younger sister, Sarah.

'Words can't express how sorry we are at your loss,' said Roscoe.

'Thank you. It's appreciated,' said Leonard. 'The family wanted to thank you both for your hard work. We realise it was a difficult case, so we're very grateful.'

Roscoe shook his head. 'Don't mention it. Every member of our team played a part, but this lady, DS Roy, played the greatest role and it wouldn't have been resolved without her.'

Among floral tributes in the chapel's pavilion, Sunita noticed a wreath of late summer flowers that Roscoe had sent on behalf of the force. It consisted of a mossed base of silver birch twigs dressed with blue and white hydrangeas, roses and chrysanthemums.

'You sent this one with the blue flowers, did you, sir?'

He shrugged. 'I chose blue because that seemed to be his colour. All the file notes described him wearing blue.'

She nodded. 'It took a while, but in the end we caught them both. Do you know, I can't comprehend how either of those women could commit such acts.'

'Nor me,' admitted Roscoe. 'Jasmine Turner's motive sprang from a lifelong resentment against her sister. But Lucy's story was very different. She pursued a journey from devoted sweetheart to broken-hearted neurotic and, finally, a cold-blooded killer.'

He led the way as they strolled back to his car. 'There's one thing I'm still baffled about, Sergeant. Why the letter *C* on the handkerchiefs? Have you any thoughts on that?'

'I figured it out two days ago when DC Khalid returned from visiting Robert Bray,' she said. 'Oliver gave his fiancée Lucinda a box of monogrammed handkerchiefs as one of her presents two Christmases ago. They were embossed with the letter *C* because Cindy was his pet name for her and she used them to mark each death.'

As they climbed into the car, Sunita glanced across to see his reaction. He was shaking his head. Then she turned away.

THE END

If you enjoyed this book, please let others know by leaving a quick review on Amazon. Also, if you spot anything untoward in the paperback, get in touch. We strive for the best quality and appreciate reader feedback.

editor@thebookfolks.com

www.thebookfolks.com

More fiction in this series

MURDER ON OXFORD LANE (Book 1)

A budding chorister doesn't return home from practice but his wife doesn't appear concerned. DS Sunita Roy becomes convinced he has been murdered but she has her own problems in the form of an ex-boyfriend who won't take no for an answer. Will she keep her eye on the ball when all expect her to fail?

MURDER OF A DOCTOR (Book 3)

Police search for the identities of people seen near the scene of a doctor's murder. And it seems like an open and shut case when a father with a grievance against him can be placed nearby. But DS Sunita Roy wants to dig deeper, and with an internal affairs investigation ongoing, she'll have to tread carefully.

OUT FOR REVENGE (Book 4)

There's a noticeable change of atmosphere in the city when a dangerous prisoner is released. He has plans to up his drugs business. But someone will quickly put an end to that. Detective Sunita Roy has the unenviable task of hunting down the gangsters who were likely responsible. But when the cops close in, they'll have an even bigger problem than they first imagined.

All FREE with Kindle Unlimited and available in paperback.

Other titles of interest

BODY IN THE SQUAT by Diane Dickson

After a bungled drugs raid, DI Jordan Carr suspects a mole in the force. Seconded to the Liverpool suburb of Kirkby, he encounters DS Stella May who is leading a murder inquiry. She has little to go on apart from the strange comments of an old woman who fancies herself as something of a clairvoyant. Can May convince Carr to support her line of investigation, no matter how odd it seems?

CODDLING MOLLY by Nicola Clifford

A teenager is found dead after a fall from a bridge on a winter night in Brecon. Nobody knows who she is and identifying her proves a challenge. DI Ben James and DS Erica Bevan manage to connect her to someone else with ties to a drugs gang. But when these crooks bother someone dear to ex-detective Heidi Holtz, she too will jump on their trail.

Made in the USA
Columbia, SC
22 November 2023

26956657R00195